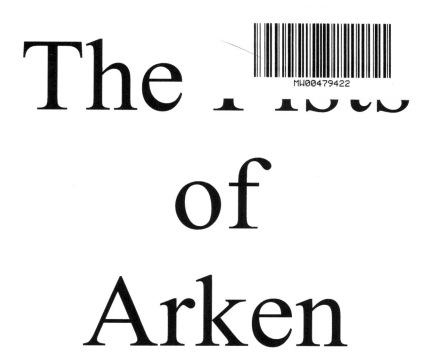

The Fists of Arken

By
Jack Keesling

1.

Blood dripped off the edge of the King's broadsword, staining the floor in wild patterns. The air was thick with the smell of the stuff. Many of the soldiers gathered in the chamber were stained in its darkened tones. The wavering light produced by the slow burning flames of several small torches danced across faces and armor, revealing exhaustion, pain and dejection. The King passed across the floor, seemingly unaware of all else as he moved toward the throne that had long been but would soon no longer be his.

That ancient chair, so cold and hard to the touch, but so welcome and comforting in times of pain or weariness when a king needed the support only a high back of iron and wood could bring. His legs were stiff and aching under the weight of the black armor that covered his features from ankle to neck to wrist. The room was silent save for the falls of his thick boots on the marble floor and the metallic click made by the scales of his armor glancing off one another as his body flexed. Not one of the nearly one hundred armed men and women in the room let slip a whisper. All eyes were on the King in silent hope that he would somehow wrest them from the certain death that waited beyond the large doors that guarded their backs.

As he mounted the white marble steps toward the seat of power, the labor in the King's movements was evident. Fatigue was demonstrated in the slump of the shoulders, the darkness of the eyes and the heaviness with which his legs took each step. The ominous song of armor and footfall flitted across the room and gained a saddened tone as it passed from ear to ear.

The King lifted his sword to his eyes, the movements more instinctual than choice, an action performed hundreds of times over a life spent at arms. He carefully checked the leading edge of the handcrafted weapon for wear and nicks. The ruler's heart was heavy as he returned his blade to its scabbard. As the King reached the top of the steps, he released a great sigh. His shoulders fell forward, and his head sank. The back of the king's armor stayed turned to the assembled gang.

"Bring me a cloth." His voice was loud and strong despite the obvious strain wrapping him. Even in the face of the certain fall of his country, and most assuredly the end of his life, the man continued to display his brawn, living up to the long-held belief shared by many in Arken that this man did not know the flavor of fear.

The borum stone walls of the massive room glowed as if they were the slow churning embers of a fire, reflecting the light of the torches and scattering it throughout the space. On a common day, when this hall was lit by the light of the sun and moon streaming through the gigantic skylights built into the high ceiling, the borum stone took to life and made the walls appear as if they were constructed of a crackling fire. The King wished to see the borum stone walls ablaze now, to enjoy the comfort of their familiar dance. Yet, on this most foul of nights, even the sky betrayed him and not a single star sent light for comfort.

Oslun, cupbearer to the Arken King, climbed the steps toward his leader and presented a white cloth. The King gripped it with an armored glove. Slowly, deliberately, the King turned his head to the cup bearer and took in his form. The young servant's fear was obvious as the lad stood by, the pressed white tunic and gray trousers common to servants hung on his plump frame. While Oslun's wardrobe was typically immaculate, the stains of sweat adorned him.

Though Oslun had been in the service of the King for nearly three years, he had a soft heart, and was not fit for battle. Thus, when the King's company went on the march, the cup bearer remained in the citadel. The young man was ill prepared for the pain heaped out by the siege of the city. The King was fond of this rotund youth despite his fearful nature, for he was always attentive, quick to respond to any command, and he kept the King's business as tightly as the tomb.

"You have served me faithfully, Oslun, son of Thom and Valis." The Kings voice was low, a shade above a whisper, though the nature of the open stone room carried the sound far, a characteristic that earned it the moniker of the Whisper Hall. "I see the fear in you, as I have witnessed many times. I have never questioned you on this, as you have always done your duty despite your fear, but now I must ask, in the hour of our greatest terror, will you fight if the fight comes upon you? Will you stand your ground in the face of your own end and pain?"

The young man opened his lips, but no sound emitted as he struggled to find his courage. Standing in the face of his great ruler, mouth agape, locked in an uncontrollable stutter, Oslun turned his eyes to the cold floor and found it unforgiving.

"I see a great potential in you, young one. I see chance for you to prove your worth, but I must have your answer." The King's voice was calm, almost warm, providing a bit of nerve for the young cup bearer.

"Your Grace," the young man's high voice quaked slightly as he spoke, despite his efforts to conceal his terror. The stutter persisted, but he forced the words to pass his lips. "I am yours to command, until the last drop of blood, the last breath and the last thought that passes as I enter into the shadow."

The King smiled down on him softly. "That is part of the sworn knight's pledge, Oslun. You need not say these words."

"I hoped it would make me brave, Your Grace." Oslun offered meagerly.

King Axeleon laid his hand gently on the crown of his servant's head. "It is alright my son, do not feel shame. We all fear what we do not know. Even I fear the end, but you will not so quickly discover its secrets. I have remaining use for your services."

Axeleon, King of the West, Ruler of the Five Fists of Arken, Commander of the Armies of Shadow raised his hand and drew the white cloth across his face, clearing away the blood and sweat that had built up over several days of fighting without respite. As he lowered the saturated cloth, a great impact struck against the large doors at the far end of the room. Wood, iron, steel and stone shuddered at the sound. Every warrior present reacted, none maintained complete composure. King Axeleon slowly turned to face his fighters.

"The end has come, and our final enemy is upon us." King Axeleon spoke deliberately, his voice booming out of his chest as if to rival the sounds of the battering ram as it impacted the great doors again. "Our enemy longs to taste our blood, to paint the walls of this hallowed room with it. He desires to butcher us, here and now."

The last syllable reverberated through the room and hung in the air like the ring of a blacksmiths final blow on the anvil. "Such has been the swiftness of our doom that many among you do not yet know how our end was smote upon us. You deserve this knowledge. We have fallen to the enemy's trap. Even my high war council did not see his plans. Our enemy attacked us in force from the south, penetrating deep into the heart of the Fire Fist. He flew his war banners and made himself known to us.

I ordered at once two full combat legions to the southern territories, and another from the Elk Fist in order that we should reinforce Fire Lady Kaowith's armies and make safe the lines, staying any further penetration into our lands. Our enemy waited until our legions were beyond the distance of recall, then landing a smaller force on the shores of the Elk Fist. So small a force that he was undetected as he passed through Elk Lord Brantus' territory and entered the Shadow Fist from the east. Only the Citadel Guard and the commanders of our highest elements remained, five hundred swords left standing for our defense."

"I sought to deceive our enemy by sending out the vehicles of my family and the high war council, containing no one of import, to the mountain castle at Barang. The convoy departed from the northern gate of the city, in full sight of the enemy's scouts. I had strong hope the enemy would take the bait and follow, giving us time for Wolf Lord Aralias and his forces to come down from the north. Barang itself is home to the reserve infantry and is, as is known to most of you, Lord Commander Fax' home when he is not duty bound elsewhere. The fortress itself is well armed and supplied, able to withstand siege long enough for us to assemble an army and come up on the enemy's rear. To our great detriment and his cunning, our foe did not take the bait. He knew, as only one with such personal knowledge would, that I would never abandon the Arkenhead."

The King paused and let loose another deep, pained breath. "Long has peace graced the fists, and I see now that we have become as the fatted sheep, basking in the summer of our long rest, unaware that the butcher was sharpening his knives while we slept in the sun."

"Lord Aralias' armies have been summoned, but they are a long march north and our reserve infantry will not depart Barang Fortress until they have marshalled their full strength. We have been cut off from communication with the armies of Elk and Fire. The final reports that were received indicate that the enemy has established fortifications and is deeply dug in, sending out only small raiding parties to keep our legions engaged. Iron Lord Nathus has refused to march his armies from the Iron Fist, stating that storms have ravaged his coast line and unoathed men are incurring heavy damage on his northern border. This is likely a lie, but there is nothing that can be done to indict this treason.

"So here we find ourselves, caught in the noose. Three thousand swords remained in the city when our enemy's banner arrived at the gate. Ten thousand stood against us. We have inflicted heavy casualties against them, and our warriors have done far more than could have been expected of the best fighters in all the world, but it was not enough.

Our enemy needs only take two more lives and he will have what he craves. If he ends my life, and that of my only heir, he will claim the throne for his own. I cannot see a path where the Lords of the Fists will be able to muster the strength to retake the Citadel once it has fallen and the Starrowlands Army has taken residence within. Now, we find ourselves in the hour of our final destruction."

Axeleon surveyed his surroundings in the Whisper Hall. Black marble floor from corner to corner leading to white marble steps, at the top of which was a large platform of hewn blood stone. On this massive platform, the seat of the King. Behind the throne stood heavy wood doors to the left and right. Over Axeleon's left shoulder, the entrance to the chambers of the King and his family. Several chambers were unoccupied, so small was the royal family. Servants numbering some forty or more took refuge within these halls. Behind and to the king's right, the entrance to the grand banquet hall and attached kitchens, as well as the chambers for the various council meetings a ruler was forced to attend.

As the King looked out into the Whisper Hall, his eyes swept over the long line of the carefully preserved remains of the fallen. In accordance with the Law of Arken, commanders of the armies, fallen in battle, were granted eternal rest in the hall of the king. Along with those posted to command, those who died in the performance of great deed to the realm were given rest here. Three hundred and seventy-two valiant soldiers from every generation in the long history resided here. The bodies of these honored warriors were carefully preserved and wrapped in clean linens, clad in the armor they wore, and armed with the weapons they carried on the day they fell. They were then placed in order to line the perimeter of the Whisper Hall, forever guarding the seat of the king.

The King's eyes ran past the remains of the warriors, pausing on those he had admired most. Vectra Oberon, renown throughout the kingdom as a tourney champion, feared and respected by all for her skill with sword and shield. She did not speak, for when she was just a babe, her father, having gone mad from the consumption of the root of the farri plant, had taken a long knife to her throat. She survived this brutality and grew to stand nearly seven feet tall, though the damage to her speech never healed. Vectra fell in battle defending Axeleon's own sister, then the oldest living heir to the Kingdom of Arken, from a band of raiders who attacked the royal convoy in route to the wedding of King Marlan of Simicot. She stood now, in the shadow armor she wore on that day, with her sword, Silent Water, as it was named, secured in her gloved hand.

Near Vectra, under one of the massive pine beams that formed the structure of the ceiling, posed Reginya Hallowfast, clad in the steel armor of a battle commander before the smiths of the realm discovered the ability to forge Shadow Steel. Reginya was a proud and fearless warrior, who fell defending Raxus, the third King of Arken in the days before the long histories were well recorded.

Amyus Colth was nearby, a famed sword in her own day, who bore a unique black sword, Nightfyre it was called, against Axise, King Axeleon's own brother, during the rebellion that took place after the father passed. Simeon Starmish stood next to her, his armored glove interlocked with hers. Starmish was likely the shortest sworn sword in the long histories, but also among the fastest. He had been rejected from service in the army due to his stature, standing barely a grain above four feet. Starmish refused to relent and used the influence of his tongue to secure training with a powerful sword's woman, Amyus Colth. In time, his skill with the blade became known and he was welcomed into the armies.

A powerful friendship formed between master and pupil that lasted the remainder of their lives. Simeon and Amyus fell side by side and were discovered hand in hand in death as they had been in life. Many whispers told that together, they sired a child, but no evidence of offspring existed.

King Axeleon's eyes followed the lines of armor, which remained in the final condition of the man or woman who had died in them. Never repaired or cleaned, many still bore stains of blood and scars of war. His eyes followed the line along the left side of the Whisper Hall to the back of the room, across the back wall and past the great doors. Each silent guardian from battles past stood unfazed as another blow of the battering ram struck its punishment against the great doors. Dust and varnish cracked off the thick wood as a few of the younger warriors in the room allowed fear to play across their faces. Oslun, who remained by the King's side, trembled as he stood. Axeleon's expression remained unchanged. He knew the construction of the hall well. It would take many blows of the heaviest ram to force the massive oak and iron doors to yield even an inch.

Axeleon let his eyes travel up the right side of the borum stone wall. He recalled the names of a few more prominent warriors, their tales long forgotten in most of Arken. The King's eyes swept up the row to the last silent figure, nearest to the white marble steps. Black Shadow armor, black bow across the back with a full quiver of arrows, a shadow steel long sword on the left hip. Around the neck, a pure silver chain which supported the most radiant citrine. One of a kind, this gem was cut with a skill and precision common only to Arken craftsman. The stone was hewn to appear as a brilliant sun, as large as a plum.

Even now, with the failing light of only a few scattered torches in the massive hall, the light emanating from this ornament traveled several feet, casting shadows off some of the warriors who stood nearby. Axeleon had given her this pendant on their wedding day, some twenty-three years before. She had never removed it, once he had placed it around her neck. Even on the day she fell, it remained with her. Alandaria, the first Warrior Queen of Arken. She was beautiful, and exceptionally passionate, in life and in war.

Axeleon had been betrothed from birth, as was common, to Julist Hallfax of the realm of Angrews. Julist was a lovely girl, a beauty rivaled by few, but she had never truly appealed to the youthful Prince Axeleon. She was not trained in war, nor was she given to strength of character. The young woman had been bred only to be the bride of Axeleon of Arken and had no design or desire of her own beyond the pleasing of man.

Alandaria was common in birth, a native of the Fire Fist, who was trained as a sword's woman. She was assigned to the citadel guard when she was eighteen years of age. It was there that Axeleon found her, and thus broke his betrothal. In the spring time of their love, confessions were made to father and betrothed. Penances were paid in full and blood was shed. In the end, a swift courtship fell away, revealing a deep love and a long burning fire that stretched beyond the grave.

Another crushing blow pounded against the doors of the great hall. No matter the construction of the doors or the passages beyond, eventually the enemy would break through. The grand hall would be flooded with warriors fueled by the blood lust so common to those who are about to kill a king. The hall of whispers would become the hall of the screams of dying men and women. Axeleon shook his head, clearing away the memories that clung to his mind.

"Oslun," The King's voice took on the quality of the highly experienced battlefield commander that he was. Every living eye was on him. The cup bearer erected his posture, standing smartly at the King's side. "Retrieve the Sun Stone from the Queen's neck."

Oslun turned towards the remains of the warrior queen, careful wrappings preserving her form. He hesitated. Where her eyes should have shown through the slit in her helm, he saw only black. The young servant breathed deeply and began to remove the necklace, but he was too short to lift it over her helm, her long red hair still flowing from underneath and trapping the pendant. A tall warrior, who Oslun recognized as Lord Commander Liam Fax, Commander of the King's Infantry, stepped forward and gingerly, despite his overlarge hands, removed the jewel from the Queen's neck.

The Lord Commander gazed fondly at the sunstone before placing it in Oslun's hand. Commander Fax closed both hands around Oslun's, staring directly into the cupbearer's eyes. Oslun hesitated, uncomfortably stifled under the commander's deadly gaze. He inhaled sharply and pulled his hand free of the commander's grasp and turned back toward King Axeleon.

"Lord Commander, bring me her sword." Axeleon requested.

The Commander respectfully removed the deceased Queen's sword and scabbard from her belt. As he calmly approached the steps of the King, Axeleon turned his eyes to the rest of his faithful few. His voice grew almost whimsical. "It is a funny thing, when a King realizes that his kingdom is lost. We have fought valiantly for three days, but both city and fortress are lost. The reign of Axeleon, son of Axlent and Santar, of the house Taymrhlyn, is over."

Axeleon grew silent, his eyes fading into darkness. Suddenly and violently, he burst out, his voice coming as if it was uttered from a young deer with the wolf's jaw upon its neck. "My own brother! He lusted for this throne from the moment of his birth! All this pain and death for what? A chair! He will have it now, at the cost of what? The lives of his own people!"

Silence filled the space again. None shifted in the entirety of the hall.

As the emotion roiled away, clarity took over Axeleon's mind. "May the rule of Axise over these lands be one of peace and prosperity to our peoples."

"I wish nothing but death to those that will kneel to Axise!" Saraf Wonr, a sworn knight in the King's Infantry shouted from the back of the assembly. Her words punctuated as another impact of the battering ram connected with the great doors. Grout and cement cracked and fell to the floor from the frame and the anchors that clung to the borum stone walls. Lord Commander Fax turned to his soldier and raised a hand to order her silence. She did not relent. "The traitor Axise and all who serve him will suffer the death of those stained with the blood of innocents!"

Saraf raised an ornamented, bright steel sword high over her head as she spoke. The blade was stained with blood and many gouges were in the cutting edges. Several others in the assembly cheered and raised their weapons. The throng of warriors pushed forwards towards the King, defiance against their impending death building in them.

"No!" Axeleon cried out, stepping to the edge of the blood stone platform. "Do not wish suffering or death on our people!" Axise will be remembered in the long histories of the world for his deeds. Long after we are gone, our bodies and souls returned to shadow, his evil will be known. You must now think of the farmers, the smiths, the gatherers, and the textileists! To resist Axise is to bring only death and pain to them and their families."

"Do you wish death on our people? Do you wish them burned fields? The slaughter of their children? Butchered husbands and wives?

We have been fortunate in this war. Fortunate that the enemy's campaign was swift and deception his most powerful weapon. While this has cemented our defeat, it has spared the lives of our people, who we are bound to protect above all else! Do not fault those who bend the knee and in so doing, defend home and family. They have not failed us, it is we, and I who have failed them." Axeleon lowered his voice and took in a long, cold pull of air. "Pray long life and safety for all the people of Arken who live under the rule of Axise."

Another impact of the ram against the door. The warriors lowered their weapons. Many turned their gazes to the floor. Oslun summoned the courage to speak. "How long, Your Grace? How long until the doors are breached?"

"It is hard to say, Son of Arken, though no doors can stand forever. Either weapons of war, or weapons of time will take them down." Axeleon placed his heavy gloved hand on the cup bearer's shoulder. Oslun seemed to melt into the comforting touch of the king. "No doubt Axise himself is directing his men in their effort to swing the ram, but do not dwell on that thought. You will not see him enter this chamber."

The king extended a hand and took the sunstone from Oslun, lifting it high. The light from the pendant reflected off his face and he smiled softly into the radiance. For a singular moment, the war weary mind of the King was taken to a better time, a time when a gentle face smiled back at him.

"Jaxus" Axeleon's voice boomed out into the room like a thunder clap. The warriors were frozen in place. After a small moment, in the very back of the expansive room, between the bodies of the silent guardians, a warrior clad in shimmering armor that seemed as if it was liquid metal emerged into the murk. This warrior bore no helm and the sleeves of his armor ended on his upper arm, contrasting him sharply to the assembly whose shadow armor covered each from crown of head, to ankle to wrist. Black leather gloves covered his hands, though no ornament or jewel was present on his body.

The man was unknown to most of the assembled warriors, though he had been in the service of Arken for many years. His skin was dark, nearly matching the tone of his armor. His deep blue eyes shown out as if they were lit from within. The man's hair was cut short, close to the scalp, and his face was clean shaven, revealing strong features and a hard countenance.

His footfalls were silent as he crossed the glossed stone floor, despite the heavy black boots he wore. At the base of the white stone steps, the man came to a position of respect, his body suddenly as if it was carved of stone, his sword drawn from behind his shoulders, held in a common salute. The blade was long, double edged, with an angular channel running the length at the center of the cord. Though longer than most swords, this blade, and the ease with which the warrior manipulated it gave it the appearance that it was of little weight.

Both the sword, and the armor the man wore were black, but not the deep, matte black of shadow steel. This metal had the appearance that it was alive, reacting to the light in the space and changing its iridescence to become nearly invisible to the eye. The armor seamed further organic as with each movement of the warriors' body, the plates seamed to change shape. There were no apparent seams, no visible points of weakness, as if one continuous piece of metal wrapped around the body and protected his every form.

The warrior stood motionless before the king.

"Come here Jaxus." Axeleon ordered firmly. The black warrior sheathed the sword and with purposeful motions, mounted the steps and knelt on one knee before the king, lowering his head in deference.

"Thyso, bring the princess forth!" Axeleon ordered, turning his head over his shoulder and shouting the command towards the door leading to the royal chambers. At once, the heavy door to the chambers of the King swung open. A young man clad in pristine shadow armor stepped out and held the door open for the princess. Thyso, handmaid to Princess Layandria, was tall, with a dark complexion and dark walnut eyes. He appeared strong and the poise of his face gave the impression of intelligence mixed with cunning.

Princess Layandria was young, approaching nineteen years of age. She had long flowing hair that shared its hue with the borum stone walls. She was light of skin and had deep green eyes that appeared to be cut from pure emeralds. She was tall and slender with long, graceful arms. Many the young man followed her as she flitted about the Arken Head. She was known, apart from her beauty, for being tenacious, well spoken, and intelligent.

The Princess was clad in newly forged shadow armor. She wore no helm, but her armor was unique in that a fan of shadow steel stood off her shoulders and collar, ringing her neck save for gap at her chin. It was a new design, forged by the royal smiths when Layandria determined traditional helms limited her field of view. She was known to be an excellent sword's woman, though that skill had not been tested beyond the practice ring.

Princess Layandria and her handmaid approached the King. Thyso stood just behind the King's left shoulder, as was the custom for servants. The King kissed her daughters head, then turned to address the assembly. Jaxus remained kneeling before him.

"Under the throne there lays a slab of blood stone. It is much the same in appearance as all the others that surround it, but this stone is much different. The blood stone slabs that make up this platform are nearly two feet thick and each took five men to maneuver into position when this hall was constructed. The stone under the seat of Kings is less than six inches thick and can be moved by one strong man or woman." Axeleon paused to survey the assembly. Slight confusion was evident on many faces, while others remained passive.

"Under this piece of stone is the entrance to a passage that was cut from the heart of the mountains by the order of Alx Taymrhlyn, first King of Arken in an age when the fortune of our fledgling new realm was uncertain. If a person were to enter this tunnel, he would find hundreds of miles of safe passage, with provisions enough for ten swords to be found at the end of each days walk. Several generations have extended the length of this passage, maintained it, and protected its secrecy." Axeleon took a long pause, examining the eyes of every warrior assembled before him. "Those of you who wish to preserve your lives will take this passage with the Princess. If that is your wish, step forward."

Not one foot in the expanse of the Whisper Hall moved. No sound was heard. The King breathed softly, as if waiting, though he had anticipated the lack of movement. The battering ram impacted the great doors again. Rather than the deep, rolling boom of a direct strike against the door, the impact was sharper, uneven, as if the strike glanced away.

Lord Commander Fax strode with swiftness to the back of the hall. The massive form of the dark warrior nearly disappeared in the low light at the back of the chamber. He removed his black helm and pressed his ear against the door. After a long moment, he came away from the entrance and returned to his place in the ranks of the assembled warriors.

"What is it, Commander?" Axeleon requested.

"They have broken the head off their ram, Your Grace." Commander Fax's deep voice seamed to the younger warriors present as if the man had a raging storm inside his chest. "If their rams are similar to that which we have seen Starrowlanders use in the past, it will take some time to repair."

"Thank you, Lord Commander, as always you prove yourself to be a most valued advisor." Axeleon paused, gazing into the darkness. Possibilities began to churn in his mind, given birth by hope for time. After several tense moments of pondering silence, he spoke. "Again, I will ask, who among you would desire to take the passage under the throne? Before you respond in your yes or no, be certain that there is no shame or weakness in either choice. Those choosing to take the passage, step forward now."

"My King!" Ramos Taymrhlyn, second cousin to the King, and Commander of the Citadel Guard broke the silence. "My steel is yours, as it has been since we were boys. I will proudly die by your side, now, this day! No secret passages or escape under the earth will delay our destiny!"

Commander Taymrhlyn drew his long, curved sword, of the type common to the city guard and held it sideways, hilt in one hand, and blade in the other. He knelt, in a similar respect to the position of honor which Jaxus still held. At Ramos actions, several other warriors, including Lord Commander Fax, followed suit. As a cascade of metal, a storm of movement, each warrior in the assembly drew their weapons and knelt before the King.

"We are warriors of the shadow. We are sworn to the service of the people of Arken. We are the last of our kind. Today, our kingdom falls, and our way of life ends but we will keep faith to oath and King until the bitter end!" Misandra Wolost, a platoon leader in the King's Guard cried forth, her tone carrying a determined acceptance of the glorious doom that awaited.

With her passionate words, every fiber of Thyso's being reacted. A cold chill of defiance ran through his spine. Pride and fury welled up inside of his chest. The words of the sworn knight's oath ran through his mind. Without willing it of his own choice, his sword was drawn, held straight up to the ceiling and he was screaming the famous words. "When the hour is dark and the enemy close, we fight! When he is many though we are few, we fight!"

Several warriors rose to their feet and took up the call, swords held high in defiance. "When blood runs cold and breath stops short, we fight! When all that is within desires to run, we fight!" Every voice, including the small, high pitch of Oslun joined the chorus. Axeleon and Princess Layandria stood by, in unabated pride. The throng of voices continued. "When the shadow calls for the souls of the brave, we fight! Until the last drop of blood, the last breath and the last thought that passes as we enter the shadow! For King and Country, People and Land, we fight!"

"I have told you that the long histories of the world will remember Axise and his deeds. This is true." Axeleon spoke to his warriors as he had on the battlefield many times. Full of love and fully committed to his cause. "They will remember Axise, but when they think of him, they will remember us first! When that door opens, the last free swords of Arken, the Fists of Shadow, Elk, Wolf, Iron and Fire will meet our enemy in his face! The long histories will know our names and they will say that few stood before many, unafraid!"

A spark of hope flew through the room. Every heart was swelled full of the fervor of it. This was not hope for victory or hope for escape, but it was the hope found in every great warrior in all the ages of all the peoples of the world. A mixture of pride, defiance and love for one another. Truly, those who have never taken up arms and fought next to brother and sister cannot know the vast amount of power held in the souls of the fighting men and women in that room. A plan took hold in Axeleon's mind.

"I cannot conjure words that would properly express how honored I am to know that I will die, my sword in hand, next to the likes of all of you. We have much to do in preparation for my brother and his men, for I intend to carve our names into the flesh of those that stand to kill us. But first, Jaxus, Thyso and Oslun, you will take the Princess into the passage." Layandria began to form protest as did Thyso, while Oslun and Jaxus remained motionless. Axeleon held his hand up, silencing both protestors. "Our line must continue, my cherished daughter. As you continue to draw breath, Axise victory cannot be completed. You may, one day, find strength to return, saving our kingdom, and long may your life be a torment to the mind of Axise. You are strong, kind and just. There is great strength in you that is yet untapped. You will find your own path, but to do so, you must go. Jaxus will lead you."

"As you command, Your Grace." Jaxus voice was cold and sharp, as if night itself had a learned to speak. He stood and replaced his sword in its sheath on his back.

The King took in the four of them. Jaxus, strong, fearless, and a mystery to all save for Axeleon himself. He alone knew Jaxus histories and his true purpose in Arken. Thyso, young, with the heart of a lion, and utterly loyal to the Princess, though challenged by shame and self-doubt. Oslun, meek, though possessing of a vast mind for knowledge. He was not fit for fighting, yet the King had long suspected that within this plump young man was a great power. Layandria, the jewel of a Kingdom and loved deeply by her people. The King feared for them all.

"I do not know what lies beyond the passage under the mountains, I have never ventured there. Be swift and seek the light of the sun as soon as a way is found." The King held out his hand to Jaxus, who returned the gesture, gripping the kings extended palm firmly. "Keep stout heart and keep moving. There are many stores of provisions along the way, but do not trust them. It has been many months since anyone has entered the tunnel and the supplies you find may well be spoiled."

"It will be as you command, Your Grace." Jaxus voice revealed nothing of his mind. "By your leave, I would gather what supplies I can before we enter."

"Of course, take any that you need. This is not the fate you had planned when you came to my service, I suspect." The Arken King released his grip on the warrior's hand and watched as Jaxus smiled, nearly imperceptibly. The tall man turned away, moving towards the door to the dining hall. King Axeleon raised his eyes back to the warriors gathered in the Whisper Hall. "Lord Commander Fax, bring me my Queen's sword?"

The Lord Commander stepped forward and presented the blade to the King. Axeleon leaned towards the tall warrior and whispered swift instructions. The commander nodded without a word and turned away. At once, he began calling orders to the other fighters. The servants in the royal chambers were brought out and began to aid in the preparations. The room was suddenly filled with sharp movements and rapid orders delegated out.

Axeleon looked softly on his daughter as a single tear formed in the pit of his eye. He opened his mouth, ready to speak his final words to the last of his family, his most beloved only child, but ceased. Oslun and Thyso both stood nearby and though they tried to conceal it, both young men were eager to hear the King's words.

"Thyso, Oslun!" Jaxus voice rang out over the din of the warriors at work, "Come lend me a hand."

The lads moved off towards the open door to the dining hall in pursuit of the phantom voice and Axeleon breathed silent thanks. Jaxus instructed the boys to take up sacks, which they set to work filling with fruit, grains and dried meat. Thyso was pensive. He did not want to leave the side of the king. He desired to stay and fight with the others, but his duty was to the Princess, as it had always been. Soldier he was not, handmaid he was.

Oslun was terrified of either fate. His hands fumbled with the provisions as he filled his sacks. He did not want to stay and be murdered by Axise' hoard, but he did not want to find out what was in the dark tunnel either. He had always been afraid of the dark, and of enclosed spaces. He could imagine no worse fate than this.

After the sacks were loaded to Jaxus instruction, Thyso and Oslun found that the warrior was no longer in the dining hall. They returned to the hall of the king and set about looking for him. It took the young men several minutes to find Jaxus, who they spotted leaving the entrance to the royal chambers. His arms held several items, surgeon's bags, packs to carry supplies, and a few waxed cloth jugs filled with water. The man took the sacks of food from his juniors and stowed them in the packs. The jugs he lashed to the outside of each pack, along with the surgeon's bags. Once secured, Jaxus hoisted one pack onto his shoulders and motioned for Thyso to do the same. The tall warrior aided Oslun in donning the third pack.

"Have you a sword Oslun?" Jaxus asked as he swiftly stepped off, moving towards the edge of the blood stone. The boys fell in step behind his wake.

"No, my Lord," Oslun stammered as he struggled to keep pace with the much taller Jaxus. "It is in my chambers."

"That is a foolish place for a sword young Sir." Jaxus chided gently. "And you, Thyso, is your weapon ready?"

"Of course." Thyso answered proudly, his eyes betraying the annoyance and superiority he felt over Oslun as he strode easily behind the dark warrior.

"Good." Jaxus stepped down the white marble steps and moved towards one of the deceased warriors that stood guard. He began removing the dead man's shadow armor. "Thyso, by what name do you call your weapon?"

"My sword has no name." Thyso bent to assist Jaxus in removing the vestment from the dead warrior.

Jaxus released the final leather buckle from its hold under the breast plate of the dead warrior and turned to Oslun. The cupbearer nervously raised his arms as Jaxus bent and began fastening the armor over the cupbearer's clothing.

"I have never seen a battle, Sir Jaxus." Thyso's pride was clearly dimmed by this admission. He had long hungered for combat, for the glory and pride that adorned warriors returned from the killing fields. He aided Jaxus in dressing Oslun and wrinkled his nose against the smell of the unwashed, sweat bathed boy.

"You will." Jaxus answered frankly. "When that day comes, you had best discovered a name for your weapon. Blades unnamed are blades unloved. An unloved blade is a poor friend in dire moments."

Thyso did not react to Jaxus words. Oslun shook with renewed fear at the thought of entering battle. He did not want to be in a war. He wanted only to read and record histories for further generations. A pain in his stomach that had been present since Axise banners first reached the citadel grew larger and the young cupbearer felt he would choke.

Jaxus, finished with his work, rose and turned back toward the throne. Oslun, now fully armored, though lacking a blade, followed at once with Thyso bringing up the rear. As the three men approached the white steps, they could see the King and his daughter wrapped in tender embrace. Both had tears streaming freely from their eyes. Axeleon caught sight of their approach and pulled away from his daughter. He kissed her brow and nodded. No other word need be said between them.

Jaxus mounted the white steps and approached the throne. He gripped the arm of the large seat and drug it to the side. It took both Thyso and Jaxus several long seconds of searching on their knees to find the lip of the slab and lift it free of the entrance. Once uncovered, the passage appeared as though it were smooth stone steps descending into nothingness.

Jaxus strode to the borum stone wall near the door to the dining hall and removed two torches from iron catches on the wall. He returned to the others, passed one torch to Thyso. He secured the straps of his pack, nodded abruptly to the King in deference and moved towards the passage to begin the decent.

"Hold." Axeleon did not shout the command, but every soul in the room heard it and stopped immediately. Jaxus foot hovered just over the first step down into the darkness. "Bring me the sword of Arielies Tarkington, the bow of Simeon Starmish, and the sword of Amyus Colth."

Almost instantly, the warriors in the room located the requested items and brought them forward. To Oslun, the King spoke, taking the sword of Arielies Tarkington from the soldier who held it. "Every warrior needs a sword, my young lad, and I believe yours has been left behind."

Oslun quaked under the intensity of the king's gaze, "I am no warrior, Sire, I am only a servant."

"Today you carry steel, not wine." Axeleon held the sword up to Oslun's eye level. It was long, the scabbard a deep blue leather wrapped around a steel sleeve. "This is the weapon of Arielies Tarkington, the first champion of the tournament of bones. The only survivor of King Prathus raid on the Elk's Fist outpost of Dwalnot during my grandfather's rule. Wounded, and alone, she traveled three days to the Imat Fortress to warn of the Prathus' assault. By her courage, she saved the fist, and possibly all Arken from great pain.

Devil's Song it is called, this blade carries with it the strength and courage of its former master. May it guide you and may her spirit strengthen yours, should hope fail."

As the King spoke, the activity of the other warriors resumed. A great commotion took over the space as the fighters and vassals prepared to execute the king's plan. Axeleon took up the sword of Amyus Colth and turned to Jaxus. "You have no name to call your lineage from. You are neither noble, nor common, nor royal. No house do you have to draw your strength, yet you are strong. This blade was carried by Amyus Colth and Nightfyre it is known, though I suspect you find another moniker for the weapon. Sir Colth was as true to the spirit and shadow as any could claim. She came, like you, from anonymity to write her name in the pages of the long histories. So, now you will go to do this for yourself."

Jaxus gripped the pommel of the sword, extended to him from the Kings hand. The sheath itself was unremarkable, black leather over dull metal. The dark warrior drew the blade out a few inches. As was his own sword, Amyus blade was black, appearing as a living metal. Jaxus recognized the weapon and knew why the king had granted it to him. It was a near exact twin to his own. There were thought to have been no more than thirty blades of this make in the known world, and less than ten armored suits of the same material. Jaxus himself had only ever seen the ones he possessed, all others were merely legend.

Jaxus smiled almost imperceptibly, and with a jolt, pushed the blade back into the sheath. Before he could sense the movement, Lord Commander Fax was at his side. Jaxus was not a short man, by any definition, but Liam dwarfed him. Without word, the Commander took the sword in his large hands moved to Jaxus back. Carefully, he attached the blade to the back of the dark armor, at an angle to Jaxus own sword, so that the hilt of each blade could be grasped over his shoulders.

"Many thanks, Lord Commander." Jaxus offered, in courtesy though his voice remained cool.

The large infantry man placed his hand on Jaxus shoulder and spun him roughly around so that the men were face to face, Jaxus' back to the King. The commander held a large finger to Jaxus lips, preventing him from speaking. "I know why you came here, Starrowlander."

Jaxus did not move or attempt speech. He gave no emotion.

"I know you came here in the service of Axise, to inform him on our moments and troop strength. Your mysterious departures and sudden reappearances in the citadel have too similar a timing to be of any other purpose." Commander Fax' voice was so deep that Jaxus could barely hear the man, remarkable considering the nature of the Whisper Hall. "King Axeleon also knows this, yet he has seen fit to entrust the safety of Princess Layandria to you. I cannot see the reason behind the decision, but I follow the orders I am given. Regardless of the King's trust, know this, man of no name, if you betray Princes Layandria or bring her to harm, the pain and suffering the Gods will bring on you will be beyond anything you have ever experienced."

"Lord Commander, what you believe of my character is incorrect. I would share the truth with you, but I see you are of simple mind and prone to assumption. I hold to no Gods whose names you can speak and no threat you have to offer will compare to the suffering my soul has known longer than yours has known life." Jaxus voice was venom, issuing from some dark place within.

"Perhaps you speak truth, perhaps not." Liam leaned in, his lips brushing Jaxus ear as he spoke. "Use your new sword as you will to protect her. If you fail, show a sliver of honor and turn it on yourself."

Jaxus watched the man as he turned and strode away. He knew the Lord Commander to be concretely grounded to ideals of honor and loyalty. Such a steadfast man was hard to find in the world of the day. Even Jaxus himself was not often troubled by such weighty concepts, and he found marvel when men truly lived by the ideals. In Jaxus summation, most men use honor and duty only as excuses for vile acts or as blankets to hide behind when their motives are less than pure.

Jaxus returned to face the king. Thyso now had the bow once used by Simeon Starmish over his back and was tying a quiver of arrows to his belt. The Princess had her mother's sword, Heart's End, in its scabbard secured to her hip. The sunstone pendant suspended from its chain around the Princess's neck. Jaxus made eye contact with the King, who held his gaze for a long moment. He could see fear and doubt in his ruler, but also strength. Axeleon nodded to him, and Jaxus moved towards the steps. One after another, Jaxus, Princess Layandria, Thyso, and finally, a hesitating Oslun, descended into the black. Axeleon watched until the light from their torches vanished and all but dark disappeared into the void.

Without word, the King gripped the blood stone slab and slid it back into place, the flesh of his fingertips painfully pinched by the stone as it fell into its crevasse. He was intently aware that the activity in the great hall had ceased. The warriors were prepared, their orders carried out. Each man and woman watched as the King drug the throne back into place over the entrance, mopping a cloth across the blood stone to remove any marks left behind. He turned and faced them, his eyes passing over each one. "Extinguish the torches."

The Hall of Whispers was bathed in sudden darkness. The borum stone walls dimmed to the glow of a dying ember. Axeleon moved about silently in the darkness, making himself ready to receive his guests while his warriors stood fast.

Axise' ram smashed against the great doors of the hall, repair or replacement now completed. No one moved as one of the great iron hinges at the bottom of the left door gave in to the force.

The ram fell against the doors again. The already weakened hinges failed entirely and the massive oak structure crashed to the floor. Outside the hall, a massive battle cry went up. Inside, not a motion or sound.

Axeleon, son of Axlent and Santar, of the house Taymrhlyn, King of Arken, Commander of the Armies of Shadow prepared his heart for what he knew would be his final battle.

2.

Jaxus movements were swift and sure despite the intense darkness of the passage and the dim light of the torches. Oslun's own movements were not so certain. Either due to the darkness or the black toned armor worn by his fellows, he quickly lost sight of the rest of the party. He could hear his own footfalls against the earthen floor, and he could see the glimmer of light ahead, but he could not see the floor before his own feet. The sounds of his fellows rapidly faded, and the light of the torches disappeared as the portly servant struggled to keep pace.

A panic started to rise in his mind. The desire to turn back towards the Whisper Hall welled in him. He broke under his fear. Oslun stopped in his tracks, spun around and ran towards the entrance to the tunnel. He imagined that he would see a point of light, some soft glow giving indication that he was approaching the king's hall, but with each step he began to feel as if he had gone much further back then he had come in.

Oslun's mind tore at itself to find some shred of information that would deliver him from the torment of the darkness. His left foot found the first stair. Oslun stumbled from the impact of his toes to stone and sprawled onto the steps. His chin hit hard, and the impact dazed him. He reached his hand to his face and found the warmth of blood coming from the flesh of his jaw. The pain filled him with terror, and he clambered up the stairs, lurching until his helm hit the underside of the blood stone slab that had been set into place.

He felt like a fool. Of course, they had secured the passage after he had entered the tunnel. Suddenly Oslun's fear conjured images of the Arken warriors left in the room above being slaughtered by the savage men sure to have broken into the Whisper Hall by now. He could see King Axeleon, proud and defiant to the last moment before Axise sword found its mark on the good king's neck. Oslun pitched backwards and tumbled down the stone steps, landing in a heap. The young man struggled to his feet, his helm falling off. He began to run back into the passage with all the speed he could find.

"Jaxus! Jaxus, where are you!" The expulsion of air from Oslun's already over taxed lungs made him dizzy. He fell hard, dirt and chips of stone digging into his hands. Pulling himself to his feet, Oslun made only four strides before returning to the floor in a spilled mess. Terror overtook him. Oslun surged into the darkness on his hands and knees. The sword, Devil's Song, clattered to the floor, its leather belt undone by the flails of the boy's terror. Blind and choking on the stale, dusty air, he began to weep.

Lurching forward into nothingness, Oslun was as a mad animal, his mind no longer an ally. The muscles in his back tightened and his knees scrapped along the floor. The grit of the stone tore through his hands, ripping the flesh. As he clambered, the armor on his knee struck a rough lip of stone. He plunged to the floor, striking his face against it with a force to rival a hammer. His ears rang, and his eyes betrayed him, showing him stars swimming in violent circles. Wrecked and utterly spent, he rolled to his side, hands grasping his battered knee. Oslun wept.

The sounds of approaching footsteps overcame the terror that filled his ears with the rapid beats of his own heart. Heavy falls of swift feet filled his mind. The boy turned his head in the direction of the sound and saw figures of men in the distance, shadowed by an orange glow that he could not place. Oslun was no longer certain which way he was facing in the passage and thought betrayed him.

Axise men had breached the entrance into the passage, knowing that Layandria had escaped. Perhaps Axise had known about the tunnel all along, Oslun knew that the man was raised as a Prince of Arken. The servants of this evil man would now be in pursuit, meaning to murder the queen and all who traveled with her. His best hope was that they would, so consumed by the pursuit of the Princess, run him through with the sword and let him die quickly. His weeping intensified as the thoughts of his certain and violent end consumed all reason and the young man urinated on himself.

The approaching footsteps were upon him. Torchlight burned brilliant that he could see it through tightly shuttered eyelids. Oslun screamed. Hands were on him, but he was powerless to fight against them. Covering his face with his battered hands, the cupbearer pulled in a great draught of air and screamed again. His terror pushed so much violent, ragged air out of his lungs, that he began gasping and choking. Over the sounds of his desperate body, he could hear a voice shouting his name. Then another voice was laughing. Not the savage laugh of hard men intent on his vicious torture, this laughter was light, amused and not at all blood lusting.

Oslun finally willed himself to open his eyes and was confronted with the last image he expected. Standing over him were not the faces of his soon to be murderers, but the concerned face of Layandria, Princess of Arken, bathed in the brilliance of the sun stone. Her face was striking in the light, her eyes sparkling as if the stars had descended from the sky to set in them. Her hair was pulled back, revealing her strong features.

"The sun stone!" Oslun's voice burst from his lips, ragged and choked though it was. "The light, how is it so brilliant?"

Layandria looked down at the pendant. "It gives off as much light as I need it to, I suppose. When we first came in here, it was dim, only enough light to see a few steps ahead, but when we realized you had fallen behind, it grew brighter, and brighter still when we heard you screaming."

Oslun was still shaking and sobbing, but the soothing voice of the queen helped to calm his tremors. Another face appeared in the light. The dark, hard face of Thyso starred down at him with narrow eyes. His voice was less comforting than the Queen's. "Did he piss himself?"

Thyso had been named handmaid of the Crown Princess on his sixteenth birthday, just over four years ago. It was custom in Arken that able boys and girls select their area of profession on their fourteenth year and begin to practice and grow knowledge in that field at once. Prior to this, all children are given the same schooling, covering all subject matter. Thyso elected the profession of arms and began to train to enter the King's Infantry. To his great dismay and personal shame, Thyso was ordered to the service of the Princess. Now, he looked quite menacing, almost rivaling the conjured images of Axise band of savages in Oslun's mind. He did not appear at all as a handmaid.

"He did piss himself!" Thyso's voice oozed disgust. "What do you make of that? Cup bearer to the King of Arken is so frightened of the dark that he scabs along the floor in his own piss like a small babe."

"Thyso, be still." Princess Layandria instructed sternly, though her words were overrun by an unrelenting Thyso.

"I will never understand, if I live to be a thousand years old, why the King would send this sniveling blob along with us. Better to have cut you then and there and be rid of your tears." Thyso's disdain for the weak boy reached its pitch. The Princess recoiled, but her handmaid did not yield. "Stop your whimpering! And where is your sword? Have you lost it already?"

"Enough!" Jaxus stepped forward into the bloom of light emanating from the sun stone. Though he was a mere step away, Oslun had not seen him, so complete was the effect of the rare armor that he wore, coupled with the dark tone of his skin. Where shadow armor absorbed the light, permitting no refection and thus aiding its wearer in camouflage, the material of Jaxus armor embraced the light, using it to create the illusion that he was not there at all, but was only the stone wall by which he stood.

"Our lad here has never been trained for war, nor has he experience in battle. He has never before been made to face true fear." Jaxus turned and gripped the shoulder plate of Thyso's armor as he spoke, commanding his full attention. "How would you have behaved if this most black of days were your first taste? Would you be strong if you were raised in his station?"

"I think not." Layandria spoke evenly, though struggling to conceal her anger. She stepped forward and though her head barely reached Thyso's chin, he shrank before her. "You will never ignore my instructions again."

"Yes, my Lady." Thyso bowed his head and stepped back, his eyes cast to the dark floor.

Jaxus turned back to the still prostrate Oslun and extended his hand. The young boy sheepishly accepted the gesture and began to struggle to his feet. The Princess gripped his free arm and helped him rise. Her movement caused the sun stone to sway on its chain, its light shifting, the shadows responding in kind. The movement of light frightened Oslun, who gasped and tucked his head into Jaxus armor for safety.

Thyso scoffed.

Jaxus spun towards the handmaid at the sound, anger springing up with ferocity in his eyes. He raised his hand, fingers joined like the blade of a knife, only short inches from Thyso's face. "You think you shame him by your words, yet you shame yourself. Withhold your insults and help your companions, lest you find yourself alone in the darkness of the world."

Thyso did not respond, his eyes fixed on the intensity of the man before him.

Jaxus lowered his hand, "Do you wish to argue the point?"

"No, Sir Jaxus." Thyso slunk back a step, bowing his head.

"Do not call me Sir, I am no knight." Jaxus offered by way of stiff reply.

The princess watched Oslun's brow tighten and his eyes narrow. "What is it, Oslun?" She inquired gently, placing her elegant hand on his shoulder.

"My Lady," Oslun stammered, "I only recall that on the sixteenth day of the fourth month of the seventh year of the rule of King Axeleon, the King did so decree that Jaxus, of no known house, lineage or parentage, having been taken as a son of Arken, should hence forth be accepted as Knight and Defender of the Fists, her people and her lands. To discharge the orders and duties give him and hold all loyalty and faith until he draws his last breath."

Jaxus stared blankly at the cup bearer. Thyso rolled his eyes. Layandria smiled.

Jaxus did not respond. He shouldered past the cup bearer and headed swiftly back down the tunnel towards the entrance steps. The hilts of his dual swords above his shoulders reminded Oslun of great horns, protruding off the back of some dark beast. Almost to himself, Oslun muttered, "they call him the no name knight. Perhaps they should call him the horned knight."

Layandria giggled softly at the boy's joke. She jabbed gently at the cupbearer's underarm with her fingers and started off after Jaxus. "I am glad you are with us, Oslun." Her voice rang as a melody as she passed.

Oslun blushed and lowered his head, "Thank you, My Princess."

A force much more severe than the jab delivered by the Princess impacted Oslun's back. He staggered forward, his breath catching in his throat as he struggled to maintain his balance. Thyso roughly pushed past him, thundering back into the tunnel.

"Mercy," Oslun whimpered and shrank away from the large handmaid.

"Come swiftly Oslun," Jaxus voice boomed down the passage. Oslun stood for a moment, the thought of his murdered king giving him pause. The image of Thyso's stalking form began to fade to shadow. Fear began to creep up the cupbearer's spine and he had to fight the urge to call out. He forced himself to move, but deep bruises were setting in on his limbs and the steps were labored. He did not have far to go, for not twenty yards ahead, round a soft curve in the tunnel wall, Jaxus and Layandria were stooped, gathering up the spilt sword and equipment left behind in Oslun's wild flight.

Jaxus stood and faced the cup bearer as he approached. With movements that seamed impossibly graceful and precise for a man so large, Jaxus reattached Oslun's weapons belt around his waist and set his helm on the young man's head. The warrior rapped a knuckle against the metal covering Oslun's chest. "This is good armor, shadow steel over hammer forged dragonscale. Do any of you know what dragonscale is?"

Layandria's eyes lit up as she began. "Dragonscale is a rare, ancient type of iron that is mined in the Derrenge Mountains, north of our lands. Many generations ago, miners and craftsman from Arken ventured into the frozen peaks to mine, explore and stake claim to new lands. They discovered dragonscale, borum stone, and other rare materials. It is said that when the first miners found a vein of dragonscale, time and pressure had rendered its surfaces iridescent, reminding the men of the tales of dragons from their childhood. Strong, but lite, dragonscale is a highly valued metal, though it is prone to corrode so it must always be covered with another metal."

"Once the Chokahr and the tribes of unoathed men began to cover the landscape, it was deemed too dangerous to mine the mountains north of the border and so, dragon scale, borum stone and other metals have become ever rarer. There is only one metal more uncommon, which Sir Jaxus swords and armor are cast from. Ploysteel."

"What is ploysteel?" Thyso asked, having never heard the name before.

"Though I know the name, I do not know the history. There are few who do." Princes Layandria responded. "Perhaps Sir Jaxus can aid us in this learning?"

Finished checking the passage floor for lost supplies, Jaxus stood. "Ploysteel is a very special material. To my knowledge, no smith of our age has yet been able to forge with it. There are but a handful of weapons and armor created from it and many have been lost through the years, though to my knowledge, none have ever been broken or heavily scarred."

"And how did you come to own such rare works?" Layandria asked in curiosity.

"These are tales left for brighter days, your grace." The man moved back to the head of the small column. "Let us begin. Oslun, you stay close to me this time, Thyso has the rear guard."

Jaxus turned back to meet the handmaid's eyes. "If the cupbearer falls behind again, I will hold you accountable."

Thyso nodded curtly. Once Jaxus had turned away, he focused his dangerous gaze on Oslun. The young cupbearer shrank away.

The four began to move into the passage again at an easy pace. Oslun was grateful for this as his limbs ached and the pack he bore was quite heavy on his shoulders.

The silence stifled Thyso. In hopes of keeping the conversation and opening distance between himself and the foul words of Jaxus' rebuke, he spoke up from the back of the small column. "Borum stone is actually a misnomer, for it is not a stone at all, but rather a living creature. I am told that every few decades, craftsmen must come into the Whisper Hall and remove several inches of new growth from the walls."

"Yes!" Oslun's voice took on a high pitch as he found, with some excitement, a topic of conversation he could share common ground with the harsh Thyso. "Many of my readings on the topic indicate that borum stone is much akin to sea coral, though much harder, and appearing more solid."

"Have you ever seen sea coral?" Thyso queried, a tone of irritation invading his voice as the cup bearer stole the conversation away from him.

Oslun did not take note of Thyso's tone, his excitement undeterred. "No, but I hope too. I would love to see the ocean."

"Perhaps someday we shall journey together to the coast off the Elk Fist. They have many great fishing vessels and warships." Layandria had been to the sea several times with her father and his court. Thyso was present for the last trip. The thought of the warm air and the smell of the pure sea brought a gentle smile to her lips, but a darker thought wiped it away. The Princess began to wonder if she would ever return to the Elk Fist, and under what manner would she return? She forced the thought down as she trudged on, unwilling to let despair take hold in her.

Silence fell over the group for a time, each man sensing the turmoil that Layandria wrestled with. Thyso grew increasingly uncomfortable. For all his experience in combat training and for all the years he had spent with the Princess, he had never learned to handle moments of painful emotion. He searched for a topic that would return the spark to the conversation. "I had always thought that the miners called it dragonscale because it was believed to be the decayed remains of ancient dragons."

Layandria giggled. "There is no recorded evidence that dragons ever existed."

"Indeed," Jaxus offered, "in all my travels, I have seen a great many mysteries, but none near as fanciful as this. Dragons are the invention of storytellers only."

"I should think I would like to see a dragon," Oslun mused from his position, just behind Jaxus, "if they were real, of course."

Thyso scoffed, "If you did see a real dragon, you'd piss yourself again."

"Thyso," Jaxus shot out from the side of his mouth, "speak only kindness and truth with your tongue, or leave it behind on the stone."

Thyso stopped short. Anger and shame fought for control of his mind. In the short moment that he had stopped, he had fallen behind. The walls of the passage seamed to close in on him in the darkness. He shuddered against the prick of fear in the small of his back and stepped off at once to close the distance to the group as they forged onwards, into the black.

3

Shattered stone sprayed into the room. The sound of a mighty door rendered to scraps echoed throughout the hall. King Axeleon did not flinch, though his eyes caught the motion as a few of his men allowed tremors. The ugly head of Axis's battering ram entered the room for a small fraction of time after the sound, filing the space with its vile imagery. The iron and bronze head, though distorted by several heavy impacts with the strong doors, resembled an iron clad warrior holding aloft a severed head in each hand, dangling by the hair. This image is one that Axise had adopted as his own after he was expelled from Arken. It adorned the shields of his infantry, the sigils carried by his banner men, and the chest plate of Axise' own armor.

Outside the hall of the king, silence fell.

Rut Prathus, a Knight of the Crux who was forced into Axise' service after his conquest of her homeland, stood outside the shattered door. She carefully peered into the Whisper Hall and observed row upon row of armed soldiers. The light was dim, and she could not see past the first ranks. "They are just standing there, Your Grace, and I see no weapons drawn."

Axise scoffed to himself. "Fool of a brother. Thinks he can pacify me into sparing his pathetic life. Thinks I will parlay with him no doubt." He searched the memories of his youth for any trap or hidden secret held in the Whisper Hall. It had been a long life since he departed this place and his memories were in fog.

No, Axise own spy was in the Whisper Hall this very moment. Word had been sent out that there were scarcely more than thirty soldiers in the hall of kings, most of Axeleon's personal guard having been scattered or destroyed. Axise knew that there were no exits to the space. There could be no trap, Axise was certain of this, though he thought it best to test for resistance before entering himself. His black eyes turned to Rut Prathus. His massive hand rose and cleared the sweat from his brow. "You, woman."

Rut turned away from the door. "Yes, My King?"

"Go forth and demand Axeleon surrender at once." His words passed through his tremendous beard as water draining through small stones.

Rut nodded her compliance and turned back to the dark entrance, pausing to observe for one last moment.

"Now!" Axise commanded harshly. Rut flinched at his sudden outburst. This amused Axise greatly and a hearty chuckle escaped from his concealed lips. He despised allowing women to fight. Women, he believed, were frail by nature, weak of heart and prone to flights of disloyalty in favor of anyone who would part their legs. The necessity to allow useless crones like Rut Prathus into his forces was born out of combat. He suffered too many losses and killed far too many fighting men during his campaigns to limit those who would rather fight than die. It did also prove of value to have such creatures around while not in battle, for his men made great sport of parting their legs, by choice or force, it made no difference.

Rut Prathus lowered her head and drew her sword. She took in a deep breath and stepped into the darkness. Her foot falls rang out, echoing through the space, seaming far louder than they should have. It was as if the expansive chamber was enhancing every sound, every foot fall, and every breath. She could easily hear her own beating heart. Rut could barely see in the dim light, the walls appearing as the dying embers of a fire, casting strange shadows and tricking her eyes. She could make out silhouette after silhouette of armored warriors standing in perfect rank and file, unmoving. She estimated that more than five hundred soldiers stood before her.

"All of you, lay down your weapons on order of King Axise, your ruler and conqueror!" Rut's voice shot through the silence with vigor. No response came. She pressed on, approaching the foremost rank. As Rut drew near, she noted a strange hollowness in the eyes of the helm before her, as if it was not a man under the plate steel, but a spirit.

"What is it?" Axise voice boomed into the space as if the king was standing just behind Rut's shoulder despite being some hundred paces back.

"I am not sure, your grace," the reply came in a lowered tone, hushed against the fear climbing inside her chest. "It is as if they are..." Her words trailed off as she closed within arm's reach of one of Axeleon's warriors. She hesitated, peering into the visor of the silver helm. Nothing but void was visible within.

"Fool." Axise muttered to himself, deciding that it was a mistake to send in the woman. "She has likely become enamored with some random beam of moon light dancing on the floor."

Confusion washed over Rut Prathus as she inched closer to the strange warriors. She darted her head left and right, examining those nearest. None seemed to move. It would take a soldier several years of dedicated training to learn completely stop the slight sway, the rise and fall of the chest, barely perceptible flexes of the muscles. Rut did not believe that the whole the Arkenhead guard would have this skill, but no other explanation for the utter lack of motion before her made rational sense.

She did not see the sword as it darted over the empty warrior's shoulder. The blade dove into Rut's neck, slightly off center to the left. The steel was eager, and it tore through the woman's body, ripping through the side of her neck.

Pain and terror crushed all thought and Rut was unable to remain standing. No chance for her to raise her own weapon existed, the damage so severe. Her knees buckled, but as she started to fall, immensely strong hands gripped her body under her arms. Unseen hands jabbed a large metal hook through the bottom of her jaw, driving through her tongue and into the roof of her mouth.

Further unseen foes pulled strongly against a rope that was attached to the hook and Rut was lifted from the floor in a sudden jerk. She felt as though her jaw was being ripped off her skull. She could not see the hands that gripped her legs, preventing her body from swinging into the ranks of soldiers that still did not move. Another yank on the rope and Rut was carried into the air. Released by the hands that steadied her, she swung forward with great speed, while several harsh pulls against the rope carried her higher.

Rut Prathus lost all thought and feeling as she swung as a pendulum, so great was the pain that controlled her. Her passing was swift, having bled rapidly and expiring before the rope brought her to the high ceiling.

Outside the Whisper Hall, all that was heard was a strange gasping sound, some rapid shuffling, and the sound of a sword clattering to the stone floor.

"What is it woman?" Axise called out into the darkness. "What do you see?"

No response reached back to Axise. "Rut Prathus! I command you to report!"

An eerie sound, much like a heavy rope being drawn over a wooden beam, followed by a ghastly, nearly inhuman moan traveled out into the passage. Some of Axise' warriors exchanged curious glances. This annoyed the King greatly.

"Tytos!" Axise called to the commander of his personal guard. "Take in a force and destroy Rut Prathus' ghosts!"

"Ah!" Tytos shouted as he leapt forward towards the shattered door. Some twenty men surged forward with him. No words were spoken between them as they moved. All communication was carried out by jerked hand motions. For a moment, the pace of the men slowed as they approached the first rank. Axise was on the verge of denouncing Rut's cowardice when a fury of metallic crashes and the screams of mortally wounded men shattered the calm. For a long moment, the sounds of some great fight shook the walls, then, as suddenly as they began, the hall fell to silence.

The thickness of the silence was dramatically broken by the sounds of many heavy ropes being pulled across wooden beams. Axise began to sweat profusely. He turned his head down the passage, surveying his remaining men. "Why are we so few?" He bellowed.

"Sire," Pheleno, a Knight of the Starrowlands spoke up from the dark hall, "You ordered the ram cleared as soon as the doors were breached. The remainder of our forces are securing the city and seeking any who would draw blades as you instructed."

Axise was silent. Anger boiled within his mind. It was intentional for so few to be next to him in this moment. His ideal was to face Axeleon alone, but this was not practical. Perhaps Axeleon did lay some trap for him. No matter, he still had some forty men behind him, and he was owed this victory. It was providence that called him to the throne of Arken and he would wait no longer for his birthright.

"To me!" The king cried out as he leapt forward toward the darkness. His huge, double headed ax held high over his head as he advanced.

Axise cry fell flat as his eyes adjusted to the near pitch blackness of the room. The borum stone walls seamed to burn out as he entered the space, reacting to a presence known to them, but unwelcome. The king could barely make out the glint of light on the edge of his axe head. None of the men he had sent into the Whisper Hall could be seen. He moved carefully as he crossed the empty floor, deep into the hall. Silhouettes of warriors in armor came into view. Hope told him that these were his men, but nausea told him they were not. These warriors did not move as Axise drew near and he began to see more of the landscape before him.

Shattered shields and broken swords lay strewn about on the black stone floor. Streaks of blood, a helm, crushed from the heavy blow of a cudgel. As his eyes adjusted to the low light, Axise began to make out row upon row of armored warriors facing him. His spy had lied. There had to be at least five hundred men, standing ready to end his conquest.

"Jaxus, you bastard." Axise muttered a curse to his spy as he continued into the room. A sharp desire for the rest of his men filled his thoughts. He should not have released them until the Whisper Hall was fully taken.

A voice both proud and strong rocked into the space, smashing the silence. "All of you, lay your weapons at your feet and surrender in the name of Axeleon, King of Arken. Do this and your lives will be spared. Do not, and you will meet the same fate as those who came before you."

Axise beat the head of his axe against his chest plate and stepped forward in defiance. "Come out Axeleon, dear brother, let us decide this together! Come forward and bow before your rightful King!"

Nothing so much as a dust spider shifted at Axise call.

"Come forward and claim your throne if you think yourself worthy, brother." Axeleon pierced the still air. The borum stone walls responded to the voice of their king, bursting in sudden brilliance and casting wild shadows about the hall, returning to their darkened state on the final sound of the King's voice.

"As I lead!" Axise exploded in rage at the sound of his unseen, estranged sibling. His long strides brought him to the first rank of armed warriors swiftly. The folly of pressing an attack when so outnumbered was lost on the man, so consumed was he with desire for his prize. Axise drew near a warrior clad in a molted red and yellow suit of armor common to the men of the fire fist as he let his first stroke fly. His massive ax collided with the warrior under the helm, perfectly finding the gap between mail and helm. The ax was already moving up and around, following what would have certainly been a deadly blow, but the soldier did not fall.

Axise was moving too quickly to stop his next stroke and the ax came crashing down onto the right shoulder of another fighter. The arm was hewn from the body, but the torso barely shifted under the impact. Axise took in the wound he had just inflicted. Broken shards of bone protruded, but the surrounding flesh appeared dry and no blood issued forth. Axise stopped his motions and brought his axe up, at the ready.

Around him, he could hear his men colliding with these suits of armor. He turned his gaze to those of Axeleon's forces standing nearest to him. None moved or seemed to draw the smallest breath.

"Hold!" He shouted to his men as a smirk began to play across his bearded face. "All of you, hold! These are not warriors! They are the empty husks of Arken soldiers long dead. No ghosts haunt this hall."

Around him, his fighters stood at ill ease. Axise had enjoyed many victories, sweeping a path of blood across the eastern nations as he marshaled an army strong enough to take the Arkenhead. He had never faltered in his vicious leadership, first made famous when he usurped the throne of the Starrowlands. He was steadfast in his brutality when he knocked back the sworn nights of the Crux, sent King Jostus of Pilfring into hiding and used his gathered strength to cut the Simicot Realm in two. He led his men with ferocity as they smashed the forces of King Counamn of Cipran, beheading the king and queen himself. In a cruel display, Axise stood before the survivors of the siege of the Cipran capital city of Reahal, holding the severed heads of their departed rulers, dangling by their hair from each of Axise upraised fists. His warriors knew him to be ruthless, though often reckless, pride deciding his tactics more often than good sense.

Axise drew in a deep breath and lunged forward, through the ranks of the dead soldiers. "To the throne!" He could almost feel the supple leather of the armrests under his fingers. He remembered, as a boy, when his father, King Axlent, had let him sit in the great chair. How he had had lusted for it! How he had turned to hatred when it was ripped from him. King Axlent, wounded in battle and suffering long before he passed, had named the cursed Axeleon as heir to the throne.

Axeleon, third born behind their deceased sister and Axise himself was to take the seat of the King of Arken. No matter, Axise mused, he was about to restore the world to its just position.

As the massive form of Axise strode on, one of his own Knights, Jussit Fike, called out from only paces behind. "My King, this hall has the smell of death! I fear this is folly!"

The words enraged Axise. The King would not abide questions to the righteousness of his path. Axise spun round and delivered a devastating blow to Fike's helm. The weight and force of the ax cleaved the knight's head in two. Axise let loose a savage cry, spinning back towards the throne and surging onward.

Axise pushed past the final row of armored bones and took in an uninterrupted view of the blood stone platform. Axeleon was seated on the throne, armor removed and stacked neatly on the floor to the side of the great chair. The King of the Five Fists wore a fresh olive tunic over dark green trousers and, with a well-groomed beard and hair, Axeleon had the appearance of one recently risen from a good rest. Axeleon's sword was securely in its scabbard, leaning against the right side of the royal seat, untouched by its wielder. Axise was stunned to see a bemused smile on his brother's face.

"You seem troubled, dear brother." Axeleon spoke softly, as if he were addressing a close companion. "Perhaps your spy in my court was ill chosen? Snakes often choose poorly in their friends."

"I know not what you mean, I have no spies!" Axise chided. "Nor do I know why you shame me with the name of a serpent! I am no snake, just a man, as any would, seeking to reclaim that which is mine."

"Even the serpent keeps his honor by calling himself thus. You call yourself brother and deny that you are snake, though all can see you for the creature you are, slithering about on your belly, taking that which you have no right."

"You will not call me vile names and shame me again!" Axise hold over his temper had never been strong, but here, so close to the throne and his rule, he could maintain no longer. The great man stepped forward, leaving the rows of dead warriors, and the ranks of his own men several paces behind.

"I must say, I am impressed with your deception. When my runners informed me the banners of the Starrowlands were flying in the south, I would have never believed you were not with them." Axeleon knew that Axise pride was his greatest weakness, but in order to destroy a thing and use it as a weapon, the Arken King had to stoke the flames. "You were never a man of subtlety or sleight of hand. You have grown in the long years you have been away."

"Indeed, I have, far more than you yet know." Axise let the feelings of power and strength wash over him. He stopped short. In the days before his expulsion from Arken, he had come to learn that if his brother was offering him deep complements, Axeleon was hiding something. He would have to ferret out what secret was being kept from him. "I should tell you then, given the grace of your tongue, that I am curious as to the fate of the scout and the men who entered our father's hall before me."

"I saw no others before you." Axeleon responded in feigned surprise. "Were they meant to herald your entry? I suppose, if you were to exit the hall, then return, I could announce your arrival as was the fashion in days past."

"Perhaps you have further grown your own deceptions in my absence." Axise determined it best to allow his enemy this momentary victory. It would not matter in the end. He would find all the answers he craved while Axeleon's blood adorned the floor.

"I have no need for deception, good brother. I am but a King, greeting a visiting royal." Axeleon took on an air of disinterest. He could clearly see the irritation filling Axise eyes.

"I am told that you are called by the people the Ruler of Long Peace, but I call you naught but a fool. Look upon the ease with which my army has cast aside those who would save you." Axise began thumping the head of his ax on the floor as he spoke. "You are unfit to call yourself king of this nation. Your army is weak, while mine is strong! Look what I have created! You were handed the finest army in the known world and still you fail! Only a true warrior may hold the throne of Arken, and I am that warrior!"

Axeleon remained unimpressed in his brother's tyrannical speech, knowing that the flames of Axise pride were nearing inferno. "If I recall, you remained home when we rode to war, left behind to lord over the cattle."

"So, I did." Axise paused, his expression growing in frustration. His brother's words brought up all manner of emotion, shame, disgrace, guilt, but predominantly rage as he recalled his father's orders to him, countless times confining him to the Arkenhead, then again as he informed his sons that Axeleon would take the throne. The large man fought to maintain control over himself. Reasons were offered, but these words were useless to Axise and he resented the implication that Axeleon were in anyway his better. Axise eyes fixed on his brother, sitting in the throne and his fury boiled. He strode several paces forward.

"Ah, careful now brother, approaching a king so armed could easily be mistaken as an act of war." Axeleon chided.

"You are a King of dishonor and of cowardice only!" Axise stepped to the base of the white steps.

Axeleon breathed a great show of relief. "You do call me your King! I am glad to hear it for I had thought your journey here was one of ill intent. I see now that I was mistaken, for you are here to swear allegiance!"

Axise bellowed and moved up several steps. "I call you no King! I call you suckling child of a weak father and a cow mother!"

Axeleon rose from his throne steadily. A passive, almost vaguely amused smile on his lips disguised the fear within. Axise was powerful, and rarely possessed fear, though he was prone to make irrational decisions based on emotion, forgoing all reason. It was for these items of character that Axise had often been left to command the rear guard and not been named to the seat of Kings. Also for these traits, Axeleon knew his brother was easily manipulated. He moved a few paces towards the edge of the blood stone platform, his sword left behind him.

"Have you no response, my fool of a brother?" Axise could not grasp the meaning behind his brother's actions. No man he had ever faced had smiled at his own certain death and this unsettled him.

Axise felt a need for something more. Some piece of verbiage that could lead his brother into revealing weakness. His thoughts reeled, seizing on a line that he felt certain would bring out his sibling's deepest flaws. He smiled at the thought. "Hold, dear brother. Where is my sweet niece? I had thought to find her hear with you."

"She is not here." Axeleon lifted his eyes away from his brother, gazing to the borum stone walls at the back of the hall of kings, his expression blank. "She is beyond all of us now."

"Of course, she is here. You attempt to deceive me." Axise stamped up another step. "I have little doubt that she is in her chamber, just beyond. No matter. We will find her out, wherever she hides."

Axeleon did not shift his eyes from the borum stone.

"How old is our dear Layandria now? I believe her to be sixteen, by my counting."

Axeleon breathed deep of the cool air. "She is now eighteen, but she will be honored to know her uncle wishes her well on her next birth celebration."

"Ah, such a tender age." Axise mused, "I wonder, has she been sullied by the touch of a man? Of course, she has. How could she have saved herself, what with the tutelage of her whore mother."

Axise lifted his eyes towards the high ceiling now, feigning deep ponderings. "Once I have ended your rule, dear brother, I will retrieve the princess from whatever cupboard you have hidden her. I shall crown her the Queen of Arken, as her lineage commands. I shall present my new Queen with the head of her vanquished forbearer. Once she has enjoyed this fruit of my labor, I will give her to her loyal subjects. Does this please you?"

Axise was grinning with a wickedness not common. Axeleon ignored him.

Sahid Hauk Khan, a Starrowlands warrior clad in dark earth robes formed of skins stood behind Axise, between two suits of dead armor. He was most curious at this turn of events. Often had he witnessed Axise gloat over his conquests, savoring the final moments before he took the lives of those he deemed had wronged him previous. This exchange was not at all uncommon to the man, but King Axeleon seamed unaffected by the display. If Axise was attempting some theatric, it appeared to be failing.

The emotions of these two brother kings notwithstanding, it appeared as if Axise had utterly forgotten those soldiers he had sent into this hall of death ahead of himself. The sounds of dying men and running rope over wood, shattered shields and damaged armor, blood streaks on the floor, but no bodies. Surely this one man, warrior king or no, did not slay them all. And where were the bodies? And why now, in the face of his brother murderer, did King Axeleon leave there by his throne, untouched, the famous sword of the King, Heart of the Fathers as it was known, forged from the blades of many swords passed down. It was as if Axeleon had no fear at all.

"Perhaps our good king remains passive because he does not appreciate how I intend to give our new Queen to her people?" Axise began a low, rumbling laugh as he turned side to side, inviting his soldiers into his great fun. "After I have crowned Queen Layandria, I will call my captains to me. I will present the queen to them as a gift. I will rid her of her robes, for surely no cloth woven of mortal hands is fit for the daughter of Axeleon. I will give her to my commanders as a prize to enjoy.

Sahid winced at the mention of this vile act. Axeleon did not react.

Should our dear Queen survive the pleasures of my Captains, I will stand her, naked and bound at the gate to this very citadel. I will offer her body up to any who desire of her. I will do this until she has passed into shadow. I expect her to be very popular, dear brother. Who would pass at the chance to taste of a Queen?"

Sahid studied Axeleon's eyes, searching for some sign of reaction, some flare of anger. There was none. The man appeared as stone, his eyes were as deep pools of water, unmolested by even the calmest breeze. Axeleon did not falter.

"As I have told you, Layandria is beyond your grasp." Axeleon's voice was collected and steady. "As for you, your vile speech shames you, just as your actions have for decades. That you would dare speak these horrible words shows the true ignorance of your mind. All that you have done, all the pain you have caused and all the lives you have taken without need, all of that I could have understood. Never forgiven, for their can be no forgiveness for the spilling of innocent blood. Power and the lust for it corrupt even the best of men, so this I can see in you. But for a man of the Arken to speak so, to intend such a fate to the blood of this earth, that I cannot ever allow."

"Piss is all I hear from you Axeleon!" Axise bellowed and moved up another step, not three steps from the top. "Your words mean nothing to me! Let us cease this pointless banter and take to swords! It is time brother bowed before the just King of Arken!"

"Call yourself not my brother!" Axeleon boomed in response, stepping some paces towards Axise in rapid, striking motions. His words poured out as rapid fire, ejecting not of anger, but of unfettered condemnation. "You are the king of spoiled children, whose toys have been taken away for ill behavior! You are angered because our good father named me heir and not you, as is his right by the law, but you never considered the why of the choice. He did so because you lack control over yourself, you lack the care for your people in favor of only your desires. You are weak and not fit to rule over pigs!"

Axise rage turned over inside of him like the churning of a great sea at storm. He began beating his ax head against the stone floor with such force that dust and small shards of damaged marble ejected and mingled with the air.

Axeleon read his brother's features and knew he had found the correct leaver to pull. A bit more force and Axise would fully lose control. "Rather than take the lesson offered by our father, growing as a man, you turned to treachery and vileness. I offered you the seat at my right hand, but second was not enough for you. You instead conspired to have your own brother, who has shown you naught but kindness and faith, murdered so that you could take from him. This should have earned you death but I, having love for the brother I grew to age with, sparred your life. You then spent the next decades not learning, not bettering yourself, but bent to evil. You grew your reach so that you may come to spill the blood of your own people! For all your ill deeds, still I called you brother. No longer. All you are is a snake, fit only to be trod by the hooves of my horse!"

"I want what is rightfully mine!" Axise screamed the words as he advanced forward. Axise pictured his next move, so simple, two short steps, a single ark of his ax and his womanly brother would be ended.

Sahid Kahn watched this display, saw the twitches in Axise legs and knew that he was stealing himself for his attack. The end of this performance was coming. Which king would emerge victorious? Sahid became uniquely aware that the borum stone walls were growing steadily in brightness. Though he had never seen a stone that could emit its own light, he was thankful for it, for in the luminance, he observed a faint shifting behind him and realized that at least some of the stationary suits of armor behind he and his fellows were quite alive. Sahid carefully inched his body to the side, nearing a black armored fighter who swayed slightly.

"I am Sahid Kahn of the Fallish region, forced to fight for Axise on cost of blood." Sahid kept his words low, barely more than a breath, confident that the bellowing of the large men on the stage before him would hide his voice from any save the one to whom he spoke. "I have no loyalty to this pig king. I ask that when the fighting begins, my life be spared."

The armored warrior did not speak, but Sahid perceived the slightest nod of the helm, which he desperately hoped was a real confirmation, rather than the conjuring of a suddenly desperate mind. He tried to prevent his breath from increasing as he waited for the moment to come.

"Rightfully yours?" Axeleon spat the words, disgust with his brother now spewing out of him like venom. "You are owed nothing! By the traditions and laws of your own people you are owed only death! You are not but a traitor to your family, your lands and your people! Now come forward and let us end your wasted life!"

Axise let loose a terrible cry and volleyed the final step towards his brother, raising his ax on high. Blinded by rage, he was certain that this would be the blow that would bring him his crown. Axeleon was unarmed and without guard. No trap or illusion of ghosts would save the man now.

Just as the ax, heavy and powerful, but slow to swing, was to impact flesh and bone, Axeleon darted forward, inside the ark of his brother's arms. A short blade concealed in his sleeve darted out, the King's fingers finding their grip on the handle easily.

Axeleon locked eyes with his brother as he drove the dagger deep into the flesh of Axise chest, just under the left arm, in the natural gap of armor left exposed by arms raised high in the swing of the ax. The steel bit deeply, splitting skin and tissue, scoring bone. The tip of the blade penetrated the heart and Axise shuddered violently, digging the weapon deeper into his vital organ. Great torrents of blood ran down the breast plate of Axise armor, obscuring the sigil that adorned it. The padded vestment underneath drank its fill, soaked nearly immediately. A horrendous rattling breath escaped Axise lips and his eyes went wide as the moon, fixed on some far-off point, seeing nothing.

Sahid found his moment just as Axise had raised his ax. The warrior pushed hard off the floor with his left leg, rolling across the smooth stone away from the throne. He came to his knees and lunged forward, his chest striking the floor and sliding further away. He splayed his arms out and held still, silently begging to be spared from the violence to come.

Genif Nitru, one of Axeleon's personal guard, was the first to react to her king's signal. At the very moment that the dagger entered Axise heart and Sahid pitched away, she brought her angled great sword to bear. The blade ripped into some dozen thick ropes lashed to a large brass knuckle anchored into the stone floor. Two of Axeleon's servants were prepared with borrowed swords that attacked similar ropes in time with Genif's stroke on the opposite side of the hall.

These ropes, having been purposed to suspend the great lanterns that kept the hall lit on even the darkest of nights, had been repurposed in preparation for this moment and with their severance it was not lights that plummeted downward towards the unaware soldiers of Axise, but the bodies of their recently slain comrades.

Sahid spun round on his chest just in time to see the horror of the trap. The armor-clad bodies of dead men and women fell from the high ceiling, crashing down onto the ranks of Axise men. The force of these bodies, falling from at least a height of forty feet, impacting hard marble floors and upright soldiers was sickening. Several of Axise men were struck directly by the falling dead. One body landed squarely on the head of one of Axise' warriors with such force that it shattered the living man's teeth into dust. Many of those who were not harmed by the corpses were stunned by the gore of the attack. Men they had fought beside for years were suddenly and terribly wrecked before them.

"The ghosts of the Arken throw our dead back to us!" One man shouted from the far left of the room. Sahid could not tell whose voice it was, only that the sound was followed by the sudden motion of steel. Living warriors materialized from the stiffly standing ranks of the Arken dead, their weapons searching eagerly for targets. Sahid watched as the knight he had so recently whispered to reached forward to grasp the silver plumage on top of the helm of one of Axise men, pulling the head backwards and exposing the neck. A long sword came around and drew across the man's throat, blood cascading from the wound and a terrible, gurgling cry escaping with it. The cut man fell to the floor, writhing as he swiftly bled to death. All around the base of the marble steps was killing. Few of Axise men were aware enough to turn towards their attackers in time to parry the first blows. They did not long survive. The ever-shifting light of the borum stone deceived their eyes as if the walls themselves came to stand against the attackers.

Starrowlands swords fell against only air. Arken swords were much more accurate. The stench of blood and bile filled the air, rendering it heavy for breath. Sahid did not dare move.

The action was over in moments and the battle song calmed. A large, dark man, dressed head to foot in black and carrying a massive long sword strode towards the front of the room, stepping easily over the dead and dying. "Quickly, check for survivors." He commanded to the others. This huge man then mounted the steps towards Axeleon, who under the weight of his brother's body, had fallen to the blood stone. Sahid watched as Axeleon and the mammoth man gently lifted Axise body and moved it to the throne. As they seated him in it and stepped back, neither man spoke.

Near Sahid, one of Axise men, a young boy of no more age that fifteen, scrambled to his feet and darted between the still standing ranks of dead Arken warriors, moving frantically towards the entrance to the Whisper Hall. The black clad bear of a man next to the King turned towards the sound.

"Stop him!" The large man boomed. "Bring him down!"

Genif Nitru took aim with a slender bow and fired an arrow at the fleeing boy. The projectile found its mark in the boy's thigh, bringing him skidding to the stone floor with a shriek. Another of Axeleon's men moved quickly to the screaming man and dragged him back to the steps.

For Sahid Kahn, the scene in front of him was little but a blur. Men that he had fought beside through countless campaigns were cut down with swift strokes. He had witnessed so much death in his years but the speed and brutality of the trap that Axise had led them into was something truly daunting to behold. He watched, motionless as some seventy-five fighters swarmed around the bodies, separating the dead from the living, keeping the Arken dead separate from the others. They bustled about, lashing hand and foot of Axise still living followers. A man, or it could have been a woman, Sahid could not tell for all the black armor, approached him and kicked him sharply in the ribs. A large knee fell on the middle of his back and rough gloved hands grasped his wrists. He felt the chord bite into his flesh as his wrists were bound behind him. The nameless warrior stripped him of his boots, tossing them aside, and bound his ankles. The heavy soldier then released hold on Sahid and moved off, tending to others. He turned his eyes to the throne. Axise body was seated upright, though his head lolled down to his chest. Axeleon stood at his fallen brother's side.

The King spoke, to no one it seemed, though all grew still at the sound of his voice. As if by some magic, the hall of kings seamed to enhance Axeleon's words, while swallowing the wails of the wounded. "Even as boys, Axise was too proud, too demanding of honors. Yet, I loved him. Perhaps not for the man that he grew to be, fueled by hate and lust for power. Not for the man who brought war to his own home, or for the man who killed so easily for personal gain, but for who he was when we were young, who he could have been had he chosen other paths."

A long silence filled the hall, none moved. Axeleon lowered his head, placing his lips on his brother's brow, and rose. "I wish you peace in the shadow, Axise, son of Axlent and Santar."

Time passed as Sahid lay bound on the stone floor. Twice, rough hands grabbed him and slid his helpless form across the floor, bringing him to the borum stone wall. Next to him was the boy who had been felled by the arrow. Axise body was removed from the throne and taken into a room at the back of the blood stone platform. King Axeleon approached the throne from one of these rooms, armed with his sword and clothed in his black armor.

"Commander Fax." Axeleon's summons was answered immediately by the huge warrior Sahid had seen before.

The commander mounted the steps, bowing his head to the King. "Yes, Your Grace."

"We must secure the citadel," Axeleon spoke swiftly, knowing that at any moment, more of Axise men could arrive in the great hall. "We must hold until Aralias arrives, and his army can scour our enemy from our walls. He is overdue."

"Sire," Liam spoke evenly, his deep voice like a great drum, "There are but ninety-three remaining among us. We cannot hope to secure the citadel with so small a force."

"And what if our enemy should find us here, no great doors to bar his entry?"

"The position is bleak, Your Grace, but we should echelon our ranks and fall back to the banquet hall if need arise. Certainly, the door would hold there for a time."

"Perhaps." Axeleon softened, "perhaps we can hold long enough. Let us at least return our fallen to their places of honor along the wall."

Commander Fax understood that this task was more to keep the soldiers occupied, rather than a true gesture of honor. Warriors want to make war, and with the enemy inside their own walls, their eagerness could swiftly turn victory into death. Liam nodded his consent to the king and exited the platform to set about the work details.

Sahid lay watching as, with care, Axeleon's men went about the hall, taking up the armored remains and placing them in a single rank against the walls of the room. This was odd to him and no such honor had been paid to the fallen in any of the worlds he had experienced.

After a time, men came and dragged Sahid, with the other survivors up onto the platform and past. They were nearly thrown into a small room, scarcely larger than a wardrobe. The door was shut and barred, closing off all light. In the darkness, the passage of time could not be counted. Only once was the silence of the wardrobe disturbed. The voices of King Axeleon and Lord Commander Fax filtered through the wooden door.

"Once Lord Aralias and his army have made safe the city, we must enter the passage and find my daughter." Axeleon's voice was hushed, but purposeful.

"Yes, Your Grace," the deep voice of Commander Fax was distinguishable as if he were standing in the wardrobe itself. "I will send my fastest rangers."

"No, Commander, you must go. Jaxus has a strong lead, so give good chase, find them and return to me."

"Sire, should I not remain at your side? Axise battalions are still engaged with our forces in the south. Should Lady Kaowith be routed, all available resources must be committed to the Fire Fist."

Axeleon knew this course to be wisdom, but he felt a great urgency in his spirit. "I share your fears, Lord Commander, but if truth must be spoken, I fear Jaxus more."

At the sound of this name, Sahid opened his eyes wide and slithered on his side closer to the door, that he might hear all. He knew Jaxus well.

"You fear Jaxus, Your Grace?" Liam's features grew tight. "I have no trust for this man, but I did not question your choice in sending him with the Princess. It troubles me to know that you also hold fear for the man."

Axeleon smiled softly. "It is not Jaxus that I fear, it is merely his dedication to his cause that need be cautioned. It is his loyalty to me that would lead him to mistrust the word of any I send after him."

The large commander did not understand this. "My King, I am saddened to hear you speak this way, for you are deceived. I believe that Jaxus loyalty does not lie with you, but rather with your deceased brother and those of his ilk."

Axeleon chuckled softly. "You are wrong about the man's character."

"That is the second time in this day that I have been told of my miss judgement, though it contradicts what my own instinct relates. Is Jaxus not a spy for Axise?" Commander Fax didn't understand this. Too much of the man's character and movements were shrouded in secrecy.

Axeleon maintained his amused countenance. "No, he is most definitely a spy."

Liam could not reason this out. The King clearly had a great deal of affection for Jaxus, but he did not offer explanation for it, and the king openly admitted that Jaxus was not as he seemed.

"Jaxus origins and purpose are not important to our current cause. All that is important at this time is for you to understand that Jaxus has served the Kingdom of Arken for many years. His faith is beyond question and that is why I fear him. Consider, my friend," the king leaned forward, placing a hand on Liam's shoulder, "Were I to have sent you with Layandria, charged with her protection above all else, you would have departed, as Jaxus did, knowing that my grave was already dug and no hope for salvation existed. Were you to be caught up by one of us, claiming that victory had been snatched out of the jaws of certain doom, would you trust the man?"

Liam straightened his posture, a smoldering resolve in his eyes. "I would think it a lie designed to lure the princess into Axise grasp and I would cut the man's tongue from his head."

"This is as Jaxus would do," Axeleon paused, considering the many instances where he had born witness to Jaxus skill with the blade. "Though I fear Jaxus would take more than the man's tongue."

"Yes, Your Grace." Liam could not fully take in the concept that Jaxus was a man of honor, worthy of the trust he was so given. He grew troubled.

Sahid was puzzled. Why would such men have this level of trust for a man of Jaxus kind? It made no sense. Sahid had known Jaxus to be highly skilled and powerful, but he was also keenly aware of Jaxus understanding of loyalty, or rather his unwillingness to be bound by it. Yet this King seamed to embrace him as one closer than blood. Sahid shifted again on the floor, not wanting to miss a single syllable of the conversation. In his movement, his bound feet found purchase against the young man with the arrow wound, who let out a muffled cry. Sahid stiffened.

"I will, as you command." Commander Fax voice was followed by footsteps, heavy on the floor. The king and his commander moved off.

Questions and uncertainty filled Sahid's thoughts. Jaxus was a confounding mystery, but more pressing was his own future. What did

Arken men do with prisoners? Would they be put to the sword? Forced into a life of servitude? Time moved slowly in the darkness and with its passing, Sahid became aware of the intense weight of his eyes. There in the darkness, Sahid slept, enjoying the momentary break from whatever would be brought on him next.

4.

Thyso rolled uncomfortably, he could not find rest on the floor of the passage. Hours had gone by since the group had reached the first of the supply stores, eaten and taken to sleep, but he could not find any for himself.

The supply cache was disappointing to Thyso's surmising. All that they discovered amounted to nothing more than a roughhewn shelf in the wall of the passage which was stocked only with grain that was long spoiled, dried beef that was molded over and jugs of water that were no longer potable. Thankfully Jaxus had the clairvoyance to pack water, fruit, dried meat and grains that would sustain them for several days, so long as they were rationed. Jaxus also had three flasks of whiskey, which he offered a mouthful of for each of them just before they settled in to sleep. He said it would help them find rest, but the burning liquid made Thyso feel as if he was about to vomit his meager diner. Though he was well of age, he had never consumed alcohol before, and he found that he did not enjoy it. Oslun, in stark contrast, seemed to savor the taste of the liquor greatly, smiling and exhaling a satisfied breath into the darkness as he swallowed his serving down.

Thyso's mind wandered much in his restlessness, its meandering largely focused on his experiences with the young princess. Most of their time spent together was in training. As Layandria learning to fight and to lead her forces in battle, Thyso trained beside her and in so doing, honed his already impressive skills. Much of the rest of their time over his years of service was spent attending council meetings and parties for visiting dignitaries. Thyso was never more than a shout away from Layandria and he knew that she trusted him more than any other, save her father.

The wandering of Thyso's mind in the dank tunnel led him through many memories, savoring those that took place in the bright sun. His eye settled on one much brighter day when he and his royal strolled across the vast fields of the cities' vegetable farms on their way to the archery range. As they walked, they came upon a large moose that had found its way out of the corals and was happily eating from the crop. Layandria suggested that they act to return the beast to its pen when several wolves appeared from the thickets of brush that ringed the vegetables. The predators closed in and the moose lowered its massive head towards each attacker, repelling them by sweeping its massive antler back and forth inches from the soil. Wolf after wolf attempted assault, but the moose was ever ready to repel the incoming fangs.

"The wolves are overzealous." The Princess whispered softly to her servant.

"How so, Your Grace?" Thyso was courteous, despite Layandria's distaste for formality and titles when the pair were away from the courts.

"The wolves attack one at a time, head on, where the moose is strongest and can defend itself well. They give all advantage to the moose." The Crown Princess spoke low, but the intensity with which her mind focused on the game being played out before her was clear.

Thyso smiled softly. "What would you have instructed the wolves as the best course of action."

"Well," Layandria never looked away from the scene. "Were I the wolf, I would go hunt rabbits instead."

Thyso laughed. "You fear the moose, your royal wolfness?"

She sneered at her servants joshing. "Of course not, I am wolf, I fear nothing."

"Ah, but you resist the hunt here, for what cause? I can see only fear."

"I can see in the wolves that they are malnourished, having been without food for some time. Perhaps at their full strength, and not driven so mad in the need for a meal, they would be more controlled in their approach, but for now, they lack the strength and control to attack this target with hope for success, so I would hunt rabbits."

Thyso laughed again. Jaxus stepped out from the brambles that lined the path, seemingly appearing from the very air. The knight was suddenly at Thyso's back, a knife in one hand, the other arm wrapping around the handmaid's neck tightly, wrenching the boy so that his throat was compressed into the crook of Jaxus elbow and Thyso had to stretch out on the tips of his toes. Jaxus pressed the side of the blade into Thyso's stomach.

Layandria looked over, amused. "Good day, Sir Jaxus."

"Your Grace." Jaxus spoke evenly, neither mischief nor malice in his tone. His grip on Thyso was firm, but not painful. "Could the moose be taken with only two wolves? Were they well fed and energized?"

Layandria focused her concentration, her eyes darting back and forth between each of Jaxus' eyes, studying him. She was quiet for a long breath. "Were I two wolves at full strength, I could take the beast."

Jaxus relaxed his hold on the handmaid. "Are you so certain, young wolf?"

"Yes, I am certain it could be done." The Princess voice carried no doubt or hesitation. Her eyes were unwavering. "I would take the moose, just as you have taken my Thyso."

Jaxus smiled. He released his hold on the man, stepping away and returning his blade to his belt. The knight gave Thyso a friendly pat on the shoulder. "Please, my Princess, tell us your battle plan."

"You used me, just as I would use the other wolf, to distract the moose. I would have my companion wolf charge in, then back off just at the last second, readjust, then charge again, holding back at the last moment. He would repeat this process many times, turning the moose away from my concealed position in the vegetables. With the moose' full attention taken by the other wolf, I would approach from the side and behind. When the moose lowered his head to defend against the next attack of my companion, I would strike at his belly, lowered to me and falling nicely to my teeth, just as you have done to Thyso." Layandria did not lose her focus on Jaxus as she spoke. Her intensity appeared to Thyso as if she were staring through the man's skull, reading his thoughts.

The warrior did not speak, matching the princess' gaze as if he was waiting for more. Layandria narrowed her eyes, rethinking her plan. "You struck at Thyso's neck first, which I though was meant to stabilize him so that he would not flinch and harm himself against your blade…"

Jaxus sighed heavily, his expression that of a stern father, disappointed in a petulant child engaged in some folly.

Layandria puzzled, "Immobilize him by the neck first. You immobilized him by the neck first."

She wrinkled her nose in concentration. Suddenly, Layandria's eyes brightened. "I would strike him by the neck, rather than the belly. The wound would give off great blood and immobilize the beast if delivered properly. If my attack were not delivered perfectly, I would disengage and allow the moose to flee. I would only need give chase for a short distance until he had bled out of his will to run or fight. Once the moose had succumbed to the wound, I would enjoy the softness of his belly."

Jaxus smiled and bowed, signifying the correctness of the Princess' response.

"Your Grace," Thyso interrupted the glee of the Princess imagined victory, wishing to participate in this exchange, "Were I the other wolf, which role would you think appropriate for me to take?"

The Princess merely starred at him.

"I should think it prudent that I take the role of the second wolf, moving in to strike, while you preform the role of distraction." Thyso spoke with an air of authority, believing that Jaxus would soon support his plan. "It is far too dangerous for a Princess of wolves to move in for the kill. The risk of injury is too high."

The Princess raised an eyebrow. Thyso starred at her, knowing that she hungered for the dangerous tasks, just as he did. He shifted his glance to Jaxus, who suddenly crossed his eyes and stuck out his tongue. Thyso recoiled in surprise at this break in the stoic nature of Jaxus, his mental control completely lost.

Layandria giggled. "No, it is better for me to perform the attack."

Thyso looked away from Jaxus, still holding the ridiculous expression on his face. "But, Your Grace, why risk yourself?"

"Because, it is her plan lad." Jaxus dropped the strange expression and his voice resumed its standard, even tone. "Should she take the roll of the bait, as it were, she risks two things." He paused, glancing back and forth between the two. "What are they?"

"One," pronounced Layandria at once, "Thyso is correct, the role I have chosen for myself is more dangerous, but I am confident I am the correct wolf for the bite. To order another to assume the role is not as a true leader behaves. If the other wolf should die, the death would be my failure, my great shame."

Jaxus nodded in approval and turned to Thyso.

"Well," Thyso hesitated as he racked his brain for answers. "I risk my diner on the hope of another's skill?"

"Correct," Jaxus nodded, "When the stakes are so high as this, why would you risk them to the hope of another's skills?"

Layandria spoke up, seconding Jaxus. "My plan was based on my knowledge of myself. Not the other wolf. You should never force one to take the place for which you are best suited."

"Indeed Princess." Jaxus folded his arms across his chest, pleased with the response. He turned to Thyso. "Our future Queen is both cunning and quick of mind, good sir. She is a perfect fit for the strike, as a surgeon would, swift and accurate."

"Surgeon I am not, but hungry I am," Layandria offered. "Thyso, you are strong and brave, with the stamina needed to execute the repeated feigns required to properly gain the moose' full attention."

Jaxus took over the instruction again, "Brave you are, but also easily taken off guard when confronted by that which you don't expect. The moose may pivot in a direction that you don't anticipate, a rabbit may dart across your path. The Princess is best suited to look past, and reason out the change."

Thyso erected his spine. He had always been at the top of his training groups for combat performance and had just last year placed fourth in the sword competition at the tournament of bones, bested in the semi-final round by Lord Commander Fax himself, a loss for which there was no shame.

"It is your pride young Ser." Jaxus commanded the handmaid's attention. "I see it in you now as you prepare to justify yourself. The true warrior is humble, and recognizes his weaknesses, for we all have them. Pride blinds us to the things that we need to learn about our true hearts. What you must learn, good sir, is to see the world for what it is. You must also learn to keep your thoughts focused, no matter the distraction. Your mind was turned to chaos by an unexpected outburst of face, this and other distractions would be detrimental in combat."

Thyso was overcome by shame. He turned his eyes to the dirt, pushing the soil about with the toe of his boot.

"Do not be distraught Thyso!" Jaxus clapped the man on the neck, bringing his eyes up to meet his own. "There is no need for shame when pride has been set aside. You have a gallant heart, and this is strength for you, but you must see all sides of a problem. You are large, and well prepared to do battle. Our dear Princess is far less physically imposing than you. Were she to take the role of the bait, she appears less threatening and may not attract the full attention of your prey. You, I dare say, cut just the fearsome image as to capture Lord Moose's full eye, thus, making safe the approach of our Princess Wolf."

Thyso smiled and felt better. It was good for him to be called fearsome by one such as Jaxus. Jaxus lowered his hand from the handmaid's neck, though Thyso still felt its presence. Rough, but cool to the touch, he was soothed by the physical memory and the aroma of the man. Thyso felt an energizing sensation welling up in him, as though he was being pulled in. He fought to conceal what he felt.

Before Thyso had fully moved past the gravity of the man, Jaxus had spoken his parting words to the Princess, bowed low and turned away. Thyso watched the man as he strode down the path, moving back toward the citadel. Thyso was taken by the movements of Jaxus body, the sensations inside himself renewing as he watched the muscles sway and flex under dark brown trousers. His mind recalled the sensations of Jaxus, as if he were breathing him in again, feeling the man's rough hand on his skin.

Layandria jabbed Thyso in the ribs with an extended finger, tearing his thoughts back to the present. The young fighter closed his eyes and shook his head, clearing away his thoughts as the excited sensation in his body began to recede.

"Come now," Layandria chided in a playful tone, "if we are delayed any longer to the archery range, father will have us stuffed and used for targets."

Thyso laughed and the pair moved off. On the edge of the field, some way off, the baleful sound of a wounded moose' mournful calls could be heard. Thyso paused in the trail and looked back, hoping to catch sight of Jaxus. None such image remained. He stood for a moment thinking of the man and found himself wondering at the softness of Jaxus lips, the taste of his skin. The sensations returned to him slowly as he pictured Jaxus body. Shame filled him, knowing as he did that these feelings were akin to a great crime.

"Thyso! Wake!" The princess voice ordered to him. Thyso was embarrassed, he had delayed their movements again. He willed that the princess could not discern his thoughts by the expression of his face.

"Thyso, wake now!"

Suddenly, Jaxus face was in front of him, a slightly playful smile on his lips. Confusion washed over him as what had only just been a bright, sunlit day, in seconds turned to near complete darkness. The man before him was lit only by a soft, orange glow.

"That must have been some woman you dreamt of my friend." Jaxus leaned in, whispering so that only the handmaid could hear his words.

As Thyso picked his head up from the cold stone floor, he could see that the Princess, and the fat cupbearer were staring at him, amused looks about them, illuminated by the light of the sun stone. He struggled to upright himself on his elbows. "T'was no woman."

"Then perhaps it was a man you were cavorting with?" Jaxus chided. Thyso grew suddenly afraid. For a man of the Arken to lie with another man was a criminal act, one that would turn him into a pariah and ruin any hope for Knighthood or glory. Thyso had long fought to conceal his desires, but had he betrayed himself in his sleep?

Jaxus looked down at him curiously for a moment, then extended his large hand and pulled the handmaid to his feet. "Well, whoever they were, I do hope they were finding the same pleasures in you, as you so clearly found in them."

Jaxus back shielded Thyso from view of both the Princess, and the cup bearer. Jaxus pointed downward. Thyso followed the gesture and found that his own member was standing fully erect, obvious in his trousers. "Perhaps you should tend to your weapons in private before we have a meal."

In the depths of his sudden embarrassment, Thyso spun away from Jaxus. The dim light of the sun stone did not aid him, and his foot caught a rough edge on the floor. He stumbled, the crown of his head connecting sharply with the low ceiling of the passage. "For the derision of all evil!"

The impact dazed him, and Thyso stumbled again, lurching back towards his companions. Jaxus' movements were like lightning in dry air. How he could see well enough to strike out so accurately in the dim cave was astonishing, but in a fraction of a moment, he had Thyso locked in his grasp, saving the man from falling directly into the Princess.

"Gain yourself." Jaxus voice was in the same, even, yet penetrating tone that it always maintained.

Thyso looked towards Oslun, expecting to see the young man in the throes of laughter at his misfortune. The cup bearer's face was honest and kind, concern for his companion his only expression. At the sight of him, Thyso cast his head down. He felt as if he were standing naked before all the king's court, on trial for the sins of his heart.

Jaxus patted the young warrior on his back. "Do not be so distressed Thyso. Dreams often wake us to disorientation."

"I have hit my head more times than I can account for in this darkness." Oslun offered sincerely.

"None of us, even the great masters of thought can control the wanderings of the mind in sleep." Jaxus spoke as he moved to sit next to Oslun, pulling a small pile of fruit towards himself. Thyso observed a portion set out for him and moved to it as Layandria took up hers. The quartet ate in silence. The sun stone did not give off enough radiance now to see more than the shadow of each face as they dined.

Layandria spoke up in her happiest tone. "We must be of good spirit and enjoy every flavor we have. The tunnel stretches long, and we have far to go until we reach the end. I fear the darkness will take our every ounce of joy if we allow it."

Each of them finished their last mouthfuls and gathered their belongings. Jaxus passed out a few strips of dried venison. In turn, they shouldered their packs and moved off, Jaxus in the lead with Layandria close behind, the sun stone illuminating their path, suspended from her neck.

"Can we sing a song?" Oslun asked from behind his Princess, Thyso a few paces in the rear.

"You may sing if Your Grace would enjoy it." Jaxus cast his eyes over his shoulder at the Princess.

"Certainly." She spoke gleefully. "Shall we sing Palish's *The Summer Sun Shines*? Or perhaps Marth's *Swallow Song*?"

"I would like to hear *The Summer Sun Shines*, if it please." Oslun offered. "Perhaps a song about the light may make this cave less dark."

Layandria scoffed in play. "Hear only Oslun? If am I am to sing, you must accompany me."

"Yes, Your Grace." Oslun cleared his throat. As his voice extended, it was weak, the pitch struggling to find balance. "*In the beauty of its face, the warmth of its embrace, the summer sun doth shine...*"

Thyso burst out in raucous laughter from the rear of the small column. "Your voice is that of a dying goat!"

Oslun silenced his singing immediately.

"I dare say he sounds better than you!" Layandria shot back in feigned anger. "I have heard you moaning to yourself in the bath all too often and I believe you to be the last worthy of giving rebuke for another's prowess in song!"

Thyso shrugged in the darkness and laughed. "I have no care for simple songs my Princess. I am but an instrument of war, not meant for music."

"You'll be whatever instrument you're commanded." Jaxus called back. "I see no warfare afoot, so you will either be a useless instrument, or one of song."

Layandria snorted in amusement. "Oslun, if you will, begin again, our good Thyso will join in fervor."

"Yes, Your Grace," Oslun's face broke into a smile as he trotted on.

"Thyso," the princess called out, "Such a fine instrument of war should be a proper loud songster."

Thyso and Oslun both laughed. The handmaid took in a deep breath and let his voice boom out. *"The beauty of its face, the warmth of its embrace, the summer sun doth shine on us, away the darkness chase."*

The sun stone reacted to the sound as Oslun and Layandria joined in, growing brighter. Happily, the group moved on, silent Jaxus in the lead.

Behind them, the darkness closed like a veil over the just vacated, makeshift camp. The air grew still and cold, bereft of the warmth of living things. After a passing of time, the voices faded away and nothing was left but deep cold and darkness.

The air shifted in the void. The quiet sound of some creature sniffing intently as a dog for scraps of meat entered the space. A low, vicious growl rumbled through the corridor, quiet, though intensely menacing. A rhythmic clicking of claws on stone began to rise, steadily moving off after the princess and her companions.

5.

Wilteph knelt on the earth, near the base of a large tree. Its bows, heavy with summer needles, cast a cool shade over him, but sweat ran into his eyes. The tips of his long, dark fingers walked along the soil at the base of the tree as if his hands were two spiders, scurrying about in odd circular patterns. The moist earth was cool to the touch, which was pleasing to Wilteph despite the dread that pooled in his stomach like a rock. It was barely perceptible, only a wisp left in the air, but the man's highly sensitive nose detected the stench of something that he and his people feared greatly.

His fingers continued their walk, leading Wilteph onward in a low crouch behind the extended digits. Every touch revealed a plethora on information. The warmth of recent presence, slight depressions remaining from footfalls, a single hair left behind and leaves just slightly bent.

Many scars and old wounds covered the man. A large scar extended from just under Wilteph's right ear, running under his jaw to the left ear. A large portion of the left side of his head grew no hair, standing in stark contrast to the otherwise full head of waist length black locks. The flesh of the scalp in this barren area was poked and churned as if it had once been badly burned. This damage extended to the side of his face, the worst of it glaring from his nose, the left nostril completely missing from mid bridge to tip. And yet, for all Wilteph's marring, he was beautiful and graceful in his motions.

His senses read the soil and he became more certain that he was tracking the enemy of his people. The short hairs on the back of his neck and the soft down on the back of his arms rose. But where had the thing gone? Certainly, it had been here, lingering in this very spot not moments ago, but as his fingers probed the turf, they lost their way. He circled this way and that, each time he found the trail, he could trace it back only to the same spot where it disappeared. The creatures were known to be cunning, but even young children know that nothing could simply vanish into the air, leaving no trace.

The man's fingers danced along the soil, probing deeper to find the mystery. His right hand moved towards the base of a thick bramble, seeking any scrap of new information with increased pressure. Without warning, the hand plunged through the surface of the dirt. Wilteph nearly lost his balance, crouched as he was, at the unexpected breaking of ground. He withdrew his hand and pushed back the bulk of the bramble, revealing a dark hole that extended deep into the earth, carefully concealed under the arms of the bush. Many moments passed as Wilteph crouched there, gazing intently into the darkness of the hidden tunnel.

He clicked his tongue against his teeth as he pondered his next action. Instinct willed him to dive in to the tunnel, giving pursuit to the creature. Wisdom cancelled this plan. The enemy was not intelligent in the way that he could create art or song, but his skills in concealment and ambush were exceptional. Wilteph let the bramble fall from his grasp, back into place over the passage.

Rocking back onto his heels, Wilteph let out a long breath, then slowly stood and moved away from the shade of the great pine tree. The man was unremarkable in stature. Neither tall, nor notably short, neither large of muscle, nor slight, but the grace with which he moved, as long grass blown by a soft breeze, made the man appear as an apparition of nature. With deliberate movements, he brought his hands to his lips, cupping them together. He blew a slow, steady breath into this instrument. A loud, melodic tone emitted from his cupped hands, ringing back and forth from rock, tree, sky and earth. After a moment, several similar sounds, though much varied in pitch and quality echoed back. Wilteph blew into his hands again, two short blasts. This was also echoed back.

"Good." He mouthed the word silently, his mind resting in the knowledge that his companions were close at hand. A shudder passed through his spine as Wilteph turned his eyes back to the bramble. He hated the darkness and the mere thought of entering this passage was unsettling. Wilteph had excellent vision, even in the pitch-black underground, but he did not believe that men were intended to venture under the surface of the soil.

Minutes or hours could have passed without Wilteph's acknowledgment. He remained still, eyes fixed on the secret entrance, breaths coming slow and shallow. The movement of the sun in the sky passed morning into afternoon. The smallest sound of a footfall on damp needles reached his ears from somewhere off to his rear. Wilteph remained motionless, waiting for another sound, giving him distance and direction. He was rewarded in short order with another small sound.

Wilteph snapped into motion, pivoting on the balls of his feet and drawing a light green bow from his back as he rose in an unnaturally smooth motion. In fractions of a second, in an action practiced so frequently that it was done without thought, Wilteph fitted a slender arrow, tipped with an angular head of obsidian and trailed with blue feathers. His eyes and weapon moved as one, finding their target just under her chin.

Her actions were as well practiced as his own. As Wilteph found his target, she too found hers, a vicious spear, tipped with onyx, expertly poised to strike the man's heart. The pair stood locked in pose, the simple twitch of a finger, the flick of a wrist, away from ending the other. They were as stone sculptures, each waiting to see the widening of their foe's pupils, the slightest increase in tension that always comes just before a blow is delivered.

Suddenly, both faces split wide into grins and laughter erupted in great torrents. They each lowered their weapons and ran toward each other, the spear cast aside to the turf, the bow clattering into the bed of needles without thought.

"Halta!" Wilteph cried out as he flung himself around the woman.

"Wil!" She echoed his joy and embraced him. The pair held each other close for several seconds, each laughing from the overabundance of emotion they felt. Halta held her eyes closed, her wide face still locked in a great smile. Tears streamed down Wilteph's cheeks.

He released his hold on the woman, stepping back slightly. Seeing his tears, Halta's expression grew puzzled. Wilteph barely breathed his response. "I cannot believe what my eyes tell me, I had thought of you as lost!"

Her smile deepened, crooked teeth peeking out. The sunlight danced off her deep black hair, braided down her back tightly, just as Wilteph's was. Several scars, though many less than those that adorned the man's body, and none so grotesque, covered her earthen skin. She stood taller than he, and slender, though she appeared just as powerful and equally as graceful.

She sensed the movement before Wilteph did, so lost was he in the pleasure of seeing her. Halta pulled her eyes away from the man and scanned the surrounding trees, looking high in the boughs. Her eyes narrowed, but her body did not tense, and the smile did not leave her lips. "Tepan," she growled, her voice low as if emanating from some large, yet melodic fox, "come down here and cease your foolishness."

Tepan did not so much as fall from the high limbs of a nearby tree as he did float down to the earth. He landed with softness and scarcely a sound despite having been nearly fifteen feet aloft. The same lightness and grace was found in him as with Wilteph and Halta, though the similarity ended there. Tepan was built like a boulder, short, and quite massive. His black hair was cropped close, though light patches of gray invaded his head from just above his temples.

Tepan's round face was deeply creased with age, though the mischievous grin he wore made him appear both old and young, weathered, but still glowing with the spirit of youth. Thick, black hair covered his exposed chest and arms, giving his body a striking resemblance to a moss-covered tree trunk. Vitiligo covered much of his neck and chest, contrasting heavily against rich, walnut skin.

"Curse you, long walker." Tepan glared playfully at Halta. "Your ears are not of this world."

Halta bowed low in and exaggerated show of honors. Rising, she moved to collect her discarded weapon. "It is not difficult to hear an elephant as it lumbers about in the tree tops."

"Pah!" Pure indignation covered Tepan. He stamped his massive foot on the earth and thrust his hands onto his hips. "I am as graceful as those foolish dancing boys at the celebration of moons turning!"

"Dear brother," Wilteph chimed in, his voice sweet as song, "grace you have in abundance, silence you have not."

Tepan glowered at him. "Were you not my Chieftain," the stout man snarled, "I would write my silence upon your brow with the tip of my foot!"

Wilteph smiled deeply as he too recovered his downed weapons, "Ah good warrior, it is a shame then that you cannot reach above my knee caps."

"Chieftain?" All humor left Halta's face, her mind immediately ablaze with questions. Wilteph too lost the amusement of his expression. He turned his eyes away, starring off into the trees. Halta looked as though she were attempting to pierce his thoughts with her eyes.

Tepan broke through the tight silence. "You have been gone too long! There is much to tell!"

"It must have been some seven long moons past, Fannin, whom you called Chieftain before your departure, made off with a party of good, strong warriors to treat with the men of the lake. They sought to join with them so that we may find shelter in greater numbers and cease this endless scrabbling for sustenance. They spoke well and were granted presence with the Gods of the lake; did you know those fools call their leaders Gods?"

"I did not." Halta answered back, but her eyes had not left Wilteph for a moment as Tepan spoke.

"Indeed, they do!" Tepan continued, paying no regard to Halta's gaze. "Fannin gained audience with these Gods. Our party was offered to feast and rest, before real talk would take place the following morning. They did so in full, enjoying the luxuries offered. Once they were well fatted, one and all slipped off to rest peacefully in the security offered to them. They were taken in the night with long knives. Only Chieftain Fannin was sparred. To him, the Lakemen gave life, but they took his arms, both, at the elbow. He was then sent back to us, bearing one message. That any of the Inohamman peoples who enter their lands will meet the same fate."

As Tepan spoke, a woman clad head to foot in armor that resembled the thick bark of a tree and armed with two long knives suspended from her belt entered the clearing. Tepan took no notice. "Fannin was cast into a deep despair at the loss of so many of our good warriors. He came to believe that there was no longer hope for our survival. Council him we did, but to no avail as late one evening, Fannin departed our camp and made his way to the high cliffs, casting himself down to the rocks."

"This is no way for a man of the Inohamman to pass." Halta lowered her head in honor to the departed Chieftain, looking away from Wilteph.

"Weakness." The woman, whom Halta knew to be called Rale'en, grunted. Halta ignored the comment.

Tepan too ignored Rale'en, as he often did. "After Fannin fell, our good brother Wilteph was filled with a great pain. He departed in the dead of night and made his way to the lake. He infiltrated their stronghold and paid the Gods back arm for arm. We have since heard rumblings in the soil that chaos and war has broken out in the Lakelands as men fight to claim power in the absence of their so-called gods."

"And for his bravery and vengeance, Wilteph was named Chieftain. The honor of which he has refused." Fash, a tall, light skinned warrior spoke up as he entered the clearing, with him several others arrived. All greeted Halta with pleased expressions and small greetings.

Halta frowned deeply on hearing that Wil had refused the role of Chieftain. This was not the first time he had done so.

"But the man cannot refuse when we refuse to allow him." Tepan exclaimed, resolute and stamping his foot again. "We simply refused to act. To eat, to sleep, to range, until Wilteph commanded it. Waited nearly seven suns before he finally took on the job. I thought I would have to eat one of the young ones if the man waited any longer to submit."

Wilteph faced his companions, a slight smile returning to his features. "Had I known that, I would have waited longer and pointed you towards Kammol." The Chieftain gestured to a young, plump man with a crooked nose who stood behind Fash.

"I am feeling quite empty today…" Tepan's voice resumed his low growl and gave a sharp lunge towards the younger warrior. Kammol took to a run, ringing the group with Tepan in hot pursuit.

"I fear we do not have time for a feast." Wil broke in as the group, now numbering thirteen in all, burst into laughter. Tepan caught the edge of Kammol's dear skin shirt and pulled him in, teeth barred and snarling.

"There is a morlt on the hunt." Wilteph said the words softly, but at their utterance, every member of the assembled group stopped in their breaths. Wilteph pointed their attention towards the disturbed soil under the bramble. "The creature has found a passage into the tunnel of the metal men. How the entrance to the tunnel was found by the morlt is unknown, but it has certainly entered. There can be only one or two of them, but if they have descended into the deep, they have a reason."

"The only reason a morlt moves anywhere is to hunt." Kepet, a weather worn, battle sore looking man who wore only a breach cloth, and bearing a long sword, spoke up in a grizzled voice.

Wilteph grew dark as he considered what must be done next. "If there are men in the tunnel, we must take extra care. We do not know from what land they have come, what direction they travel, their strength or their intent."

"We must kill the beast," Tepan shouted with fury, "before it turns it's hunger on one of us!"

"Yes, my brothers and sisters," Wilteph stood taller, growing larger and discernably fierce as he spoke. "Those who hunt men will now be hunted."

6.

Lord Commander Fax sat heavily on the floor, leaning back to rest his head on the white marble steps before the throne. Aralias' army had not yet arrived in the city, and the King did not dare to send out a scout. Though it was uncomfortable for the soldiers, not knowing the movements or proximity of their enemy, the risk far outweighed any potential of gains. Over a day had passed since Axise was slain and morning was beginning to rise. The men had managed to stand the great doors roughly back into place, though if they were struck with more than a breath, they would be rendered to kindling. The soldiers slept in shifts, half resting, half alert.

The bodies of Axise' dead were taken, with the body of their king, into the banquet hall where they were wrapped in heavy canvas to prevent pests from setting in. Remarkably, no Arken warriors had been felled in the combat, though a few were wounded to varying degrees. The bodies of the honored commanders and knights had been returned to their positions around the hall, though some care and reassembly would be required once the citadel was made safe.

One of the Starrowlanders that had been suspended from the ceiling prior to Axise entry had not fallen during the attack. The rope that held it aloft was caught in a joint between two of the great beams supporting the high roof. Commander Fax ordered one of his men to climb the timber supports and free the remains. Once loosed of its bonds, the body crashed headlong to the floor, landing with a tremendous impact. The dead man had worn no helm and the Lord Commander caught glimpse of his facial feature as the body plummeted. The warrior had been scarcely more than a boy and though dead, his face looked serene, perhaps innocent.

Liam forced his mind off the boy and the image of his falling body. He recalled instead the moments before Axise entered the great hall. He tried to remain in the spirit of defiance and power that dwelt in him in those final moments. In that time, he felt as if all the pain of a long life in battle was to be ended, and in that strange place, Liam found a strange peace. He longed for that calm in his soul as he lay on the stone, but it proved elusive.

His mind unwillingly flashed back to the young boy. He could see every detail as the soldier's face had impacted the floor. His head was reduced to nothing, as a fruit that had been run over by a wagon many times. The hook, placed though his lower jaw just as with the others, was dislodged and bounced on the black marble floor. It played over and again in the Commander's sight. He could not shake away the scene no matter the effort he exerted.

"Lord Commander." The King called out softly from the throne. Liam responded to the call at once, rising and mounting the steps. As Liam approached his king, Axeleon noted a troubled look about him. "What ails you, my friend?"

Liam did not respond for a moment, his dark eyes unfocused, and his mind seeing the boy impacting the stone again as if it were freshly occurring before him. When he spoke, his voice was grave. "It is nothing Your Grace. I am only restless knowing that our enemy breathes still within the walls of our city."

The King nodded from his seated position. "Is this all that weighs on you?"

"Your Grace?" Liam had no other words. Long had he served the King, first, as a boy, being the same age but much greater stature, Liam had been assigned as Prince Axeleon's sparring partner. Later, the young Liam Fax had been named handmaid to the Prince and from then on was never far from his side. The two had trained together over all their years and fought as one in many wars. Each one learned how the other thought and the instincts that governed, honing this understanding into a bond closer than that of the womb. Attending banquets, tournaments, and battles together, their friendship grew as well as their respect for each other's abilities in combat. When Axeleon took the throne, he named Liam Commander of the King's Infantry, Lord of Barang as one of his first acts.

Though the Lord Commander had been the striking blade of death many times, no death he had witnessed had haunted him as the fall of the boy. Liam had not seen him die, this was done in the darkness before Axise entered the hall. He did not know who had taken the life, and did not want for this knowledge, for there was no blame to be placed. The boy had entered combat bearing weapons and he was cut down, as is the way of warfare. Yet, Liam was deeply challenged by the thing in a way that he had never experienced.

"You are finding no rest, though your face betrays great fatigue. Long have we stood beside each other and easily can I see when you are not well." The king spoke softly, willing his friend to confide in him. "Many times, we have been forced to hold our attack surrounded and cut off from aid, and never have I seen you so agitated."

Liam's brow furrowed as his mind turned over on itself. "It was no way to honor a soldier having died in his duty."

The King raised an eyebrow. "Who is it that has been dishonored?"

"My sincere apologies, My King, I have spoken out of turn."
The massive Commander bowed his head. "I am, as you have noted,
fatigued and I find that I am unable to still my mouth."

"I would bid you speak your mind Liam." The king rose from
the throne and approached the Commander, his countenance gentle.
"You have never withheld from me, I see no reason for it now."

Liam hesitated, unsure of what words he could say, unsure of his
own emotion. His body felt as if a great weight were pulling it towards
the floor. "The boy, Sire, the one cut down from the rafters. I cannot
unsee his face as he fell."

"Ah, you gave me concern, my friend." Axeleon smiled softly,
gripping the Commander's large arm with his hand. "When you said a
soldier had been dishonored, I feared it was one of ours that you meant."

"It is not, My King." Liam's eyes remained steady, meeting the
King's.

"Then all is well!" Axeleon clapped the big man's arm again.
"Shall we to rest then? You will have the watch again soon."

"It is not well, Your Grace. I cannot get the boy from my mind.
He haunts me and will not leave my sight, no matter if my eyes are open
or closed." Commander Fax felt the King's hand leave his arm as the
words tumbled out. "I know that we have done what we must, that we
have wrested victory from the very moment of our death, but I am not at
ease with all we have done."

King Axeleon narrowed his eyes. "We owe nothing to the dead,
Commander. As you say, we have torn victory from certain defeat.
There is no honor paid to those who enter our sacred halls to do us
harm."

Liam's eyes grew cold, "We have always honored the dead, Your Grace, it is the way of soldiers."

"Our dead, yes." The King stood, his eyes reflecting the shifting flame of the borum stone. "We owe no honor to those who struck with Axise."

"My King, they were but soldiers for their Royal, just as I am to you." Liam felt rising anger like a poison in his flesh. Though he had climbed to nobility, in his heart, Lord Commander Fax had never existed as more than a soldier. His heart was still committed to battle and those who fought. "These men followed the orders given them and served as they were commanded, just as I do. It is no fault of theirs that they were pressed to serve a mad man, vile and wicked. We should honor them, just as we honor our fallen."

"Surely those who fought for Axise did so out of the same loyalty and honor that we here fight for you, for the same values that drove you and I to war against nations with which we had no personal quarrel, but war we did, out of love and fealty to your father, King Axlent." Liam lost control of his emotion and did not take in the impassive, calm expression of his King, nor the many pairs of eyes that were fixed on him throughout the Whisper Hall. "King Axlent once told us both that those that fall on the orders of a King are a gift of the highest order. He said that we would always respect that gift, and that Arken warriors would ever fight for the dead, just as we fight for the living."

"My father was a great man, a valiant king, of this there is no question." Axeleon gripped his friend's forearms. "You and I have drawn swords together for our entire lives. I have trusted you above any other in all things. Will you trust me now?"

Liam fought his anger down, controlling his voice. "I do not now, nor have I ever questioned you, My King."

"What you are experiencing is not uncommon. Human beings are not meant to take the lives of our fellows, though we often do. Taking a life strips away a piece of the soul that can never heal. Too many lives taken and man will lose himself entirely, becoming no more than a beast. How much killing a soul can bear is varied for each, though I suspect your soul is telling you that you are coming to close to your limit." Axeleon's words were warm and comforting, taking much weight from his friend. "Now, my faithful brother, you must take what rest you can, for when Aralias arrives, we will strike out and there will be much more killing needed. Are you prepared to do this work?"

Liam bowed his head in deference. "I am yours to command, till my death come, My King."

Liam bowed again and turned away, moving back down the steps to join his men on the floor. Several restless hours passed, but the Lord Commander could not find sleep. Each time his heavy eyes began to close, the image of the plummeting boy jutted into his thoughts, bringing wakefulness back to him.

The faint sound of a great war horn drifted into the hall, passing through the damaged doors. The sound was nearly imperceptible, and Liam was unsure if he had heard it at all. Again, the horn sounded. Joined by other horn blasts, the note grew stronger. Liam sat up, leaning on his elbow against the black floor. The sound of the horns was joined by the sounds of war drums. These sounds were much stronger, closer to the Whisper Hall, certainly within the citadel itself. Commander Fax recognized the drums. They were the same that announced Axise' arrival at the gates of the city nearly five days ago.

The horns continued, gathering more in their ranks as the drums rose in answer.

"To your arms!" Lord Commander Fax commanded across the hall as he stood. The warriors responded to the order at once. Liam looked back to the throne and found Axeleon meeting his eyes. "With the coming of the new day, the wolf-son returns to the Arkenhead. Lord Aralias has arrived."

7.

"Flowers bloom, pestles grind.

Falcons plume, passing time.

Old and young, meek and bold.

Weak and strong, time will hold.

Time calls, we answer.

Death comes, we answer.

There is no escape, run ever faster!" Layandria's voice swelled, filling the void of the tunnel. She let the final note fade from her lips as if it were the last grains of sand filtering through an hour glass. The princess paused, letting the walls of the vast tunnel return her voice back to her. She did not normally sing so freely, as Queen Alandaria had not considered her daughter's singing voice to be one of her finer qualities. Here in the tunnel, with her three companions, Layandria could not help but free her songs. She belted every song she knew, from the happy songs of her childhood nursery, to excited ballads of men marching off to war, to the somber lyrics of death, she sang them all with fervor. No one had complained, in fact, both Oslun and Thyso had joined her when they knew the words. Jaxus remained silent. The Princess asked him about his silence once, but as way of response, he muttered to her that it was better to die by the sword here and now than to be slowly ground to death by his atrocious voice.

The Princess drew in a great breath and began again.

"Flowers bloom, pestles grind.

Ravens plume…"

"It's breakfast time!" Oslun burst in, his high voice completely devoid of musical tone, though it dripped with enthusiasm.

The Princess laughed freely and spun around, jabbing at the cup bearer with a finger.

"Must every word that comes from your lips be concerning food?" Thyso grumbled from the back of their small formation. "By the earth and iron, you have already eaten enough in your days to last a lifetime."

"Thyso, watch what you speak!" Layandria shouted at her handmaid, stepping towards him in immediate anger. She spun back around and turned to Jaxus, "Why does he feel the need to insult others so? Is this a trait of all soldiers?"

Jaxus did not respond, keeping his pace into the darkness.

Layandria turned sharply back towards Thyso. "Why are you so cross with him? Has he committed some offence against you that we are not aware of?"

The handmaid stopped before the princess, his eyes meeting hers, but he did not respond.

"Answer me!" The Princess anger showed through in her voice, the intensity multiplied many times over by the walls of the tunnel. Well illuminated by the sun stone hanging from her neck, her features hardened and her stance commanding. Thyso and Oslun were visibly stunned.

"Your Grace!" Thyso stammered, unprepared for the fury of his Royal. "I beg forgiveness, I did not intend to anger you."

Layandria turned away, moving forward and passing Jaxus. This was the first time in her life that she had truly shown anger to one of her vassals. It made her uneasy. She walked alone in silence, embarrassed that she had let her emotion drive her words. She was the crown Princess of Arken, but in truth, she did not believe herself fit to be a leader of a nation. Her heart desired only to sing, to train with sword and bow, to be free.

"My Lady." Jaxus approached the princess' back, leaning in close to her ear that only she may hear his whispers. "It is best to give your men the reason for your rebuke. Tell them why their action was incorrect and allow them the grace to learn from it. Without this they will grow to resent you, thinking you are of hot temper."

Layandria turned to look into Jaxus eyes. She could not remember when Jaxus had come to the capitol city, only that he seemed to appear one day, at her father's side, whispering council to him. That was why she trusted him so. Other than her own mother, and Lord Commander Fax, she had witnessed no other to be so trusted by her father. Now, as the man's rough face was lit buy the glow of the sun stone, Layandria saw a strength, tempered with softness in his eyes. Jaxus seldom spoke, and shared no personal detail of his life, but she felt comfort in his words and wisdom gained over long, hard years. She nodded to the warrior and turned back, approaching Thyso softly.

"Forgive my aggressive response, my friend." The Princess took her handmaid by his arm. "It is important that we show respect to all, and that we build up those we stand beside. Every person has the basic right to be treated with kindness, no matter your perception of their weakness."

Thyso found the Princess' eyes. She showed no anger, but her young features appeared to him to be those of one much past her age. He felt small in her presence, though strangely to him, he felt no shame. "Yes, My Lady."

"I believe that each of us had something that we can teach the others, some area of strength not common to us all. Thyso, what is your strength that you believe Oslun lacks?" The Princess drew the cupbearer into the conversation as she spoke, a small gesture of her elegant hand bringing him in.

Thyso hesitated. He knew immediately what this area of weakness for Oslun was, though he did not want to answer incorrectly. "I believe, Your Grace, that Oslun lacks the hardness of spirit needed to be a man of war."

The princess looked over her shoulder, in Jaxus direction. "Sir Jaxus, do you believe hardness of spirit is needed to be a man of war?"

"No, My Lady." Jaxus emotionless voice answered back from the darkness. "Hardness of spirit can aid a warrior in battle, but it is grace, mercy and patience, one's ability to think through a challenge faster than his foe that makes him victorious. A warrior without heart will become a tyrant. A warrior who possesses feeling and sharpness of mind will be a hero to his people."

"Well spoken, Sir." The Princess turned back to her men. "You, Thyso are gifted with blades, though Oslun has much more of a servant's heart. He possesses the soundness of mind that is needed to complement your fierce heart."

Thyso turned his eyes to Oslun. He was disgusted by the idea that this small, plump boy would somehow surpass him in any facet. Though he took pain to hear it, he knew that he lacked the quality of mind that Oslun had demonstrated. The cup bearer returned his gaze, and for the first time, he did not look away.

"From this moment, you will strive to teach Oslun what you know. Pass your skills on to him that he may gain strength and confidence." The Princess' voice did not carry the sense of an order, but that of wise instruction. She turned to the cup bearer. "And you,

Oslun, will strive to learn all you can, while you must also teach Thyso those skills you possess. You think quickly, and your mind sees past the surface of a problem. You must teach Thyso to look deeper, as you do."

Both men bowed their consent. Layandria did not know what else to say. Jaxus took cue from her silence.

"It is not yet time for breakfast." Jaxus voice came as a spirit from the darkness. "We have much ground to cover and I feel, though I do not yet understand the cause, that we must increase our speed. Perhaps it is only my hunger for the light, but I must insist that we move on."

Layandria was surprised to see Jaxus face emerge from the darkness, coming into the luminance of the sun stone as he spoke. He stood before her, waiting for her command, as she had seen him do with her father many times. This day, or night, she was not aware which it was, had given her strange and new experiences. Thyso bowing before her, and now Jaxus calmly awaiting her order. She felt ill prepared for this leadership and a strong churning rose in her stomach.

"May we take rest to eat, though quickly?" The Princess asked, unsure if the question was correct.

"We are yours to command, Your Grace." Jaxus bowed sharply.

The four travelers sat on the cold floor in a small circle. Oslun was nearly overcome with happiness at the prospect of food, though it waned slightly when Jaxus passed out meager portions of grain, a single strip of dried beef and half an apple for each. The dark warrior informed them that this was the last of the fruit. The princess took the sun stone off her neck and placed it on the floor at the center of the circle, giving its light to each face. Oslun let his eyes pass over his three companions as he ate, trying to savor the final bites of apple, wondering when he would taste another.

The cup bearer felt weak. His hand brushed his cheek, finding naught but smooth skin. Jaxus and Thyso had both developed a thick scruff of new beard on their faces, making them look even more menacing. He himself had only the deep cut on his chin to add to his appearance. He felt the grime on his skin and hoped that the film of dirt that adhered to his features made him appear less soft.

Oslun longed to be strong, like Jaxus. To be unafraid like Thyso and confident like Layandria. He wanted it desperately, but for all his wanting, he was still unable to stop himself from crying in silence as the group traveled. He also greatly wanted a hug. Human contact, beyond the good natured, but insufficient pats on the head that Jaxus offered, or the encouraging hand on his shoulder that the Princess gave when his pace slowed. The young man had only been truly embraced four times in his memory.

Both of his parents had been in service of the armies when Oslun was born. His mother was a soldier in the Wolf Cavalry, carrying her broadsword, known as Vioquil, which Oslun remembered meant loyal blade in old Carenbon, the language of their ancestors. His father was a crafter of wood and iron. At the height of his career, Thom Panteon was chief builder in the Wolf Fist, often sent abroad to build and repair the great structures of the Kingdom.

When Oslun was but eight years of age, his mother, Velis, was dispatched with the Wolf Cavalry to replace the forces holding the outposts on the norther border of the fist. She was due to be gone for one year. Oslun and his father carried on well, and the young cup bearer remembered it as a happy time. Four months after his mother left for the border outposts, Oslun's father was summoned to the fortress at Dubner, the seat of Arkral Landers, then the Lord of the Iron Fist. Thom was ordered to make large scale upgrades to the fortress walls and expected his absence to last nearly eight months. Oslun was sent to the Arken Head, to be in the care of his mother's sister, Hellin Pollunt, who was cupbearer to Queen Layandria. Thom had thought this a great chance for his son to learn alongside the children of high officials and make a name for himself with his sharp mind. Oslun enjoyed his time in the citadel, but he longed for the comfort of his own bed and his family.

Velis was the first to fall, killed in battle far away from her son and home. Oslun never learned the details of his mother's end, only that her body was never recovered. Merely ten days after being told of his mother's death, Aunt Hellin broke news that Thom had also passed into shadow. While working the high walls of the Iron Lord's holdfast, a support beam gave way, causing a great collapse that took the lives of many builders. Thom died never having been told that his bride preceded him to the shadow.

Only four hugs. One from each parent, given to him when they departed on their separate orders. Aunt Hellin had embraced him when he learned of his mother's death, and again when news of his father's passing reached the capitol. Perhaps he did not want a hug, the young man thought. They come only with grief.

"We should be moving on." Layandria picked up the sun stone and placed its chain around her neck. She spoke softly, her eyes darting into the darkness, in the direction they had come from. "I am beginning to feel Jaxus unease and I would like to cover a large distance before we rest again."

The group quickly gathered their effects and reset their packs. Oslun was finding it easier to bear the weight of his weapons, armor and baggage. He hoped it was due to his strength increasing and not due to the lack of remaining food and water. Thyso and Oslun stood fast, waiting for Jaxus to lead off as he normally did, but the tall man was standing still, next to Layandria, staring intently down the passage, back into the darkness they had already traversed.

"I think it is time for Oslun to lead us." Jaxus spoke without looking away from the darkness. Oslun's body went cold. He did not feel ready to lead at all, feeling much safer in the center of the group. Jaxus sensed the hesitation in the young man. "Oslun and Thyso will lead, side by side. The Princess will follow, and I will take up the rear."

Jaxus drew his voice in tight, emitting barely a whisper, "I have a growing fear in my mind, a presence I cannot describe at our backs. Perhaps my instinct is influenced by the darkness, but I would feel better to take the rear guard for a time. Step quickly lads and let us put some distance on."

"Yes Sir," Thyso nodded in consent. He stepped forward but noted Oslun hesitating in his place. He thought to berate the younger man's fear but recalled the Princess' rebuke. He paused in stride and gently took hold of Oslun's arm. "Come on now, there is no need to be afraid. Stay next to me and I will guard over you."

Oslun gave in to the encouragement and stepped off. Layandria smiled at her men as they led into the darkness, the light of the sunstone at their backs. Jaxus allowed the others to create some distance before he followed. He could not be sure if he heard the sound, or if his mind conjured it, but he thought his ears caught the faintest impression of an animal snuffling along the ground, deep in the darkness behind them.

8.

Wilteph crouched onto his toes, pushing the brambles back from the secret entrance. Wil was taken in surprise by the size of the gap. It was easily as wide as his arm span in any direction, though astonishingly well concealed. There could be no doubt that this opening was constructed by the metal men as a ventilation tube.

Tepan was busy fixing a rope around the large pine that shaded the group. He handed the coiled braid to Wilteph, who loosed it into the darkness of the passage. No one was certain how far they would have to descend before they came to the floor. The Chieftain himself had only been in the tunnel of the metal kings once before, when he was very young, a trespass for which he was well punished by his father. Perhaps that lone experience was the reason for his distaste for the dark places of the world.

The spring air whistled around them as the sun concluded its slow decent, the first stars of the night beginning to show their faces in the sky. Wilteph thought of her as her prepared to descend. Chandr, his beloved and forbidden. To be a warrior of the Inohamman Tribes, each man and women bound themselves to the law. They could take no lands, hold no ranks in the leadership of the tribe, parent no children and devote their days solely to the arts of warfare. Wilteph's father was the Chieftain of their tribe, and as such, Wilteph had grown his early years believing that he would follow in his father's path as a leader of the Wanoak Tribe of the Inohamman, but fate had other plans. The council of elders handed down the stations for each young man and woman to serve on their thirteenth birthday and though it shocked many in the tribe, Wilteph, the only son of Chief Talin, was ordained to serve as a warrior.

Chandr was two years the younger of Wilteph. She was a quiet woman, who worked in silence as she fashioned weapons for the warriors. She was gifted with metals and had produced many of the finest in the tribes, including Wilteph's own sword. Though she rarely spoke, Chandr's smile, the brightness of her eyes and the way she smelled of honey and fresh blooms always took hold of Wilteph's attention. They knew each other for many years, but their romance bloomed in the summer of Wilteph's twentieth year. Within months, the two began secreting out of the village at night to be together. Though it was forbidden, the two rapidly came to passion. They lived out their love in the secret of the night for nearly two suns and only a precious few were aware. Chandr became pregnant in the summer.

Wilteph approached Chief Talin in the dead of night and informed him of the love that he held for Chandr and their child. The Chief ordered Wilteph to take his young love and their unborn child far away from the tribe, into the high mountains, but Wilteph would not leave, believing that Chandr and their offspring would perish in the wilderness. Talin, knowing that child would soon be discovered, called a tribal council. The penalty for a warrior to father a child is banishment from the tribe and Wilteph began to prepare for that fate. Talin announced to the council that it was not his son, but he himself that had lain with Chandr and fathered the child. The council called for Talin's execution immediately.

In desperation, Wilteph gathered his closest companions and most trusted warriors. He told them the truth of his crimes and the impending death of Chieftain Talin. He requested that those willing would go with him to stop the execution of his father and allow him to take his just place in payment for his deeds. Some thirty warriors agreed and moved under arms to the village center.

As the warriors entered the village, they found Talin bound to a post, prepared to be executed by spear. Wilteph and his friends formed a protective ring around Talin, though the council had anticipated some sort of rebellion and warriors loyal to the law were at the ready. Few of Wilteph's group survived. Talin was put to death and those who escaped were banished from the tribe.

Wilteph, along with six others traveled into the high mountains to the east. Upheaval followed in the tribe after Talin's death and within the first weeks, many more warriors sought the outcasts out, joining their ranks. In the end, Jordache was named Chieftain of the Wanoak and he ratified the banishment of Wilteph and those who were loyal to him. Chandr birthed her son and the two remained in the tribe, no penalty given to either.

The outcasts of the Inohamman grew to a total of fifty-six, naming Fannin as their Chieftain after Wilteph refused the title. Many challenges were found in the high peaks. Food was scarce and difficult to hunt; many predators called the mountains their home and shelter was not easily established. Morlts were the biggest cause of concern. These creatures were a vicious manner of wolf that dwelt in caves and other deep places of the earth. There were larger than most wolves, strong and able to move with a silence of no other kind. Morlts were terribly difficult to kill, able to withstand many blows that would bring normal beasts to the ground. The Inohamman had fought these menacing creatures for many generations, but the morlts rarely traveled in numbers more than two or three and had long been driven away from the villages. Wilteph and his group did not fare was well. They were much closer to the caves the morlts dwelt in and the Outcasts were far fewer in number. To combat this threat, their camp was constructed high in the boughs of ancient trees.

The death of Fannin and those who accompanied him to the Lakelands thinned their ranks and three more lost their lives in the cold of the winter, dying of exposure and starvation. As the spring came on, the outcasts numbered only twenty-three.

Game returned to the mountains with the coming of spring, and the morlts, who favored the cold and darkness of winter, withdrew. Relative safety allowed the Inohamman outcasts to range further and stockpile supplies. Many long months of tenuous safety stretched out before them, but Wilteph never stopped fearing for his people. They were too few to survive another winter. Fannin had sent Halta to range over the mountains and gather what information she could about the lands to the east, in the hope that better climes would sustain their future. Wilteph argued against the dispatch, but there was little else they could do. Keep hunting, keeping killing morlts when they appeared. Keep fighting to survive.

Wilteph took the lead, swinging his legs down into the passage, gripping the rope tightly as he cautiously descended into the darkness. Tepan, Halta and Rale'en followed in quick succession, the remainder of the party sent back to the camp. Wil was surprised when his feet found the stone floor of the main passage after only a short decent. He stood off to the side of the entrance, giving room for his companions as his eyes adjusted to the black of the tunnel.

The passage was full of the stench of the morlt. Wilteph did not need his refined senses to be sure that the thing had come this way.

"How far is the creature?" Halta asked in a hushed whisper. Her eyes were better than Wilteph's, but her nose was not nearly as strong.

"I believe it is at least one-half days walk." Wilteph spoke louder, not concerned that the creature could hear them with so much a lead. "There is human warmth here two. The beast is chasing someone."

"Then let us chase the beast." Tepan spoke low, uncomfortable in the darkness. Wilteph and Halta took to the lead, Rale'en in the rear. The darkness and silence were confining. Wilteph shuddered slightly as he walked.

"Shall I tell you what I have found in the east?" Halta sensed the discomfort of her companions and reasoned that conversation would aid them. The group moved swiftly, needing no light to guide them.

"I could not possibly wait any longer to hear the great adventures of the long walker." Tepan answered eagerly.

Halta grinned. "The Iron Kings have a vast region spreading out from the mountains. Massive dwellings that dwarf any built in our lands rise out of the ground and dot the entirety of the world. Their warriors are well organized, wearing suits of metal and armed with all manner of weapons. The people are vastly successful farmers who appear to transport their crops throughout the lands. I walked among them, even in their chief city, called the Arkenhead. No one challenged my origins despite my appearance. I was not denied entrance to any area of their city save for the massive fortress that houses their King, which they call the citadel."

Rale'en interrupted from behind the group. "What of food? Do they have decent food?"

"It seems that food is plentiful in the lands, though if a person does not grow or hunt their own provisions, they must be purchased using coins they call rashes." Halta did miss the comforts of the great cities of the Iron King. While she walked among them, she had found easy means to gain rashes, purchasing for herself many fine meals, soft beds and warm lodgings. "They have an incredible drink that they call whiskey that makes a person feel a kind of warmth that spreads to all parts of the body. They have a meat that they call lamb that is both flavorful and tender when roasted over a strong fire."

"So, what are waiting for?" Tepan broke in. His mind especially interested in the whiskey. "Let us leave this awful passage and seek out some of Halta's rashes so we may sample some of this fine comfort for ourselves!"

"We must kill the morlt before any other courses can be decided on." Wilteph broke in, his mind never far from the threat ahead. Halta spoke of a land that he and his people could thrive in, but there were many considerations to be analyzed before any course could be decided. "Would these Iron Kings grant us stay in their lands?"

"Of this I cannot say." Halta's voice grew softer. "War was upon them as I departed. I thought to stay among them longer as the cold of early spring had not yet left the foothills, but a great threat was approaching them. The armies of the King were dispatched to the southern region, called the Fire Fist, moving off to counter an enemy of which I heard no name. I departed at this news, but on my second day of travel, being high in the peaks, I could see clouds of smoke rising from the Arkenhead."

Wilteph thought through this news slowly as the group moved swiftly though the darkness. "We will present this news to the assembly and decide, though I would be hesitant to take our people into a war-torn region."

"We find no safety in the mountains alone" Tepan called up. The old man had followed Wilteph willingly over the long year since Talin's death, much of this out of loyalty to the departed Chieftain. Wil had proven a good and true Chief, but the old warrior had grown weary of the constant fight for bare survival.

"Be still Tepan." Halta called back. She had no doubt that the winter had been harsh for her companions. Guilt found its way into her heart as she remembered the ease with which she passed the snows in the cities of Arken.

"Let us find the morlt." Wilteph's voice took on an air of a leader, stilling Tepan. "We will discuss this news with all and decide what we must do, but only after we have ended the threat and discovered what persons travel this lusterless road."

9.

His muscles ached against the rough cords that bound him. They burrowed into this skin and stole the sensations from his fingers. He could smell rotting flesh, though he couldn't be certain which of two men that lay bound in the small closet with him birthed the odor. The darkness did not allow for a measurement of time, its slow passing interrupted only by sporadic bouts of uneasy sleep, his mind ever rebounding between tormented wakefulness and arduous rest. One of the other captives tried to speak to him, to suggest a method of escape, but Sahid ignored it. The man's voice was familiar, but in the darkness of their confinement, Sahid did not attempt to discover the identity of the speaker.

The sounds of horns and drums rising in the distance confirmed what Sahid had long suspected. The deception that King Axise used to secure his entrance into the capitol city was certainly a stroke of tactical genius, but it lacked focus on the end game. With the bulk of the Starrowlands forces committed to the fight in the south, there was little manpower to hold the citadel once it had been secured. Indeed, more than half of the forces that were committed to fight at the Arkenhead, some 10,000 in all, had been killed over the three days fighting that lead up to Axise death. The remaining 5,000, possibly a strong estimate on Sahid's part, were spread throughout the city, some no doubt engaged in the age-old tradition of taking war spoils. The remainder were committed to the security of the perimeter, a foolishly small number of swords against the wrath of Arken weapons.

Axise had been a fool, that fact was all too clear now, but Sahid had held to that knowledge long before he watched King Axeleon burry his blade in the man. Axise believed that the people of Arken collectively held him as the rightful King and once word was passed that he had vanquished Axeleon, most would lay down their arms and weep tears of great joy at the return of their true King. The loyalty and ferocity that the men and women of Arken fought with disproved that belief. Had Axise triumphed over Axeleon, Sahid and many others in the Starrowlands vanguard believed that they would not long hold the citadel, and now, Sahid knew that the meager number left committed to the security of Axise in the citadel would not be enough.

The Armies of Arken were well known to be vast, each of the five fists holding combat power similar to those of many other independent nations. The army of the Shadow Fist, being the seat of the King, held twice that many or more, though most were dispatched south to the Fire Fist. Sahid held little doubt that these armies would return rapidly to the seat of the King once word was given to them.

The armies of the Shadow fist had a full ten days march to reach the southern outpost of Lamath, their staging ground for counter attack against the main Starrowlands force, as did the forces of Lord Brustic in the Elk Fist, but Axise spy had told him the armies of the Wolf and Iron fists were not marching. As result, the Starrowland King expected Lord Aralias Taymrhlyn to remain in the wolf fist, unable to come to his King's aid. The lie given over by Axise spy sealed the fate of the Starrowlands soldiers now in the citadel. When Axise forces arrived at the Arkenhead, Aralias was four days march.

Heavy footsteps entered the banquet hall. The door of the closet was wrenched open and Sahid was blinded by the sudden light that streamed into the hall through large windows. The intensity of this breath of luminance was overpowering and he shuttered his immediately watering eyes against it.

"You, Starrowlander." Lord Commander Liam Fax' voice crushed the isolation of the small cupboard. The tip of his boot found Sahid's ribs with a similar damage. "Can you stand?"

"I am bound and cannot move." Sahid's voice quaked, his mouth dry with thirst and his lips cracked. So long had he gone without water or speech that it was quite painful for to form the sound of words. Liam bent and loosed the bindings on Sahid's feet and hands. As the massive Lord Commander gripped Sahid and lifted him to his feet, unbearable pain flooded through his entire body and he moaned sickeningly. Having been locked in position for so long, the muscles protested mightily against the movement. Blood renewed its rushing passage into appendages that had nearly forgotten the feeling. His feet found the floor and he wavered, nearly falling, though the commander's strong grip steadied him.

"Set me free and I will obey all order." The captive that had attempted to speak with Sahid so many dark hours or days ago spoke up. The man's voice was broken, his mouth parched, and his limbs bound as Sahid had been.

"Perhaps later." The commander moved Sahid away from the door, shutting it firmly behind them.

As the door swung closed, Sahid looked past the threshold. The young man that had taken the arrow to his leg was alive, his eyes wide with fear as he lay bound on the floor of the closet. The wound on his leg was indeed the source of the foul smell as it appeared festered. The large commander bolted the door. "Do you hear the horns, Starrowlander?"

"I do." Sahid quaked with weakness and fear, unsure what this massive man was planning for him.

"The horns signal the arrival of Lord Aralias and the Armies of the Wolf Fist. They have surrounded the city and are preparing to enter by force." The commander towered over Sahid, still steadying him with his massive arm. "We are going out to meet your army from the rear and I have decided to give you one chance."

"What is this chance you offer?" Sahid felt the blood coursing through his limbs and he massaged his damaged wrists, pleased to find that the abrasions left by the rough cords were not infected.

"I have been told that before the bodies were cast down on your men in the Whisper Hall, before Axise tasted his death blade, you gave your surrender to one of my soldiers." The Commander's voice was low but menacing. "Why did you make that choice?"

Sahid chose his response and the tone of delivery carefully, knowing full well that his neck was still very much in the hangman's noose. "I am not of the Starrowlands. I am Sahid Hauk Kahn of the Fallish Realm. I am a tribal leader of the men of Wallanpom."

"How came you to be in the service of King Axise, Fallish man?" Commander Fax brows raised in suspicion.

"Axise came to my lands some three years past with a force both large and powerful. The tribes of the Fallish region are many but dispersed over a vast landscape. We were unable to repel him and he slaughtered a great many brave warriors. Our women he took as slaves, our men were forced to serve in his armies, or put to the sword. The leaders of the tribes were required to serve in the vanguard. It was this order that brought me before your king. I have no malice in my heart for your people and my greatest desire is to return home to my lands." Sahid's breath nearly ran out as he spoke, so weak was he.

"Have you committed crimes against the free peoples of this earth or put to the sword the innocent during your forced time under the command of Axise?" Liam leaned down to meet Sahid's eyes as he spoke. "Answer me truly, I am deft at detecting a lie."

Sahid breathed deeply, delving into his soul for the courage to be truthful, knowing that death would likely be his reward. "I have put many to the sword. Axise was ruthless in his command. Any that refused to fight were beaten to death in view of the other soldiers. So, fight I did, and many lives stain my hands. I can offer no words that will assuage the blood I have spilt, though I can say, with my honor intact, that every man or woman I have laid to rest was bearing arms."

"If your words are true, there may yet be a way for you to prove your honor and secure your passage home." As the Commander spoke, he withdrew a skin of water from his belt, handing it to Sahid. He watched as the man ripped the cork from the top of the flask and pressed it to his lips, his eyes filled with hunger. Liam raised his hand and took the flask back, water spilling from the man's rough beard. "Too much and you will be sick."

Sahid's eyes were locked on the flask, thinking of only the water.

"I give you this one chance, Fallish man." Liam commanded the other's attention. "You will come with us as we move out. You will cross the enemy lines and deliver a message to Wolf Lord Aralias on behalf of the King. If you succeed, your life will be returned back to you."

"Thank you, my Sir!" Sahid nearly fell in his excitement. The commander reached out and steadied him, drawing him so close to the black armor on his chest that Sahid could smell the man. Sahid looked up into the Liam's burning eyes.

"If you betray us in any way, or attempt to flee," the Lord Commander's voice carried a sort of malice that only few could muster. It shook Sahid. "The pain I inflict on you will make your stay in this closet trivial."

Sahid could only nod his consent. He gestured to the barred door of the closet. "What of the other men?"

"The young one should have never been made to fight. He will be fed, and his wound looked upon shortly, though the stench of that closet gives me feeling that he will lose his leg. As for the other man, where does his loyalty lie?" Commander Fax inquired stoically.

"Of that, I cannot be sure. I was not aware of his identity until you pulled me from the room, and I saw his face in the sunlight. I know that the man's name is Jarren Shaff and that he is a man born of the Starrowlands. I have been told that he has been with King Axise since the beginning of his reign over that kingdom and it has been said, though I do not know for certain, that he took part in Axise assumption of the throne in that land." Sahid answered honestly, though he suspected that his words may have condemned the man.

"Stand aside." Commander Fax brushed Sahid away and yanked the door open, revealing Jarren laying bound. The young boy shimmied his body across the floor, away from Jaren. "State you name."

Jarren blinked hard in the sudden light as he struggled to find his voice. "I am Shaff, Jarren Shaff."

"How long have you been in service of Axise?" The Commander was brisk, unemotional as if he cared not what the answers were.

"I have been with Axise since he first came to the Starrowlands, before he claimed the crown." Jarren hoped that his long-standing loyalty would be favorable for him.

Liam did not stop to ponder the response. "Did you volunteer to serve him or were you taken into service by force?"

Jarren did not want to appear weak, and he did willingly serve Axise, perhaps Sahid knew that fact and would call out any lie. "I was in service by my own choice."

"It is good that you were honest." Commander Fax looked down on the man, bound as he was, without emotion. No message passed over his face. Liam turned to Sahid and drew a short dagger from his belt, laying it in Sahid's palm. "Kill him, then come into the Whisper Hall. You must take in food before we move into combat."

Sahid remained frozen in stunned silence, dagger in his hand, watching the huge commander stalk to the exit. He did not turn back to the closet for some time, turning over the blade in his hand as he considered the order set before him.

"Sahid, you know me!" The man began to whimper as a child. Sahid looked down on him curiously. "We have fought side by side for years! You know that I am a good man, do not do this thing!"

"Why did you volunteer to serve Axise?" Sahid asked coolly. The Commander had seemed fixated on this point, as if that one question was the deciding factor for death over life. Sahid was drawn to it as well, the quality of a man's heart being of high import to him.

"I..." Jarren did not know what to say and he stuttered heavily. "I thought it better to serve at the hand of a mad man than to than to die by him."

"Speak in truth to me now." Sahid narrowed his eyes, thinking through the past three years of war. He had seen Jarren take delight in the slaying of others many times. He certainly did not resemble a man forced into service by circumstance. Sahid stepped towards Jarren slowly. "I have been ordered to end your life, and my own survival depends on the execution of this command. Though, I have never taken a life not deserving of death and I refuse to do so now, take me to the grave or no."

Jarren's eyes grew wider as Sahid entered the closet and crouched next to him. He wildly searched for any way out of this terrible position. "I believed Axise would be victorious and I had hoped that he would grant me title and land!" Jarren nearly screamed the words, so filled with terror was he. Sahid's expression never changed. He conveyed simple curiosity and that was all. "I beg of you Sahid! Think of the victories that we have enjoyed together! Think of all we have been through! Spare me from this blade Sahid!"

Sahid stooped low, next to the bound man. He cupped the Jarren's face in his free hand and looked softly into his eyes. "I fought that I may one day return to my home, which was taken from me by men like you."

Sahid watched as the man's eyes widened in renewed fear. Sahid raised the dagger into Jarren's line of sight. He slowly lowered it, the tip of the blade pushing back the collar of Jaren's shirt, finding skin just over his heart. "So, I am to know that you fought for personal gain and the power that you felt lording over others. There is no honor in this."

"I am repentant!" Jarren screamed as the tip of the blade, under just a slight amount of pressure from Sahid's hand, split the skin on the man's breast. "Our imprisonment in this cage has given me time to examine my heart and I am repentant! I am an honorable man! I have a wife and children! I beg of you!"

"I pray your family may enjoy the gift that I am about to give them." Sahid spoke evenly, his tone betraying nothing of his intent.

"You're going to free me?" Jarren shuddered as the pressure on the knife increased slightly. Blood formed a slow stream, moving down his chest. Jaren took no note of the increasing wound, so filled with terror was he. "Sahid, you will be repaid many times over for the gift of my freedom, and when we return to the Starrowlands, all will herald you as a great champion!"

"No, that is not within my will. Heralding means nothing to me. Many believe that honor and glory is obtained behind a sword, but it is not. Honor is a gift presented to those who show restraint and mercy. As you have spoken, we have fought together through many great battles. I have seen neither restraint nor mercy in your heart and I find that now, in this final hour, no honor exists in you."

Sahid lowered his face, coming within inches of Jaren's ear. "The gift I give to your family is the chance to take a new husband and father who is driven by true honor and kindness not one who looks only for the self."

Jarren screamed out in terror. "Sahid! My blood will stain your soul! I am bound and unarmed, if you take my life, yours is forfeit and you will die bereft of all honor!" Sahid leaned forward, his weight pressed into the dagger as it penetrated Jarren. The blade passed easily between the ribs, entering the heart. Sahid forced it until the hilt met Jarren's skin. The man's eyes went wide in the pain and shock of the cut. As the blade bisected Jarren's heart, his body shuddered violently.

"Did you not hear the Lord Commander's words? My life is to be returned to me. It is yours that is forfeit." Sahid gripped the handle of the knife and wrenched it, turning the blade and opening the wound wide. A great torrent of blood ran freely. Jarren shook and a hollow gasp escaped from him. Sahid did not take his eyes off the other man as the life left him. "As for honor, I suspect that only now are you finding the true definition of the word as your own soul slips away."

He freed the knife from Jarren's chest, wiping most of the blood off on the dead man's trousers. He stood and threaded the blade through his belt. Sahid turned to face the wounded boy, still huddled on the floor. "You will be fed and attended to by a surgeon, those words were given by one of the Lords of this land. Do not attempt escape or any subterfuge. I believe these people will hold to their word and I may be able to secure our passage home."

The boy nodded his silent, labored consent. Sahid turned and moved, somewhat unsteadily towards the large door to the Whisper Hall, following in the path of Lord Commander Fax. He smiled slightly to himself as he swept a straggling lock of hair from his eyes. The Commander had spoken of food and there was a powerful hunger in his belly.

10.

The group walked on in silence. The light of the sun stone had dimmed, forcing Oslun to squint into the darkness ahead. Thyso was still next to him, which gave him comfort, though the barrier between the two stood firm. Oslun bumped his shoulder against the large man's armor, for what seemed to be the thousandth time. Thankfully, Thyso had quit complaining about it hours ago.

Jaxus had not let them slow for a second. Every time one of them suggested a break for rest, the dark warrior would insist that they continue. He would mumble about a darkness pursuing them, though he offered no specifics. If either Thyso or Oslun protested, Layandria would stop them, stating that she sensed the threat and that they must trudge on.

Oslun thought it strange that the Princess was in agreeance with Jaxus. Certainly, the man was strong and intelligent, but Layandria was clearly long weary of trekking. Jaxus too thought it strange that Layandria supported him. He had watched the Princess carefully over his years in the capitol. She was wise beyond her years, skilled with sword and bow and gifted in many small areas of field craft. She had shown great promise in the torturous world of politics and her people seemed to respect her.

All of this gave Jaxus a great deal of hope for her future as a ruler, and he harbored no doubt that she had the corner stones of an excellent warrior leader, but he still found it unusual that the Princess could sense the same threat that he did. Jaxus puzzled long over this as he walked on, in the rear of the small formation. Unless the young royal could sense his mind, he could think of no answer to this new puzzle. There were rumors in the wide world of individuals who could perceive the thoughts or emotions of others, but he had never seen this or met anyone with this gift.

Layandria too had been puzzling in the long dark. She did feel the presence of a growing threat. She could not put a name on it or explain what it was that caused her to feel as if she were constantly being chased by some monstrosity that was mere inches from locking its jaw around her neck or racking its massive claws down her back. She felt naked and vulnerable despite the strength of the armor that she wore.

The conversation had been sporadic at best over the past few hours and the silence made the distance grating for Thyso. The one positive motivation for the handmaid was Oslun. He was quickly proving to be stronger than his soft appearance suggested. After the first hours, Thyso's legs began to protest and he started to want for more sustenance than the few strips of meat that Jaxus rationed. Oslun continued to plod along next to him, keeping pace and not complaining. It was Thyso that first requested a rest, and when rebuffed, was proud to see that Oslun was unfazed by the distance or the time. Thyso was beginning to think that he had judged the cupbearer too harshly.

Unaware of the impression of strength he was putting out, Oslun felt weaker than he ever had. He missed the sounds of the Princess' singing voice that made his steps feel lighter. Also, he had noted that when the Princess sang, the sun stone was brighter, making forward progress in the darkness much easier. He summoned the courage to ask her to raise her voice. "My Lady?"

"Yes, Sir Oslun?" Layandria was shocked at the sound of the cup bearer's voice. It snapped her mind as if roused from a nap. She found herself wondering if it was possible to sleep while walking.

"Would my lady care to sing for us?" Oslun asked hopefully.

"I would that I could deliver you lighter steps, my dear Oslun." She answered sincerely, though it pained her, "but my legs and lungs are weary. I fear my songs would be little more than the sound of a voiceless cat being struck by an angered foot."

Thyso's heart sank. He too felt that the Princess beautiful voice made the drudgery easier to take. "Would Your Grace be willing to but speak the words of a song or rhyme?"

Layandria sighed heavily again. She wanted to take care of her men, as she knew they suffered for her, but she felt so weak, as if she were slowly turning into stone. None of them, save for Jaxus had ever undertaken such a journey. Jaxus. The Princess realized that the large man had not sung or spoken, save for telling the others that they could not stop to rest, for several hours. "Sir Jaxus, what of your rhyming?"

Jaxus raised his eyebrow, cocking his head at the Princess.

"Certainly, such a well-traveled man has learned songs or poems along the way." The Princess did not look over her shoulder for she knew the man's unique armor would render him nearly invisible in the crushing black of the tunnel. She also knew what expression the man wore without needing to look at it. She could not explain it, but somehow, she could feel Jaxus thoughts. Not hear his words, but she could feel the impressions, or perhaps the essence of the man. She wondered if that was why she could feel the same threat as he.

"I am not one for poetry, Your Grace." Jaxus voice was rough, not having been used in many hours.

"Save for the poetry he writes with the tip of his blades!" Thyso called back playfully.

The Princess smiled, enjoying the levity for a moment. Jaxus was silent. Layandria thought over fact that she knew of Jaxus past. She was saddened to find that she knew very little about him. In fact, all that she knew was memories of things she herself had witnessed. She knew nothing of him before he came to be in service of her father. She didn't even know where he was born.

The Princess decided that she should remedy that lack of knowledge. "Where are you from, good swordsman-poet?"

Jaxus sighed in resignation. He would never admit it, but he had been wearying for the past hours. He too longed for respite from the endless trudging, but he could not shake the gnawing fear on his mind. "I have called many realms my home."

"Yes, I know." Layandria breathed heavily. "We all know that, but where are you from? Where were you born?

"Your grace," Jaxus thought carefully before responding. To give the Princess enough information to satisfy, but not enough to give away his true history. "I am from a place that has no name. At least no name in common tongues."

Layandria turned her head back, her eyes narrowed, peering into the darkness. She could not see Jaxus, but she hoped that he could see her. She could feel that while Jaxus response was not a lie, it was not wholly a truth either. She decided to press the point. "Describe it to us, if you please."

"Must I?" Jaxus voice was flat, as it always was. The Princess was silent. Jaxus again sighed out his resignation. "Where I was born is far from here. I do not remember it well, though what I do recall feels as though it was a place made of magic. It is far from Arken, on the sea. The summers were mild and warm, the breeze carrying the ocean spray through the entire place. The foliage seamed to radiate the sun's brilliance as if the great light had set itself down on the soil. A pantheon of colors, purple, blue, yellow and the deepest greens a man could see coat the hills."

He forced himself to keep going, not allowing the searing pain of his memories to overtake him. "When the winter comes, everything is covered in snow so deep that a man saddled on a great horse would vanish under its surface. The sea is ever rising and crashing. It is not but rolling mountains of deep green capped in pure white. Everything smells new and refreshed."

Though the group continued walking, each one found themselves dreaming deeply of this land, of any land where the sun was shining and they were not trapped underground.

"Sir Jaxus?" Oslun called back, breaking the images in each mind and forcing them back to the dark underground.

"Yes, young master Oslun?" Jaxus responded with a voice that suggested a deep pain.

"Why do you never speak of your life before you came to Arken?" The cup bearer questioned easily, his voice free of the typical fear and hesitation that plagued him when he spoke to the dark warrior.

Jaxus scoffed, all traces of personal agony lost from his countenance. "I have just told you a great deal about my childhood home, have I not?"

"You have, Sir Jaxus." Thyso joined in the probing. "Though, to know the starting point of a tale and the current location, but to lack the in between is a poor tale, and a poorer telling."

"Some tales are not worth knowing." Jaxus more grunted the words than spoke them.

"Come now, Sir Jaxus," Princess Layandria spoke up, hoping to edge the large man into more beautiful stories.

"My Lady," Jaxus voice lost all perceived softness. "Some nightmares are best carried to the grave."

"Maybe later." Oslun muttered.

The group walked on in silence. After a time, Layandria began to hum softly. With each stanza, her volume grew. With each increase in sound, the sun stone reacted, building its radiance to match. Just at the point where it seemed the Princess was about to abandon humming and burst out into song, she stopped all together.

Thyso looked back at Layandria in surprise at her sudden silence. The sun stone slowly faded back to the same dim glow that it commonly held. He was just about to loose a query when she broke the deafening silence.

"Jaxus?" The Princess asked in her sweetest tone.

"My Lady?" Jaxus responded carefully, uncertain as to what the next demand placed on him would hold.

"Will you sing for us? My voice is worn, and neither Thyso nor Oslun could hope to carry a tune further than they could carry a castle." Layandria spoke in humor, though her face carried none. The young men in the front of the small formation both blushed at the insult.

"No, Your Grace." Jaxus was as a statue.

"Certainly, you can sing." Layandria was curiously annoyed by Jaxus. Though she had never noted this before, the Princess realized that no one had ever directly refused her before. She did not enjoy the sensation.

"Not everyone can sing, My Lady." Jaxus voice carried no hint of feeling as he spoke.

"Sir, everyone can sing." Layandria was beginning to become angry. She could not see why this man was being so resistant.

Jaxus cleared his throat. "Not everyone can sing *well,* Your Grace."

Layandria stopped in her place and spun around, facing Jaxus, the sun stone barely illuminating him. "I did not ask if you can sing well, Sir Jaxus."

"Your Grace," Jaxus sighed out his resignation for the third time, something he was not accustomed to doing. "I am not a musical man"

"Save for the music he makes with his swords!" Oslun interrupted, mimicking Thyso's previous joke with glee. Thyso laughed. Jaxus and Layandria did not.

"I am not a musical man," Jaxus continued. "But if it pleases My Lady, I will do my best."

Jaxus took in a slow draught of air as Layandria spun and resumed her plodding. *"The climbs of winter in the deepness of snow..."*

"We've already done that one, several times." Oslun called back. He wanted to hear something new.

Jaxus again inhaled and began, his voice rough and without any energy. *"The little frog, leapt over the hill, in search of flies and flowers fill."*

Thyso and Oslun burst out in laughter. Layandria could not suppress a smile despite her lingering irritation.

"What is this?" Thyso burst out between his guffaws. "Jaxus the Vicious sings out child's nursery lyrics?"

"Keep going, Sir Jaxus!" Oslun joined in excitedly. "I look much mightier by compare when you sing the words wet nurses use to soothe upset babes!"

"Good Sir Jaxus," Layandria broke in, her voice smooth and welcoming, like soft butter on warm bread. She stopped and turned to the warrior again. Her delicate hand taking hold of one of the warriors large, worn hands. His skin was pleasantly warm and astonishingly soft to the touch. The Princess marveled at the feeling rising inside of her chest. Though she had not noted it before, the aroma of the man reached her nostrils. He smelled of richness and calm water. The Princess' heart was fluttering so that she could feel it moving against her armor.

"My Lady." Jaxus answered evenly, slowly withdrawing his hand from her grip. Her eyes sparkled up at him, lit just so by the sun stone. He could feel her mind, pondering and examining him. Jaxus became intensely uncomfortable in the closeness of her, and yet, he did not want to pull away.

"Sing us a song that we have never heard before. Truly, you must have gathered one in all your years." Layandria's eyes locked into Jaxus'.

Jaxus bowed his head and gestured that they should keep walking. Layandria kept her eyes fixed on his for a moment longer, before she slowly turned and started off again. Jaxus spoke low, his voice somehow gentler than any of the party had ever heard it. "I have one song, My Lady, though it is a dark lyric."

"Dark places call for dark songs, Sir Jaxus." Oslun offered hopefully.

"Very well," Jaxus nodded and gathered his breath. He started out low and soft.

"She was to him as the sun is to the new birthed flower.

He sang her name, he sang her power."

As Jaxus tranquil voice filled the emptiness, the sun stone seamed transformed, the color changing markedly. When Layandria let her songs free, the stone was almost red, deep in hue and strong in radiance. Jaxus tones caused the thing to mimic the first light of daybreak, that fantastic golden glow that rocketed over the treetops, shattering the darkness of night.

"When she had crossed, below mountain far,

He called for her, longing hour after hour.

Return to me, love of my soul,

Return to me and never go.

She was to him as the rain is to the soil,

He refreshed in her, ceasing all toil.

Without her he withers to dust,

Nothing but her, nothing alone.

Return to me, breath of my life,

Return to me and never go.

Return to me, love of my soul,

Return to me and never go.

As the final words climbed out of him, a deep sadness took hold on Jaxus. With long fingers as ice it wrapped around his heart. The sun stone faded slowly back to the meek lantern that it was before.

"Jaxus," Layandria had to fight the urge embrace the man, so challenged was she by this first taste of his true emotion. She felt a heaviness on her heart and felt a need to reach out to the man. "That was just fine. And your voice is so very beautiful."

The Princess turned away from the warrior as a tear formed in the corner of his eye. Layandria did not understand why, but she felt wrong to see Jaxus in his sadness, as if somehow, she felt that the powerful man did not wish to share his hearts pain with anyone.

Jaxus forced his face back into impassivity. The song was the only memory he held of his mother and the only true memory of his home. He thought of her now, wishing he could remember her face, the feel of her skin, even the smallest sound of her voice. He wondered if she would condemn him for all that he had done, for the man he had grown to be. He felt certain that her spirit would be crushed to see how deeply he had wasted his years.

As the group walked on, they were unaware that scarcely fifty yards behind them, a creature of a ferocity none of them could believe sat rubbing its eyes fiercely with the back of its foreleg. Matts of thick, bristly fur helped soothe the beast's eyes from the brilliant light that had flooded the tunnel only moments before. After a few minutes, the rubbing slowed, and the creature stood, sniffing the air. Slowly and with a sinister patience, the beast started inching forward in the depths of the passage.

11.

After he had dealt with Jarren, Sahid did as the Lord Commander instructed and entered the Whisper Hall. He had offered the blade back to its owner, but Liam looked away. As the Commander stepped off, he muttered under his breath that Sahid should keep the weapon, claiming that one can never know if someone will need to be stabbed, or if you would find something to eat. Sahid could not get a read on the strange warriors of Arken. At moments, they appeared ruthless, capable of ordering the death of bound men without hesitation. The next second, they would show kindness, easily given trust, even warmth. Sahid thought these men as a pure enigma, a contradiction of all that he knew of the nature of soldiers.

The large commander sprinted across the open courtyard. Sahid marveled at the speed of the man, despite his sizable build. The shadow armor combined with his midnight skin concealed Liam well in the darkness. Aralias men had penetrated deep into the city and were scarcely more than an arrows flight from the gates to the citadel courtyard. Two days the wolves had fought, but they encountered heavy resistance and bogged down, taking many losses against a well-entrenched, though numerically inferior enemy.

Largely due to the fear instilled in them by Axise, none of the Starrowland's soldiers had dared set foot in the fortress itself, a great stroke of luck for Axeleon's men, as they were able to move about the castle freely, albeit away from the windows. Axeleon determined this the proper time to strike at the enemy's back, turning their attention from Aralias and his soldiers and opening the battle ground for advance.

The King had offered up his plan, the assembled fighters were allowed time to ask questions, and to Sahid's bewilderment, the King altered his plan to suit the ideas brought up from even the lowest ranking among them. Sahid had never witnessed a ruler who was willing to listen to the thoughts of his lesser. Even in the Fallish tribes, the chieftains seldom took council from any besides the highest levels of the tribal ranks.

Many men wish that in the moments leading up to battle, as they move to their fighting positions, their faces would appear hard, focused, ready to draw blood. Sahid had learned that very few men possessed this composure. Most wore the face of a young child facing the darkness. This, to Sahid did not make them weak, but simply human. Warriors were naturally afraid as they approached the meeting of life and death, knowing that these two primordial forces would be engaging in a vicious battle for their souls. It is the mark of a warrior that he be in fear and yet still he moves forward against the swords meaning to slay him. Most men trained for war were like this, but not Lord Commander Liam Fax. Sahid observed that this man's face wore neither the expression of fear, nor the desired hardness. The man's face was a new canvas, untouched by stroke of brush or blade.

Sahid sped across the courtyard, towards the Commander's position. He expected that the big man would have drawn the attention of some off Axise marksman, who would be waiting for the next man to expose his silhouette to their arrows. No shots came in and Sahid chastised himself for his minds conjuring as he slowed his pace, entering the shelter of the high wall behind the Commander. The sounds of battle were growing louder, though still some distance off.

"Have you your blade?" The powerful Lord Commander inquired in a hush.

"Yes." Sahid breathed back. He instinctually reached to his belt and touched the grip of the knife.

"Come forward." Liam gestured to his side. Sahid moved as instructed and peered around the corner of the wall. He could make out the outlines of the Axise soldiers, in position at the rear guard. The Starrowlanders were arrayed on a wooden scaffolding that stood behind a ten-foot stone wall. This wall formed the outer ring of the citadel courtyard, which was some two hundred yards across. "Can you get around them without being seen?"

Sahid swallowed hard. He knew himself to be fleet and quiet when needed, but these men were Axise own. Men who he had fought with for three long years. Increasing his hesitation, Sahid was certain that beyond these soldiers on the scaffold were hundreds more of their companions. Still, the Commander was not one to be refused and Sahid knew he was still a prisoner. He swallowed his parched fear and forced the words, "Yes, I believe that I can."

The Commander turned to meet Sahid's eyes. "Aralias and his men will think you a spy of Axise."

Sahid swallowed hard. "What am I to do?"

"Aralias most certainly believes that King Axeleon is either captured or dead. He will not know that we have survived." Liam spoke quickly, his voice as silent as falling snow. "He must receive word that the King fights on, else his men will spend all costs in the recapture of the citadel. Such action could cause great damage and loss of life, as well as the death of our soldiers by the hands of our own countrymen."

Sahid nodded, confirming his understanding. "How am I to make myself known to them that they would trust my words?"

Commander Fax's eyes narrowed. "Do Fallish men hold to a God?"

"Many do, but I have no strongly defined vision of such things." Sahid was immediately confused. Was this impassive war fighter suddenly concerned for the afterlife?

"What is it that you hold to then?" Liam's voice was steady, showing no doubt. "What gives you comfort in the cloud of battle?"

Sahid found it odd to speak of this, so close was their position to the enemy, but he consented to the commander's request. "I hold to the earth, to the water and stone. I believe that we are subservient to these. When a man passes from life, he returns to the earth and takes a place according to the way in which he lived. If he lived with honor, he will be as a tree. Should he die in shame, he will dwell under the surface of the soil where he cannot be a blight to the sun."

The Commander gripped Sahid's shoulder, "You will need all strength you can draw and every scrap of steel within, but if you succeed in the task I give you, on your death you shall become the largest of trees, standing for all the ages of this world."

Sahid nodded but remained silent. This poetic side of the Lord Commander was yet another contradiction to all he had learnt of the man's character.

The Commander turned back to peer around the wall. "Skirt the left edge of the court and come under the canopies of the shopkeepers. Use these facilities to screen your movements. At the end of the shops, you will cross some fifty yards of open terrain before you come to a sewer trench. I and my men will provide the enemy with distraction, allowing your passage unseen. Enter the sewer and move westward until it passes under the wall of the citadel. Aralias will have set his personal vanguard just off the central gate. You will know it by sight as it is a structure of two turrets, unique to our city."

Sahid nodded, begging his mind to recall every word.

"You must move as the wind as you approach, do not allow yourself to be stopped by the Wolf Lord's men until you have reached the man himself. Any others you encounter will likely kill you, thinking you a deserter or spy of Axise. Aralias will be known to you by his vestments, he bears the large head of a wolf mounted to the left shoulder of his armor. The men of the Wolf Fist wear armor similar in material and design to that worn by I and my men save for the color. Wolf soldier's armor is light gray with molted patches of brown. It appears in low light as the fur of the beast for which the fist is named. Look for the Lord Wolf."

"What am I to say when I find this creature?" Sahid's body was preparing for the coming movement. He felt alive with energy, his fingers and toes tingling. There is a special sort of calm and focus that comes to a man prepared to make war. Sahid was living in that space now, both aware of every detail, and immune to unneeded distractions.

"When you come to the wolf, tell him you were sent to bring a message from Lord Commander Liam Fax. That will stay his hand, but only for a breath." The Commander drew his massive face inches from Sahid's. His voice barely audible even from the short distance. "You must immediately ask him about the health of his dear wife, Anoxamall. He will know this to be a genuine message from me and me alone."

"I will do as you order, Lord Commander." Sahid steadied his breath, looking away from Liam's eyes towards the low structures of the shops.

"Best speed to you, Fallish Man." Lord Commander Fax gave Sahid a quick shove and propelled him from their position of cover.

Sahid darted across the terrain with every ounce of swiftness his legs could carry. He kept his left shoulder to the stone wall and held his head low as he shot towards the shopkeepers stands.

Liam turned back and signaled for his men to move up, joining him at the wall. He held his breath as the shadow of the infiltrator darted through the narrow gap between stone wall and wooden structures. As Sahid approached the final shopkeepers' stand, open terrain exposed like an ocean of grass before him. He hesitated, looking back to the gap where the Lord Commander and his forces waited.

Liam leaped out from the cover of the wall and advanced at a run across the courtyard towards the backs of Axise men. The men of the Shadow, six in all, followed their Commander's advance at speed. As he crossed the open terrain, Commander Fax let out a savage bellow. His voice cut through the night, tearing it open and exposed to his presence. He drew his sword, Falchon as it was known, drawing in a massive breath and letting fly another guttural scream. Axise men on the wall turned in confusion as the commander approached, some fifteen long strides in the lead of his small formation.

The men on the wall did not understand the sight before them. The massive form of a mad man rushed towards them, a humongous sword in his hand, screaming like the most criminally sickened creature they had witnessed. The demon and the men behind him wore the armor of shadow soldiers and approached from within the citadel itself. Though no word had been received from King Axise since he and his men entered the throne room, this was not unusual. His forces had no reason to doubt the victory of their King. Confusion overtook them, and they stood on the scaffolding transfixed.

As Liam drew near the wall, he planted his feet and launched himself into the air, landing on the wooden scaffolding next to one of Axise men. The Commander curled his fingers into the underside of the man's helm and wrenched upwards lifting the man off his feet, extending his torso and spreading his armor plates. Liam plunged his sword into the exposed stomach, the metal of Falchon gliding against the thin metal of the man's armor breeches. Upward force on the man's helm while Liam spun to the side propelled the body off the structure.

The men arrayed on the wall reacted fairly to the assault and as the Commander raised his sword to meet his next target, weapons were raised against him. Liam's huge blade swept aside an attempted counter and arced around, two sure hands drove Falchon's length eagerly through a chest plate. The enemy reeled, falling back into two others and creating standoff distance. Liam withdrew his weapon, spun to his opposite side and shot the tip through the visor of new foe's helm. The blade entered with lust, producing a tremendous wail. The Commander continued through the stroke and raked the blade to the left as it punctured through the back of the dead man's head. The tip of the sword found its mark on the throat of another soldier. This man dropped to his knees, rolling off the wall in a gurgling scream and a spray of blood.

Falchon became entrapped in head and helm, the metal marrying and refusing to be parted without force. Liam stepped back and kicked the man fully in the chest, divorcing his sword from the dead man as the body flopped away. One of Axise men charged in, bearing twin blades in wide circling patterns. Liam lowered his shoulder and rotated side face, raising his sword skyward in front of his face. The first of the blades impacted the armor on his back, glancing downward and causing no effect. Liam knew that the first strike was unimportant, a mere distraction for the second. The second weapon came in slashing high towards his face, its trajectory intended to find Liam's jaw. It found instead the raised edge of Falchon. Liam delivered his armored elbow into the man's face, crushing bone and causing the man's eye to explode from its socket. The man lurched and tumbled off the scaffolding, while Liam surged forward paying no further time to the dead. Chaos broke out as Lord Commander Fax' men mounted the scaffolding in various places. The enemy did not know where to turn to defend themselves.

Liam looked out into the darkness of the courtyard and saw the shadow that could have been no other than Sahid passing over the edge of the courtyard into the sewer. He let loose a savage cry and buried his sword into the chest of another faceless foe. He observed Genif Nitru several paces away along the scaffolding, several enemy soldiers between them. One of the Starrowlanders had concealed himself in terror, cowering in a crook in the stone wall. Genif charged past the coward, unaware of his presence. She parried an incoming attack, raised her blade and brought it down on the attacker's arm. Limb and man feel as Genif volleyed them, charging away from the Commander to challenge a large fighter armed with a spiked cudgel. The coward exited his concealment and raised a curved dagger towards Genif's back.

Liam saw the coward for what he intended and knew at once that his friend would not be prepared. He lowered his shoulder and crashed through any that stood against him, calling her name with thunder as he advanced. A short enemy clad in chain mail caught Falchon with his own sword, curving it around and lodging it into the wood of the scaffold. The short man simultaneously spit a knife towards the gap of armor under the Commander's arm. The knife found its mark and passed into the side of Liam's chest. The Commander jerked against the sudden pain and yanked Falchon free of the wood, bringing the hilt up into the man's jaw like a battering ram. The jaw collapsed and the man fell away wailing. Blood rushed down the inside of Liam's armor as he closed the distance to Genif.

He watched as she tore her blade from the man who had born the cudgel. The coward closed on her and pushed his weapon into Genif's lower back, just between her back plate and armor breeches. She spun against the wound, the force of her movement yanking the blade out of her. A jolt of dark blood bathed her armor as she fell to her knees.

Liam was but ten steps away, one enemy stood between them.

The Lord Commander moved like a starved beast closing on a meal. He drove his shoulder into the lone fighter's chest with so much power that he felt the man's breast bone snap like many small twigs. He called out to Genif again, but his words would not save her. The coward gripped Genif's hand, exposing the underside of her wrist. He drew his dagger across the tissue, severing tendon and letting lose a jet of blood. Genif did not scream, her free appendage searching for her sword on the floor of the scaffolding. The coward gripped Genif's helm, pulling her head back and exposing her neck. As Liam closed within striking distance, he knew he was too late. The coward drug the curved edge of his wicked tool across Genif's throat. Blood shot from the wound and the proud warrior, so menacing and strong, keeled from the scaffolding, landing on her back in the low grass as a sea of blood disfigured her graceful face.

The sound that emitted from Liam's throat was no longer the war cry that he had sent up so many times, but a true wail of rage. He wrapped his massive arm around the coward's body and pulled him tightly against his chest. Liam dropped his sword and closed his hand around the man's throat. He jerked the man's body to the right as he chiseled his fingers deep into the man's neck. The passionate force tore the man's neck open as a starving child tears into a rind fruit. He cast the dead man off the scaffold.

"Lord Commander!" One of Liam's men called out to him, "the enemy has turned to move on our position! We must return to the King!"

Liam bent and recovered Falchon, returning the long sword to its sheath as he stepped off the scaffold, landing as a great stone in the grass. He stooped low and took up the body of Genif Nitru under her arms, pulling her onto his shoulder. Sorrow broke across his face as the beautiful warrior's blood ran across Liam's armor. Time to mourn would later come, but the weight on the man's shoulders was infinitesimal compared to the burden on his soul.

"To the King!" Liam shouted and took to a run, though slowed by the weight of Genif. He pushed his pain down, as he had countless times over the decades. Many more would die before the sun returned its face to the sky and death held no care for your feelings on the matter.

12

"And so, he returned home, rich in tale and in treasure. Full of pride and glory, only to find that his own cousins believed him dead or gone mad. These relations had seized his home and were selling off his accouterments at auction on the front lawn! He ejected them post haste, full of confidence from his battles with orcs and dragons galore, none of them the wiser as to his dealings away." Oslun beamed as he finished his story. He had been telling it for hours, thrilled from start to finish and enjoying his enraptured audience.

"That, was an amazing story!" Thyso's countenance overran with awe. "You tell it with such detail! I believe I could feel the mountains of gold and jewels beneath my feet as you described them, and I nearly felt the dragons flame at my back!"

"It's my favorite adventure." Oslun basked in the warmth of Thyso's approval. "I learnt it as a boy."

"You're still a boy." Thyso cut at Oslun, though his tone was much transformed. His words carried no venom, no disdain for the soft cup bearer. His voice carried a note found in friends who tease each other in fun.

"I dare say you are both men now." The Princess smiled, "Wouldn't you agree, Sir Jaxus?"

The warrior did not respond. Layandria looked back to find that the man could not be seen.

"Jaxus, what are you doddering for?" The Princess demanded in her best feigned royal annoyance. Thyso and Oslun both sniggered.

Again, Jaxus did not respond. Layandria was beginning to experience slight irritation with the ease of Jaxus disappearances. "I swear it, I will have to find a bright pink sash to affix to your armor, so you will always be within my sight!"

"My Lady, be silent," Jaxus voice came as a low hiss from the shadow.

Layandria started towards the sound of the man's voice, the others keeping pace behind her. As Jaxus came into view, Layandria stopped frozen. She could not put words to it, but Jaxus stance and the tenseness of his expression spoke clearly of imminent danger.

"To arms!" Jaxus shouted suddenly as he lifted his arms above his head and drew his twin swords. He planted his feet and made ready for an unseen attacker's approach.

Without hesitation Thyso brought his own sword to bear. He advanced towards Jaxus and placed himself in front of Princess Layandria.

Oslun froze in place as fear swept over him like a wave.

"Fight on your feet or die on your knees!" Thyso shouted back, demanding the cup bearer take action.

Oslun fumbled with the hilt of his sword, finally freeing it from its scabbard and bringing it up. The weapon felt heavy and awkward in his grip. "I don't know how to hold it!"

"You'll learn!" Thyso shouted the order without looking back. "Follow me and do as I do!"

In a flash of fluid motion, Jaxus wheeled, his twin blades sang as they cut the air. The weapons collided with a strange foe that appeared as an over large dog. The beast was silent in its approach, invisible and arriving with no announcement. How Jaxus had anticipated the beasts first lunge was a mystery to all. Thyso steadied his grip and lunged forward, hoping to pen the animal between himself and Jaxus, using his own body to shield the princess. Oslun followed him, mimicking Thyso's movements, placing himself between the beast and his royal.

Layandria's heart raced. As her breathing increased, the sun stone reacted, increasing its brilliance. The entire passage came alive with the dancing orange radiance.

Jaxus pivoted to his left, prepared to levy a new strike. In the light of the sun stone, he saw his enemy for its truth. It was canine, or some similar form, with patches of pale gray skin exposed between clumps of dull fur. The light of the sun stone dazzled the creature's small yellow eyes and it blinked heavily.

Jaxus took the chance afforded him by the creature's resistance to the light and let his strike fly. He plunged his blades towards the thing's chest, but as he struck, the creature leaped into the air towards Oslun.

Thyso saw the creature in flight and reacted without thought. He lowered his right shoulder and drove his armor into Oslun's side, sending him reeling across the narrow tunnel into the rough wall. The creature slashed out with its foreleg, the claws on its gnarled paw finding Thyso's breast plate. They tore through the shadow steel and Thyso cried out, falling to the floor.

Jaxus caught sight of Layandria just over the beast's back. She was staring at him, her eyes fixed on his with intent. No terror invaded her face. Jaxus felt her as if he were hearing her voice aloud, though her lips did not part. She instructed him to move left and strike, while she would take the opposite angle.

Jaxus threw himself at the creature, carving his body sideways as he flew, his swords swinging round like the crack of twin strikes of lightning. Layandria planted her foot squarely on the back of the downed Thyso's armor, propelling herself off the man as if from a catapult.

Jaxus blades slashed out, the first blade cutting deep into the monster's spine. His second sword took the things right foreleg, just below the shoulder joint. Layandria's outstretched blade found its target and the steel opened the muscle on the back of the great dog's neck eagerly. Still, the creature did not fall. As Jaxus moved to bring his blades around again, the beast reared and sprang towards the Princess.

Oslun saw the creature move towards his royal. The scene brought up a great flood of rage, the likes of which the young man had never experienced. He surged off the stone wall with all his strength and crashed headlong into the creatures back, toppling both to the floor in a horrendous cacophony of steel and breaking bone. Oslun found himself on top of the creature as it writhed under him with fury.

"Kill it Jaxus!" The cup bearer begged as he struggled to pin the beast's snapping mouth.

Jaxus stepped forward and crossed his swords over the things neck with a precision only possessed by few. He wrenched the blades against one another and cleaved the beasts head from the still writhing body.

The head rolled off towards Layandria, the great jaw of yellow teeth snapping one final time at the feet of the Princess of Arken. Life left the headless body and Oslun struggled to his feet. Thyso rolled to his side and moaned as blood trickled out from the gouges in his breast plate.

Jaxus found Layandria's eyes as many troubling questions filled his mind. How had he heard her thoughts and how had she behaved so decisively? He knew Layandria to be gifted with the sword, but she had never faced such a foe. Few hardened warriors could maintain such poise in the forge of sudden battle.

He looked down at the creature's head, still impaled on Layandria's blade. He stopped short, his breath caught inside of him. Something else was approaching.

13

"Be swift." Wilteph hissed to the others. "We are nearly on it!"

A strange voice went up in the empty expanse of the tunnel ahead of them calling for arms. A brilliant orange luminance flooded the passage ahead as if it were water rushing through a pipe. The sounds of combat rang through the air, the tight stone walls causing the sound to surround the charging warriors, distance unable to be ascertained. Wilteph silently begged that they were close enough.

"Kill it Jaxus!" Another cry, desperate and wet with fear, crashed over the ears of the Inohamman warriors. As they rounded a bend in the tunnel wall, a splash of harsh orange light nearly blinded them. Halta's vision reacted before the others. "Wait!" She ordered to her fellows.

Highly skilled warriors can move with incredible speed, which is magnified when the enemy is at hand. What some of these experienced fighters cannot readily do is curb this immense momentum. Tepan, being the largest of them, smashed headlong directly into Halta's back.

The woman turned to her side, dropped her spear to one hand and wrapped her free arm around the speeding Tepan's shoulders. She swung him around her own body, peeling off his energy with impossible grace and accuracy. She readied her long spear and took in the image that filled the passage.

The sight filled Halta with wonder. A man, clad head to foot in iridescent black armor that she could barely see, holding twin swords aloft. Another man, tall, but portly, in ill fitting, matte black armor, stood unarmed, his eyes darting back and forth between her and his tall companion. A third man lay crumpled on the floor, blood slicked over the chest plate of his armor. These three were near to what Halta expected to see, save only for the blank expression on the first man's face. The fourth figure was not at all what Halta expected. What she saw first of this person was the pendant. Halta could only understand the thing as a shard of the sun itself set against the backdrop of matte black sky. It hurt her eyes to look directly at the jewel.

Next, she saw the sword, held aloft in two hands, ready for use and adorned with recent blood. At her feet, the severed head of a morlt. The morlt's fangs were turned out, the creature's eyes wide and menacing though devoid of life. Halta glanced quickly to her companions. Their faces expressed what she felt. Astonishment.

"How did you..." Wilteph started, but the words failed him. He had known a single morlt to slay several men before falling.

"By the Gods!" Tepan took up where Wilteph fell off. "How did you kill the thing?"

"With an expertly timed volley of precision attacks delivered by the known world's best swordsmen." Thyso spoke the words through teeth clenched against much pain.

"This one is of hard spirit." Rale'en laughed heavily from the rear of the Inohamman group. Tepan snapped his head towards his companion, his eyes wide as he looked at the hard woman. He had never heard her laugh before. None of them had.

"Explanations can wait. We must see to our man." Layandria stepped towards Thyso, but she did not take her eyes off Wilteph and his fellows.

"If your intention is to strike, do so without delay." Jaxus spoke calmly, devoid of emotion or inflection. "So that we may kill you and tend to our wounded man in peace."

Wilteph took in this man, clad in the blackness of the night sky as he appeared. He understood that the words were spoken not as a threat, or as a display of arrogance. This dark warrior believed what he spoke as utter truth.

"Our intent was to strike the morlt." Tepan spoke with a hint of disappointment in his intonation. "Seeing that you sturdy fellows have taken that joy from us, I suspect that the striking is well and done."

"For now." Rale'en added coolly.

Jaxus did not move so much as an eyelash. His eyes drilled into Wilteph's, sizing the man's intent, judging his ability. A killer knows a killer's heart, Jaxus recalled words long ago said to him in a similar contest. He saw no malice in the other man, and yet, he saw a killer, tried and capable, standing before him.

"For now." Jaxus confirmed, his tone as sharp as his twin blades. He sheathed the weapons over his shoulders.

Oslun walked slowly, crossing the distance to his lost sword. He felt the eyes of the strange woman watching his movements. Her gaze was penetrating, and he felt exposed to her as he turned to meet her eyes. He took her in and found that she was beautiful in a way no woman had ever appeared. She was taller than Jaxus, but not as heavy in build. She wore very little, only a short, dark brown cloth skirt at her waist and a similar cloth vest over her shoulders. Much of her earth toned skin was revealed. Her hair was black and smooth, igniting her sparkling golden eyes. They shone so lively in the light of the sun stone that Oslun could not help wondering if they were of the same magic and the pendant.

Oslun felt himself wishing that he could stop in this moment and memorize every detail of her form. He was so transfixed by the sight of her that he nearly tripped over his own sword as it lay on the stone. He bent and sheepishly scooped it up, struggling with the weapon as he wrestled it into its scabbard. He blushed deeply to see that she was still watching him. The woman lowered her spear and smiled at the young cup bearer. Her teeth were slightly crooked, but in a special way that made her smile so utterly perfect to the young man's perception.

Layandria moved to Thyso's side and began releasing the clasps holding the wounded man's chest plate into position. Tepan joined her. Layandria hesitated, unsure of the squat brown man. She pushed past the doubt as another pained moan escaped from Thyso's lips.

Oslun put his back against the roughness of the wall and let out a deep sigh. The adrenaline that had rushed through him in his first trial of combat was leaving his body. His stomach rolled and sweat drenched his tunic. The young man leaned forward, bracing his hands on his knees. He silently begged the spirits of his ancestors to keep him from vomiting. The spirits declined. Oslun's stomach emptied, is dignity lost with his food. He slid his back down the wall, the armor scraping terribly as he sat, his head hanging between his knees.

Thyso coughed weekly, "Little lord lost his lunch?"

Oslun felt tears well in his eyes. 'Please don't let her see me cry!' The cup bearer screamed inside his head. He felt a warm hand on the back of his neck. He knew it was the woman the moment her skin touched his.

"It's alright, brave one." Halta whispered to him in a voice that felt to his ear like a silken garment. "I too became sick after my first fight."

Oslun looked up just enough to see her face, so close to his own. She was smiling at him, the softness of her hand still on his neck.

"And the second." Rale'en offered. She stood behind the rest of her companions. Her long knives lowered, but not stowed.

"And the second." Halta's smile brightened at the obvious insult. "It gets easier young warrior, you will see."

Layandria struggled with Thyso's breast plate, her hands struggling to grip the metal and the leather bindings, slick with blood as they were. Tepan was next to her, squatting on his heels rhythmically clicking his tongue against his teeth as he watched the young woman.

"Get the high ones, under the arms." Thyso moaned his instructions, only half lucid, such was the pain that took over his mind. His hands pawed at the clasps holding the armor in place.

"No no," Layandria fought to control her nerves as she pushed Thyso's hands away. She felt as if she were unraveling and kept turning her face to Jaxus for help, but the tall warrior still stood with his back to her, locked in some wordless battle with the apparent leader of these new folk. She returned her attention to her handmaid, "Let me do that. Please Thyso, stop touching them."

"Hold his hands together and lift them high above his head." Tepan's gruff voice instructed her. As he spoke, he rolled forward on his toes and withdrew a wide, oval bladed knife from a leather sheath concealed beneath the skirt of animal skin around his waist.

Layandria saw the blade and became immediately afraid that this boulder of a man with the voice of a bear would kill Thyso. Perhaps in some sort of show of mercy, perhaps in a disguised attack, the reason was unclear, but she recoiled at once. The Princess lunged forward grappling for Tepan's wrists, struggling to keep the blade away from her servant. Tepan rolled his body, causing her balance to fail. Layandria wrapped her left hand around the angry blade. The knife dug deeply into her fingers and blood ran across her knuckles as she struggled against the man's strength.

Wilteph observed the struggle, turning back to the greater threat in the tall warrior with the impassive eyes. He had no doubt that Tepan could easily crush this small female, even though she had apparently killed the morlt or at least taken a part of the feat. Before Wilteph could react, Jaxus had drawn his twin blades and was advancing on Tepan, who was unaware, focused as he was on the Princess. Rale'en leapt in front of Jaxus and brought her daggers inside of Jaxus swords. She lifted and pushed outwards, swinging Jaxus blades in a wide circle and trapping the hilts against the grips of her own blades. The tips of Jaxus swords impacted the floor and to Rale'en's surprise, the swords scarred the stone. Jaxus was prepared for this and lowered his head, driving the crown of his skull directly into Rale'en's nose. He was rewarded with a shriek of pain and the sensation of crushing bone that was not his own.

"Stop this at once!" Oslun shouted as he ejected himself from the floor. With his fists clenched and his eyes burning, he stomped towards Jaxus. For the first time, Oslun looked the dangerous knight in the eyes. "What are you doing? These people came to our aid!"

"Yes," Halta stood at his side, though she rose much more gracefully than the cup bearer. "We can kill each other later, if that is your desire Master Black, though I would prefer to make that combat in the light of the sun, above ground and free of the foul smell of this dead cave critter."

Tepan released his grip on his knife. He dug his hands under his skirt and removed a soft white cloth. The man gently took Layandria's damaged hand in his. The young Princess' eyes were fixed on Oslun and the woman next to him. She barely noticed as Tepan gently bandaged her wounded fingers, so taken was she by the sudden appearance of Oslun's assertive courage.

"You have quite the strength, young lady." Tepan broke the tense silence. Though I dare say that your intent is skewed."

Layandria heard the man, but she did not truly understand his words, so bewildered was she by the cupbearer's conduct. "I…What?"

"Generally," Tepan's low voice sparkled with amusement, "if your intent is to damage someone, you should cut them, but you, sun bearer, have thought it better to damage yourself. You must correct this if you wish to fight me again."

Rale'en rustled herself off the floor. She paid no attention to her damaged nose, or the blood streaming down her face and neck.

Tepan looked up at her and burst into laughter. He turned his beaming face to Jaxus. "Master Black! You are certainly my hero! Finally, someone has found a way to make Rale'en's appearance much improved!"

The woman glared down at her short companion. She barred her teeth and licked the blood from her lips. Tepan grimaced in comic exaggeration while Wilteph and Halta both chuckled.

Tepan stilled his laughter and returned his intention to Thyso. He held his hand out to Layandria, who after a moment of hesitation, placed the knife in his palm. The short warrior quickly cut loose the clasps that bound Thyso's armor in place and lifted off his breast plate. He carefully inserted the blade under Thyso's cloth shirt and cut it away, revealing shallow rips in his chest that were dark and oozing a greenish yellow puss.

Wilteph stepped in and looked down on the wound. He lowered his face and smelled the torn flesh. After a moment and several analytical sniffs, he turned to Halta. "Have you any marantus root?"

"Of course." Halta scoffed the words. "Only a fool would face a morlt without it." She withdrew a small brown pouch from within her vest and tossed it to Wil. Jaxus noted that the warrior raised his hand and caught the pouch without looking at it, his eyes focused entirely on Thyso and the care of the boy. He handed the pouch to Tepan as he extended his long graceful fingers and began separating the flesh of the wounds and gently pushing the puss out of the torn flesh with his finger nail. Each probing movement of the man's digits produced pained moans and quivering limbs from Thyso.

"Steady your heart, good soldier, this will bring you much pain." Tepan opened the pouch and began to sift the contents with his thumb. He pinched a small amount of coarsely ground dried root between his thumb and forefinger, sprinkling the powder into the open wounds that Wilteph had cleared. As soon as the substance contacted the exposed musculature, Thyso writhed in fresh agony. Wilteph began to push the powder into the tissue with his fingers, following on as Tepan added more.

Layandria looked away, tears running freely from her eyes.

"Look on, My Lady." Jaxus spoke evenly, as a patient scholar to his pupil. "A leader must share in the pain of those who sacrifice for her."

Layandria slowly turned back to face her handmaid. He was struggling against his pain, his body wrenching under Wilteph and Tepan's force. Thyso's eyes frantically searched the interior of the dark passage for anything that would ease his agony, coming to lock onto the face of his royal. The two men who held him down were expressionless as they worked, adding more of the powder and grinding it into the wounds.

Thyso found that as his pain intensified, his vision began to fail him. He could no longer feel his limbs. His hearing departed, and he was left with only the massive pain in his chest. His thoughts began to swirl around him. Thyso's ragged mind conjured an image of the cup bearer's face. He pictured the boy, grinning from ear to ear. The delighted sounds of Oslun's laughter, having just finished the telling of his favorite adventure flooded his entire reality. Thyso felt himself calming in the sight of the smiling face and the pain subsided as the grand tale dominated his thoughts.

"He will recover." Tepan spoke slowly as he whipped his hands on his skirt. "A morlt's strike can be devastating, the beasts grime turning the flesh to poison, but the wounds were shallow and this young one is strong."

"Without question." A small smile crossed Jaxus face. "Any deeper and those wounds would have ended the life of any man, no matter what creature delivered them. I have seen these creatures before, far in the east."

"And now, travelers from the metal kingdom," Wilteph's voice, quiet though it was, commanded the attention of all. "Would you like to escape this dark passage and feel the warmth of the sun again?"

"The sun!" Layandria burst out in desire. She paused in her delight and looked to Jaxus. "Do you think it wise to leave the passage, Sir Jaxus?"

Jaxus bowed his head to the Princess. "I am yours to command, My Lady."

Layandria looked to each face. All were waiting her order. "To the sun."

14.

As the water swirled around his feet, Sahid was forced to move at painfully slow rate preventing any splashes. He could not see over the stone edges of the sewer trench. He had no idea where Axise men were or how far he had yet to travel. The feeling that tells a person that they are being chased by some hungry beast or murderous killer crept up the back of his spine, strengthened by the powerful stench of the refuse that filled his path.

He felt as though he had been in the sewer for hours, making little progress. He knew that this was only the lie of his mind as he slowly made his way past the floating fecal matter and decay. He could see the shadow of the massive city wall, but the darkness destroyed his sense of distance. The Fallish man was keenly aware that if he was found by Aralias men before finding the Lord himself, he had no hope of survival. With each step, he passed further from one danger, but closer to the next.

The sounds of combat were all around him some near and some far off, hidden from his view by the trench walls. Sahid thought of the Lord Commander and his men. Just before he entered the sewer, Sahid saw Commander Fax and his men engaged with Axise fighters on the low wall of the courtyard. He stood witness as the massive commander, distinguished from the others by his size and the dark tone of his skin, gripped a smaller man around his chest and throat. Sahid shuddered as the memory of the commander tearing the man's neck apart with only his hands flooded his mind.

Sahid had no doubt of the Commander's ability to strike men down with little care, but there was something else lingering in the man's character. A strong contradiction to the image of a brutal man, bereft of feeling. This was the image that Axise had wanted for himself, though in his own way, he was overrun with emotion. This Lord Commander did not seem to care what image he presented. Allowing him to keep the blade that was given him in the banquet hall, feeding him well, trusting him with the message to Aralias. The Commander was more than a killing dog to be sent out by his master. He quite possibly possessed the strength lusted for by generations of dead Kings and Emperors. The man was royalty, in the image that Sahid imagined that royalty should be.

The outline of a body floating in the water came into view ahead. Sahid tensed and lowered himself as he approached the corpse. Sahid saw that the dead man was clad in the armor of a Wolf Fist fighter, so described to him by Commander Fax. He rolled the body over onto its' back. The man's chest plate had been punctured by a heavy spear. The froth on around the man's lips indicated he was alive when he entered the sewer. How horrible an end this man must have faced, unable to clear his head above the surface, overcome by pain and breathing in his last of this rancid liquid. Sahid searched the man and found that he was without sword, but a long, angled knife was still sheathed on his belt. Sahid took this, prepared for an encounter with whom ever had downed this wolf.

Sahid moved on, resuming his slow pace. The water formed calm circles swimming about his thighs. The sounds of combat grew as he moved forward. He slowly rounded a bend in the trench and in the darkness found more bodies, partially submerged under the weight of their armor and weapons. Sahid determined that he needed to get a better bearing on what was happening above. He approached the right wall slowly. The stone was taller than suited his need. Carefully, taking pain to not disturb the water, Sahid slid one of the bodies closer to the wall. He raised his foot onto the person's back. Sahid tried to keep his motions steady, but as he stood up on the man's back, reaching for the edge of the trench, the body beneath him waggled and Sahid was forced to leap upwards. His fingers found grip on the lip of wall and he pulled himself up. The waters splashed about greatly as the dead man bobbed and moved away. Sahid was caught between the desire to drop back down and hide, versus the desire to gain some sort of information. The need for facts overrode his fear and Sahid pulled his body up the wall, raising his head over the edge.

A young man, clad in the dingy steel armor of the Starrowlands knights, was looking directly at him as Sahid's eyes cleared the edge of the trench. Drawn by the sounds of splashing, this young insurgent drew his blade and marched towards Sahid, who panicked and released his hold on the wall, splashing down into the sewer with great commotion. He slid against the wall four steps to the left and lurched up, his left hand gripping the wall's edge again. He could hear his enemy's foot falls approaching. Sahid drew his newfound dagger and gripped it securely.

Sahid judged that the man was two steps away and he made his gamble. If the man was where he expected, he would be victorious, if he was not in the anticipated position, Sahid would likely die. He kicked off the wall hard with his right knee, swinging his body to the left, his left hand the fulcrum. At the peak of his swing, Sahid again kicked off the wall with his left knee, pulling with his left arm upwards as hard as he could. The Starrowlander's light blue eyes appeared against the night sky just as Sahid kicked off. His sword was in his right hand, pointed down towards where he expected Sahid to be. The Starrowlander was wrong, Sahid was not.

The Fallish man soared up towards his target, dagger at the ready. He reached the apex of his trajectory just as the enemy realized he had been fooled. His eyes went wide, but he did not have time to scream. Sahid drove his dagger deep into the man's neck, just below the jaw line, driving upwards. The blade penetrated the brain stem, internally decapitating and severing all communications between brain and body. As Sahid began his decent, the soldier fell with him. Both men crashed into the water like projectiles fired from the long-barreled cannons of fighting ships.

Sahid knew that the sound would rapidly bring other enemies to investigate. He took in a deep breath, drawing in as much air as he could hold. He closed his eyes and slowly slid his head under water. He kept his dagger in his hand as he carefully moved across the bottom of the trench. He would not open his eyes for fear of the disgusting water.

The trench was shallow, the water only rising to his hips when standing which forced him uncomfortably close to the bottom of the sewer. Coating the bottom was a thick, putrid muck formed by years of carrying the filth of the citadel away. Despite his caution, Sahid struck his chin against the floor of the sewer trench. The pain was instant, but the warrior kept his discipline and did not allow his body to react. Vomit rose in his throat, but he kept convulsions at bay.

As his lungs began to run out of air, Sahid rotated over to his back and let himself slowly rise to the surface. He broke evenly, making scarcely a sound. As his nose cleared the surface, he forced himself to release the air slowly. As he drew in a steady breath, he opened his eyes and gently lifted his head. He could see that he had traveled some thirty yards from where the slain man fell. Three others stood on the edge of the trench watching while one of them jabbed at the dead bodies with a long spear. Sahid drew in a deep pull of air and rolled over again, gently easing himself back down to the floor of the trench and continuing along the bottom as he had before, using his toes to propel himself forward.

As his lungs started to scream for air again, Sahid started easing himself upwards. Suddenly his head impacted against a solid structure so sharply that he bit his tongue. He could not see, refusing even in sudden pain to open his eyes within the waste. He reached his empty hand forward and found that he had impacted metal bars. He gently rotated his legs under himself and pushed his head past the surface. As he opened his eyes, he found that he had reached the outer wall of the citadel as Lord Commander Fax had described.

The wall had a narrow opening to allow the flow of the sewage away from the sensitive nostrils of the royals. That small tunnel like passage appeared to be blocked off by iron bars. Sahid slid his feet forward, attempting to feel out path through the thick grate. As he suspected and much to his dismay, he found that the bars connected to a crossing bar close to the floor of the trench. Sahid closed his eyes and sighed. He would have to slide under that crossing bar, in the slime and muck along the floor. He knew, as most warriors did, that hesitation will kill quicker than the blade. Drawing in a breath, Sahid eased under the water.

Sahid gripped the crossing bar with both hands and shoved his feet under, pulling with his arms to move himself through. The gap was not as wide as Sahid had believed it to be and his hips caught on the crossbar. He wriggled against it and pulled with all his strength, but he did not make any progress. Panic rose in his consciousness. He struggled against the entrapment, to no avail.

Sahid determined that it would be better to move back and reassess. He pushed against the bars with his hands but found that he could not move in either direction. The bar pressed against his body and he could not find release. Sahid began losing control as his lungs screamed for air. He thrashed out with his arms and legs wildly.

The irony struck with a strangely calming force. He was going to die, trapped in nothing but human waste and excrement. Likely, his body would not be found until long after this war was concluded. He continued to struggle against the bars, refusing to accept this terrible demise. His strength began to fail him, and his arms grew weak as his air ran out. Need for oxygen bypassed fear and Sahid breathed in the filth of the sewer. It invaded his eyes and made him convulse, only drawing in more of the scum.

Sahid felt his body relax as the life left him, though his mind was still screaming for release from the trap. As his body let go, Sahid thought he felt the pressure on his hips lessen. He struggled to lift his arms and find the cross bar. He wrapped his fingers around the iron and pulled. He felt spent, and he had little faith that his effort would be rewarded. An immense feeling of dread took over him.

He let his hips relax and pulled against the bar again. Sahid was rewarded with the slight forward movement of his body. Though it was mere inches, hope sprang inside of him. Sahid adjusted his hips and pulled again. He moved several more inches, adjusted and pulled again. Less effort was required and Sahid found that he was nearly free. He let go of the bar and put his arms under it, pushing against the back side of the grate. His head cleared and he was free. Sahid planted his feet and burst out of the water, so great was his thirst for air that he lost fear of an enemy. The new air flooded into his being and he felt alive with its refreshing hope as he spewed out the vileness that filled his body.

He opened his eyes and looked around, but he could see nothing. Sahid became concerned that he had somehow gone blind by the impact of his head against the bars or the poison of the trench that still invaded his body. He began to slowly realize that this was a foolish fear and he reasoned that he must still be under the wall of the citadel.

Sahid gained his composure and slowly started moving forward again. A dim glow of the night sky appearing at the end of the tunnel. Hope returned and Sahid increased his speed as much as caution would allow. As he neared the end of the wall, no threat was apparent. The sewer trench continued, no doubt taking the waist well away from the city. Sahid started scanning the edges of the trench for a place to climb out.

"Hold man," A voice hissed in the night. "Hold fast or you'll be run through."

Sahid looked up to find that some ten Wolf Fist soldiers lined the edges of the trench, each with a long spear ready to engage him. He froze.

"Who do you serve?" The voice hissed again.

"I seek audience with Lord Aralias!" Sahid called out, desperate to avoid an end in this disgusting trench, having just escaped the same repulsive fate. "I carry a message from Lord Commander Liam Fax!"

"The Lord Commander is dead," the voice hissed again.

"The Lord Commander lives!" Sahid pleaded with the hissing warrior, "King Axeleon lives! Please, take me to Lord Aralias and I will make all known to him!"

"He lies." Another wolf hissed from the right side of the trench.

"I carry a message from Lord Commander Fax that will stand as proof of my word!" Sahid begged the men surrounding him.

"Deliver this message to us and we will decide it." The first voice, to the left, hissed again.

"I must give this message to Lord Aralias alone!" Sahid began to consider fleeing from these men, back into the tunnel under the wall, but he doubted his ability to pass under the bars again.

Without warning, a rope looped around Sahid's neck and pulled him violently towards the left wall of the trench. Sahid kicked out violently as he was pulled up the wall, his hands grappling with the noose. His back arched against the edge as he was pulled over it and several excruciating jolts shot through his spine. He opened his mouth to scream at the pain, but the rope was so tight that no sound emitted. He came to rest on the turf next to the sewer, but the pressure of the rope did not subside. He fought for air but could draw none. His vision failed and Sahid was lost to all thought.

15

Wilteph stayed close to Jaxus at the rear of the line as they passed through the darkness. Both men spoke in a hushed conversation of some obvious substance, though unknown to the ears of the others. Oslun longed for the Whisper Hall, where all but the very softest of spoken words carried to every listener. During the time he spent at the feet of the King, Oslun heard all manner of things not meant for his ears. He knew which politicians were conducting foul dealings, which inappropriate relationships were taking place, he even knew which nobles were taking from the royal purse, through deception and other means. Here, in this new company, he had no knowledge and that emptiness only intensified his unease.

Tepan led the group, with Rale'en just behind. Thyso had come to consciousness some time ago and walked under his own strength, though he seemed in a daze and did not speak, dragging his feet across the rough floor. Halta and the Princess walked side by side, each telling of their respective cultures and histories in a spirited exchange. Oslun was left to trudge on in silence.

In time, the group came to a small crease in the rock walls of the tunnel which appeared to be nothing at first glance but was in fact a carefully concealed branch from the main passage. Jaxus explained that many such concealed entrances were necessary to keep air in the tunnel and they had likely passed several without knowledge. The excellent low light vision of their newfound Inohamman companions allowed for discovery of the crease with ease.

To enter this branch, each person had to turn side face and pass forward, then back, zigzagging into the darkness. Thyso needed help getting through the tight turns, but Halta gently assisted him along.

Oslun entered behind this pair and found himself suffering irritation at the attention Halta paid to his fellow. This feeling was overtaken as Oslun found the series of hewn switchbacks far too narrow for comfort. He began to imagine the embarrassment he would feel, and the ridicule he would face from Thyso, if he got stuck in the rock. It was Halta's disappointment he feared the most, though the young cupbearer could not understand the depth of this feeling.

The passage brought the group into a narrow alcove, which contained a small wooden ladder formed of pine boughs bound together with leather cords. Dust covered the ladder from decades of disuse. Oslun doubted the ability of this ancient article to hold them.

One by one, the group climbed the ladder towards a narrow exit, concealed in a rock outcropping at the base of a small cliff. Oslun struggled to make the climb, hampered by the weight of his armor and weapons, fearing with each step that the rungs would snap.

Clearing the opening, he found that the sky was dark, though lit by far more stars than he had ever seen. The air was cool and fresh, the smell of pine and moist soil filled him. Oslun breathed deeply of it and found that with each breath, he felt lighter, almost clean. Being above ground and no longer bathed in stuffy, dank air felt to the young man much the same as the feeling of first breath after holding under the water for too long.

Layandria had taken to laying on her back in the rough grass that surrounded the outcropping, her boots cast aside and her toes playing freely in the water of a gentle stream. She laughed freely at nothing as she hungrily took in the clean air and dug at the dirt with her fingers. Jaxus was the last to exit the underground, a great smile appearing on his face in the starlight. Layandria looked at the man and was astonished by the freedom painted on his face. She found that the normally hard feature of the man was quite handsome when it conveyed true joy. That expression quickly faded away as Jaxus began to survey their location. Layandria turned her eyes back to the stars, keeping the image of a smiling Jaxus in her mind.

After a short rest, Wilteph roused the group, saying that they should not tarry long in the darkness. Tepan and Rale'en assumed the lead as the small formation wound its way through thick trees and rough under growth. The breeze was cool, but not bracing, a welcome guest for the Arken travelers. The turf was soft and covered in fallen needles from seasons past that crinkled pleasingly underfoot. Every sensation was like new to Layandria and her men. Jaxus estimated that they had traveled underground for some nine days. Wilteph explained that the passage was not at all straight and the journey over the mountains, would they return to Arken, was a much shorter five-day march.

After what felt like hours, the group was led to a grove of trees, each one so large that several men linking hands could not stretch around the base. Tepan moved to a particularly massive tree, gripped the bark with his hands and swiftly climbed the trunk, disappearing into the high boughs. Oslun knew at once that he could not climb this tree. He could barely summit the short ladder that took him above ground. As if answering back to Oslun's concern, a thick rope fell from above, jerking to a stop just above the turf.

"Those who can climb will do so. Those who cannot, will be hoisted by those of us already aloft." Wil turned and gracefully mounted the rope, using only his arms to swiftly ascend into the night.

As Rale'en followed suit, though not nearly as gracefully, Oslun found himself wishing that he too would one day be as powerful and with movements as light as the men and women he found in his company.

Layandria took to the rope next. She struggled to make progress, pinching the rope between her feet and pushing up with her legs. The young princess refused offers of assistance as she toiled the long way up. Once the rope ceased moving and the royal image removed from view, Thyso was led to the base of the tree. Jaxus tied the rope around the handmaid, passing it under his arms and securing it to his weapons belt. Thyso fell limp as his damaged body was hoisted upwards.

Oslun stood motionless as the rope was dropped down. Halta approached and gestured for him to go next. Oslun looked into the churning golden sea of her eyes and found himself lost in the depth just as he had been in the passage. He found that the woman appeared even more beautiful in the natural light of the stars. The young man summoned his courage and walked to the dangling rope. He gripped it in his hands and pulled himself up, catching it between his feet, mimicking the motions Layandria used.

His muscles burned as he struggled upwards, but he refused to quit. He felt like he had climbed hundreds of feet, but when he looked down, he found that he was barely above Halta's head. He reached one hand at a time, pulling against the rope and drawing his body upwards. He looked back to Halta. From his angle, Oslun could see that the woman's vest was parted. The top of her breasts shown in the light of the stars. The cup bearer had never seen a woman's breasts before, though he had imagined them often in recent years.

Halta saw the young man's gaze and frowned up at him. Oslun became immediately embarrassed. He turned his face skywards and reached up with his hands again. In his shame, the cup bearer missed the rope with his hand. He grappled wildly for grip but could find none. He spilled onto the turf and the air was forced from his lungs by the impact. Oslun fought to draw breath but found that he could take none. He panicked, trashing his arms and legs. Halta's face appeared above him, smiling down with a beaming brilliance. Oslun fought to focus on her face, but he could still bring no air into his lungs.

Halta looked over her shoulder and saw that Jaxus was some distance away, studying the surroundings. She turned back to Oslun and smiled deeply. Her hands moved to the leather laces tying the halves of her vest closed. She gently untied the knot and parted her vest, leaning in over the young warrior.

Halta watched in amusement as the young man's eyes grew wide and his body ceased his thrashings. Slowly, he began to breathe in, though he was not consciously aware of the new air. His eyes did not leave her body. Halta let out a small laugh and closed her vest, refastening the laces. She moved to Oslun's side and helped him to his feet. "Let me fasten the rope so they can pull you up."

Oslun stood carefully, struggling to raise his courage. He began to feel the disgrace of failing before this transfixing warrior woman. "No, I want to climb."

"It is alright, brave one." Halta's voice was as silk, soft and welcoming. "There is no shame."

"Please," Oslun asked in earnest. "I want to try again."

"As you please, Oranku." Halta gestured to the rope.

"What is that?" Oslun inquired, certain it must be a vailed insult, "what is Oranku?"

"It is a word of the Inohamman, of my people." Halta smiled deeply. "One day, I will teach you its meaning."

Oslun shied away from her face, but refused to give in. He mounted the rope and surged upwards, fueled by sheer refusal to fail before this beautiful creature a second time. He toiled against the weight and his muscles ached with fire unlike any he had ever felt, but as he continued his accent, Oslun came to find a wooden platform carefully constructed and concealed in the thick bows of the tree. As he drew near to the structure, he found that Layandria and Tepan stood by to help him over the edge. The young man collapsed onto the wood floor in complete exhaustion.

It felt like seconds to him before the still deeply pleased face of Halta appeared over the edge. Seeing her, Oslun sat up and fought to calm his rapid breaths, attempting to maintain an impassive expression. A mask he hoped would appear similar to the strength displayed by Jaxus. The woman paid no mind to the cupbearer's windedness, offering her hand to Jaxus who summited the rope with little effort. Once the dark warrior was aboard the platform, the rope was pulled up and coiled near the edge.

The platform was massive, extending out from the trunk of the tree and connecting to several others by way of simple plank bridges or wooden stairs, though the darkness made it impossible to determine how many platforms, or how large this treetop dwelling was. The shadows of other Inohamman moved about on other platforms and a few approached to speak in hushed whispers with Wilteph. There were woven baskets piled against the tree, which Wilteph and Rale'en opened and began passing out fruits and leaves of greens that were cool and refreshed the tongue.

Halta set about laying mats that were soft and gave off a comforting fragrance in a circle around the trunk of the evergreen. Each man and woman took to eating in relative silence, though Halta moved to sit next to Layandria and the two women resumed their previous conversation while they dined. Oslun wished he were nearer to Halta, but he felt too awkward to dare an approach.

As he finished his meal, he noted that Thyso had already fallen asleep on a mat. Jaxus moved to his side and draped a large blanket made of several billowy furs over the handmaid's resting form. Jaxus then took to his own mat. Oslun looked on while the warrior took off his armor piece by piece, arranging it next to his assumed bed in particular order, checking over each piece for damage with a weather eye.

Wonder overtook the cup bearer as the man took up each of his swords in turn and inspecting them with precision, cleaning them with a soft cloth from his pack and returning them to their sheaths once satisfied. Jaxus then bowed his head, raised the weapons to his lips and whispered words in an old, possibly foreign tongue that Oslun could not decipher. Jaxus then laid the blades on either side of his mat and settled his body down. The warrior pulled a fur blanket up to his shoulders and closed his eyes.

Oslun looked around the platform. Wilteph and Tepan stood near the far edge, huddled in some deep conversation with another man, Oslun heard him being called Fash. Halta and Layandria were both settling into their beds and blankets. Oslun watched Halta as she so gracefully moved around, preparing her bed. A mat lay, unoccupied, next to hers. The young man summoned his courage.

Oslun stood and moved to the mat next to Halta's. She looked up at him and he expected her to order him back. She smiled and lifted her hand, gesturing to the mat. The warmth of her presence felt as though it melted into him. Oslun breathed deeply of the scent of her. Halta smiled and turned back without a word laying her head on her mat.

Oslun began slowly taking off his armor and weapons, trying to inspect them as Jaxus had done, though he had no idea what to look for. He arranged the pieces next to his mat in a way that seamed sensible to him, though again, he had no idea what order to place the parts, or why the careful ritual. He slowly drew his sword and checked its edges. Seeing nothing of significance, he sheathed it. Recalling Jaxus moves, he supposed he ought to say something to the weapon. He knelt and raised it to his bowed head.

"Devil's Song, you are called." Oslun whispered, feeling foolish and certain that everyone was watching him. "You have been carried by the mightiest of warriors. Though I am not strong, I will carry you with the best of my being."

Oslun kissed the scabbard, as Jaxus and done, and laid it down next to his mat. He looked up and found that Halta had a blanket pulled up just under her arms, her eyes closed. Oslun sighed and shimmied himself out of the now filthy servant's tunic that he wore under his armor. The garment was yellowed with sweat and smelled terrible. The cup bearer wanted to pitch the thing over the edge of the platform, embarrassed to have been wearing it so openly.

He laid down on his mat and found that it was soft and comforting. His eyes felt heavy and his limbs weak as he pulled the blanket laid out at the foot of the mat. The blanket was heavy. It smelled of the earth and all good things. Oslun turned over on his side, his back to Halta. He knew he was acting foolishly. She was a woman, strong and brave. He felt certain that she saw him as no more than a child, the kindness she offered him much the same as the grace given him by Lord Commander Fax and the other great warriors of Arken. They were powerful and skilled in battle, showing kindness to the weak child that scurried about with the wine. He closed his eyes and began to feel sleep overtaking his thoughts.

"Sleep in peace, Oranku." Halta's lilting voice came to his ears like a warm breeze.

"Sweetly rest, Agal'le." Oslun whispered, nearly lost to sleep. Thankful that the word he used was old Carenbon and would not be known to the woman at his back. He doubted the word she used for him, Oranku, was of similar meaning to his chosen noun. Oslun supposed it was a moniker for a favored child. The thought weakened his spirit as he gave into sleep.

16.

They moved swiftly down the narrow road, darting from one building to another, moving in sequence not unlike the legs of a centipede. Commander Fax had the lead, followed closely by King Axeleon. Twenty warriors followed every move of their leaders. The remaining Arken Warriors were ordered to stay in the citadel, holding that sacred location until Aralias could clinch the needed victory.

Those now weaving their way along the streets of the Arken Head were moving to ambush a force of some thirty or forty men who were manning the mortars and catapults on the southern wall of the city. While Liam had taken Sahid to the sewer, Axeleon had gone to the top of the southern tower of the fortress to survey the battlefield. Aralias and the men of the Wolf Fist were making good progress and had fully ringed the city. The Starrowlanders had been too widely distributed when Aralias arrived and had been ill prepared for an attack which allowed diminished resistance against the wolves, but reactions were swift and the enemy, though severely outnumbered, was well entrenched. The Starrowlanders fought with tremendous tenacity, knowing that no mercy would be offered to them at the tips of Arken blades.

Axeleon wished to end the fighting as quickly as possible. He had little faith that the Fallish man Lord Commander Fax had dispatched would complete his mission and Lord Aralias would likely sack the entire citadel if needed to ensure that Axise would not long hold the throne. He would fire his own mortars and burn the fortress from within if he could not break the enemy. Axeleon did not want to see his beautiful citadel destroyed before him, nor his men ripped from life by their brothers in arms. So Axeleon and twenty strong fighters would take the fight to the Starrowlanders from the rear once again.

It had been Commander Fax's devising that the man, Sahid, be sent to infiltrate Aralias lines and bring the message of the King's survival. Axeleon knew that the man would clear Liam's line of sight and run straight to the others of the Starrowlands. The coward would tell them of Axeleon's survival, and they would enter the Whisper Hall in force. Commander Fax was persistent, stating that he had trust for the Fallish tribal leader and that he believed this course was the safer for all. It had been hours since Liam returned, carrying Genif Nitru's body across his shoulders, and yet, no news of the Fallish man's mission had returned. Again, Liam advocated caution and patience, stating that he did not deem it likely that word would be given across the enemy lines, but Axeleon had grown jaded towards long waits of inaction.

The south mortar battery fired, the powder charges launching deadly iron projectiles wrapped in greased canvas high into the air, raining fire and death down on the men and women of Wolf Fist. The element moved in this sort of zig zagging pattern, closing on the mortar towers as a worm, extending out its head, then waiting for its rear to catch up.

Soon, only one row of stone cottages separated Axeleon's men from the guns. There were seven mortar towers, each standing ten feet tall. Two men were needed to load and aim the mortar, while a third man would light the fuse and fire the weapon. One more stood half way between the platform and the ground, on narrow stone steps, handing up the ammunition and powder to the loaders, while two more men stood at the base of the tower, bringing the needed items out from the stores underneath. The towers were twenty yards apart, with unused trebuchets standing between and slightly behind each tower.

Lord Commander Fax moved up and down the line of Shadow warriors, giving them instructions as silently as possible. Three men were to strike at each tower, moving under the shadow of the trebuchets, using the structures for concealment as they took up positions as close to the towers as possible without alerting the artillerymen. King Axeleon and Commander Fax would take the last tower together. When ready and into position, Liam would let out a deep blast on the war horn he kept on his belt. Once the teams of three heard the blast, they were to move in and strike the men on the ground as the next volley of mortars was fired, then mount the platforms and take those firing the weapons as they looked to reload. For the plan to work, all the teams needed to strike as one lest the numerically superior mortar men be warned their demise was at hand.

The King and Lord Commander moved down the dark alleyway, no longer as a worm, but as a two-headed snake. Their movements were rapid and in tandem, no signals or communication needed as the pair found the harmony only known by fighting men who had trained and made war together for decades. They arrived at the corner of a two-story stone building, directly behind the seventh mortar tower. Liam checked the street for presence, then stepped into the open so that all his men could see him. He formed a fist with his left hand and quickly raised it up, pumping his arm up and down three times. On the last, he turned back towards the mortar tower and darted down the alley way. Axeleon was scarcely a step behind him.

They arrived at the south eastern corner of the building and saw the mortar tower for the first time. There were not only six men manning the tower, but an additional four, standing watch from slits in the Citadel wall. These men were relaying instructions back to the mortar team for aim and firing. Axeleon looked back down the line to the other mortar towers and found that this final tower appeared to be the only one that was over strength. He turned to Lord Commander Fax. Liam's face was blank, his eyes narrow and focused on the enemy.

"I will take the onlookers." Liam whispered to his old friend. "You take the artillerymen."

King Axeleon nodded.

Liam lowered his posture and darted across the wide street towards the trebuchet that stood between mortar tower seven and six. He took cover under the structure of the weapon and motioned King Axeleon forward. Liam surveyed the scene again and prepared his mind. He held the war horn to his lips and waited.

The mortars fired a volley. Commander Fax loosed a brief, steady breath into the horn and a rumbling tenor emitted. The Starrowlanders had not heard it, so deafened were they by the sounds of the mortars. Liam released his grip on the horn and let it fall to the grass under the catapult. With his sword in two hands, he rushed out from under the structure, moving directly for the onlookers at the wall. All four had their backs to him as he approached, none were aware of the reaper bearing down on them.

Liam aimed for the center of them, cutting his sword through the air in a wide arc. Three inches of Falchon's blade bit into the back of the middle right onlooker's neck and continued, impacting the middle left man's neck in the same position. Both men went down. Dead or not, Liam did not stop to check. He let the momentum of the huge sword carry around to the left. He curved his wrists, reversing the blade and charging it back to his right as he pivoted on the balls of his feet. He stepped right and pulled the blade low, slashing across the belly of the onlooker on the far left as the man turned towards the sudden motions. Falchon was rewarded with a burst of blood as its victim's abdomen split wide and his intestines spilled out onto the stone. As the Commander turned away, he witnessed the man drop to his knees, desperately attempting to scoop his organs back into himself.

The final observer had time to his advantage and was bringing his own sword, a rough, poorly maintained weapon, down in a hammering motion towards the Lord Commander. Falchon was not in position to block the blow, so Liam raised his elbow, the enemy's blade impacting his shadow steel armor, scoring the metal and releasing a show of sparks. Commander Fax reared back and kicked the man in his knee with a heavy boot. The man splayed back as the joint failed and bent sickeningly in the opposing direction. Liam pounced on the man, driving downward with his knees. The magnitude of the huge Lord's impact utterly pulverized the Starrowlander's chest. Liam took no time to observe his own destructive power.

Commander Fax sprinted towards the King, ready to take his back and finish the men on the mortar. He watched in horror as the man charged with igniting the fuse dove down from the tower and took Axeleon by the chest, bringing both men to the ground. The other two men leapt from the platform, landing between Liam and his downed King, swords in their hands, their attention on Axeleon who had managed to come to his back and was ably defending himself from incoming blows.

Liam charged in to the left and loosed a powerful stroke from Falchon that cleaved one of the soldiers' legs from just under his pelvis.

The man let out a terrible bleat, teetered and fell, blood erupting from the severed limb. Commander Fax found his next target with his head, driving the crown of his skull directly into the man's teeth. Liam mildly registered pain as the man's denticules penetrated his scalp, but the sensation did not cause him to waver. The enemy was not so steadfast, going to ground heavily. Liam planted his left foot on the turf, inside the man's left armpit and raised his right leg, smashing the boot down on the man's throat with unimaginable force. He was answered back with a sensation not unlike the crushing of pottery beneath his sole.

Axeleon screamed out in pain. Commander Fax wheeled and saw that the fireman who had driven the King to the turf was on him, a short knife in his hand. The King's sword was pinned to the soil with his assailant's foot. Liam raised his sword high and stepped in, letting the full force of the heavy Falchon fall towards the attacker's neck. The blade missed its mark high, striking the man in the base of his skull. Falchon was not deterred and tore through the man's head with fervor. Liam kicked the man's remains away from the King and knelt. Blood gushed from beneath Axeleon's armor. The enemy had passed a short knife between the gap of the King's chest plate and back plate. Liam let Falchon rest on the grass while he removed Axeleon's armor and cut open his shirt. He wiped the excess blood away and saw two distinct punctures wounds. King Axeleon howled against the coursing pain.

Liam stood, looking down the line of mortar towers. The combat was all but ceased and warriors were already running towards their fallen royal. As the first arrived, Liam recovered Falchon and took Axeleon's arm, ordering another soldier to aid him. The two men gripped the King's weapons belt as they hoisted him up while another gathered the King's dropped blade and chest plate.

"Back to the Citadel!" Commander Fax bellowed out the command. The men moved off with all haste, stealth no longer their need. The cries of their wounded King would have afforded them no secrecy in movement. Liam looked to Axeleon's face as he moved. The King was ashen, sweat covering his features and soaking his beard. There was little time if his life was to be saved.

17

"Come to yourself man!" A rough voice ordered just as a large draft of water was thrown into Sahid's face. The velocity carried the liquid into his sinuses, and he choked against the intrusion.

The wolves had stripped him completely. His ankles were bound together, his wrists bound to the ankles. A board was jammed between his knees, forcing him to remain upright in a sort of rough tripod. Sahid found that he was inside a dwelling, likely the home of a prominent family of the Arkenhead. On all sides stood men clad in the armor of the Wolf Fist. Sahid could identify no individual as their armor and helms were alike. The molted pattern of color on the armor, coupled with the detailed design of the helms, resembling the head of their namesake, caused the wolf soldiers to appear as vicious beasts. Fear rolled over Sahid's body, intensified by the water on his skin and the cold air of night.

"What is this message you carry, Starrowlander?" A gruff, bestial voice demanded just as the tip of a sword was brought under Sahid's jaw, forcing him to raise his chin.

Sahid swallowed hard, keeping his head still for fear of the blade so close to his throat. "My message is for Lord Aralias alone."

The sword moved back slowly, tracing the outline of Sahid's jaw, scraping over the rough stubble of beard that grew on his neck. The harsh voice assaulted him again. "I will have your message, or I will have your head."

Sahid could barely make the words come out, and when they did, his fear rendered them broken and weak. "My message is for Lord Aralias alone."

A large man entered Sahid's restricted view and stooped low in front of him. The man's dark brown eyes locked on to his, the snout of his helm inches from Sahid's nose. The wolf soldier held up a small carving knife, just to the left of his face where Sahid could see it. He gripped Sahid's genitals and pulled them taut. Sahid winced against the pain. The sword at his neck nibbled on his skin, and blood began to bead on the shallow wound. The kneeling man did not speak, but remained still, holding Sahid's manhood and staring into his eyes, the knife just in the edge of view.

"Lord Aralias." The name came out as little more than breaths and Sahid's body began to shake. He felt more fear than if all his darkest days were made one.

"Halton!" A high pitched, but strong voice called out. "I'll have this damned message."

The kneeling man released his grip on Sahid's genitals and slowly stood as the sword was drawn away from his neck. Sahid looked in the direction the order had come form, expecting to see a massive man, similar in stature to Commander Fax, with the pelt of a wolf on his shoulder and a massive tangled beard falling from his face. Lord Aralias did indeed have the preserved head of a wolf on his shoulder, but that was all that bore similarity with Sahid's image.

The man was young, not more than twenty-five. His face was naked, not even a shadow of beard. The man's hair was the color of wheat and pulled back on his head, crowing large ears that protruded from the sides of his head. The strange Lord approached Sahid and stopped before him, looking down at the bound man expectantly. Sahid could not speak. His genitals ached with intensity and he could not bring air into his chest.

Lord Aralias did not show patience. "I will have you message, or I will feed your balls to the dogs."

"I carry a message from King Axeleon and Lord Commander Liam Fax, for you, Lord Aralias." Sahid found his air, his words sputtering out like a geyser, begging with every syllable to keep the torturer's hand stayed. He knew he was to ask after the health of the Wolf Lord's wife, but in his fear and pain, he could not recall the name. His mind clawed for this critical scrap of detail, but as fear intensified in him, clouding his memory further.

"Do not speak the names of our honored dead!" Aralias kicked out with his boot, smashing it into Sahid's chest. The force lifted his knees from the floor and spilled him onto his side. The board between his knees tore into his flesh and his head impact the floor. His mind swung around in bursts of intense pain and flashes of cold. The Wolf Lord turned from Sahid and stormed away. "Make this man pay for the pain of our fallen King."

Desperation set into Sahid's thoughts as men ripped him up from the floor, propping him back on his knees. He felt as he had under the sewer when he was mere instants from drowning in human filth. Perhaps influenced by the memory of that terrible moment, Sahid's body relaxed and his mind slowed. Anoxamall. The name floated up into his consciousness.

"Lord Commander Fax inquires after the health of your wife Anoxamall!" Sahid screamed out the words with all his force, desperate that the Lord would hear his message before the wolves could end his life.

Lord Aralias stopped in place and snapped back. "What did you say?"

Sahid swallowed, willing his voice to save his life. "Lord Commander Fax wanted that I ask after the health of your wife, Lady Anoxamall."

Aralias reared back his head and burst out in hearty laughter. He crossed the floor to Sahid swiftly, erupting in humor as he did. "Liam Fax! Only he knew of that embarrassment! Untie this man and clothe him!"

"My Lord, how can you give faith?" The wolf at Sahid's right questioned the order.

"Only the Lord Commander himself knew of my folly and only for a purpose such as this would he share of it." Aralias continued to guffaw between his words. He knelt before Sahid and helped him to stand as his bonds were removed. He draped a thick coat of wolf skin over Sahid's shoulders. "When I first came into my manhood, I became greatly interested in women, but my father wanted that my time be spent on study and training. So, I would sneak out of the fortress and seek women who would share bed and discretion in exchange for coin, a highly salacious activity for the son of a Lord."

"When I first went south to the Elk Fist, it was as aid to the Lord Commander as he surveyed the readiness of the armies. I was but nineteen and highly involved in my scandalous acts. Women of my desired repute were uncommon there, but I quickly found a beauty by the name of Anoxamall who sold my desired merchandise. Anoxamall was nearing her forty fifth year and her look was hard, but I reasoned that under cover of dark, all women must bear resemblance. I paid her the asking price and went to her chamber. When the woman disrobed, I rapidly discovered the error in my desire."

Several of the Wolf Fist troops began chuckling as their Lord spoke. He was undeterred. "I swear it to you; this woman had more fur than all the wolves of all the forests of Arken! Her breasts reached her knees and her skin resembled stressed leather! As I stood there, this road worn old beast licked her lips and beckoned me to her bed with the gesture of a gnarled finger. I shrieked at the sight and ran from her chamber, leaving my coin, and trousers behind!"

"When I exited in disgust and out of pant, who should be there waiting to great me in my hour of triumph, but Lord Commander Liam Fax." The men burst out in laughter, such a strange image to Sahid, surrounded as they were by the death of war. "The good Commander deemed that my loss of coin, knickers and the permanent damage to my sight to be payment enough for my lack of honor and swore to me that he would keep this knowledge to himself alone."

Sahid pulled the blanket around himself tightly, not wanting the warmth to be taken from him. "My Lord, I do not wish to dishonor you before your men, I only repeat the words of the Lord Commander."

Aralias clapped Sahid on the shoulder and laughed freely. His high, clear voice full of amusement. "Have no fear, you'll keep your balls for today. My father has long gone to the soil and I find that I no longer care who knows of my encounter with beast of the Elk Fist."

Sahid smiled slightly and allowed the tenseness in his back to ease, though fear remained in his spine.

"Now," Aralias lowered his volume and stepped in towards Sahid, looking up at his face. "What is the message you carry?"

Sahid quickly told his tale, all the events that had taken place since Axise and his men entered the Whisper Hall. Aralias did not stop him, his fare face changing as new information gave him thought.

When Sahid finished and announced that King Axeleon still bore the crown of Arken, Aralias turned away, issuing orders swiftly to his men.

"Pass the word to cease bombardment. We must abandon caution and patience." Aralias spoke quickly, handing out order for troop movements to the assembled men. The Lord of the Wolf Fist faced Sahid again. "We have been waiting out our enemy, harassing him with mortar and denying him rest, hoping to limit losses to our own, but if Axeleon remains, he may be discovered at any time. Certainly, he cannot defend the hall of kings against a second strike alone."

"I will lead the main assault and we will move on the citadel at first light." The little Lord's eyes connected with Sahid's again. "You are certainly brave to have crossed the lines to us, but judging by the garb you wore when captured, you arrived in the Arkenhead as a servant of Axise. I have no concept of what reason would possess Lord Commander Fax to trust you with this most critical message, and until he explains it to my own ears, I do not share the trust. You will fight by my side and prove your worth, or you will die as a newly made woman. The choice is yours."

18

Jaxus rose after a short rest. He had, over his years, come to find that he no longer slept for longer than a few hours. His dreams were troubled by dark memories of terrible deeds and sorrowful experiences, making wakefulness, no matter how exhausting or pained, the preferable experience.

The sun was not yet rising as Jaxus slowly cleaned his body with a soft cloth from his bag, dampened with water. He dressed himself and carefully donned his armor. The pieces, when set aside, looked unremarkable. Standard shapes for chest plates, shoulder guards, braces and all manner of attachment. Yet, as Jaxus connected one to another, the pieces appeared to meld, as if forming a singular suit, seamless and without weakness.

Jaxus took up his swords and carefully ran a honing stone along the edges. He learned the blades as they learned him. Jushash, the blade he had carried all his life, was handed down by his father, though he had no memory of the man. The blade was older than most fortresses, but it shown alive and new in the early morning rays. Fine markings scrolled the length of the sword. Words formed of characters that were not of a common tongue told the story of the weapon and the names of all who had carried it. Jaxus carefully worked over Jushash's edges and returned it to its long familiar home on his back once it was perfect.

He took up the blade given to him by King Axeleon and examined it. Ragnashon, it was called in the Jurin tongue, roughly translated as truth. Jaxus knew the word held a much stronger concept of life acted boldly, in the pursuit of the true character of man. His eyes took in the long line of the names of warriors who wielded Ragnashon.

Jaxus smiled softly as he honed the blade, contented in his religious practice. Finished, he laid it across his lap and removed a small, pointed chisel and a similarly delicate hammer from his bag. Carefully, Jaxus began adding his name, and the name of Amyus Colth to the list. He found it fitting that he would carry both Ragnashon and Jushash. Truth and Vengeance.

Layandria entered the warrior's mind. He turned to look at the princess as she slept across the platform, her blanket pulled up to just below her chin. He found Layandria's face soft and arresting in the light of the breaking dawn. Jaxus had, in all his long years, never felt drawn to a person, but this young woman seamed to grip his conscious. The man could not understand how he could feel her thoughts in his mind, what caused this unfathomable connection, or the need he felt for her.

These thoughts troubled Jaxus mind as he stood and moved to the edge of the platform. He sat, letting his feet hang off the edge. With a flourish, the black warrior rotated his body and dropped, his hands gripping the edge of the platform as he dangled underneath. He worked his hands along the support structure until he reached the trunk of the tree. Much as Tepan had done the previous evening, Jaxus bit his finger tips and the inside edge of his boots into the bark, quickly making his way down. On the ground, Jaxus began to range out, making long, wide circles ringing the tree, moving some thirty yards out from the trunk with each pass. He was looking for nothing of any specificity, but the air cooled him and helped to clear his mind.

The rising sun's small rays shot over the eastern peaks. Jaxus knew that just over these mountains, no more than five days march away, stood the Arkenhead. For a moment, he stopped and wondered after the fate of the King and the men in the Whisper Hall. The thought chilled him.

"I see you." Wilteph's voice called out softly, disrupting Jaxus thoughts. The black clad warrior did not turn or react to the voice. "I know what you hide."

"I hide nothing, Inohamman." Jaxus spoke calmly, still gazing at the high peaks. Wilteph approached the man, coming to just off his right.

"I see many things, Jaxus. Would you care to know my sight?" Wil cooed softly, his voice carrying no further than needed.

"I would," Jaxus agreed, cocking his head curiously, "as you are so intent on sharing and I may hope that this divulgence would silence you further"

Wilteph sucked his teeth and bored holes into the back of Jaxus head. "I see that you are much older than you reveal to your companions."

Jaxus nodded in silent confirmation.

"I see that you care for your friends, though you do not know where to lead them." Wilteph wanted to pull more information from the man, to gauge his character, but the silent warrior only nodded again. "I know that you have stained your soul with the blood of the innocent. I know that you desire to do right by these you travel with, though you feel that it will not assuage the grief that covers your mind."

"You see much, Inohamman." Jaxus consented. "Though, I fear your vision is much crossed. It is a wonder that you can walk in a straight line."

"Perhaps." Wilteph ignored the insult. "But I must know, how far will you go to reclaim your honor?"

"I care not for honor." Jaxus scoffed lightly. He turned his face to meet Wilteph. "Honor is a construct those in power use to coerce the masses to do their bidding. Though the people believe the choice is their own, honor is the deception that gives them the lie."

Wilteph furrowed his brow. "What then is your moral? What is it that drives you forward if not for honor?"

Jaxus pursed his lips and raised an eyebrow but said nothing.

"Is it blood lust that drives you?" Wilteph was growing irritated with the man who would not give him a direct answer. "I see a love for the fight in you, but I do not believe that is the sole purpose of you. You embrace violence and do not fear to inflict pain, and yet, you do not show the color of a man who seeks only for the kill."

"I do not enjoy killing nor acts of pain." Jaxus turned his face away from Wilteph. He hated conversations like this. Speaking of the violence that a man is forced by circumstance to perform did not sit well with him. He found that when he spoke of death, all his mind would conjure were the images of those he had slain. Every face, every dying scream, from the very first, bludgeoned to death with a stone, to the very last spilt by Jushash the morning Axise arrived at the door to the Whisper Hall. The memories unsettled, conjuring feelings of self-loathing and guilt.

Wilteph's irritation turned to anger. "You are in my camp, among my people, I demand to know. What is it that fuels you?"

Jaxus turned back to Wilteph, studying the man's eyes. He spoke after a long wait that pressed the ragged edge of the other man's patience. Jaxus was amused, by this man's tenuous grip on his emotions. "I will tell you of my histories and lineage, if you will settle yourself and cease this mindless chatter."

Wilteph did not speak, but abruptly sat down on the ground, his legs crossed. He starred up at Jaxus expectantly, his expression hiding none of his frustration.

Jaxus smiled and lowered himself to the ground, mimicking Wil's position. He could see the astonished look on the Inohamman's face at the ease with which Jaxus' armor flexed. "I am, as you suspected, far older than I appear. I am in fact two hundred and twenty-nine years of age."

"How is this possible?" Wilteph started in disbelief, but Jaxus cut him off with a raised hand.

"I am a Jurin man, from the now uninhabited island of the same name. Jurin men live far longer than other peoples, the longest living among us is recorded to have celebrated his nine hundred and ninety third year. The people of Jurin were travelers and teachers of the world for thousands of years, sharing their vast knowledge of science and nature with all who would listen. Some five generations of my people past, our leaders determined that we must stop our travels, as the world had grown hot and full of the thirst for violence."

Wilteph hung on Jaxus every word, having never heard such magical tales.

"And so, my people faded from the eyes of the world. We spent our years studying nature and recording all that we learned. Our people became one with the land, developing many technologies and materials from the knowledge. We grew in number and thrived in isolation." Jaxus paused, going through the details in his mind, allowing Wilteph a chance to soak in the tale.

"To the north of Jurin lay an island known as Carenbon. The men of Carenbon were hard, struggling to build civilization on the rough, sulfuric terrain. The Jurin men shared our knowledge with those of Carenbon and aided them in building a society that would grow in peace, but it was not to last."

Jaxus lowered his head slightly, his voice taking on a rougher feel that Wilteph could not read. "Some fifteen hundred years ago, the men of Carenbon built ships and began to sail, exploring and conquering the neighboring islands of Ralun, Carenphail and Naughton. These lands were home to their own populations, primitive and untouched by the outside world. The men of Carenbon did not spare their cultures or lives as they sought to control and assimilate."

"After a time, the men of Carenbon deigned to take Jurin for their own, craving to seize the knowledge and technology of the Jurin people. They fell on the island like an evil wave, casting my people down. Many died in the fighting and my people knew they could not hold their home."

Sadness took over Jaxus features as he spoke, as if he felt the pain of those long dead. "So, we took to our seafaring ships and departed, traveling far from the Carenbon people. The men of Jurin came to the black isles and found that they were uninhabited. The islands were rough and inhospitable, but our people took to them as shelter and began to rebuild. They watched as the world around continued to change. Tribes and bands of men joined together and fought over the land. They forged wicked weapons of war, fashioning new methods of killing. Kingdoms rose and fell, and the earth was bathed in blood."

"What of the Carenbon people?" Wilteph asked, totally given in to the sad history.

"They grew in number and strength, though the earth did not forget their violence. The island of Jurin did not welcome them and the Carenbon men found naught but death at the hands of waves and the beasts of the isle. They abandoned the island and took to ruling over the others as little sea tyrants, attacking ships and destroying all that came near enough to their grasping claws. The earth had not finished punishing them for their war making. Carenbon erupted some nine hundred years past, casting the men out to sea to escape its fire. These men sailed west, landing on the iron coast, never to return to the isles."

Wilteph spoke up again, his curiosity peaked fully, "Did your people return to Jurin?"

"No, we did not, though I have walked its cliffs and forests." Jaxus forced himself to remain in the present, not allowing his mind to return to Jurin, as it was never far from doing. "We were long isolated from the world and did not know the fate of our home. In time, we were ever fewer. When I was very young, before my memory, it was decided that my people would leave the isles and seek life elsewhere, in hope that we could preserve our race. My mother and I sailed for Jurin with a few others of our kind, intent on studying all that remained of our culture and knowledge."

"Where is your mother now?" Wilteph questioned, interested in meeting this woman and learning from her.

"She is long dead." Jaxus stood and walked away, coming to hold his back to Wilteph several paces off. "I will speak no more of her."

Wilteph lowered his head by way of empathy.

Jaxus was silent for a time. When he spoke again, his voice was distant. "I lived alone on Jurin for many years. In time, I determined to leave the island and seek out any of my own kind. I have lived in many nations and traveled much of the known world."

Wilteph stood and approached Jaxus. "Have you found any others, any Jurin men?"

"No." Jaxus voice grew sharp. "After the first fifty years search, I held to hope, but after one hundred, I abandoned all."

Wil nodded in sadness. "How came you to be in the service of Princess Layandria?"

Jaxus sighed. "That is another long tale, better left to rest. Suffice to say that her father, the King of Arken, found trust in me, and I in him."

"So, after all the years and all the travels, a warrior of more than two hundred years finds himself bound to the service of barely adult age Princess." Wilteph found irony in Jaxus fate comestible.

"I am bound to no one." Jaxus faced Wilteph again, the fire of defiance in his eyes. "All that I do is by my own estimation of correctness."

"And it is correct for you to serve her?" Wilteph grew curious again, confounded by Jaxus sense of morality.

"It is my choice to give her my strength." Jaxus eyes did not waver. "Until I see her set on the throne of her father."

"I see." Wil opened his hands to Jaxus, "I see no reason why our objectives would cross."

"Then I see no reason to kill you." Jaxus bristled. "For now."

The two men stood, their eyes boring into each other, motionless and rigid. There was no hostility between them, only the intensity of hard men, examining each other. Time passed slowly.

"Wil!" Halta burst into the clearing at a run, Tepan close behind her. "Wil, come quickly!"

Wilteph turned to the woman, as did Jaxus, both men's hands instinctively twitching towards their weapons.

"Men have come from the Wanoak! They tell us that Lakemen have invaded our lands and are burning our villages to the ground!" As Halta spoke, Layandria, Thyso, Oslun several of the outcasts entered the clearing.

Wilteph seemed to grow taller, his shoulders widened, and his nostrils flared. "We are outcasts, unwanted and rejected by the Wanoak."

"Wil, please!" Halta interrupted. Oslun moved swiftly to stand by her side, a fierce look in his eyes. "Our people are in need!"

Wilteph raised his hands. "We are outcasts, we have no people."

Layandria stepped forward rapidly, drawing her sword as he approached Wilteph. "I and my men will go in defense of any in need, with or without you. Though we do not know the way."

Wilteph turned to Jaxus, certain that the man would not allow his charge to enter combat. Jaxus moved to Layandria's side and turned back to stare at Wilteph. The black clad warrior then reached his arms across his shoulders and drew his twin blades in a flurry. Thyso and Oslun moved to just behind Layandria and Jaxus, both young men drew blades, at the ready.

Wilteph stood in stunned silence as Halta, Tepan, Rale'en and several others moved to stand with Princess Layandria. Anger brewed in his heart, but he knew that he could not afford to lose face before the outcasts. "We will go to the aid of the Wanoak. Though they have forsaken us, we will not forsake them. Halta, gather our people."

Wilteph lowered his eyes. He knew that this small group of assembled warriors were not enough to break the tide of an invasion, but his mind began to turn over the various options. Wilteph knew that for any of his plans to bear fruit, he must first find a way to be rid of this metal Princess and her irritating companions. "We move now."

19.

Lord Commander Fax paced the blood stone platform, uncertainty filling him. With the mortars felled, Aralias men had rallied and breached the western wall of the citadel courtyard. The fighting was still heavy, but Liam estimated only hours remained until the Wolf Soldiers made safe the city. Scouts reported that the Starrowlanders were falling back, breaking south en masse as they attempted a retreat. They would not get far as the Lord of the Wolves had echeloned a portion of his army to deny escape.

Undoubtedly, Jaxus would have moved the Princess along rapidly in the passage and Liam knew that they had likely exited by now. If they had returned above ground, there was little way to find them and any number of unknown threats could have appeared. Men would have to be sent after the Princess, but were the King to succumb to his wounds, all possible strength would be needed to hold the throne until Layandria could be returned. Liam felt trapped like a rabbit in a snare. The one thing he desperately needed, he could not do, but none other could be trusted to do it. Desperate fear wrapped around the man.

A scout by the name of Runlan entered the hall at speed, the doors held open by two others set to guard them. "Lord Aralias is coming! He has entered the citadel and is moving unopposed!"

Liam breathed a sigh of relief. He stopped pacing in front of the throne, though not touching it. He did not want it to appear to Aralias that he was attempting to claim it for himself, no matter if news of the Kings grave injury had reached his ears or not.

Commander Fax held great affection for Lord Aralias, though he would admit this affinity only to the silence of the night. Aralias was an excellent warrior, his skill in combat surprising due to his small stature, fare features and soft voice. In his youth, Aralias compensated too greatly for the perception of his weakness by leading with brutality, often bending to methods of torture and coercion no longer tolerated in Arken. These tendencies lessened as he aged and gained experience, but his violent nature still surfaced when given chance or cause. None the less, the Wolf Fist had grown in strength and prosperity under his leadership and the citizens loved him. Axeleon and Aralias often came to energetic words over issues facing his fist, and Iron Lord Nathus openly detested the Wolf Lord, but Liam could not fault a man who stood with passion for his perceptions.

Some thirty minutes passed while Commander Fax stood, waiting for the arrival of the Wolf Lord. He was updated on the condition of King Axeleon twice in that time by surgical aides, offering up the words of their betters in carefully concealed murmurs. The King was not well. The small blade had done large damage, penetrating the King's intestines and allowing the mixing of the acids and fluids that should not be permitted. Liam knew all too well that survival from wounds of this type was difficult. Surgeons could repair the physical damage to the organs, but infection was a much more persistent threat. He was unsure what would happen if the King did not survive and the Princess could not be found.

According to the law, if the King was to be injured and be rendered unable to rule, with no blood heir present, the commander of the King's armies would sit the throne until the proper ruler had regained strength. If the King were to die and no blood heir lived, the law stated that the eldest Lord or Lady would take the throne.

There were five Lords and Ladies in Arken. Each fist was controlled by one, with the Commander of the King's Infantry being counted as the Lord of the Shadow Fist by King Axeleon's order. Lord Aralias Taymrhlyn controlled the Wolf Fist, though he was the youngest of the currently seated Lords. Nathus Marshan sat the lordship over the Iron Fist. Eldest of the Lords and Ladies, Nathus had often expressed little interest in participating in the government of the realm, choosing instead to remain behind his own borders.

Several times during Nathus leadership of the fist, taxes due the crown had been withheld, orders for troop movements had been refused or ignored, and dignitaries from the capitol were refused entrance into his holdings. This fact greatly displeased Axeleon throughout his rule, having dispatched armies to the north several times to correct Lord Nathus course. Were Axeleon to succumb to his wounds, Liam could not anticipate what the Iron Lord do. He hoped that Nathus would cede the throne and remain in his northern territory, though dread told him this would not be so.

Holding control over the Fire Fist was Lady Kaowith Bernat. Lady Kaowith was the eldest after Lord Nathus, though her armies were heavily engaged with the main body of the Starrowlands army in the south. Even if Lord Nathus were to cede the throne, it would be months before the Lady could claim the crown. Lord Brustic Taymrhlyn controlled the Elk Fist. He was only months older than Lord Aralias, and he was often felt to be weak in his rule, his people failing to obtain support from their Lord and often feeling no enforcement or protection under the law. Lord Brustic was far fonder of parties and drink than he was of performing his duties, though he did admirably marshal his army to counter the Starrowland incursion into Lady Kaowith's realm.

Liam realized that he had not considered his own place in the line of succession. Though he had been named Lord Commander many years ago, he had never considered that he may be one day forced to assume the throne. He hated the idea, believing wholeheartedly that his place was in the field of battle, leading his men and fighting beside them. He had no desire for a chair in a grand hall, though his Lordship did come with a vast stronghold at the fortress of Barang, a day's march north of the Arkenhead. Barang was well furnished with servants and aides, but as Liam had not wife or children and seldom took comfort there, the fortress had never felt his own.

Now, the thought of the throne passing to him was worrisome. He was older than Lord Nathus by three years, though his titleage as Shadow Lord was by act of King Axeleon and not without possible contest. Dread welled up in him and he began pacing again, beads of sweat forming in the creases of his brow. This was potentially problematic for multiple reasons, chief among them being that Liam was the only member of the nobility present when Axeleon fell. Often, in times of power struggle, those with secondary claims to thrones will seek to supplant or cast accusations. Could Liam withstand these toils long enough to return Layandria to her proper post?

"Lord Commander," one of the men holding guard over the door called up. "Lord Aralias approaches to enter."

"Open the doors and welcome him in!" Liam ordered, momentary hope springing up in him like a wave of cool water.

The heavy doors swung open, creaking and dragging damaged spars of wood across the black stone floor. As they parted, Aralias strode in, his eyes gleaming and a massive grin crossing his features. Even from this distance, the man looked comical. Aralias was small, though he possessed a much larger man's ears. The angular features of his face coupled with the twin protrusions on his head resembled drawings by the hands of young children the Liam's perception. As small as he was, and as odd as he looked, Aralias was not a man to be underestimated.

As the Wolf Lord swiftly crossed towards the throne, Liam could see that his face and armor were heavily soiled. Aralias held his sword, unsheathed, loosely at his side, the blade well saturated with the marks of human death. A large slick of blood matted the Lord's light hair down on one side if his head and he was obviously bleeding, though not heavily, from a wound on the side of his neck.

Much to Commander Fax' astonishment, striding in step with Lord Aralias was Sahid Hauk Khan. The man was quite the worse for wear, a large gash on his chin visible from a long way off and a slight limp adorned his gait. He wore the armor of the Wolf Fist, though he wore no helm. Sahid carried a longsword of the Wolf Fist to complement his vestment. Liam was astonished that Lord Aralias had allowed Sahid these armaments, though the Wolf Lord was well known for his unconventional decision making and unpredictability.

"Lord Commander Fax!" Aralias shouted in exuberant greeting, the high pitch of his voice coming as an excited youth. "How surprised I was to hear of your continued existence, and how glad I am to see that this word was true!"

"As am I, Lord Aralias." Liam answered back, quite surprised at the fact himself.

"Of course," Aralias stopped just before the white steps, his face transforming to one of feigned anger. "You may not long exist, for I have payment to bring on the man who betrayed the trust he swore to me some years past."

Liam was exhausted and war weary. His mind could not decipher Lord Aralias' words, though he knew them to be in jest. "I must offer my apology, Wolf Lord, I do not know what trust I have broken."

Aralias scoffed and stamped his foot. His tone turned musical in the reverberations of the Whisper Hall as a sinister grin crossed his face. "Are you to tell me that it was not you who divulged my secret to this man beside me? Are you to tell me that this man has lied to me? His testicles beg for his words to be true, but if they are not, all shall be dealt with in correctness."

Commander Fax furrowed his brow, commanding his typically sharp mind to find its edge and understanding. The answer came to him like an arrow. He burst into loud, deep laughter, his sound filling the hall from corner to corner. "My deepest and most humble regret, my young Lord, I had assumed that you would have taken the good Lady Anoxamall as your wife by now and we would have an end to this secret."

Lord Aralias scoffed again. "I would sooner wed the rear of a burro then that woman, if it is woman that you call her!"

Commander Fax' deep laugh boomed out again. "Come now, Aralias, Anoxamall would make a sensible bride for you, as I am told, she is the only woman who has seen you unclothed and not cried out in terrible laughter!"

"She could not!" Aralias dropped his conjured anger and laughter as well. "I dare say that I departed her chamber before her withered eyes could take in the sight of me!"

As the two men jested, some two hundred of Aralias wolves entered the hall, forming lose ranks behind their Lord. These men took humor at the sight before them, the fight had been short, but vicious, and the joking of their leaders was welcome.

"Indeed, I would have left much destruction in the wake of my flight, were I forced to see Anoxamall undress." Commander Fax stepped forward, coming down the white steps towards Aralias as he spoke. "We should have placed her at the front gate to the city. Just the sight of her, in all her womanly beauty, would have sent Axise and his men straight back to the Starrowlands, tails tucked willingly between their hind quarters."

The two men embraced, the comradery they shared clear to all who observed. They separated, and Aralias face grew darker. He lowered his voice to a wisp of a breath, all too familiar with the quality of the hall. "What news of King Axeleon, I had expected to see him seated on the throne."

Liam lowered his head, not wanting any of the more quick-witted wolves to read the words on his lips. "The King was gravely wounded in battle and is now in the care of our most skilled surgeons."

Aralias nodded slowly, considering the situation. He, like Lord Commander Fax, did not want word of the King's wound to escape this hall. He raised his voice to its former volume. "The city and the citadel are secure. My men have taken some two thousand prisoners and are currently sweeping the Arkenhead for any who remain bearing weapons against us. I have dispatched a few of my fastest men to give orders for the citizenry to return."

"Good." Liam too raised his voice to its regular volume, for now, showing the assembly that all was within control and there was no further cause for concern. "There is much to be rebuilt and we must soon send out reinforcements to the south to meet Lord Brustic and Lady Kaowith in the Fire Fist."

Aralias nodded. "I have left half my strength in the Wolf Fist, holding the territory, should our enemies to the north wish to take advantage of our moment of weakness. I will leave half of my force here, under your command. The rest of my army, I will lead south. Do you know the strength of the Starrowlands armies engaged in the Lady Kaowith's holdings?"

"If I may, My Lords," Sahid stepped slightly towards the men. They both nodded that he should speak his mind. "Our Army numbered near two hundred thousand. Axise took only ten thousand of the force to move on the Arkenhead, leaving more than one hundred and ninety thousand engaged with your armies in the south."

"This is as I have been told." Commander Fax confirmed Sahid's account.

"How many have we dispatched to the fighting?" Lord Aralias asked, his mind forming calculations and battle schemes.

"Lady Kaowith's army was nearly sixty thousand strong when the Starrowlanders set upon them, though their losses were deep by all report. Elk Lord Brustic ordered the bulk of his soldiers, approximately fifty-five thousand strong, to meet Axis hordes. I and the King followed suit, sending all but the King's guard and the city watch. Eighty-three thousand souls departed the Shadow Fist not three days before Axis came to our stoop. I have received no news of losses or victories of late, closed off as we were under Axise assault, but I would hazard to say that the armies are nearly evenly matched. By last report, the Starrowlanders were stopped at Yarran and lines had been dug in, the pace of combat slowed."

"Evenly matched is less than ideal, old friend." Aralias looked up at Liam. His eyes were full of thought. "Do you know if the Iron Army has set to march?"

Commander Fax shook his head. "We received word from Lord Nathus that he deigned to keep his men in the Iron Fist, fearing an attack by sea. King Axeleon sent back word ordering the march, but that was eleven days past and we have no word from the north since. I fear that they are at least ten days march away, if they were swift in departure or if they took to the order at all."

"Then my fifteen thousand will have to break the tide. We will move at once, it is ten days march to Yarran." Lord Aralias was energized anew, a plan formed and orders to be given.

"My Lords," Sahid broke in again, not waiting for permission this time. "When Axise army landed on the Elk shores, we observed hundreds of sailing ships at anchor in their harbors. If we were to move with all haste, we could arrive at the harbors in four days march. We could then take to the sea and in three days, if my geography is correct, land behind the lines of the Starrowlands army, attacking them from the rear and by surprise."

Both Lords contemplated this idea. Liam stroked his beard and Aralias eyes darted about as he reasoned out the plan "The troop ships were meant to carry the Elk and Shadow armies north to the Iron lands if need arise, so long is the march, but they have not been used for more than the occasional sailing to freshen up the sailors."

"Fifteen thousand behind the lines of the enemy, who's strength we estimate to be likely near one hundred and thirty thousand, accounting for losses." Liam thought through the problem aloud. "That is a small force for assault, and a large risk."

"I like it." Lord Aralias reanimated as he came up with the final course of action. "We will land behind the enemy and we will strike in smaller forces, attacking their rear elements as bandits in the night, rushing through and killing all we can with swiftness, then withdrawing into the cover of dark, only to move on to other encampments and repeat our attacks."

Aralias turned to his men, summoning his leaders and issuing orders for each to carry out. The hall emptied as swiftly as it filled. With the security of the city now assured, the remaining Shadow soldiers departed the hall as well, going off to survey the damage to the city.

Sahid was shown to the banquet hall, where a kindly spread of cold food was laid out. Lord Aralias and Lord Commander Fax ate little and with less speech, rapidly departing to attend to their wounded King. Sahid ate in plenty, alone as he was with the comparative feast.

As the two men entered the King's chamber, Aralias noted the stench of infection hanging in the air. Axeleon slept under the rest of herbal mixture, uneasy and shallow. The men stood at his side in silence while those attending the King departed for a much-needed respite.

Aralias grew restless. "Where is the Princess?"

Liam sighed heavily. "King Axeleon sent her and three others into a passage built by the first kings of Arken. The passage leads under the mountains, though none living know where it exits the underground."

Aralias face grew ashen. "If the King should die, he has no living heir present to take up the crown."

"That knowledge has troubled me deeply." Commander Fax did not take his eyes from the King's face as he spoke, his voice dark and full of the dread that suffocated him.

"She must be retrieved." Lord Aralias spoke the words as if they were rule of law, without option. "Our King is not long for this life."

"I know." Liam could think to say no more.

"You must remain here, old friend." Aralias turned to face the large Commander.

"I must go in search of the Princess." Liam answered back, still holding his eyes to the King.

"By my view, Axeleon will live for one day more, perhaps two." Aralias spoke evenly, concealing the sorrow that teamed under his gentle face. "You must bar access to the king, permitting only those you most trust. Keep this number small, for you must deceive the entirety of the realm."

Liam looked away from his King, his eyes narrowing as he faced Aralias. Deception was not something he found honorable, even more so when the lie is given by those sworn to rule in truth.

"With the returning of the families to the city, the high councils will also return. You must make them believe that the King lives on, no matter the cost, for as long as you can. If the council is allowed to see the King, they will know he is soon to die. This must not be allowed to happen."

Liam was at a loss for understanding. "I am three years senior to Lord Nathus. Were I to take the throne, knowing that upon Layandria's return I would yield, would not Lord Nathus remain in the solitude of his northern tundra?"

Lord Aralias raised his eyebrows in much exaggerated mock surprise. "That is the word of a fool. Think, old friend, why would Nathus refuse to set his armies marching to the aid of the Arkenhead? For fear of an attack at sea? This is beyond reality. In the current season, the seas off the Iron coast are cold and violent. Much of his coastline is cliff and treacherous rock that is barley possible to land in the best of conditions. The oceans protect Nathus' shores from invasion, he has no need for soldiers in this task. So too does the winter guard his norther border as the Derrenge Mountains are enfolded under tens of feet of snow. They are without doubt completely impassable and still Nathus hold his forces back. What could cause the man to act so?"

Lord Commander Fax bristled with barely controlled fury as he processed the logic of the Iron Lord's cause. "I can think of only one reason."

"Yes, now you see it." Aralias high voice carried a note of malice with it, though far less than that of the Commander. "If word reaches Nathus that the King has fallen, he will march in force to the Arkenhead. Nathus is not of our mind, my brother. He is of the old blood and will not honor your title or claim. I have not the strength in my fist to hold him back and the Arkenhead could not survive another incursion. Those loyal to Nathus are few, but their support for his treason would sound as wisdom and cooperation with the law."

"Should Layandria return after Nathus has gained control of the Arkenhead…" Liam pondered, already aware of the fate she would suffer.

"Nathus would no doubt think of some reason to have the Princess put to death, much the same as he would do with you." Aralias spoke as if he were saying that water is wet. "Were I him, I would have the Princess tried and put to death for treason and desertion. She is of able body and age, many would argue that her duty was to remain in the Arkenhead, no matter the doom before her. Were you crowned, Nathus would likely spin some tale in which you caused the King's demise. He has enough support in the councils, mostly through fear and bribery, that he may be able to secure such outcomes."

"When this is over, the Princess on the throne and the strength of the fists regained, Nathus will pay for his treachery." Liam snarled.

Aralias let out a slow breath. "Indeed, the man must be held accountable for his actions, or rather, his inaction, though I dare speculate that getting council support for his prosecution will be nearly impossible. Nathus has planned his coup well. If he succeeds, it will look to our people as the just course of law. If he fails, he will hold to his story that he feared invasion and did not comprehend the drastic need of the Arkenhead, or that word of the King's orders did not reach him in time. It is a near perfect trajectory, and I am forced to admit that I am jealous of the old bastard's cunning."

"We will deal with the man when the time has come." Liam voice grew impossibly cold. "We must send out our fastest couriers, carrying word that Axeleon lives, Axise has fallen and the war in the south progresses well for our side. Nathus must believe that there is no cause for him to march south."

"If the ruse fails and he comes to the citadel, you must find a way to kill him." Aralias eyes burned in the darkened chamber.

Liam's voice matched the fire of his companion. "I will end the Iron Lord before he has a breath out in greeting."

20.

Halta and Tepan imparted the history of their tribe as the group hurried down the mountain. Oslun was amazed that these people could speak at all, his own breath extremely labored. The Inohamman people, the warriors explained in short chops of verbiage, were divided into four separate tribes, each lead by their own Chieftain. The tribes were once a singular nation, but the bonds of old were wisps of memory now. Each tribe had its own territory, holding most of its population in a large village, with several smaller camps located near steady sources of water and game.

The Inohamman tribes held to their own knowledge of law, though the tribes were forbidden from making war against each other. The Inohamman tribes had not been united in many generations and most viewed it unlikely that the tribes would do so again. Breeding between separate tribes was forbidden by law, and any trading of goods, unless for the purpose of making war with outside forces, was also forbidden.

Wilteph told the details of the Outcasts expulsion from the Wanoak, and of the death of Chieftain Fannin. Tepan informed the little group that the western village of the Wanoak was not more than one hour ahead. Once arrived at this small encampment, they would mount horses and move to the central village of the tribe.

Layandria had much experience riding on horseback, as did Thyso and Jaxus. She knew that Oslun did not. She worried about the young cup bearer, glancing over her shoulder to see that he was some twenty paces behind her, struggling along next to Halta. The young man was visibly winded, his face red and his mouth agape. Layandria watched in amusement as Halta turned in stride to look at Oslun.

Seeing the woman's movement, the cupbearer pulled his shoulders back, raised his head and forced himself to take even breaths, as if he were not fatigued. Halta smiled at him and turned her face away. Oslun relaxed his posture and resumed his ragged breathing. Layandria found the effect the woman had on the servant fascinating. She could feel Oslun trying his best to be strong for her eyes. She wondered what about Halta brought this out in him.

Ahead, Jaxus moved along the terrain behind Wilteph. Layandria could see the ease of his movements, the way his feet danced over the rough undergrowth with seemingly minimal effort. His armor flexed and moved along with every motion of his muscles. Layandria wanted to be next to him, to feel the energy given off by his presence. Layandria felt her pace quickening, despite the protests coming up from her legs.

As Layandria gained on Jaxus, he felt her presence and looked over his shoulder towards her. Layandria was overcome by embarrassment. She slowed her pace and resumed her place in the loose formation. She began to understand, at least in part, what Oslun felt under Halta's sight.

Come, join me. Layandria felt the words in her head, as if Jaxus were speaking aloud.

Why? She answered back silently, though she did not expect the man to hear her.

Because you want to, my Princess. Jaxus voice entered her mind again. Layandria was amazed, and slightly frightened. She had heard Jaxus voice in her mind before, and she knew that he had heard hers, though she did not know how either person had done this. She quickened her pace again, coming along Jaxus left side.

How can I hear your mind? Layandria forced herself to focus on the thoughts, willing them out to the man.

I do not know. Jaxus words entered her again, his voice strong and clear, though the man had not turned his head to her or parted his lips. *Perhaps we are connected through our nature.*

Layandria was confused by this. What nature could connect a person to another that allowed them to hear without word? *Have you experienced this before?* It seemed to her that though she had been able to communicate to Jaxus through thought before, she had never done so with intent, only in moments of duress. Now, it was as though by concentration alone she could speak with him at ease.

No, I have not. Jaxus voice carried the same curious uncertainty that Layandria felt. *Have you?*

Layandria shook her head. *No.* She could not understand this gift, and though she found it frightening, she found comfort as well.

The group passed through thick brush into a sun-soaked clearing. Small structures of wood and animal skins dotted the bare terrain. A small fire smoked out its dying embers in the center of the clearing. Several horses were tethered to posts imbedded deeply in the turf. Hushed whispers of shock passed among the few inhabitants as the Outcasts entered the village. Several older Wanoak gathered the others and pulled them into the buildings. Wilteph became visibly angry, flexing his hands repeatedly. None of the other Outcasts appeared to react to the rejection.

After supplies were loaded onto horses and relief taken, Wilteph drew the small group together and explained that they would ride for some hours, reaching the Wanoak home village just as the sun began to fall. If the village was uncontested, they would take rest, riding out to meet the enemy at first light.

The Princess approached the horse that was to be hers gently, petting the animal's neck as it sniffed out her character. These horses were taller than those in Arken, and while Arken horses were predominately black or brown, these animals were many tones of white, gray and caramel, patched over the skin as if the animals were assembled from the parts of many others. Layandria's horse was steady, waiting patiently for her to mount.

The Princess watched as Jaxus aided Thyso in mounting his horse, then moved to his own. The man gently sprang up onto the horses back without apparent effort. Layandria was again amazed by the ease with which Jaxus moved, his body having a strange fluidity to it, as if the man never exerted effort.

There were fewer horses than needed for their group, so Halta and Oslun were mounted together, the woman in front, and the cup bearer's arms around her waist. Oslun was clearly satisfied with the arrangement, and the contact he had with the vixenous woman. Rale'en sneered at the pair, but the fierceness of Halta's eyes silenced her and kept any ill words at bay.

Wilteph trotted his horse to the front of the group and turned to face them. He raised his arm high over his head, bringing it down in a swift motion pointing them in their direction of travel. The Inohamman let out a great shout and surged off, kicking their horses into speed. Dust kicked up around them as they charged down a slight decline at a full run. Layandria gripped the reigns and kicked her horse off gently. As if it were waiting, the beast took to a full gallop, rushing off after the others.

Layandria found herself riding next to Jaxus on one side, and Thyso on the other. Halta and Oslun were in front of them and the Princess could see the young man struggling to keep his place behind Halta, having no saddle or stirrups to aid his balance. The Princess turned her eyes to the right. Thyso rode with confidence, a look of pride on his face. The poison of the morlt had left his body, aided by herbs and his strength returned rapidly. Looking now to Jaxus, Layandria found his face impassive as he easily rose and fell, in step with his horse. She faced forward again, silently preparing her mind for the combat that she knew they would soon face. She hoped with all her strength that she was not leading these three brave men to their deaths.

The ride was long, but easy on rider and animal. The Wanoak village came into view as the party crested a low hill, the sun setting behind and casting long shadows that seemed to reach out in welcome to the warriors as they sped across the open terrain towards the buildings.

Given the leather cloths and simple skin shoes worn by the Inohamman, Thyso expected to see shabby structures, made of branches, or woven grass. Instead, the buildings were formed of hewn trees, beautifully adorned fabric, and a dark brown type of brick made from mud. A large log wall ringed the city. It was a city, as it was much larger than something called a village should be. Thyso estimated the population to be near twenty thousand.

Layandria was also quite shocked by what she saw. Not the structure of the city, for she had spoken at length with Halta about the makeup of the cities of the Inohamman lands. What shocked her was the size of the black smoke plumes that rose over the skyline.

Wilteph smiled broadly at the sight, so long had it been since his eyes rested on the home of his people. The smile crashed into great fear and concern as he took in the smoke. A gentle tap of his heels increased the speed of his mount. The other riders followed suit and took to a full gallop as they crossed the plain. The group rounded the high wall to the south of the city and drew towards the gate. The gate itself was massive, formed of the mighty trunks of pine trees. The strength of the trees was no longer intact as the gate itself had been set to flame. It was now only the smoldering memory of its former self.

The riders wheeled around, led by Wilteph, passing through the broken gate and the shattered remnants of the wall. Several of the buildings had crashed to the ground, smoke belching through the fallen roofs. The horses drove on, coming to the center of the city. Wilteph reigned his horse and turned around several times, taking in the scene before him. The bodies of dead warriors and citizens lay all around.

Wilteph let out an anguished cry. His voice carried high into the air, wrapping the destruction in a blanket of suffering. Drawn to the sounds, survivors began to filter into the area. Many were wounded, others were blackened with the smoke of many fires that raged still in the city.

Shock was evident on the faces of many as they saw Wilteph and the other outcasts. The shock was rapidly overtaken by anger. Shouts went up, announcing the presence of the outcasts to all alive within the city. Wilteph and the others said nothing. Halta and Oslun dismounted their horse. The cup bearer followed Halta as she ran to embrace an elderly woman who was limping heavily, a bloodied bandage wrapped around her right calf. Halta's face broke and she wept openly as she wrapped her body around the injured woman.

Oslun approached the woman and bent to check the damage to her leg. As his fingers unwrapped the bandage, he found that an arrow head was lodged deep in the muscle. The shaft had been broken and protruded from the wound. Halta carefully set the woman down on the turf. She withdrew a small pouch from her vest and opened it, placing small dried leaves on the wound. The woman cried out at the contact, but soon began to relax in ease. Halta indicated that Oslun should remove the arrow and she gripped the old woman's leg on either side of the damage.

Oslun pressed his fingers into the wound, fishing for the head of the arrow. He pulled against it, sliding the stone out of the flesh. The woman scarcely let out a sound and Oslun knew he must find out what leaves Halta had used, so easily had they ridded the woman of pain. The arrow removed, Oslun carefully spread the laceration, probing it for any remaining shards of the arrowhead. Satisfied, he bound the wound in a fresh bandage from his pack. Halta helped the woman to rest against a log near the edge of the city center.

Layandria surveyed the area and saw the great number of wounded citizens that needed aid. Her heart felt like shattered glass and she could not bear it.

"Bring the wounded over here!" The Princess shouted, directing to an open area with short, soft grass. She jumped off her horse, removing packs of supplies from its back. As she moved towards the grass, several citizens came near. Halta and Oslun, Tepan, Jaxus and Thyso joined her and all set to work caring for the wounds of the people.

Three men entered the city center carrying the body of another. The man, who was no doubt large in life, was now broken and diminished. The men presented the body before Wilteph and stood back, letting him take in the image. Chieftain Jordache he had been in life. Now, in death, the Chieftain's arms and legs had been removed roughly with the savage strokes of a dull blade. He had bled to death from so many vicious wounds.

Wilteph starred at the broken body. The realization of the cause of Chief Jordache's death reached his mind. Anger built up inside Wilteph to a level he had never known. The images of his broken home swirled around him, their deaths fueling his enraged spirit. The anger and clear blame directed at him on the faces of many Wanoak citizens shamed him and he could no longer contain the fury.

"They will pay for this evil!" Wilteph's horse reared up. He drew his sword and raised it on high. "Let us ride out! Let us put down those who have brought death to our people!"

"What are you saying?" Layandria called out from the grass. She was kneeling next to a man, wounded in his stomach by a slashing sword. The wound was shallow, and she was cleaning it so that it could be sutured. Wilteph and the other Wanoak turned towards her. "We must tend to the wounded and provide security before we can strike out!"

"The time of healing will come after our enemies are put to ground!" Wilteph shouted back in defiance of this small woman who dared to challenge his authority. Several of the Inohamman raised their voices, jeering Wilteph's vengeance.

"Look around you!" Layandria stood as she screamed the words. "Look at these people you call your own! The need aid, not revenge!"

"How am I to aid them while those who caused this pain still breathe?" Wilteph directed his horse towards the young princess. He picked his way through the crowd, stopping the beast just in front of her.

"It is for weak minds to think that the only aid they can give is at the tip of a sword!" Layandria cried out in passion abundant. "You would ride out now, taking with you all able men and women, to do what? To make war on an already departing enemy? Your people need strength here, now, not there, later!"

"I am not their Chieftain!" Wilteph shouted as he reared his horse again. Layandria did not step back in the face of the angered animal. "They rejected me and slew my father!"

"So, you abandon us now?" Another voice, soft and meek, came from the shadows. A young woman stepped forward into the grass. She was blackened with smoke, a large bruise adorned her cheek and her clothes were torn open.

"Chandr!" Wilteph dismounted his horse and rushed to the woman, calling to her in desperation. He reached to embrace her, but the young woman backed away from his touch. "I have not abandoned you!"

"All of this is of your making!" Chandr wailed as she stepped away.

"How am I responsible for this evil?" Indignation covered Wilteph and fury renewed in his feature.

"I begged you to let us leave, just we two, holding no one else accountable for our choices." Tears poured over Chandr's face as she spoke the words, deep lines cleaned from the soot on her face.

"I had no choice!" Wilteph begged from her, buckling as if heavy blows fell on him.

"There is always a choice!" Chandr was defiant. "We could have left. Our lives may have been short, but no other would have suffered for us. You chose to tell your father, knowing that his love for you would spurn him to action in your defense. Then, when he had accepted his fate, you chose to bring others into the path we made. The death you see is on your hands alone!"

All around, the gathered people had grown still, watching the exchange before them. Wilteph's shoulders sank. The weight of the destruction around him crushing. "I only wanted to save you and our child!"

"Our child!" Chandr cried out, as she stepped towards the weakened man. She raised her hand and struck him heavily across his face. Her eyes welled with mournful outrage. "Our child died at the hands of the enemy you brought down on us! We know that it was you who turned this evil against us! With every stroke of their blades, the Lakemen spoke of it! You could have stayed your hand against the Lakemen, heeding the warning that was so clearly given, but the great Wilteph, son of the Chieftain, refused. Now look what you have brought on us! The death of our people and the death of our child!"

"Our child is dead?" Wilteph slumped towards the ground. Chandr starred at him in silence.

Layandria approached the man softly. She kept her voice lowered and even. "The time for vengeance will come, now is the time for healing."

"What should I do?" Wilteph looked up to Chandr, his spirit breaking. She turned her face from him.

"There will be a time to strike out to your enemy." Layandria maintained her calm demeanor. "But your people need a leader who will care for them and help them in their time of despair."

Jaxus stepped towards Wilteph, opposite of Layandria. "I would suggest that you set those able and not skilled in medicine to rebuild the wall and put out what fires can be stilled. Once completed, these men and women can set to finding food and comfortable resting places for the others. Those with knowledge of wounds and treatment must care for the people. Once all are mended as possible, graves must be cut and the dead laid to rest."

"I must see our child." Wilteph looked to Chandr again, as if he did not hear the words spoken to him. Chandr gestured that he should follow and Wilteph slowly rose from the grass. The outcasts looked around from one to another, uncertainty filling them.

"Who among you knows how to treat wounds?" Layandria turned to address the Outcasts as Wilteph departed. Several hands went up. "There is more than enough work to be done tending to those with hurts."

Several villagers moved to join Layandria on the low grass.

"Who among you has knowledge of building?" The passion of Layandria's voice ebbed into calm. Several gave their acknowledgement. "Jaxus will take you to the gate where you will set to work rebuilding it, then you will tend to the fires and the structures as best you can."

As the builders moved off, Jaxus dutifully leading them, several remained in the city center, staring blankly and the young royal. Layandria quietly instructed them to begin gathering the dead and preparing them for burial. Once they had departed to their tasks, Layandria turned back to the wounded.

Halta watched the young Princess and she moved among the gathered citizens. Layandria gave soft words of comfort to the weakened, while she offered words of strength to those who needed it. Halta was surprised at the grace she displayed and the way the people responded to her presence. Halta felt drawn to Layandria, much the same as she had been to Chieftain Talin when she was young.

Over many hours, cuts and burns were bound, limbs were cared for and those who could not be saved were given herbs to ease their passing. While Layandria was busy tending to the people, Jaxus and the men and women with him had felled new trees and rebuilt the gate. Most of the fires in the city were put down, food and water were brought up for all. The bodies of the dead were gathered, and men began digging graves.

The recovery was slow, but the spirits of the people seemed lifted with the effort put in by the outcasts and their foreign companions. Night had long fallen by the time the work was done. At Jaxus insistence, Layandria and the others with her took to rest. Jaxus alone stayed awake through the darkness, keeping watch over the village. No word of Wilteph was brought forth.

Halta took Layandria off to another hutment where Oslun suspected they would continue their conversations and enjoy each other's company. How he wished to be in Layandria's place, to share the privacy of four walls and the night air with Halta. She was more beautiful to the young cupbearer than any image his mind could conjure. He fell into rest with her sparkling eyes and brilliant smile fixed on his mind.

The sun rose slowly, and with it, Layandria came to Jaxus, concern deeply troubling her. The course ahead was unclear. None among her could be trusted for council more than Jaxus and he alone of those of Arken had experience in war.

"Should we ride out?" She softly approached the dark knight. The man faced away from her, his arms against the massive supports of the gate. He starred out into the distance, gazing through the spaces between the beams. He did not move at the sound of Layandria's voice.

"Jaxus?" Layandria hesitated, coming to a stop several feet behind the man. He did not respond to her. Though Layandria was fond of Jaxus and felt a deep connection to the man, she was forced to admit that she knew very little of him. She could hear his thoughts when he willed them to her, but she could see no further than the blank slate that he presented. She pressed on, undeterred by his silence. "Jaxus, I need your council."

"What kind of royal do you want to be?" Jaxus did not turn away from his view of the sky through the gate.

Layandria did not understand her companion's sharp tone or his refusal to look upon her. She stepped forward, just behind the man's shoulder. "What are you asking, Sir?"

"It is a simple question, your grace." Jaxus betrayed more concern than he intended. He could not control it, so much was his fear for her future. "What king of royal do you want to be?"

Layandria starred at the man's back, the rising sun glinting off his hair and the skin of his neck. "What kind of Royal do you think I am?"

"It is not of importance what I think, what matters is what you believe in your being that you will be." Jaxus was stern, perhaps even irritated. "I have walked this earth far longer than you can know. I have seen many rulers. Men who called themselves Emperors, Kings and Czars. I have seen cruel queens, soft kings, men governed by selfish gains, ideals of useless moral constructs and others who ruled by brutality and fear. I have witnessed entire populations laid to ground for the wishes of mad men and I have seen those who deserve to die raised to positions of power. Precious few of the men and women I have known to call themselves royals were worthy of the title. So, I ask you, Layandria of Arken, what kind of royal do you want to be?"

Layandria stifled the feelings welling inside of her. She fought to keep her voice controlled. "Why do you hate us for the deeds of others? I believed you were fond of my father, he thought highly of you."

"I have no hate in my heart for you, or for you father, nor did I state such feeling." Jaxus turned his eyes to Layandria. She was astonished to find not anger on his features, but rather a countenance that conveyed a long-held sadness. "In King Axeleon, I believed that I had found the virtue of a man worthy of his crown."

Layandria stepped forward again, clenching her fists, less from anger and more from sheer confusion as to where Jaxus was leading this exchange. "My father is a great man and a good king."

"I have never spoke that he was not, or less than." Jaxus turned his face back to the gap in the gate, staring out onto the horizon again.

"Speak plainly man!" Layandria shouted, leaning towards Jaxus back. "And look at me when you speak! If you have no respect for me as your Princess, then at least give me the respect of a woman!"

Jaxus spun around suddenly, his nostrils flaring and his features tight. "Your father ceased to be a good king the second that he gave up hope and accepted the death of his kingdom. He sent his only daughter underground to run as a rat, abandoning his people to torment and cruelty at the hands of Axise, whom I know too well. What was the end state of his plan? What are you to do now? Even if through some force of magic, you were to gather strength and return to your kingdom, retaking the throne from Axise and his hordes, you would bring yet another war on your people. More death, more suffering on people who trusted in him to protect them."

"And what, My Lady, do you think Axise will do once he has scoured the citadel for word of your whereabouts?" Jaxus held his ground, not advancing on Layandria, but he showed such a fire that he spit as he spoke. "Do you think he will not put to death any whom he suspects have the slightest knowledge of your location? Eventually, after the bodies of those loyal to you have been stacked to the sun, someone will tell of the passage under the throne. Axise will gather his armies and strike out into this land. He will raise these cultures to dust to find you, so consumed is the man with ending your father's blood line and any claim to the Arken throne that is not his. So, the selfishness of your father will bring death and pain to worlds that have never heard his name. That, My Princess, is the failure of Axeleon."

"This is the same failure I see in the good Chieftain Wilteph. His desire to preserve his own caused his own father to take the death that was owed to Wilteph alone. Then, he refused to accept that result and brought death to many more that were loyal to him. How many did he say joined him in the mountains? Fifty? Of whom slight more than twenty remain. And, because his pride was damaged by the harshness of the Lakemen, he struck against them, not in justice, but in anger. This wrath has now turned back on his own people and brought great suffering to them, or did you miss the words of the woman who bore his now deceased child? Another life lost that is laid at the feet of a flawed ruler."

"To be a ruler is to accept that your pride will be damaged, those you love will be killed. A true leader must understand that his life does not belong to him, in any way. It belongs to his people and even in death, a royal must serve them. This is the sad truth of a crown. Nothing you hold dear is yours alone, all you are belongs to those you rule. You must always, in every moment, put your people and their safety above your own. So, I ask you again, Layandria, Princess of Arken, what kind of royal do you want to be?"

Layandria stepped backwards, her eyes wide in the shock of Jaxus tirade. "I have never wanted to be a royal at all."

Jaxus sighed heavily, his posture relaxed, and his breathing slowed. "That, my Princess, is the only answer I could hear that would give me hope in your leadership."

Layandria did not release her anger, though she paused long enough to collect her thoughts. She did not understand this tirade and found Jaxus account of her father deeply disturbing, but there were far more pressing issues at hand. "So, do we ride out against the enemy?"

Jaxus softened further, resuming the calm demeanor he frequently held when guiding those around him. "I would suggest that we send out a scout to find out the enemy's location and intent. If the enemy is departing, there is nothing to be gained by attempting to fight. If the enemy shows he intends to continue his persecution of these people, we must go to meet him as far from the village as time allows."

"You speak with wisdom." Layandria slowed her speech, regaining her controlled, even tone. "You will be my scout."

Jaxus nodded to her, accepting the assignment. Layandria turned away from him, moving back towards the city center. She stopped several paces away from the man and turned over her shoulder. "When you come back, I expect to know how it is that you can speak so well on these Kings and Czars you have witnessed over a life not much aged past my own. I would also like to know who you can so well determine the actions my uncle will take in my absence."

As Layandria turned away, Jaxus breath caught short. He knew of no words that he could convey that would explain his history in a way that would not destroy all trust. He called after her, determined to make all known though he himself lacked the strength. "Ask the cup bearer. He knows my history as well as any, though he will deny this knowledge."

Layandria did not pause in her step as she strode away. Jaxus words troubled her deeply, and she found herself buried under doubt of one whom she so desperately needed to be steadfast. "Find the enemy, report their movements."

Jaxus felt the heat of her words as they reached him. He closed his eyes and let out a slow breath, turning slowly back towards the gate. With ease and silence, Jaxus hoisted himself up over the gate and dropped to the turf. He broke into a run, crossing the open terrain low and swiftly.

Layandria heard the man's foot fall as he came to the ground from the top of the gate. She stopped and turned back, knowing she would not see him. Dread filled her. Too many questions surrounded the man. Their deep, seemingly inexplicable connection, his intimate knowledge of Axise motivations coupled with his frequent absences from the Kingdom conjured horrible thoughts. She began to consider the possibility that he was not the ally he seemed. There were rumors in the citadel that Axise had a spy carefully placed high in Axeleon's government. The more she puzzled over Jaxus, the more deeply concerned she became that he could be this spy. Were this true, how could she possibly kill him? And how many would die for the effort?

21.

"Lord Commander!" A young woman burst into the Whisper Hall, shouting as she passed from within the King's chambers. Liam snapped up from the throne, pressing his extended finger to his lips and bidding the girl to approach the seat of the king in silence. She was pretty, young and full of vibrancy. She had long, sandy hair that fell over her shoulders in sheer waves that framed a lovely, youthful face.

Liam threw a quick glance around the hall of kings, but he knew it was only occupied by three. The young girl approached him, dwarfed by his immense size. "What is it?"

"The King has passed, My Lord." The girl said the words with her eyes downcast and sorrow on her face.

Commander Fax closed his eyes and breathed out his sorrow. Some four days past, the King began to stir, showing signs of life and calling for his trusted Commander. Liam knew that he was not to last, but he seized the opportunity. The King was seen by many on that day, in improved spirit and showing signs of recovery. Liam knew all too well that Axeleon would not recover. The infection had set too deep.

Often, in the cold of late winter, the sun will rise strong for a few days, even a week, melting off the winter snows, bringing on the warmth and fragrance of summer, only to be replaced by a blowing storm and frigid temperatures. This was often true for men gravely wounded. A burst of hope, recovery of slight strength brought on by the bodies attempt to revive what had already been sentenced to death.

The false summer of King Axeleon served Liam well. At the King's revival, he took council from the man, discussed the happenings and what courses of action would be best taken for the kingdom's preservation.

Axeleon agreed with Lord Aralias' interpretation of potential pitfalls before them. Knowing he was dying, the King, in the presence of Sahid Hauk Kahn, to whom he took a strong liking, and Lord Aralias, named Lord Commander Liam Fax King Regent. This decree would aid Liam and provide him safety if the King's death was discovered, but Axeleon urged that no word be given of his passing for as long as it could be held back. Axeleon seconded Aralias' judgment that if word of his death reached Lord Nathus, he would contest the throne, or at the very least attempt to secure the Iron Fist for his own, declaring himself separate and independent from Arken. Liam begrudgingly accepted his fate, remarking to the King that this course of action would likely bring him to the noose.

Under the guise that their King no longer needed great attention, given his recovery, Liam sent away the surgeons and aids that tended the man. Only one remained at his side. Second cousin to Princess Layandria, Ilsla was her name. This young woman refused to abandon the King's side until he was fully recovered and back on his feet. Liam was powerless to refuse the commitment and Axeleon seemed to rest easier in her company.

The surgeons and aids who were sent away reported throughout the Citadel that the King was recovering, was awake and giving instructions to the Lord Commander. This news reached the ears of those loyal to Lord Nathus, which Lord Commander Fax fiercely hoped would stay the man's hand in any action against the throne. Any movement of the Iron Lord would be sped quickly to the Arkenhead and Liam rested in the knowledge that Nathus would not be riding to the citadel any time soon.

With the councilors and masters believing the King would return to his seat within a few weeks, one month at the most, they were contented. The pressure now somewhat staved off, Liam formed his plans.

Sahid approached the throne, moving up the steps from the black stone floor. The Whisper Hall was dimly lit, the lanterns not yet returned to the ceiling and the sun having faded into dusk. The borum stone walls glowed warmly. The Fallish Warrior had embraced the armor of the Shadow fighters, replacing the tattered leathers he wore when he first entered the citadel and casting off the ill-fitting armaments of the wolves. An ugly wound graced his chin, a reminder of his trek through the sewers. The wound had been treated, the cleaning process one of great pain, though long term damage was prevented by the suffering.

Ilsla stood waiting for the Lord Commander's instructions, her eyes to the blood stone floor. Liam gently cupped her face in his massive hand, paying no mind to Sahid's approach. "Did he pass in peace, daughter of the Shadow?"

Ilsla nodded softly, tears running easily down her new cheeks. "Yes, My Lord. He passed in sleep."

"This is well." Liam spoke softly, his mind not on the woman to whom he spoke. "You have served the King well and will be long rewarded for the grace of your care."

Sahid handed Liam a silver cup, filled with the juice of peaches and grapes. Liam lowered his hand from the woman's face and took the cup, presenting it to her. "Drink and take rest."

Ilsla followed the Lord's gesture and sat on the edge of the throne of the king. She sipped from the cup and found the juice to be light and delicious. She had stood by the side of the king for several days and had taken little for herself. She felt refreshed by the fragrant beverage. "What will we do now, My Lord?"

Liam smiled softly at the young girl, watching her drink deeply. "We have much to do, young daughter. We must go in search of Princess Layandria. We must send word to Lord Aralias in the south and ensure that he, Lord Brustic and Lady Kaowith return as soon as may be allowed."

Ilsla did not react to this news, the sadness of the loss of the King too deep on her heart. "What shall I do, Lord Commander?"

"You, my dear, I am sorry to say," Liam stepped towards the girl slowly, taking her free hand in his, "will pass into a calm, easy sleep. When you wake, the world will be clean and new. All of your pain will pass away, and you will be united with the King you so love."

Ilsla's face grew heavy in confusion. She puzzled over the Lord's words for a moment, her mind muddled and slow. Realization came on like a cold wave. "Am I to die?"

"I am sorry, daughter of Arken." Liam's voice carried sadness and pain. "None can know of the King's death. We must preserve the throne as long as we can, protecting it from those who would wish to claim it for themselves in the absence of the rightful Queen."

"I will tell no one." Ilsla sat forward, withdrawing her hand from the commander's touch. Her voice was strong, but her words were slurred, as if she struggled to fully open her mouth. "I will tell no, any, person."

"I believe you, dear one." Commander Fax stooped towards the girl. "But the survival of the throne cannot rely on that faith. You wear the news of our King's passing on your face as if to announce it to all who would see you."

"Then let me leave Arken!" The young woman pleaded as tears filler her eyes. "Send me to find the Princess and with her return, all treacherous news that I wear will be of no import!"

Lord Commander Fax sighed heavily. He took a knee before Ilsla, drawing close to her and laying his hands on her knees. "Would that I could, dear one. I must send only those who can travel at haste and track well in the wild."

Ilsla began to cry in earnest. Her head lolled to the side and her mouth fell open. Her eyes fixed on Liam's, burning in hate as the poison took hold on her organs.

Sahid stepped forward and eased her shoulders back into the seat. He gently stroked her hair and began humming softly in her ear.

"When Layandria has returned to us, she will be told the truth of your sacrifice. She will know that you alone stood by her father to his end and that you gave your life to preserve her throne." Liam's features grew hard and grim.

The fire in Ilsla's eyes did not fade, though the color drained from her face and her breath grew shallow. She attempted to swallow, but her tongue fell into the back of her throat. She began to convulse against the obstruction. Sahid steadied her, as her muscles failed.

Liam swallowed hard. "The Queen will likely order me put to death for what I have done to you, and I willingly accept that fate. If you take nothing with you to assuage the injustice of this day, know that I will pay for your life with my own and while you will rise in grace, I will fall to dwell among those stained with the blood of the innocent.

When you wake, the veil of shadow will fall away. All goodness will pass to you."

Ilsla's breath caught, then jerked back into her chest. A long, ragged gasp escaped from her as her body tremored. Liam stood and gently lifted her from the throne. Sahid moved before him, holding open the door to the King's chamber to allow him entry. The large commander laid Ilsla next to the King's body and covered her with a white cloth.

"Tonight, under cover of darkness, we will move them to the catacombs. We will seal their bodies into the tomb of King Alx, where none will find them until the return of Queen Layandria." Liam looked to Sahid, though he spoke as though he were far from the chambers of the king. "I did not wish this throne for myself. I would have the King returned to life, and all of this cast from me."

Sahid cleared his throat, the sound bringing Liam's focus back to him. "It is never the wish of good men to be burdened with a crown."

"Perhaps, friend." Liam's voice carried the death his soul felt. "Perhaps. Though I am not a man fit for good words or hopeful thoughts. My place is among the damned."

"You will see in time," Sahid lifted his hand to the Commander's arm, "the sadness you feel over that which must be done, that is what makes you a man worthy."

Liam turned away and strode from the chambers. "We must not leave the throne unattended."

Sahid touched the cloth over Ilsla's head gently, whispering in his own tongue, some small thanks for her sacrifice and bidding her safe passage to the world beyond. He turned and followed the Lord Commander out. Liam paced in front of the throne, a custom he had taken to in the days following Axeleon's injury. As he approached, the large man stopped and faced him.

"I want you to enter the passage under the throne and go out in search of Queen Layandria." Liam's voice was strong, but forced, his mind still dwelling on Ilsla and other pains.

"My Lord," Sahid hesitated. "How am I to find one that I have never seen, in the company of violent men who will not trust the words I bring to them?"

"I cannot go, Sahid." Liam spoke in frustration, his large fists clenched at his sides. "I alone was entrusted by King Axeleon to rule in his daughter's stead. I am now under oath to hold the throne and cannot do the one thing that is most needed. Would that I could dispatch Lord Aralias, for he would certainly succeed where many others could not. There remains but one choice before me. You must go."

"I am willing, Lord Commander." Sahid stepped forward, offering open hands in submission, "It is only that I do not know how to accomplish this task."

Liam carefully removed a ring from the small finger of his right hand, giving it to Sahid. The ring was black, made of some strange metal that seamed solid, and yet liquid all the same. It bore no mark, adorned only by a single stone, small, though it shone with the same glowing light of the borum stone walls.

"Look for a man by the name of Jaxus. He wears armor of this same make. You will know him by this." Liam watched Sahid's eyes as he spoke, studying them for understanding. "When you find him, present him with this ring and tell him that when I gave it to you, I told you that it must be united with that from which it came. The man will know the meaning of the words and will trust you in this."

"I will do as you command." Sahid fitted the ring around his thumb, finding that it was too large for any of his fingers. He chose not to inform Commander Fax that he was already quite familiar with Jaxus. He also kept concealed his confusion. Did they not know that it was Jaxus who had given King Axise word of the citadel's troop strength? That is was Jaxus who had been ordered to befriend and become trusted by King Axeleon? It was he who was ordered to murder the Princess as soon as Axeleon had been slain? That all of this was ordained years before Axise came to the shores of the Elk Fist?

Liam studied the man for a long moment. "You must return the Queen to her throne, no matter the cost to you or any other."

Sahid nodded as he processed the information. Without a further word, Commander Fax turned and dragged the throne aside. He knelt and wrested a slab of blood stone, revealing a dark passage that lead away to the west. "How is your vision in the dark?"

Sahid coughed slightly, looking into the deep black that stretched away from him. "It is well, though that is more than dark, My Lord."

Liam strode to the wall and took up a torch, bringing it back to Sahid. The Fallish man accepted the light and stepped to the passage without hesitation, descending into the darkness. The commander returned the slab to its position and pulled the throne back into place. He stood, frozen in space and time as his eyes locked on the throne.

"I am again the fool." He spoke quietly to himself in exasperation. "Now I will have to move the bodies alone."

22.

The Princess stood at the log gate to the Wanoak City, letting her eyes pass far over the clearing, her mind turning over on itself. Six days had passed since Jaxus departed for his scouting. Layandria had pressed Oslun for information at first, insisting that the cup bearer tell her what he knew. Despite her persistence, Oslun stuck to his silence, citing the oath of silence he once swore to her father.

As Layandria knew no other who could speak to Jaxus history, she had no information to temper her anger. By the fourth day, she began to question the wisdom of sending Jaxus out alone. As the days moved on, Layandria began to worry deeply that Jaxus had met some ill fate, or that her suspicions were true and the man had abandoned her.

The sounds of swords colliding somewhere in the city shook Layandria's focus off the black clad warrior. She turned away from the gate and nodded to the Inohamman men who stood guard on either side. They returned her gesture respectfully as she strode away. As the Princess approached the city center, she observed Thyso and Oslun rushing towards each other with blades raised high and intensity in their expressions. Several of the Wanoak stood by, forming a circle around the two men. Oslun brought his sword down in a swift ark, speeding towards Thyso's knees. The larger handmaid countered in time, meeting the stroke and sweeping his opponent's sword up and away.

Oslun anticipated the move and as Thyso lifted his weapon, the cup bearer stepped in to Thyso's right, pulling the weapon down and across Thyso's chest. The blade connected with the armor heavily, though heavy cloth wrapping prevented the blade from causing damage. Thyso stepped back quickly, raising his sword in salute as Oslun braced and pointed his weapon towards the handmaid's heart, prepared to strike again. At the salute, Oslun smiled and relaxed his posture. Thyso smiled brightly, shaking Oslun's hand and clapping his shoulder. "Well done! Very well fought!"

Halta stepped forward, congratulating Oslun on his strike while several of the men and women gathered offered free congratulations. The two young men had endeared themselves to the tribe over the past days with their youthful exuberance and constant activity. They were nearly always together, save when Oslun took leave of his companion in favor of moments shared with Halta. They aided the village greatly, with more than their smiles, as each had lent the strength of their backs to rebuild the damage brought on by the Lakemen.

Layandria smiled as she approached, glad to see the two men forming a bond. In Jaxus absence, Thyso had taken to instructing Oslun in sword play, archery and empty hand combat. Oslun had learned quickly, his mind able to retain every move and every counter, playing it back and analyzing every instruction. Thyso too had sharpened his skills, finding that teaching the art of war made him examine his own form, refining, and adding to his skill.

"The armor on my shoulders is restricting." Oslun said, flexing his arms in wide circles. "I wish I could take them off or modify them."

Thyso examined the black plates. "You can take them off if you wish, but it will leave you exposed. I would suggest leaving the left alone, as you rarely raise your trailing arm high. I think we can cut your right plate down a bit at the top so that allows more flex at the joint."

"That would be good." Oslun agreed, flexing his right shoulder again. "I wish I had known I could modify my armor, I would have done it days ago."

"Of course!" Thyso laughed. "You have to fight in your own armor, so it must work for you. There is no set form that will work for every soldier."

Layandria took pride seeing the comradery forming between the two men. She stepped forward, entering the circle and slowly drew her sword, making no sound. The two men were before her, looking away and discussing their moves and counter moves. Halta's eye caught Layandria's movement, but she only smiled, not giving away Layandria's intent. The Princess took up a ready stance. "Let us begin!" She shouted at the two men. Both wheeled around and readied their swords.

"Her sword is not wrapped, take caution!" Thyso called to his companion as he circled around Layandria's right.

"I am not afraid." The cup bearer called back as he circled to the Princess's left, bringing her to the center between the two of them. His hand quickly checked the heavy cloth wrapping that covered the blade of Devil's Song. The thick canvas dulled the edges of the weapon and added weight, unbalancing the sword and forcing the wielder to exert more strength to control it. Layandria's sword had no such wrapping, her weapon deadly.

Thyso moved to strike first, his sword low and parallel to the ground. Layandria easily blocked the stroke. Oslun seized the opening and drove forward, ready to slash Devil's Song across her back. In a stunning move, Layandria yanked Heart's End upwards, over her head and down her back, blocking Oslun's strike and spinning to the left.

Thyso followed the move closely and dipped in to cut his weapon across Layandria's ankles. She was slightly faster and avoided the move. Oslun jumped forward, pressing Devil's Song towards

Layandria's belly. The tip of the sword caught Layandria's armor as she moved. He did not celebrate, for the hit would not have been fatal and Thyso had trained him to never relent until the foe was fully downed or yielded.

Layandria countered the stroke, gripping Oslun's chest plate under his chin. She yanked downwards, pulling Oslun off his feet. The young cup bearer took the move well, rolling forward onto his shoulders and springing back up. Thyso wheeled around the Princess as she stepped to the side of the falling Oslun. He brought his sword up and swung toward her arm, the dulled blade connecting with the armor on Layandria's bicep. The strike would have done significant damage to her arm were the sword not dulled.

Layandria reacted to the hit, turning in and bringing her sword up. Typically, in such a combat spar, once seriously wounded, the opponent would cease combat, render the salute and concede victory. Layandria did not follow this ruling. A sly grin crossed her face as she stepped in and attacked. She caught Thyso in the armpit with the hilt of her sword. The man cried out in pain, wrenching away. Layandria chased the move, arcing Heart's End upward savagely. As the blade found its mark, just above Thyso's groin, Layandria loosed her wrists, preventing the blade from digging into the armor.

Oslun saw the blow fall on Thyso and reacted instantly. He stepped in from the side and jerked Devil's Song up, lifting Layandria's sword off his companion. He followed through the cut, wrapping around and dragging Layandria's sword backwards, against the control of her wrists. She lost her grip and Heart's End crashed to the dust. Oslun stepped forward and drove his shoulder into Layandria's breast plate, throwing her over backwards. The Princess smashed to the ground in a cloud of dust, her breath escaping her. She gasped terribly as she struggled to regain her air.

Thyso and Oslun rushed in, reaching to help their royal to her feet. She waved off their advances and their concerned expressions. She slowly recovered her lungs and rolled to her knees, standing. As she turned back to her men, a large smile broke across her face and she sharply hoisted her weapon in the required salute.

"Well fought!" The Princess congratulated both men heartily.

"You would have saved my life and ended the fight with that counter!" Thyso spoke sincerely and Oslun basked in the praise. "You have learned swiftly, and I measure that you are rapidly becoming an excellent swordsman!"

"I am only doing as you show." Oslun lowered his head, embarrassed by the praise he received. He had spent much of his life in the shadows, never receiving attention and certainly not praise.

"Oranku!" Halta shouted, flinging her arms around Oslun's neck. "I am so very proud! You are not the boy I met in the tunnel; you are a man of war!"

"Progress is good. Combat will come on us quickly." Wilteph broke into the circle. Hushed whispers passed from mouth to ear. The man had not been seen since the day of the outcast's arrival in the village.

"What combat do you expect?" Layandria turned towards the man, her eyes narrowed.

"We must ride out and strike the Lakemen. We must repay them in blood for the death they have wrought on our people." Wilteph spoke the words of fury, though his voice was flat and his eyes dark.

Layandria stepped forward. "I have dispatched a scout to report on the actions of the Lakemen and I think it unwise to move until he has returned."

Wilteph gestured Layandria back. "I have no interest in the words of your scout. These are not your people lying dead. They are mine. I order that we take our vengeance to our enemy in his own home, and we prepare for this war now."

"Those dead of whom you have spoken were laid to rest by my hands and the hands of these living people." Layandria swung her arms out, drawing the crowded Inohamman in. Though only some thirty stood by, the sounds of shouting drew more in rapidly. The early morning air was light and cool, but the intensity of Layandria's words increased its heat. "While your people lay dead and dying, where were you?"

"It is no business of yours!" Wilteph shouted, lunging forward. He came within inches of Layandria. Though the man bore no weapon, Thyso and Oslun took his move as threat. Both young men stepped in, cloth wrapped swords raised. Thyso caught Wilteph in the side with the flat of his blade, sending the man spinning to the soil. Oslun was on him in a flash, the tip of Devil's Song inches away from Wilteph's left eye.

"Get these foreign goats off me!" Wilteph called as he scanned the observers, looking for someone to step to his aid. None moved.

"Be still Oranku." Halta's gentle voice cooed to Oslun. The cup bearer lifted his blade and stepped back, allowing her approach.

"Thank you, my sister." Wilteph sputtered as he pulled himself to his feet. He turned to face Halta, an inferno in his eyes. "What is our strength, how many can we move with?"

Halta fixed her eyes on his, examining the man's thoughts. "We have three thousand, two hundred and eleven alive."

"That will be enough if we plan our attacks and move in secret." Wilteph turned away and began surveying the crowd. "Tell me, do we have weapons in plenty?"

Halta did not answer. Wilteph turned back to face her in irritation at her silence.

"There are three thousand, two hundred and eleven alive." She repeated the words coldly. "More than twenty thousand called this land home before the Lakemen came to them."

"Yes, I see." Wilteph answered flatly. "Why do you repeat yourself?"

"Brother," Halta softened her voice and lowered her eyes. "The scouts reported the enemy moving on our home and more than eight thousand set out to meet them as the crossed the Bandir River. None survived."

Wilteph stared blankly back, unfazed by what he was told.

"Following this defeat, five and a half thousand met the enemy one day's ride to the west, hoping to stop them before they reached our home." Halta continued. "These were not warriors, not fighters, but men and women fueled by fear and need. They were slain. I have walked on the field where they lie. The birds and scavengers pick at them. They find no peace. Each day, those among us who are able lay them in the soil that rest may come to them. Our enemy murdered more still as he tore through our city. There are three thousand, two hundred and eleven left alive."

Wilteph pushed towards Halta in fury, forcing her to step back. Oslun raised his sword, but Halta stilled him with an open hand, held at her hip where Wilteph could not see. The young Chieftain continued his charge. "I do not care if there are only thirty! We will not let the deeds of the Lakemen go without blood!"

"The blood has already been spilled!" Layandria stepped in between the man and woman, rage pulsing out of her with every syllable. "Thousands on thousands of the people you call your own lay dead and you demand war! These who remain are not warriors! They are the old and the very young! They are the innocent and the wounded! They cannot lift swords!"

"I am Wilteph, son of Talin!" Wilteph pushed Layandria away with his forearm across her chest as if he did not hear her. He shouted to all the gathered Inohamman Wanoak. "I am your Chieftain and I command you to prepare for war! All will march, and all will fight to avenge those who fell before us!"

Tepan and Rale'en strode towards Wilteph, each blazing with intensity. Wilteph turned to them, pleased to see his most loyal companions joining his cause. Rale'en struck Wilteph squarely in his chest with her foot, the impact sending him sprawling back, towards the center of the circle, all his grace and poise lost as he heaped on the ground. Tepan sprang off the ground, soaring as if he were a much lighter and smaller man. The old warrior landed next to Wilteph's head, planting one hand on the Chief's chest and cocking the other high, as if to drive his palm down into Wil's face.

"Hold your tongue, or I'll hold it for you." Tepan snarled the words, his voice menacing even to the enraged Wilteph. "None can claim authorities which they are not given."

"You are no longer my Chieftain!" Rale'en shouted the words for all to hear, her eyes focused on Wilteph.

"Release me!" Wilteph screamed. Release me now!"

Tepan pressed down hard, forcing the breath out of Wil's chest. He suddenly released his grip and stepped back. "Be warned, old friend, I will strike you down if your words suggest the need for it."

"How can you come on me like this?" Wilteph called out, overcome by anger and an immense feeling of shame that only further fueled his madness. "My father was Chieftain of the Wanoak, wrongly put to death! Chieftain Jordache is dead, as are his sons! By blood, I am your Chieftain, wrongly outcast, but returned now in your hour of need! I demand your service!"

"Wrongly outcast?" A grizzled old man shouted from the sideline of the circle. "You willfully violated the laws of our tribe. Then you traded on the love of a father to free yourself from justice. You have no place here."

Halta gently stilled the old man as she approached Wilteph slowly, her empty arms held out at her sides. Wilteph looked at her, but he did not lower his tense stance. "Wil, take a breath and hear me."

"I hear you Halta!" Wilteph cut back.

"You hear my words, but I need you to hear my heart." Halta stopped some ten feet away from the man, her arms still outstretched.

"What is your heart then?" Wil's eyes still blazed, and his face was dark as if he wore a mask.

"Wil, you must put aside your anger and your pride." Halta spoke softly, her voice as a cool breeze. "The pain you must feel at the death of your child, whom you so desperately fought to protect. I cannot imagine this devastation."

"Do not speak of him!" Wilteph screamed and charged at her. He closed the distance fast, his moments precise. He extended his hands and grabbed her by the throat and pulling her into him. Her eyes went wide in the pressure and she fought for air, though none would come. Oslun, Thyso and Tepan charged in, but Halta maintained her composure and warded them off with raised hands.

The woman choked from the grip and Wilteph burned into her. He stepped forward, his leg between hers, catching her heal as he pushed her back. She fell, the man falling with her, his grip never breaking. Halta's legs began to kick out wildly under Wilteph's force, though she kept her hands raised, holding back Oslun and the others.

"I will not let him kill her!" Oslun spoke to no one, but he words were loud and forceful. He swiftly unwrapped the cloth from his sword, watching Halta's face for any sign that she was failing.

"Be still lad." Tepan instructed. "She knows what she is doing and needs no aid from you now."

Wilteph continued to squeeze, his eyes boring into Halta's. The strength in her limbs began to fail under the lack of air. Her legs slowed their movements and her arms lowered to the ground, still Tepan held Oslun back.

"What was his name?" Tepan asked softly, his focus on Wilteph's back. "Wilteph, what was his name?"

"Taolin!" Wilteph screamed. The sound of his son's name escaped from his lips without will, his hands still bearing down on Halta.

"Say it again." Layandria asked calmly.

Wilteph eased his grip slightly, allowing Halta a shallow breath. "His name was Taolin." He said the words as he fully released the woman beneath him. "My son's name was Taolin and he is dead."

Wilteph fell to the ground on his side and began to weep. Halta rolled away, curling in on herself as she drew in air. Oslun rushed to her side, and took her head in his lap, stroking her hair and whispering to her. "Do not leave me Agal'le."

"I'll not leave you Oranku." Halta managed between sharp draws of air.

Layandria knelt near Wilteph's face. The man wept freely, overcome. She looked on the weeping man as she spoke, but her voice carried to all as if the words were meant for each one.

"Your grief is great, as is mine. My father and all who served him are dead, my home taken over by evil men, yet there remains hope for you and I." Layandria's voice grew in strength as she spoke, the words drawing in all those who were near. Wilteph opened his clinched eyes and watched her, though his body still racked with anguish.

"I am faced with choices, as are you." Layandria continued, gathering her own courage. "I choose to act out of love and faith in my companions, not out of the fear and pain that lives in me. I have seen great strength in you, Wilteph, son of Talin. I believe that when your grief has ebbed, you will find inside your heart the same choices. What has happened cannot be mended by swords or blood. Those who have died cannot be reclaimed. All that we can do is guide and protect those that still live."

Wilteph could not speak, his body still shaking with pain. He forced a small nod, knowing finally that his son's life was on his hands, adding to the blood of his father and so many others.

Layandria stood. She turned in a slow circle, taking in the faces of all that were assembled. "We will wait for Jaxus return. He will report on the enemy's movements and we will use that information to guide our own."

"The enemy will return if he learns we have survived!" One of the Inohamman called out from the crowd.

"I am certain that he will." Layandria answered, her voice sure. "And when he does, he will be met not by the shattered remains of a defeated people, but with strong swords and hungry hearts!"

"My Lady," Oslun spoke up, still holding the weakened Halta. "Where will we find these hearts and swords? All that remain are not fit for a battle."

"I propose that we send out riders to each of the Inohamman Tribes." Layandria watched the surrounding Inohamman faces as she spoke, looking for any sign of resistance. "We must go to the Chieftains of the Inohamman and ask them for aid."

"Such a thing has not been done in the lifetime of all our people." Tepan spoke low in council. "Only a Chieftain may order such requests."

"Then we must decide who will lead us." Rale'en spoke the words expectantly. Several of the Inohamman looked back and forth amongst themselves, uncertain of what they should do.

Halta struggled to her feat. She drew in a deep draught of air and forced the words against her damaged throat. "I choose to follow Layandria, of the Metal Men. I will take Layandria as my Chieftain!"

Several voices went up in a low roar of confusion and uncertainty. Thyso stepped to Layandria's side. Oslun followed suit and Halta moved to her back. The four stood in silence, waiting for the response.

"I will follow Layandria." Tepan called up in his unique voice. "So long as she remains the kind of Chieftain that bandages the wounded and cares for the weak."

"I will, with all my strength." Layandria answered confidently, though she did not expect this turn.

"That is enough for me." Tepan grunted and moved to stand next to Thyso.

"And I will follow Layandria." Jaxus voice rose above the crowd as he burst through the gathered masses. He entered the city center and moved to stand before Layandria. His face was badly bruised on one side, his left eye swollen nearly shut. Blood and other human matter clung to his armor and his knuckles were damaged as though they had been used as a hammer.

Layandria smiled, extending her hand to greet Jaxus. Oslun moved side face, opening a space at the Princess' side. Jaxus stepped in and stood proudly next to Layandria.

"What say you, people of the Inohamman Wanoak? Do you choose Layandria, Queen of Arken and Lady of the Shadow as your Chieftain and leader?" Jaxus voice reverberated across the clearing

Layandria cast Jaxus a sideway glance at his addressing her as queen. He turned his face to her, lowering his eyes and his voice. "I feel in my heart that Axeleon is dead and I know that you feel it too."

Layandria nodded in grim confirmation, then raised her head and turned her eyes to the Inohamman. "I will be your leader, if you will choose to follow me."

"Who will stand with us?" Halta called, her strength returning. "Who will follow Queen Layandria?"

Several Inohamman stepped forward, moving to stand behind Layandria and the others. Others hesitated for a moment, then moved to join.

"Queen Layandria!" Tepan screamed savagely, his voice climbing above all others. "Queen Layandria!"

Other voices joined Tepan's as he repeated the address. The sound grew as many more voices rose into the air in unison. They shouted her name and surrounded her. Layandria's face grew hard, hiding the fear she felt.

As the crowd continued to shout her name, hands raised high in the air, Layandria turned to face those closest to her. She looked on Halta, Oslun, Jaxus, Tepan, Rale'en and Thyso, focusing on each one as she spoke. "I cannot lead these people alone. I will need all of your council and all the strength you can give."

"We will give all." Rale'en clapped Layandria on the shoulder of her armor.

"Then I will give my life to the service of yours." The weight temporarily lifted from Layandria's heart. "We must send out to the other tribes at once."

Layandria narrowed her eyes and lowered her voice, speaking only to her close companions. "Two riders will go to each Chieftain. I and Tepan, Oslun and Halta, Thyso and Rale'en, Jaxus and one other."

"My Lady," Halta spoke up, adopting the courtesy Jaxus used. "The Xonar are south and their village is a three day ride."

"Rale'en, do you know this land?" Layandria waited for Rale'en's confirmation. "You and Thyso will go there."

Halta continued. "The Takkar and DaVasl villages are hours apart. It would be best for one group to go to both. Takkar Chief Warrot is friendly to us and will be easily swayed, but you will need his support to convince DaVasl Chieftain Barbas."

"I and Tepan will go there." Layandria decided. Tepan dropped his chin sharply in agreement.

"The Nordan Tribe is slightly more than a two day ride and I have dealt with Chieftain Zinan before." Halta planned out quickly. The fervor of the crowd was dying around them, the people losing interest in this quiet conversation.

"My Queen," Tepan broke in. "I am old and well trusted by our people. I should remain here and continue to rebuild the structures and their spirits. Let Jaxus go with you. I should think Chieftain Warrot would respond well to Jaxus manner."

Layandria considered this quickly, Jaxus return bringing freshness to her anger with the man, coupled with a strange comfort and delight that she could not shake. "It will be as you say. Look after Wilteph. I fear he has not come to the end of his turmoil."

Tepan again dropped his chin in compliance, please to see the young woman taking heed of council. This was not something either of his recent Chieftains were often willing to do.

Layandria lifted her eyes to the gathered crowd. She drew in a breath and sent her voice out, silencing the murmuring crowd. "We will ride to the Chieftains of the Inohamman tribes to gain their support for our defense. Until I return, Tepan will lead you as you continue to rebuild and comfort your families. When we return, it will be with the gathered strength of the Inohamman at our backs!"

The crowd sent up a cheer that shook the earth. Layandria swelled with a mixture of pride and the weight of the responsibility now thrust on her. Packs were readied quickly, and horses were mounted. Tepan mapped directions for Jaxus. The guards at the gate opened the heavy structures and they rode out at a quick pace.

As the pairs began to separate off in their needed direction, Layandria called out to them. "Be swift and sure. Do your best to gather the tribes, but do not delay long against resistant hearts."

Halta spurned her horse into a rapid pace. Oslun, mounted on his own beast, matching her pace, his confidence soaring and his joy complete to be with her on this quest.

"Is there hope, Jaxus?" Layandria asked in earnest. "Real hope?"

"There is, Your Grace." The black night answered back, "There is hope as long as you believe in it."

"I choose to believe." Layandria stared directly into is eyes.

"And that is why you are different." Jaxus answered back, returning her solemn gaze. "That is why I follow you. Backs against the wall and only a whisper of a chance remaining, the strong cling to hope."

23

Aralias smiled as the towers of the Argarnoth Stronghold came into view. The Wolf Lord knew from the number of civilians that his armies had encountered during their travels that the stronghold had been overrun and flame set to the buildings. Despite the charring, the bones of the fortress were reported to be intact. More important to Aralias, Argarnoth was near enough to the Starrowlands rear elements to be used as a base for his striking teams. The city around the fortress was completely abandoned, allowing the wolves to move without detection.

The trek from the Arkenhead was a long one and the ships had not been full of comfort. Lord Aralias hated being on the ocean. As a boy, his father had often told him that their ancestors were great travelers on the water and had come to Arken by ships when their island home of Carenbon was destroyed by volcanic eruption.

None of this gave the Wolf Lord any comfort as the rocking of the massive ships turned his stomach several times over. Once on land and recovered from his unpleasant disposition, Lord Aralias marched his troops at once. A full day covered the distance and now, as they approached the stronghold, the men let their fatigue wash over them. They passed through the city, the empty buildings and remnants of life surrounded them. Bodies lay wrecked in the place, flies and scavengers eating their fill. The men took in the sights but let them pass away, choosing to save these torments for another day.

The Wolf Army was well experienced in death. For centuries the unoathed savages and the Chokahr Tribes that called the Derrenge Mountains their lands had been a nuisance. Twice in Aralias life they had mounted serious forces and attacked towns and villages, giving the men and women of the Wolf Army great experience in death and warfare.

The troops took to bed on the cold stone of the stronghold while Aralias and his commanders moved to the keep. In just hours the first striking force would depart. The concept was sound, but Aralias was not free of concerns. Sending out small forces allowed for swift movement, quick strikes and less chance of the whole force being discovered. Of course, the small forces were highly vulnerable. Aralias did not want to see his men destroyed, but failure to act would likely result in the defeat of the Fire and Elk armies. To assuage his guilt over the risk he forced on his men, Aralias committed himself to leading the first assault.

He laid down on the floor, soot sticking to the palms of his hands. He did not bother to remove his armor, knowing that he would not find comfort or sleep. He closed his eyes and let his thoughts drift. In what felt like less than minutes, a young boy roused him, calling softly as he shook the Lord's shoulder. "Lord Aralias, it is time to move out, as you requested."

"When you wake a man," Aralias spoke gruffly, brushing the boy's hand away and sitting up. "Shout loudly and rouse him. I thought you were attempting to rock me to sleep with the soft touch of a wet nurse."

"I could put a wet nurse to good use about now." A large, barrel chested warrior across the room growled with feigned ferocity.

"Why?" Aralias stood and rubbed the weariness from his eyes. "Have you recently given birth? I was not aware you were with child."

The big man laughed, and several others in the room chuckled. Aralias walked across the room causally, examining the man's belly as if curious.

"Now, I understand how a person might not see that you were carrying an infant in you." The Wolf Lord prodded the man in his stomach. "I would not be surprised if you had an entire smithy in there, which if true, is a great benefit and I demand that you begin producing new blades at once."

The group laughed hearty. Another wolf stepped in and jabbed the large man's stomach. "Do you have a brothel in there? I could use something good to feed my other hungers!"

Aralias turned to the new jester. "So, you are saying that the hunger of your loins can only be satisfied by what is inside Goganr?"

Goganr struck a seductive pose and giggled in his best impression of a loose maiden. They all fell into deep laughter, several hardened men and women breaking into poses and catcalling the others.

Aralias was glad to see his warriors in good spirits. It would not be long before many of them were dead. Perhaps himself as well. He pushed the thought down. The Wolf Lord carefully checked his weapons and tightened the straps of his armor. "Goganr!"

The barrel-chested man dropped his seductive pose at once, coming to attention. Goganr towered over Aralias, his molted grey brown armor making him resemble a fur wall or a large blanket hung up. Aralias focused on the warrior's small eyes. "Rouse the men, get them water and good meat. We will move in the hour."

"Yes, My Lord." Goganr turned with a snap and strode into the adjoining chambers. Aralias removed a folded map from inside his breast plate and spread it out on the charred top of a stone table.

It was a two hour walk north west to Yarran, where Lady Kaowith camped her reserve forces. The Starrowlands reserves were said to be only thirty minutes from Argarnoth, dispersed in a wide line from east to west. The line of combat was somewhere in the space between, though local informers could not pinpoint the exact distance.

Apparently, the combat had grown stale, with both sides taking heavy losses as they gained territory, then fell back. Fighting was brutal, with many dead spent on each scrap of dirt won. The Starrowlanders had cannon and mortar at their disposal, but they were countered by Lady Kaowith's flechette launchers and catapults.

"Lord Aralias." Goganr ducked under the door frame, his massive body dominating the entrance. "There is a runner from Lady Kaowith."

Aralias looked up from his map in shock. He did not think anyone knew they were here, but this runner had found them within hours of their arrival at the stronghold. "Send him in."

A woman, clad in the armor of the fire fist, concealed under a sandy brown cloak stepped past the massive wolf solider and approached the Lord. Her face was homely, large cheeks and a sharp chin contrasting to eyes that were the hue of mud. There was the hardness of combat in her and Aralias noted several scars on her armor. She bowed stiffly to the Lord.

"I ask your name, messenger." Aralias asked in slight suspicion.

"I am Kellen, Wolf Lord." The woman rose from her bow. Her voice was airy and beautiful, not at all what Aralias expected to emit from a woman who appeared so. "I bear greetings from Lady Kaowith and thanks for the aid of your army."

"Tis a little army, and I fear not much aid." Lord Aralias spoke calmly, examining the woman's eyes, watching for a glint or a feeling that might tell him if she were to be trusted.

Kellen looked around the room hastily and leaned in towards Lord Aralias. "Lady Kaowith bids that I ask after Lord Nathus. She also sends her thanks that you did not travel with him as his stench would likely give away your position to the enemy."

Aralias chuckled in good spirit. He recalled how two years past, during the annual summit in the Arkenhead, Lady Kaowith was seated next to Lord Nathus in banquet. The Lord had given great flirtations to her and she was repulsed by them, remarking that he had the smell of a man who rolled in the shit of a pig. Nathus became angry and stormed from the hall, withdrawing from the citadel and returning to the Iron Fist immediately. Later that evening, after the Fire Lady and Wolf Lord had shared of their bodies, Aralias commented the Lady was the bravest he had known to so accurately and viciously describe Nathus stench before the King. The moment became a point of some hilarity between the two nobles for that moment on.

"Indeed, the man smells of pig shit and the Lady Kaowith is quite welcomed for our leaving the vile man in the north." Aralias offered, accepting that this woman could be trusted. "How is it that you have come to find us so easily?"

"My Lord Wolf," Kellen bowed again, "there are many left alive in the south that send word back to our forces. News of your arrival reached us nearly as your boots touched the docks."

"I am glad to hear that your networks remain." Aralias allowed. He was concerned though. Information had its keen way of finding ears that were not meant to hear. "So what message does the Lady of Flame send to the Wolf's den?

"My Lady sends word that we would be best served if you and your men could determine where the enemy leader is and once identified, infiltrate and kill him." Kellen stood by, waiting for the response expectantly, though what she was given was not expected.

Lord Aralias reared back his head and laughed mightily. "This is nothing! We will have it done within the day! If the task she wishes were so simple, why has Lady Kaowith not done it already?"

The Wolf Lord's humor surprised Kellen, but she chose to ignore this child Lord and press on with the delivery of her message. "Word of Axise death has not yet reached the Starrowlanders. Those we have captured remain in the belief that their leader holds the throne. They further hold to ideal once our lines are swept away, they will be welcomed into our capitol as vanquishing heroes. Though, their taste for combat is waning and they engage us only in small harassing elements, testing for weaknesses and no doubt, hunting the Fire Lady and Elk Lord personally, seeking to break our leadership and morale."

"Is it your belief that if their leaders were to be dealt with, the whole of the army would then, do what, surrender to us in weeping mass?" Lord Aralias looked at the woman with an expression somewhere between disbelief and an accusation of all out lunacy.

Kellen maintained her bearing. "My Lady is not so foolish as to think that. What we believe is that once their leader is killed, the Starrowlanders will be thrown into chaos. We have learned that while Axise was with them, he insisted that no other would issue orders for movement or combat. Whoever is leading them now commands much the same way. This commander has not shown his face in battle, which leads us to accept that it is critical that his life be preserved, having no other, or only few to replace him."

Aralias narrowed his eyes, thinking through the ideas that fluttered through his mind. "The Fire Soldiers have learned a great deal, and the knowledge will be put to use, though I am curious, how is it that you have not discovered the location or identity of their commander from those you have captured?"

"The soldiers we have captured are curiously unwilling to give information that is of use, even under the threat of death." Kellen allowed a shade of irritation to show through her voice and expression.

"That is because you have not followed through on the threats or offered up a path that would make death seem the more desirable course." Aralias voice carried the scorn given to children who do not know simple facts.

"It is against the laws of Arken to kill prisoners without fair trial." Kellen stepped back slightly against the brace of the Wolf Lord's seditious statement.

"I and my men have kept the northern borders safe for generations through cost of blood. The Wolf Lord did not raise his voice, but the intensity increased by a large margin. "Do not quote the law of war to me, I have no time, nor enough men to operate in this manner. We will conduct our skirmishes and discover what we must, in our way, free of judgment from those whose taste of battle is new."

"Yes, My Lord." Kellen bowed in deference to the Lord's authority. She struggled to conceal her distaste with this odd looking, little Lord who so easily violated the honor of law.

Aralias softened his stance. "You may tell Lady Kaowith that when the sky is lit in green, she must attack at force along the full line of the enemy's front. She must have her forces, and those of Lord Brustic prepared, for this is the signal that we are moving on the enemy commander."

"I will inform My Lady of your needs." Kellen bowed and turned away. She had to duck under the massive Goganr's arm as she passed through the door.

As soon as Kellen exited, Aralias addressed his commanders. "We will continue forward as we have planned. Though we must put in effort to find the identity of the commander."

Aralias moved out of the keep, gathering his men for the first assault. The soldiers stretched and gathered their gear, following their Lord. They assembled in the charred courtyard of the fortress. Aralias briefed them on their mission and the responsibility of each. Once the needed information was disseminated, they departed, spreading out their formation as they passed through a damaged portion of the wall.

The men walked on for nearly two hours in what seemed too many as a random wandering series of switches and cutback. Finally, after a long, sweeping loop, Aralias maneuvered them into position some one hundred yards from the pitched tents of a small reserve camp. There were few guards patrolling the perimeter, the rest of the force under cover, taking rest.

Aralias looked to his left and right, seeing that his men were in position. He raised his arm and dropped it quickly. On the signal, his designated archers fired their arrows at the patrolling guards. Experience and the strong light of the high moon aided the archers. Their arrows struck true. As soon as the arrows were fired, Aralias signaled again, three quick motions of his arm. The wolves rose and surged towards the tents as a great wave builds in silence before it breaks.

Aralias estimated that there were some two hundred men in the camp. His thirty five soldiers would charge straight through the camp, killing all they could without getting bogged down. Aralias drew his sword as he pushed forward, reaching the first row of tents in the lead. As he passed between two tents, a soldier exited on his left. The man did not see Aralias and the sword found his chest before the enemy could acknowledge the attack. Aralias kicked the man in the stomach, freeing his blade, Ancient Fire as it was known. He dug his feet into the silt and moved on. The sounds of his men finding targets reached his ears. Torches were put to tents and screams of fear and pain went up.

Aralias pushed deeper into the camp. The Starrowlanders began to react to the sounds of fighting, exiting their tents with weapons at the ready. Aralias closed on a large woman who wore no armor and no clothes but wielded a menacing back cut sword. The woman had clearly been sleeping, roused by the sounds of incursion. Aralias was impressed that she had taken to combat without worry for clothing. Many would not have reacted with this priority.

Aralias dove in, sweeping the woman's blade down and away with his sword as he buried his knife into her chest, just above and inside her left breast. The woman screamed horribly and fell to the dirt, a large cloud of dust coming up around her. Aralias pushed on, entering the center of the camp. Several of the wolves followed almost in step with Aralias. The enemy was beginning to form organized resistance and Aralias determined that the wolves must change their course.

"Ramulith! Ramulith!" Aralias shouted the code word and his men immediately began to repeat it. Ramulith Outpost lies on the north western border of the Wolf Fist. Its twin, the Mallin Outpost is near the eastern edge of the fist. The soldiers of the wolf fist understood that calling the name of Ramulith directed them to turn, departing the camp to the west, while Mallin would direct them to move to the east. Were

Aralias to call out Derrenge, the men would press through to the north and Kanamar directed them to cut back south.

Aralias darted across the center of the camp, seeing four enemy soldiers take up a loose formation in his path. As he ran, he sheathed his sword and drew a short bow from his back, fitting and firing three arrows in short succession. Two of the enemy were felled, the arrows striking their exposed faces. The third arrow missed its mark low, grazing the man's neck, but causing no serious damage. Aralias closed the distance and returned his bow to his back, drawing his sword. He moved to the right, as if to take the man on that side first. The defending Starrowlanders shifted their stance to counter.

At the last step, Aralias darted left. His smaller frame was more agile than most and his speed was stunning. The two Starrowlands defenders were not prepared and Aralias slashed his sword across the belly of the man on the left. He did not pause to attack the other, pressing through and granting the defender his life for another day. Aralias entered the tents again, smoke billowing up from several that were blazing away. His eyes caught sight of a large cache of powder used for cannon and mortar. The powder was stored in waxed canvas bags which were piled higher than most men.

Aralias spun and took up a torch from one of the tents, wheeling back around and sprinting towards the cache. A stout looking man stepped out from between the tents as Aralias passed. The man raised a large ax to strike, but Aralias was faster, smashing the flaming end of the torch into the man's face. The man let out a terrible scream and dropped his weapon, raising his hands to his damaged face. Aralias sped on. He closed the distance to the powder and threw the torch into the pile. The canvas bags caught slowly, affording time for escape.

As he turned back, Aralias saw that the man whose face he had burned was still standing, stumbling in slow circles, unable to see and screaming madly in pain. The Wolf Lord neared the edge of the camp as the powder cache exploded. The blast was far more powerful than he had imagined, throwing flaming canvas and wood high into the air. Aralias smiled, knowing that some of these remnants would fall on the tents in the camp, no doubt igniting and spreading destruction.

As Aralias passed between two tents, coming to the edge of the camp, he could see the backs of his men moving away at a rapid pace. They would continue until the camp was far behind, then turn south, making their return to the Argarnoth slowly to ensure that they were not followed.

A young woman, clothed in soft, billowy white stood by the mouth of the last tent. She was dark skinned, with long dark hair falling down her back, tied with a white ribbon. She was clearly frightened and uncertain, unable to find safety. Aralias grabbed her arm, pulling her forward.

"You will come with me and do as I say. If you struggle or attempt to escape, you will die." Aralias naturally high voice took on a hissing menace as he pulled the woman along. She stumbled, but his firm grip on her arm prevented her from falling. "Do not make a sound, or your throat will be cut."

The woman did not speak as she struggled to keep pace with Lord Aralias' stunningly fast motion. The pair moved off after the wolves as others exited the village behind them. Three hundred yard ahead, the raiders took up positions beyond a low rise in the loose soil. Aralias glanced over his shoulder and saw that behind him were nine of his men, pursued by some fifteen Starrowlanders.

Lord Aralias launched himself over the rise, dragging the woman behind him. He threw her down on the silt and ordered one of his men to bind her. Aralias drew his bow and lay down, barely seeing over the rise. As the last of his men passed him, he loosed an arrow aimed at the pursuing enemy. His men followed suit as he fitted another arrow and fired. The Starrowlanders were downed in three volleys. Aralias stood and directed his men to move south, cutting towards a large outcropping of red stone that would give them cover from the enemy and offer no footprints.

Smoke rose from the camp and he knew no more would come. He counted his men and was gladdened to see that all were accounted for. He ordered one to get the woman to her feet and bring her along while those with bleeding wounds were cared for. A single careless drip of blood on soil could lead the enemy to their doorstep.

It took the raiders nearly three hours to reach Argarnoth, winding through several cutbacks to disguise their destination. Once returned to relative safety, Lord Aralias ordered his men to rest and discovered that several other raiding parties had already departed, another preparing to move out as the first returned. Based on reports, the wolves counted sixty eight enemy slew or seriously wounded in the first attack. This positive result was due largely to complete surprise, a benefit that would not long last.

Aralias approached the woman, kneeling next to her as she sat, propped up against the charred wall of the keep. Her white garments were heavily soiled with sweat and soot from the burned out fortress.

"No harm will come to you." Aralias spoke soothingly. "Answer my questions, attempt no escape and all will be well with you."

"Please, sir," The woman shook in fear as she spoke. "Do not bed me."

Aralias scoffed. "Bed you? If you mean that I would take your body by force, have no fear. Men of Arken are forbidden from this vile act under penalty of death."

The woman's eyes did not convey belief. "Is that not why you took me?"

"No, it was not for your body that I took you." Aralias moved to sit, stretching his armored legs out in front of him. "I have need for information, not victims."

"And your men," the woman cast her eyes towards the others in the room who were in varying states of rest, "what are their needs?"

Aralias allowed a kind smile. "They have no needs of the kind you fear. Though I do wonder, what is your role in the army of the Starrowlands that you would be dressed as you are?"

The woman's expression grew pained. "I was taken from my home in Gilfring, far from this place. I and my sister were made to dress well and dance for the men after they returned from battle. Our bodies were often used for their pleasure. My sister was hanged when it was found that she had become with child."

"Good woman, I give you my word as Lord of the Wolf Fist and a son of Arken that no harm will come to you of this kind. You will be kept well unless you force my hand by deception or subterfuge." Aralias kept his voice calm and even, reassuring the woman with his tone. "I need to know where to find the man that commands the armies, that is all."

The woman's eyes grew wide with renewed fear. "I do not know this my lord! Please do not hang me!"

"I have already given you assurance that you will not be harmed." Aralias confirmed softly. "I am to leave now. You will remain here with my men. Though you will be bound, you will be fed and given a place of comfort to rest. While I am away, think on all that you have seen. Try to remember who gave orders, who the soldiers feared. You may know things through observation that simply have not occurred to you. We will speak on this when I return."

"Thank you, My Lord!" The woman sputtered between her tears.

"There is no need for thanks." Aralias stood and tightened his sword belt. "You have suffered at the hands of vile men. You may thank me when they are all ripped from this life by the swords of my wolves."

Aralias turned without further word and exited the room, joining his men as they prepared to move on another camp in the cover of the waning night.

24.

"My people tell me that you have come to my feet with request for my aid in war. Is this true?" Chieftain Warrot sat in a large chair at the end of a massive rectangular table. He was a tall man, with skin darker than that of the Wanoak and hair of golden sunlight falling carelessly around his shoulders. The Chieftain was older, his skin bore creases of deep wrinkles and his belly jutted out over the waist band of his dark leather pants. He wore no shirt exposing a light dusting of golden hair that adorned his chest.

"Yes, Chieftain Warrot." Layandria started out with a deep breath, unsure of how to handle the conversation. She had witnessed her father giving such briefings several times but seeing did not equate to confidence. "The Inohamman Wanoak have been invaded and attacked by the Lakemen. Their population has been reduced to barely more than three thousand and they cannot withstand another assault."

The old chief considered the news for a moment, scratching at the short stubble that grew on his chin. "If the attacks have come and gone, the death already done, what need do you have for my warriors?"

"I have sent a scout to determine the intent of the enemy." Layandria was surprised at the ease with which she found the words. She was nervous, her palms sweating, though she felt in control of her thoughts. Perhaps it was her lineage that gave her the sense for this type of dealing. "My scout has reported that the enemy determined the ease of their victory was an omen. They are now rearming and preparing to move out, intent on furthering their conquest to control all that the Wanoak call their own."

Chieftain Warrot narrowed his eyes suspiciously at the report. "How did this scout find such detailed information?"

Layandria nodded to Jaxus.

"I am the scout who gathered this report." Jaxus face was impassive as he addressed the old man. "I followed the tracks of the enemy for two days which brought me to their encampment at the lakes. I infiltrated the holding during the night and stole into the dwelling of their leaders. They were unaware of my presence and were not cautious with conversation on their plans as they took freely of strong drink in celebration of their victory."

Jaxus paused as a servant presented him with cool water. "The armies were dispatched on the Wanoak to exact revenge, in payment for blood spilled by the Chieftain of the Wanoak Outcasts. Their orders were to raze the Wanoak villages to the ground. When the armies returned to their masters on the lake, reporting good battles and easy victory, the so-called Gods of the Lake determined that they should take the land of the Wanoak as their own, expanding their borders and increasing their power. Their soldiers will take rest in their homeland, replace the losses to their ranks and move within four to six days' time."

The Chieftain picked up a wooden cup filled with a deep red liquid. He drew a good swallow before raising his eyes to ponder Jaxus. "I see this from the two sides of a stone. I cannot allow land that has belonged to my people for more generations than are recorded to fall to any other, though the law of our nations has long held that each tribe wars of its own accord and this conflict was begat by the Wanoak."

"If what you say is true, your skills as a scout rival any I have ever known. I see also that your armor aids you in this task, though the marring of your face suggests your escape from the home of the Lakemen was one of great excitement." Chieftain Warrot let his gaze linger on Jaxus damaged face. The dark warrior did not shift. "Still, you survived to bring this report, suggesting uncommon skill. Also, though it may surprise you to know this, your metal skin is not a new sight to me. You are a Jurin man, or at the least, you have killed a Jurin and taken his clothing for your own, either way, this is an impressive piece of information."

Jaxus eyes widened slightly and his face changed to a mixture of barely perceptible surprise. It had been several decades since anyone had identified his origin. "I am Jurin."

"Then it is of no surprise to me that you are able to move as a ghost." The Chief swallowed of the red drink again, setting the cup down on the table harshly, the liquid sloshing out. "Some forty suns past, when I was not yet Chieftain of the Inohamman Takkar, a Jurin came to us. His name was Taleel and he wore armor much the same as yours."

"I knew the man, when I was very young." Jaxus regained his impassive countenance. "Though, I've no memory of his word or deed."

"He stayed with us for some years, teaching my people knowledge in the arts of agriculture, writing and building. We wished greatly for Taleel to stay with us, but the man never seemed content among our people. After a time, he departed to the west, venturing on into lands we have never explored. He has not been heard of by my people since that age." Chief Warrot grew silent, letting memories pass over his mind.

"Jaxus," Layandria spoke tentatively, in hushed words from the corner of her mouth. "How old are you?"

The Knight turned his face to the Queen, his eyebrow raised. He did not speak.

"I had thought you to be possibly as old as twenty nine or thirty, possibly as young as twenty two, but if you knew this Taleel, who was here forty years ago, you must be older than I imagined."

Jaxus sighed and folded his hands on the table while Chieftain Warrot gnawed gristle off a bone of some unknown animal. "I am two hundred and twenty nine years in age, My Queen."

Layandria smiled deeply and let slip a small chuckle. "Jaxus, be truthful."

Chieftain Warrot cleared his throat loudly, speaking past the bone that was still clenched in the corner of his teeth. "Lady, the Jurin men do not age as most others, often living several hundred suns. Taleel himself was nearing his five hundredth summer when he departed our land."

"How can this be?" Layandria's mouth hung open in awe and she chocked on her breath. "I have heard the stories of the Jurin men, but I must confess that I considered them to be nothing more than exaggerated children's tales."

"They are truth, My Queen." Jaxus confirmed without a shade of emotion, though inside his mind, he was a whirl with memories shrouded in the impenetrable mist of time.

Chieftain Warrot took the bone from his mouth, throwing it to a small black dog that circled the legs of the table. "I do not know these children's stories that you speak of, but I know that the Jurin men are not fable. If you have one on your side, I suggest that you keep him there. These men make powerful allies, though they often make much more powerful enemies."

"Thank you for your wisdom, Chieftain Warrot." Layandria acknowledged the advice, though her mind was wild with thoughts of

Jaxus and the strange character he presented over the years she had known the man.

The old Chieftain rubbed his clouded eyes, bringing Layandria back into focus. "While the presence of a Jurin in your council gives me comfort, I am curious as to why a Queen from the lands east of the mountains is here asking for support on behalf of the Wanoak. Where is Chieftain Jordache? Or one of his leaders?"

"If you will allow me, My Queen." Jaxus shot his words out before Layandria could speak. She nodded her consent. "Chieftain Jordache was felled in battle. We were with the outcasts, led by Chieftain Wilteph, son of Talen, when we discovered the plight of the Wanoak. Chieftain Wilteph abstained from taking leadership of the tribe and the people chose Queen Layandria until such a time as peace had been regained and the tribe has strengthened."

"So, you are Chieftain of the Inohamman Wanoak now? Am I correct in this?" Chief Warrot lowered his brow to Layandria.

She cleared her throat softly and leaned forward. "I am."

The old tribal leader drummed his fingers on the table several times, staring intently at Layandria. "Is it your intent to keep this title for yourself?"

Layandria did not hesitate. "No. My intention is to see the Wanoak through this conflict and to aid them in selecting a new leader who is one of their own."

"Hmm." Warrot resumed scratching at the stubble on his chin. "You do not intend to stay in this land?"

"My home is to the east, over the mountains. I was forced to flee for my safety, and I know not what I will find when I return, but every moment I spend away from my people, I feel a pull on my heart growing." Layandria's eyes shown earnest and her voice was steadfast. "I will see the Wanoak through the fight before them, but as soon as may be done, I and my men will return to our home."

"This one has no home to return to." Chieftain Warrot gestured to Jaxus as he spoke.

Layandria furrowed her brow. "His home is in Arken."

Chief Warrot grunted. He felt it strange that this Queen did not know the most basic facts about the man she traveled with, yet so adamantly spoke of his belonging to her. "It is said that the Jurin never find rest in any place, ever seeking the comfort of home, but never finding. Taleel told me once that he did not think he would ever find true peace unless he returned to his homeland, though he believed that this was not possible in the current age."

"Did Taleel ever say why he felt this way?" Layandria wanted to understand, but all she could recall of the stories of the Jurin had said they left their home to spread their power and influence throughout the world, but their arrogance forced them largely into hiding as their numbers diminished.

"We are forever drawn to our homeland, but the world is full of those who would not see us regain it." Jaxus took over the telling, his voice growing dark, his eyes distant and empty. "The Jurin developed great science and knowledge. The leaders of the kingdoms of this world fear that if the Jurin returned, they would become more powerful than could be contained. They fear the knowledge that could be cultivated. For that reason, the island that my people call home is ever watched and any who return to it are hunted."

"Perhaps when we return to Arken, we can take an army across the sea and help you secure your home." Layandria spoke the words with hope, though she knew there was little to spare.

"That would not be possible, My Queen." Jaxus spoke sternly, no longer desiring to speak on his home. He turned his eyes to the old chief. "We must move out in the morning to make our way to the Inohamman DaVasl in search of their support. Do we go with the strength of the Inohamman Takkar at our backs?"

Warrot cast his eyes back and forth from Layandria to Jaxus. He was silent for several minutes. "You will have five thousand of my warriors. They will be prepared to move to the Wanoak city in two days. I will go to Chieftain Barbas. He will not listen to any other, though I have sway over his eyes and can secure his support. He will not grant us his men if he knows the Wanoak are led by one who is not of our people, so you must not reveal yourself at this time. I will come myself to the Wanoak lands in no more than four days, with all that Chieftain Barbas can spare."

"Thank you, great Chieftain Warrot." Layandria was grateful and her voice broke as the weight was lifted from her heart.

"The Inohamman tribes have not been united in many generations. We do so now for the Wanoak people and their need." As the Chieftain lifted his voice, he seemed to grow younger and stronger in his chair. "Do not take this as a gesture of loyalty to you. When the fighting is over, release your hold over the Wanoak and allow them to find a leader of their own blood or the weapons at your side will swiftly be turned against you."

Layandria's eyes widened. She began to think of what assurances she could offer this man, but he held up his hand and silenced her.

"If your intention is pure, the threat need not be regarded as more than words." Warrot lowered his hand and softened, seeming to shrink back into his seat. The wrinkles and sun spots on his skin seamed to deepen. "If you wish to remain here for the night, I will have beds laid out for you."

Layandria considered the conversation quickly. She glanced to Jaxus. *Should we depart and return to the Wanoak, or would we be better served to remain and see Warrot off as he leaves for the DaVasl?"*

Jaxus eyes remained focused on the old chieftain. His expression did not change, though Layandria heard his response clearly. *"I do not doubt this man or his words. I believe we would be better served to return to the Wanoak as they will likely need the support of their Queen."*

Layandria turned back to Chieftain Warrot. "We will depart back to the Wanoak. We will make camp on the plains tonight, but the courage of the people will be much raised at the news of your support."

"My men will see you out of the city when you are ready. Be glad, Layandria, Queen in the East, you do not stand alone." The Chieftain rose and exited the tent.

Jaxus and Layandria followed suit. They were led out of the city by two young warriors who provided them will full skins of water before they departed. The sun began to descend behind them as they moved away. Layandria estimated that they would have three hours of light to travel by before they would be forced to make camp for the night.

As they walked on in silence, Layandria's mind churned over the information she had gained about her companion. Knowing his true age seemed to fit in her mind. Jaxus had a wealth of knowledge that few others could rival. His field craft and skills with all manner of weapons were above any equal. The man understood the histories of many cultures in a way that suggested personal experience rather than scholarly learning. The man had lived several lifetimes, but was, by all she had learned, in the younger years of his expected span.

The sun fell faster than Layandria expected and soon, Jaxus stopped and began to set up camp. Layandria stood by, watching his graceful motions. She knew she should down her pack and begin to set up her bed, or prepare a meal, but her mind was so full of questions and wonder that she found herself frozen in place. Jaxus did not appear to notice her lack of action.

"Do you find it lonely?" Layandria broke the silence as Jaxus began to strike his tinder against the flat of his knife, sparking the kindling of his carefully set fire.

He raised his eyes and investigated hers. The intensity of his gaze made Layandria uncomfortable, though she did not know why. "Do I find what lonely, Your Grace?"

"To live so long among people who at their best live only a fraction of your time." The Queen let her voice trail off, her thoughts not fully formed. "So many you have known have died. That cannot be an easy life to live."

"It is not." Jaxus returned his focus to the fire, stoking it and adding sticks from his pack as he saw fit to coax the perfect flame.

"Why do you never speak of your history? Layandria asked in trepidation. She felt that she had learned more on this day than she had ever known of Jaxus, but the information also made her feel as if the man was more a stranger to her than he had ever been.

"There are many who would not be pleased to know a Jurin walks among them." Jaxus did not look up, turning to his pack and removing his rolled mattress. "Though I find myself pleased that you are not among them."

Layandria grew silent, her mind driving off. She downed her pack and slowly removed her armor. She looked to Jaxus several times as she smoothed out the mattress and began to gather a meal for herself, wanting to speak, but not finding the correct words.

Jaxus finished his preparations and sat on his bed, his meal before him but untouched. He watched Layandria. "What is it that troubles you, My Lady?"

"It is nothing, Sir." Layandria looked down at her food and though she was hungry after the days walk, she found it unappealing. She looked up and saw that Jaxus was still starring at her across the low fire. The light of the flame shown off the man's face and Layandria was struck by the curves and angles of his features, softened by the short, dark beard that had grown in the days since their departure from the Arkenhead.

She summoned the courage and the words ran out of her like a strong flowing river. "I would think it lonely and hard to live such a life. Would I want to marry and have children, knowing that I would outlive my husband, and my offspring? Would I know if my blood carried long life to my children? Would I want it to, knowing the hardships that it would bring to them? Would I be able to find even friends to spend my days with knowing that I will outlive them all?"

"I have been on this earth for two centuries, My Lady, but I would not say that I have lived the time." Jaxus voice hung in the night air, sadness lingering in the cool breeze.

"I do not understand." Layandria responded quietly, her mind struggling to see through Jaxus mask.

"A person has need to feel alive." Jaxus voice was hollow, as if he were not speaking to Layandria. "I remember that feeling, when I was a boy, with my mother. She has been dead longer that I care to say, and I have not felt as though I have truly lived since her passing."

Layandria was embarrassed to admit that she could not grasp the feeling her companion conveyed. She said nothing, allowing the man silence in his thoughts.

Jaxus stood and came to Layandria's side. He towered over her, his eyes dark and full of pain. "Do you trust me?"

"Yes." Layandria said the word without hesitation, though her body was alive, tingling in fear.

"I will show you." Jaxus breathed the words. He slowly lowered himself to his knees and sat on the mattress in front of his royal. He took her hands in his without word. Layandria's breath came in sharp bursts. She felt a strange hunger and desire building inside of her as the man touched her skin. She felt him in her mind as she looked into his eyes. *Close your eyes. Walk with me.*

Layandria felt fear and intense hunger climb up her spine in tandem. She starred into Jaxus eyes, uncertain, but she felt as if he were pulling her into him. As she let her lids fall closed, she could see as if she were looking through Jaxus memories. People and places that were foreign to her swam about as reflections on a pool. She saw a woman, strong and beautiful smiling warmly, her face youthful and full of love. The woman embraced her and held her close. The warmth of the tender body spread through Layandria and she felt as though she were safe, both comforted and loved in a way that she had never felt before. The woman released her and Layandria saw her features transformed, weariness and sadness in her expression. The woman stepped backwards, fading away, entering a fog as she moved, tears running freely down her face.

An intense emptiness filled Layandria as she watched the woman disappear. The Queen walked among massive trees, larger than even those in the outcast's home. Strange structures and stone with writing of a language and symbol that she had never seen. The emptiness persisted, growing stronger as time passed. She boarded a small ship and pushed out to sea, looking back as a lush island fell away, swallowed up in the mist. The emptiness turned to a feeling that was biting and cold inside of her. She wanted to separate from the intense loss that enraptured her heart, to climb over the edge of the boat and slide under the water, letting it cleanse away the pain and sorrow. The desire was not quenched. Layandria was rooted to the structure of the wooden boat as the waves churned around her.

She came to land on a foreign shore. Peoples that resembled no other she had seen greeted her. She walked among them and learned of their ways, though the hollowness in her soul remained. After a time, she began to feel as if she were wrong to walk among these people. She was not one of them, theirs was not her home, so she left their land.

As she moved on, finding new peoples and new lands, the emptiness of her heart grew. A longing for the comfort of the woman's embrace accompanied her everywhere she moved. She watched the people that she traveled among. She saw kindness and love among the cultures, but these images were quickly replaced by cruelty and death. She witnessed leaders ordering the blood of their rivals spilt to the earth. Men forced into combat at the whim of those in power. She saw women abused for pleasure, men forced to fight to the death for entertainment. Fury built with each scene. Layandria could take the injustice, the pain of it all no longer and she pulled away from the people, walking alone in high mountains.

Her anger ebbed in solitude, but the desperate need to fill the void inside only grew in intensity. She returned to the worlds of people and walked among them again. Though the faces changed, and the terrain moved ever onward, the sequence did not. At first a leader would be virtuous and strong, but the hope that welled inside Layandria at the sights gave way as violence and greed hardened the hearts of men. She pleaded with them to act differently, to remember their former selves, but they would not be swayed.

She fought with the sword. She found that at the edge of the threat of death, the hollowness faded. The closer she stepped toward death in combat, the dimmer the hunger grew, sated as it was by growing intimacy with death. Not for glory or honor, Layandria lost faith in these constructs. She found nothing of pleasure, nothing sating the rage that dwelt on the ragged edge of her empty heart.

She joined armies in war, fighting with them until their quests were completed. Moving on as the soldiers celebrated victory. Where they found comfort in an end to their conquest, Layandria felt only nothingness. She walked on until she found another nation at war, joining their cause without regard for the purpose. She pushed her skills and courage ever further, embracing the most dangerous and precarious challenges with fervor.

Every time Layandria escaped death, the need to face it again intensified. In the quiet of the night, Layandria felt utterly nothing. The knowledge that she was no longer alive, but merely existing came like the dry air over the desert. She came to know that she no longer felt sadness. The desire for the woman's touch was gone. The want to belong amongst the peoples and cultures of the land was no longer present. She felt no pain, no sadness, and no joy. She was dead, though her body walked on.

A new face emerged from the gray haze that had become her world. A strong man in gleaming shadow armor stepped towards her. Layandria's heart felt the faintest glimmer of hope as the man became clear. She saw her father, King Axeleon, clothed in glory and virtue. Feelings long lost to the void of a deceased existence awoke. She fell to her knees before him, offering her loyalty and service. The spark of hope inside was infinitesimal, but it was alive. Her father's face smiled down on her and she began to feel less heavy, less burdened by the nothing that she had become. The King's face began to fade, growing dark. Suddenly, it was gone. Rage and despair crashed over her heart and she could not control it. She began to desire death. No longer seeking only closeness with the end, Layandria longed to join it, to end her incessant walking alone on the soil.

She journeyed alone to the wilderness. She removed her armor and cast it aside. She took up her sword and braced the hilt on a small rock. She began to lean forward, the weight of her body pulling her down towards the hungry blade. She was stopped, just as the comfort of death was upon her, by a single shout. A strong voice calling the darkness. The voice called her name and Layandria answered. The voice beckoned her to follow and she did, though she did not know why her feet chose to move. Her mind stayed on the sword and the blissful end it held.

The voice issued commands and Layandria complied without hesitation or understanding. In time, she grew to need the voice, to want deeply for its leadership. She realized that the voice was no longer her commander, it walked beside her as a companion. She forgot the sword on the rocks, ready to free her from the pain of an empty life. As she walked along with her faceless companion, she began to feel again. Slight pangs of anger, sadness, hope and even small bursts of happiness came to her. When the voice fell away, the nothingness came back, but the voice always returned. Layandria begged to see the unknown companion that kept her and made her feel alive, but she was denied. Finally, the voice revealed its form and Layandria saw her own face staring back. An intense wave of comfort washed over her and Layandria felt her own expression crack, mimicking the warm smile of the image before her.

The images and emotions she felt slowly left Layandria as her eyes softly opened revealing Jaxus in the place the memories occupied. His expression was hard, despite the warmth carried by the touch of his hands on hers. As the memories faded, Layandria felt a great wave of exhaustion wash over her. She felt as if she had walked for days without food or rest. Jaxus withdrew his touch and stood, stepping away from the Queen and the light of the fire.

She rose and moved after him. Her body fought her, but she pushed past the pain in her joints and the weakness of her muscles. She came to the man's side. "Was I seeing through your eyes?"

Jaxus nodded, his body heavy as he stared out into the darkness. "I do not know how much you could see. I have never attempted it before, having only heard others speak about such things when I was a boy."

"I understand." Layandria whispered. Sadness and longing took over her heart. She stepped in, next to Jaxus. His hand hung at his side and she took it in her own. She could feel the man's muscles tighten as he began to pull away from her. She tightened her grip and the man relented.

"She was your mother? The woman in the beginning who held you?" Layandria watched Jaxus face in the dim light of the half moon. He nodded. "Why did I see myself at the end?"

Jaxus said nothing, but she could feel him squeeze her hand gently.

"You loved my father?" She watched him nod again. "But he broke your trust."

The man remained silent, offering only a small nod in response.

Layandria watched him carefully. His face did not move or change, his eyes fixed on some far point. The feelings she experienced in Jaxus mind were overwhelming and she felt a strong pull to him that she could not explain. The desire to know the meaning of what she saw filled her. She wrestled with herself.

"Jaxus, look at me." Layandria barley breathed the words, desire winning over all other emotions. The man closed his eyes and turned his face to her. When he opened them, Layandria could see a softness there, a sparkle of tenderness that she was drawn to. She stood there, her eyes locked on his, trapped between hesitation and need for understanding. "Do you love me?"

Jaxus remained silent. Hesitation shown on his face. His hand quivered and so did hers. A small nod of his head confirmed. Layandria could think of nothing to say. The warmth of Jaxus hand on hers, the scent of his breath that climbed into her nostrils. She felt a deep need inside of herself unlike any other. Layandria rose on the tips of her toes and put her hands around Jaxus neck. He dipped his head to meet her. She closed her eyes and kissed him.

She hesitated, suddenly afraid that she would anger the man. She pulled her face back and opened her eyes, though she did not release her hold on the back of his neck. Jaxus looked down on her, his face blank as always. Layandria nearly let go, certain that giving into her feelings had been wrong, but Jaxus leaned into her and kissed her.

His lips were soft and warm, a contradiction to the hardness the man displayed. With their touch, an electricity flashed through Layandria's body, every cell of her alive and aware. The man released his touch on her lips, but she craved them still. She rose to him and kissed him again. Jaxus wrapped his arms around her back and she felt his large hands grip her. She felt weak, but strangely strong, connected to the man and feeling so much of him. She kissed him again, parting her lips.

She did not think about what she did or how, her conscious mind given completely to him. She felt with every inch of herself. His hands on her, the gentleness of his lips, the smell of his skin and the taste of him. Every sensation flooded through her and she floated on the calm waters of this perfect hour. Her heart was pounding like a great war drum, but she could not feel his. Jaxus still wore his armor and it blocked the sensation.

She pulled her face away from the man for just and instant. She opened her eyes and looked deeply into his. Layandria probed for the edges of Jaxus armor, finding the concealed gaps and searching for the bindings. Jaxus withdrew from her touch, and moved to his mattress, gracefully removing the plates of his armor. Layandria stood by, watching with anticipation nearly overwhelming as he partook of his careful ritual. She desperately wanted him to hurry, so deeply did she want for his touch on her body, so intense was the feeling of loss when the contact was removed.

Jaxus bent and set the last plate to rest. He stood and turned to face Layandria again, his white tunic moving gently in the breeze of the desert. She took a moment to take in the shape of his body, drawing in every possible detail from the broadness of his chest, to the slight tremor of his thighs under his black trousers.

She pulled him towards her and felt his chest on hers through the cloth. She kissed him deeply and he returned her passion. Their comfort and tenderness grew with each touch. His strong hands found her back again. Layandria felt his heart thrashing in his chest, the cadence rapid, matching hers. The kisses did not satisfy the hunger she felt, and she wanted more. Layandria lowered her body to Jaxus bed.

"Lay with me." She whispered, her desire completely in control. Jaxus joined her, his movements slow and graceful. She starred into his eyes for a time. His face lacked expression, but the man's eyes told her volumes. They conveyed the same feeling that she experienced while looking on herself in his mind. She asked him again, her voice strong but quiet as the surface of a great river. "Do you love me?"

Jaxus nodded again, his face next to hers. His eyes were soft and full of something strong and warm like the first sun after a deep snowfall. The sight of the man's feeling on display washed over Layandria and she wrapped herself around his body. She felt his arm around her and his legs intertwined with hers. She kissed him again and felt his body melt into hers. Layandria let herself go completely in the sensations. There was no fear or hesitation in her, only passion and hunger.

The small fire began to fade as the two lay in embrace. As the flames died, the fire of their passion intensified. Layandria took Jaxus, guiding his touch to her breast. Pangs of the deepest need ran through her at his touch and she kissed him ever more, exploring his neck with her lips, her hands finding other places to discover.

Layandria could not measure time's passing, so given over to the power of the moment was she. All knowledge of the surrounding world disappeared as the two became one. The man was gentle, yet immeasurably intense as they writhed together in shared passion. The sounds she emitted were new to her and carried far in the night as their energy reached its pitch. Sleep came on both in time, though it's passing was not noted as they remained wrapped in the warmth and peace of each other.

The Queen slowly woke to the light of the new sun. Jaxus was not present and his armor was gone, though the small fire had been nurtured back to life. She rose and donned her armor. She rolled both mattresses and packed them away. She took up her uneaten diner and nibbled at it, surprised that she was not hungry, finding her mind and body renewed. She was light and free in spirit. The weight of the Inohamman was still on her, as were the worries she carried for her home, but Layandria felt less alone in her concerns. She finished her meal and carefully smothered the fire with dirt.

Jaxus returned just moments after the fire was completely put out. As she saw him approaching, Layandria stood and donned her pack. Jaxus came near and took up his as well. "Are you ready to move, My Queen?"

"I am." Layandria answered and the pair moved off, though they walked closer to each other than was their established pattern. Layandria began to think of the Inohamman and what must be done to prepare for the armies that would be moving towards the Wanoak city. She pushed thoughts of the night shared with her companion aside and focused on the looming tasks.

"Do you think these will keep until we rest for lunch?" Jaxus asked slyly as he held two silver fish out for Layandria to see. They were suspended from thin twine, wooden hooks in their mouths.

"Where did you get those?" Layandria asked in surprise both at the fish, and the knowledge that they had been in Jaxus possession since he returned to the camp, but she had not seen a single fin or scale. "I have not had fish since we left Arken!"

"I found a small stream this morning and caught them for us to break our fast." The dark Knight explained. "I had thought to roast them over the fire, but I found that someone had smote it out."

"I'm sorry!" Layandria squealed. "I didn't know!"

Jaxus smiled. "They will not keep and the smell that they will give off in the high sun will be revolting. Perhaps the hunger for fish will help us push for home with greater haste."

Layandria watched as Jaxus whipped his wrist and flung the fish away. She imagined some scavenger finding them and enjoying the feast. In her mind, she saw a raccoon, though she doubted they lived in this arid climate. She smiled at the thought, but Jaxus words came back to her and gave her pause. "Is Arken home to you?"

"What?" Jaxus asked in confusion at the sudden shift in conversation.

"You said that the fish would hasten us home." Layandria stopped in her tracks. Jaxus echoed her pause and turned to face her. "Is Arken your home?"

Jaxus sighed and his eyes grew dark, the spark of amusement and affection they held seconds before lost. "Jurin is my home, My Queen."

"I see." Layandria did not know why, but Jaxus words saddened her. She knew it was unreasonable to think that she had somehow lifted his burden, but she could not fight the feeling. She did not know what to say. The emptiness of Jaxus eyes was no longer an accepted part of his persona to her, but she did not know how to bring life back to them. She could think of nothing else to do, so she turned away and began walking again. Jaxus stepped off next to her.

"I know it is not my place," Layandria spoke strongly, the force of her will evident in her voice, "but if I could, I would help you find your home."

Jaxus reached his hand out and took Layandria's. He felt her skin and she did not resist his touch. There were no words that could be said between them, so they walked on, hand in hand as the distance ranged out before them. Jaxus steadily increased his pace, but he did not let go of her. The confidence with which they moved, hand in hand, told both far more than any words.

25

Liam listened to the masters of coin as they went over their figures. He did not have a mind for numbers, and he found the conversation tedious. Once per quarter year, the masters of coin from each of the fists journeyed to the Arkenhead to give report as to their finances, pay all dues and make any requests of the council. The masters of the coffers in the Arkenhead, of which there were five, reported on the financial health of the entire realm and made recommendations on the requests of the fists. The result was a great deal of speech on senseless numbers that bored the Lord Commander to the point of lunacy.

The men and women droned on in their particular style of bland while Liam forced himself to stay awake. He could not help but let his mind wander. He was playing a very dangerous game, keeping the councilors and various ministers away from the King's chambers. Were the King's demise to be discovered, there was naught that would prevent his immediate death and Lord Nathus seizure of the throne.

Though he had guards posted to prevent any from accessing the King's chambers, he could not settle. He had not been sleeping, his mind wrestling with the precarious situation he dwelt in. In the few small seconds where his mind found any comfort, the image of the Starrowlands boy plummeting from the ceiling attacked him and the death of Genif Nitru wrecked his hearts hold. The exhaustion he felt complicated his thoughts and worsened his fears. He could take only small scraps of food, no sleep and he felt in his heart that there was no escape. He longed to depart the Citadel, to journey south and join Wolf Lord Aralias in combat. That was his place, on the fields of battle, not sitting in endless meetings and council sessions, giving direction over topics for which he had no understanding or interest.

The coin master from the Elk Fist continued, but the Commander grew restless. He cleared his throat and stood, his chair squealing as it slid back. "Can I be assured that the Fists will maintain their fiscal integrity until the King has regained his strength?"

The coin masters looked back and forth amongst themselves, uncertainty covering the myriad faces. Liam was satisfied with their lack of response, taking it for confirmation enough. He turned from his chair to leave the room. Grand Master Hale Niwcurt, chief coin master of the Arkenhead, stood quickly and darted to the door, closing it and barring Liam's exit. He was old and frail, having been a master of coin for nearly fifty years. Liam fought the urge to smack the brittle man aside. Grand Master Hale's small dark eyes shown out of his thin face, wreathed in large gray brows that stood in high contrast to his dusky skin. The expression presented was one of stern disappointment.

"If you insist on keeping up this charade, you must at least do us the kindness of pretending to care about our business." Master Hale spoke as if her were scolding an unruly grandchild.

"What charade is this?" Liam's mind reeled; his usually quick mind was disarrayed by the strain on him. "I have made no secret that I lack skill with numbers and finance. Trust when I tell you, Grand Master Hale, my ignorance is no charade."

"Commander, I would ask that you sit." Hale motioned back to Liam's chair at the head of the table.

As he turned to retake his seat, unable to find the words to excuse himself further, Liam found that the other masters were all leaning forward in their chairs, looking at him expectantly. He sat, though he did not move in on the table.

The old coin master patted his shoulder gently. "You have done well, Lord Commander, though I fear you cannot continue this deception alone. Too many ears have heard too many details and suspect far too much."

"I know not of what you speak." Liam let the words out, but he knew they were useless. These masters were sharp of mind and he was far too exhausted to fight. He knew he would soon be put to death and without Aralias here to stop it, Lord Nathus would take the throne. There would be no kingdom for Layandria to return to.

"Please, Lord Commander, do not insult us." Master Chopin of the Wolf Fist spoke up. She was younger than most, though she possessed the long nose small, darting eyes and egregious brows common to many of the coin masters.

"I am certain no insult was intended." Master Hale patted Liam's shoulder again. The man's tone made the Commander feel as though he were but five years old. "I am certain that the Commander's intent was pure, but intent often leads to folly."

Master Hale hobbled to the left of the table, passing behind the backs of the seated masters. "The surgeons who attended to the King on his deathbed were certain that he would not survive. Yet, we were told promptly that the king was stable and healing, a miraculous recovery made. Several among us even took audience with our dear Axeleon, reporting back his good spirits. Within the day, new reports stated that though recovering well, the King would receive no further visitors. The King's niece, who had attended his side at all hours, strangely disappeared shortly after. I find the timing of these events troubling."

"I fail to see what you are moving towards." Liam's eyes were downcast, his massive fingers picked at the varnish on the table.

"Tut tut, Commander." The scolding tone of Master Hale's voice increased. "Let us all agree that we will cease deceiving each other, shall we?"

Liam nodded his head in agreement.

"For example, Master Pleuin has told us that the Iron Fist has generated less revenue this year due to an over cold harvest. He further stated that several of the ships belonging to the Iron Navies required rework and as result, Lord Nathus is unable to provide his due for this quarter year." Master Hale paced behind Master Pleuin, who looked markedly uncomfortable.

"While the good Commander has stopped our council in progress, I would suspect that most of you have let slip some small deception or another, and if you have not, you would have before the conclusion of our meeting." The old man's left eye seemed to enlarge, staring from one face to another in exaggerated suspicion. "But now we are come to agreeance, we will all speak in frank truth for the remainder of our time together. Commander, answer me honestly, is our good king healing peacefully in his chamber?"

Liam felt like the air had been sucked out of his chest and the ceiling caved in on him. The edges of his vision faded black and he felt like his heart had stopped. A hollow wind rushed through his ears and his stomach rolled.

"Come now Commander, let us hear your answer." Master Hale stepped to Liam's back and squeezed the massive man's neck.

Liam summoned his courage. He sat up in his chair and straightened his shoulders. He held his head up and let his voice come out with all the strength he had remaining. "All that I have done, I have done for the good of the Kingdom."

"Of that, I am certain." Master Hale returned to his seat, folding his hands on the tabletop.

Liam drew in a breath and steeled his heart. "King Axeleon is dead. I am alone in that knowledge. Prior to his passing, the King sent Princess Layandria into the passage under the mountain and as of this day, she has not been located. I feared that if word of the King's passing broke, with no blood heir able to claim the throne, Lord Nathus would ride in force from the Iron Fist and attempt to seize the rule of Arken. I do not believe this the just course for Arken and her people."

"Who are you to decide what the just course for the kingdom is?" Master Pleuin demanded, pounding his small fist on the table. "Perhaps your short time seated on the throne has made you hunger for the power and you attempt to secure it for your own."

"I have no desire for power." Liam forced himself to maintain his composure, despite the waves of fatigue and the undertow of anger that rolled over him. "My only desire is to preserve the throne until the rightful ruler can be sat upon it."

Master Pleuin scoffed and stood, his wooden chair toppling behind him. The Iron Fist coin master was young, but his unkempt, faded hair, his sharp nose, exceptionally pale complexion and narrow face gave him the impression of a much older man. Contempt shone like acid in his eyes. "These things are not for you to decide. You have no knowledge of the Princess whereabouts, or if she still lives. Lord Nathus is the rightful ruler and your deception will not go without reward."

"Is not Lord Commander Fax the rightful ruler?" Master Chopin chimed in, earning a snarl from Master Pleuin. "He is three years senior to Lord Nathus and a true Lord by the law."

"King Axeleon pioneered that law!" Master Pleuin shrieked, stomping towards Master Chopin. "As if the fates smiled on him themselves, this dog of a man finds himself not of noble birth, of no right, honored and given Lordship over a fist that needs no Lord, for it holds the seat of the King! This is deception and treachery at its highest! Lord Nathus will not stand for this peasant to sit upon his throne!"

Master Hale raised his eyes to the younger iron coin master. "What is it that you intend to do Master Pleuin?"

"I intend to return to my holdings and inform Lord Nathus as once!" Master Pleuin stepped towards the door. "My Lord will see that all those responsible for this treachery are put to death and justice is served to all who had knowledge."

Master Hale returned Pleuin's stare evenly, though absent the younger man's lusting. "I think that is an unwise course of action."

"I do not care what you think!" Master Pleuin stamped towards the door. "Lord Nathus will be here with all haste. You will bend your knee to the rightful king, or you will be removed."

"What of the Princess?" Master Hale questioned softly.

"What of her? I see no Princess!" Pleuin feigned looking around the room as if searching for Layandria. "She abandoned her people in their darkest hour to flee! To where? I do not know, and even this so-called Lord Commander has no knowledge of her location. If she returns, and I do stress if, she must answer to Lord Nathus for her crimes!"

Liam stood sharply at the last sentence, though Master Pleuin was so engrossed in his anger and open disdain for Master Hale that he took no notice.

"So, you see, dead or alive, Princess Layandria dug her grave the moment she abandoned her people, a crime for which there can be only one course." Pleuin turned and strode towards the door, having to turn his shoulders to Commander Fax to pass by him.

The heat of the small coin master's passion radiated so powerfully that sweat dripped off the end of his narrow nose. Anger lit inside Liam like an inferno. He did not process thought, no clear reasoning formed in his mind, only animal need to protect his kingdom. This need was fueled by absolute unwillingness to allow harm to be perpetrated on the Princess, in word or design.

As Master Pleuin moved past him, the massive Lord Commander spun. He raised his left hand and caught the narrow-faced accountant by the neck. Liam drove him around, slamming his back into the table and pinning him down. Pleuin shrieked as his limbs shot about at random. Pleuin's mouth attempted to form words, but the pressure of the large hand on his neck prevented all but the most desperate wheezing noises from escaping.

Liam looked up to see that the masters of coin were seated, save for Master Hale who appeared completely calm, stroking his thin beard thoughtfully. A few of the younger masters bore surprise on their faces, but most wore only solemn looks and hard eyes.

"You will pay." Master Pleuin managed to force out the words raggedly.

Commander Fax raised his right hand and touched the Iron coin master's lips with his index finger, silencing him. Liam closed his fist with all his strength around the man's thin neck. Cartilage and bone crushed under his grip. Pleuin's eyes bulged severely under the pressure of the Commander's vice. Liam released his grip and Pleuin's body slumped to the floor.

Commander Fax raised his eyes to the council. He wore no guilt and strangely found that much weight was lifted from him. He looked to Master Hale. "I am Lord Commander Liam Fax, Commander of the armies of Shadow and Lord of the Fist. I am sworn to the service of Arken. Layandria lives, of this I am certain. I take not this throne for myself and I will rebuff any who attempt it for their own until Princess Layandria is returned. All who oppose this will fall."

The room was silent for a time. The coin masters looked at Liam, most impassively.

Master Hale broke the silence. "My good Commander, you misunderstand. We do not wish to oppose you. We wish to aid you."

Liam narrowed his eyes in suspicion. "How can this be?"

"Be seated, Lord Commander, and I will explain all." Master Hale sat and waited for Liam to follow suit. He watched intently as the large man moved the body of Pleuin to the corner and returned to the head of the table. "As is common, the masters of coin arrive several days prior to the official timing of the council. We do so that we may confer with our contemporaries and shore up any planned request for funding before they are presented to the King. Naturally, Master Pleuin does not take part in these early conferences. He is not truthful with the finances of his realm and wishes to limit his exposure to those that would know better. This is of great benefit to you as we were able to come to agreement early on."

"As for your secretive dealings, we first grew suspicious when we were told of the miraculous recovery made by King Axeleon. Then, when I inquired about his niece, whom I knew to be attending him, none were aware of her location. Of further concern to me were the guards placed at the King's chambers. I can recall no time in all my long years that a practice such as this has been undertaken." Master Hale paused and sipped from a small flask withdrawn from his cloak.

Liam listened intently as the man continued, confusion the only emotion he experienced.

"I must confess, Lord Commander that I grew suspicious. I began to consider all possibilities and I was forced to examine one in which you wished to claim the throne as your own. I knew Lord Aralias had been in your company and I have no trust for a man of such youth and savagery. So, I began checking the dark places of the citadel. In the crypt, I discovered the remains of our departed King and his loving niece."

A small flash of shame crossed Liam's face. Hale continued, unfazed by the Commander's display of remorse. "At first, I took this as confirmation that you, Lord Aralias, or perhaps both, were conspiring for the crown. I brought this information to the council of coin and I was shown the error of my thinking."

Master Jessuck, the coin master of the Wolf Fist, took over. "I have known Aralias for many years and while the man is uncouth, he is loyal and has shown no desire for higher glory. I have also known you, good Lord Commander, for many years. I have seen in you a progressing burden as you have risen in leadership and I did not believe you would desire the throne."

Commander Fax nodded, appreciative for the show of faith.

"So, we reasoned that you must be aware of Lord Nathus desire for the throne." Master Hale took over the narrative. "We, who are often overlooked by those who believe we know only of numbers, have long been aware of Lord Nathus disdain for the King. We are equally aware of the disasters that would follow if the Iron Lord assumed rule."

"We have all come to agreeance and we know what must be done." Master Hale paused long enough to see interest and intensity play on Liam's face. "The ruse that you have set in place must be maintained. It is critical that Layandria be returned in all haste, and I trust you have sent trusted warriors to accomplish this?"

"I have." Liam answered evenly.

"And whom have you sent?" Master Jessuck asked in earnest.

"I have dispatched one called Sahid Hauk Kahn, a man of the Fallish lands." Commander Fax said the words easily, though he did not expect the looks of disappointment and shock that passed through the group.

"Commander, that news does not sit well." Master Hale's voice grew concerned.

"Allow my reassurances masters." Liam laid his hands on the table and leaned forward. "This man is worthy of the trust. It was he who moved in secret through the lines of the enemy to deliver word of the King's survival to Lord Aralias. The man then fought bravely at the side of the wolves as they retook the citadel. He has proved himself both strong and quick witted. Further, he has nothing to be gained from deception as the man's only desire is to return to his people in the Fallish lands. He understands this desire cannot be achieved if he is being hunted by our people and the Starrowlanders, to whom his betrayal is well known."

"And you are certain of his loyalty to our cause?" Master Challin, a woman master of coin representing the Elk Fist spoke up.

"To our cause, the man has no loyalty." Liam let the words fall like a hammer before he continued. "But to his own, his loyalty is as steadfast as my own. As his great desire requires safe passage through territory held by Arken and her allies, the man will do whatever he must."

"We have sworn to him passage home?" Master Jessuck inquired.

"We have." Commander Fax waited for another inquiry. There were none, so Liam raised his own. "What part will you play as we move forward?"

Master Hale sipped from his small flask again. "We will provide credibility to the story. We will tell many of our contemporaries that we have been in to see the King. We will pass on news that he is healing, but that his wound is challenging and will require much time for full recovery. Word will pass quickly. It will assuage the suspicions of most, though there will be some among the government who will desire to see the king for themselves."

"How then do we deal with these visitors?" Liam asked. "Is it not better to limit word of those who have seen the King, passing on that he wishes to heal in solitude?"

Master Hale's face showed his irritation. "No, that would not be wise. Others would grow suspicious as I have and would be less sympathetic to your aim. We must allow these visitors to see the King. There is in the village Prapan, a man who is the image of Axeleon, though his is shorter and of less weight. This man, Markols is his name, is loyal to the kingdom and will act as we need. We will bring him here and gain him entry under cover of night, in passages known to precious few. He will stay in the chamber of the King and be our proof, as it were, of the King's life."

"How will this man be able to play the part and be ready for all that may come to see him?" Liam was growing uncomfortable with the plan. He felt it was too complicated and offered too many chances for discovery.

"I am aware of a poison that when consumed in the proper amount, leaves the drinker sedated and quite weakened. We will give this to Markols and it will render him confined to his bed, unable to speak. His skin will take on the look of the ill. As Markols is several years older than Axeleon, the needed look will suffice. Visitors wishing to see the King will be allowed entry but will be told that the King must be afforded his rest." Hale seemed pleased with the conspiring. "This ruse will likely only work for a short time, a month at most. Layandria must be found in this time."

"I see." Liam sat in silence, ignoring the eyes on him. He turned the angles of the plan over in his mind. There were too many people involved and too many possibilities of exposure, but Liam felt that he had little choice. "A trusted surgeon must be found who can tend to the man in Axeleon's chamber and administer the poison in the proper dose."

"That would have been easier, had you not murdered the King's niece." Master Hale pointed out sharply.

"Perhaps, but I had little option at the time. Lord Aralias and I thought it the only course before us." Liam was burdened with the guilt of the girl's death but did not question the necessity of the act.

"Lord Aralias is aware of these goings on?" Master Challin asked quickly, sitting forward in her chair.

"He is." Liam answered. "It was Aralias who first suggested that the Fallish man be sent to reclaim the Princess."

"That is an advantage to us." Master Hale considered this news carefully. "Should the worst come to pass and Nathus grow aware of our deception, the Wolf Lord must return to the Arkenhead at once. The Iron Lord has no love for his westward counterpart, and a lesser respect, but I dare say that he would hesitate to challenge the Lords of Wolf and Shadow united under the same cause."

"Aralias expressed his intent to return with all swiftness before he and his forces departed." Liam confirmed the master's thoughts. "Of course, if Lord Nathus does seize the throne, I will deny any involvement of Lord Aralias in this deception."

"You will deny any involvement of ours as well, I trust." Master Hale looked at the large commander intensely. "Do you consent to the plan we have laid?"

Liam paused, considering all details again, and as before, arrived at the conclusion that there was no other path to be taken. "I do."

"Good. You must return to the throne and continue to lead the people. Take them in and hear their requests. The better you can aid them and make them feel validated, the less they will cry for their King. On matters of great import or cost, you must excuse yourself to gain the King's council. You will go to his chambers and let time pass, returning to inform the people of the King's order." Master Hale instructed as if it were but a simple task, though Liam felt that it would be much more difficult in practice. A performer, he was not.

Master Hale rose, and the other coin masters followed suit. "Aside from this, you must take rest, and hope that this Fallish man you have trusted is good to his task."

Liam nodded. His eyes fell on the body of Master Pleuin, crumpled in the corner of the room. "What of him?"

Master Hale's face grew hard, his eyes dark. "We will deal with this man."

26

Sahid felt as if he had been walking for days. He had lost track of time, unable to see anything other than stone and black air. He rested when he grew tired, ate when he was hungry, and he walked. Endlessly searching for any sign that would indicate the location of the Princess and her companions. Sahid was deeply grateful for the torches he gathered along the way, no doubt left behind by the princess and her men. When he woke from sleep, or when a torch extinguished, he found the darkness suffocating and beyond penetration. He felt like a fool, fumbling around for tinder in hurried movements that were less than efficient.

Still he walked on. There was no possibility for error as he had yet to find a branch in the passage. He perceived rises and falls in the floor of the tunnel, but there had been so many that he had lost track of them and had no way of knowing his depth relative to the surface of the earth.

Though he was grateful for the honor of the shadow armor bestowed on him by Lord Commander Fax, it rubbed fiercely on his neck as he walked. The sword he was issued, a cruel looking blade, was heavy and cumbersome, not at all the thin, agile weapon he was used to. His hip ached under the imbalance of the sword hanging off his side.

Shadows in the light of the torch disturbed him. He would see images, branches off the main passage, the silhouette of a human, laying in sleep on the floor and other creatures, intent on ending his life. At first, these images had frightened him, but as the time passed, he became desensitized to the terror of the darkness. Even now, ahead in the cold black, Sahid could make out the shape of some monstrous dog, laying on the floor as if in sleep. It began to amuse him how the shadows played tricks on the mind, so common these insane sights had become.

Sahid grew fascinated by the shape. Strangely, it did not change as he grew near. The flame reflected off the floor and Sahid could see a mass quantity of dried blood bathing the stone. He quickened his pace and found that the shadow was not an apparition of light against rock but was in fact the headless corpse of some strange wolf. The body had sickly pale skin, abhorrently large feet with cruel claws and an oddly curved spine that made Sahid picture a grizzled dog of war once used by enemies long dead.

There were footprints in the blood, which had long coagulated and dried. Some of the prints were smooth, as if made by some sort of thin sole, while others resembled those made by the boots common to soldiers of Arken. Sahid realized at once that this creature must have been downed by the Princess and her company though he could make no discerning of the smooth soles.

He raised his torch, scanning the surroundings for any other information. Slightly ahead of the carcass, against the right wall he found another pool of blood smaller than the first and separate from the random splatters that littered the floor. Several bloodied bandages and cloths lay discarded. Someone had been seriously injured in the fight with this creature. Sahid hoped, for his sake, that the wounded party was not the Princess he was charged to find and retrieve.

Sahid continued to search, now lowering himself much closer to the floor. He touched one of the discarded bandages. It was dry and stiff, long past use. A trail of small droplets of blood seemed to lead off into the passage. He kept his eyes low, continuing the search of the area. A burst of glare in the darkness caught his eye. The sight before him shocked him so deeply that Sahid shouted and rocked back on his heels. Sahid flailed onto his back, losing grip on his torch in the process. The flame failed and the tunnel was bathed in darkness.

Sahid struggled to his knees, wrenching a fresh torch from his pack. In movements that he had never expected to have such experience with, he clenched the torch between his knees while he dug flint from inside his chest plate. He removed the cloth wrapping from his flint and striker, holding the canvas swatch in his teeth while he sparked the torch to life. As the light grew, Sahid nearly dropped the flint, his eyes confirming the sight that caused his tumble.

The head that once belonged to the deceased beast's body sat upright before him. The eyes were open, though they had shrunken and darkened in the sockets. The lips were pulled back, dehydrated by time, revealing yellowed, jagged fangs. As his heart rate slowed back to a normal pace, Sahid examined the head. It had been severed with some sort of dual cut from both sides with an uncommon precision.

Sahid took some time for himself, letting his heart settle. He searched the floor again, finding the trail of blood. The drops were small and hard to spot in the shifting fire light, but he searched the floor carefully on his knees and was able to follow the breadcrumbs on into the passage.

As he crawled along, his knees began to ache. Pain distracted the man's concentration, causing his focus to wane. He almost missed it, so accustomed had he become to the frequency and forward pace of the droplets. The trail doubled back and seamed to disappear into the right wall of the passage as if the wounded man had vanished into the living rock.

As Sahid drew near, he found that carefully concealed in the wall was a branch off the main body of the passage. He entered the branch and stepped sideways through a series of cutbacks in the stone wall, coming to a slightly wider opening that had a well-constructed ladder against the far wall. Careful examination showed several prints of foot and hand marring the thick dust that coated the ladder. Sahid was certain his quarry had taken this climb.

Despite his intense desire to be free of the dark underground, Sahid reasoned that there could be any number of threats above and he was not aware if it was day or night. While the body of the canine monstrosity haunted him, Sahid felt that if he took his rest here and if a threat approached, he would be able to mount the ladder quickly.

He downed his baggage and unrolled a small straw mat. He carefully laid down and rested his head on his pack. The first signs of his quarry that he found renewed his hope. As he drifted into shallow sleep, Sahid thought of his home, which now, though he was the furthest he had been from it, felt closer than it had since the day he was forced to leave.

27.

"Queen Layandria." A stone-faced warrior stood at the doorway to the burned-out residence that had once housed Chief Talin, passed then to Chieftain Jordache. Layandria rolled over in her makeshift bed, sitting up slightly. The morning sun had barely broken the horizon, casting a purple glow into the room.

"Yes," Layandria answered as she rubbed her eyes, "what is it?"

"Halta has returned with your man." The warrior kept his face averted from Layandria as he spoke, not wanting to see the Queen in a less than flattering time.

"Thank you, I will be with them in a moment." Layandria waited until the man had departed before she rose from the thick furs. Jaxus had gone sometime in the dim hours of the morning. He had come to her in the night, long after all but the watchmen had taken to rest. They had discussed little else but battle plans, though the dark warrior had eased her to sleep as he spoke of the culture of Jurin men. In the days since they returned to the Wanoak village, the pair had not spoken about the passion they shared in the desert. Layandria greatly desired his touch but she also knew that such pleasures were unwise so close to the eyes and ears of the Wanoak people. They did not need to be handed a reason to question her leadership.

She rose slowly and washed her skin. She braided her hair tightly, dressing in a light green tunic over dark trousers. The generosity of the beleaguered Wanoak was astonishing. Food, bed and clothing were all given freely by the tribe. Her armor lay untouched in the corner. She hung the sun stone around her neck, letting the familiar weight fall on her chest. Halta advised the Princess to keep the power of the sunstone hidden, given the superstition of many Inohamman elders, so Layandria concealed the pendant under her shirt.

Halta and Oslun were seated on logs, chatting cheerfully with Jaxus when Layandria approached. Oslun inquired after Thyso and Rale'en, but disappointment crossed his face when Jaxus informed the young man that the handmaid had not yet returned.

Layandria explained briefly of the encounter with Chieftain Warrot and his promise to bring the forces of Chieftain Barbas with him.

"There, you see!" Halta turned to Oslun in glee. "I told you they were marching here to reinforce us!"

Layandria and Jaxus both starred at the pair, waiting for an explanation.

"Yesterday afternoon, we crested a hill and saw a huge group of warriors moving this way, maybe a half day's march behind us." Oslun explained. His eyes shown with confidence and his face seemed to have grown stronger, some of the plumpness of royal servanthood vanished. "I thought they were the forces of our enemy, moving to strike us, but Halta insisted that they were the armies of the Takkar and DaVasl Inohamman."

"He did not believe me, doubting my ability to recognize my own people." Halta smiled at the cup bearer.

"But they were so far away!" Oslun retorted playfully. The young man placed his arm around Halta's waist, and she drew near to him.

"What is this development?" Jaxus asked sternly, though the cracks of a smile could be seen at the corners of his eyes.

Halta smiled deeply and looked away. "We have grown close."

"More than close!" Oslun exclaimed. Halta shot him a narrow look that silenced him, though neither lost the happiness that was written on every part of their skin. Oslun regained his composure and turned to Layandria. "Chieftain Zinan has committed to sending five thousand of his warriors, who should arrive in a day."

"The Chieftain rides with his men and though he comes, he does not trust the thought of a foreign woman leading the Wanoak. He will contend that his chosen commander must lead the armies in battle." Halta already anticipated what reaction the Queen would have to that assertion.

"That will not happen." Layandria spoke sternly. "While I am not of this land, I do not send men to fight and die before me. I will lead them, and I will do so from the front and center of the fight."

Jaxus turned away as obvious concern played across his expression.

"In the Inohamman tribes, the Chieftains do not enter battle. They send runners forward to give instructions." Halta was correct in her assumption of Layandria's response, but she knew the young Queen must see the peril she placed on her head by the act she intended. "To lose the Chieftain in battle is seen as a great dishonor to the tribe and none will support this decision."

Layandria looked directly into Halta's eyes. "Luck would seem to be on my side then as I am not a Chieftain. I am but a foreign woman who calls herself a Queen."

"It will be as you say." Halta responded easily. She was impressed with the willingness of Layandria to embrace the people and to gently enforce her will. She hoped that strength of character would hold when the other tribes arrived.

"What of Wilteph?" Oslun asked, attempting to appear nonchalant, though he could not forgive the man who had so willingly strangled Halta. That persistent anger burned across his eyes like wildfire.

"He has barred himself in his home with Chandr." Jaxus responded quickly. "She has come out to gather food, but he has not shown himself."

"It is good for his health to stay inside." Oslun growled.

"From what depth of your soul has this aggression sprang, meek cup bearer?" Layandria asked in surprise. "I have never known you to speak in anger."

"I am merely concerned for the man's wellbeing, My Lady." Oslun softened, embarrassed for the outburst. He knew it was wrong to hold such anger for the man, and he knew that Halta had loved Wilteph as a brother for many years, but he could not keep his feelings held down.

"Certainly." Layandria let Oslun's words go. He was growing into a warrior, and was no longer a simple, doughy servant who skittered about in the shadows of powerful men. She watched him now, seeing the transformation that had overtaken his body in the weeks since they left Arken behind. Strength shown in his arms and chest. His face was harder, the youthful innocence leaving him. He still grew no facial hair, which made him look younger than his eighteen years, but his eyes shown with the confidence that was rising in him.

"Tepan has been busy readying those with the strength and will to fight." Jaxus took over the conversation. "He believes that the Wanoak have just more than two hundred ready for war. The dead have been cleared off the fields and have been given rest. Weapons and provisions are ready for the arrival of the other tribes. Those unable or unwilling to fight are prepared to move to the Takkar lands if we fail in battle."

"We move in three days." Layandria's voice took on the air of command. "The Takkar and DaVasl are, as you report, a half day away. I suspect the Nordan and Xonar tribes will be shortly behind them. Our strength should be nearly sixteen thousand. Will it be enough, Sir Jaxus?"

Jaxus turned to the Queen, his eyes dark as he focused his mind back to his scouting of the enemy several days ago. "If we meet the enemy in open conflict, at their full strength, we will fail, My Queen."

"How then can we divide their numbers?" Layandria asked, her eyes focused on his.

Jaxus knelt and began to make a rough sketch in the soft dirt. "This is the Wanoak village," he explained, pointing at a circle in the soil, then moving his hand south. "This is the Lakelands. We know that the men of the lake are preparing for war, but we also know that the leaders never move with the infantry, choosing to stay sequestered far from combat. The army will depart their homeland in the morning, making a long march using all hours of light available before taking camp. That is our time. We must split our strength, with our main body setting sword to the sleeping army, wearied as they will be from their long march. A smaller number of our strength will set upon the leaders in their dwellings. I believe a force of some three hundred could easily bring death on them."

Halta followed as Jaxus traced the lines of approach in the dirt. "If we are to trigger simultaneous assaults, separated by great distance, how will we coordinate our assaults?"

Jaxus did not look up at her as he measured the distances in his mind. "If our forces move swiftly, taking full advantage of hours of darkness, each should be in position in three days. We will hold until the final ray of the sun has dropped below the horizon."

Layandria knelt over the map, her eyes moving over the other three warriors. "This plan will work, and I have confidence in Jaxus knowledge of our foe."

Oslun leaned forward, pointing towards the southern lake. "Couldn't we all just attack the main force as they sleep, then move to the commanders when their main force is defeated?"

"No, that will not work in our favor." Jaxus explained. "The so named gods of the Lakemen are new, following the death of their predecessors at Wilteph's hands. From what I was able to glean in their presence, these gods achieved the rule they hold by spilling much blood. They fear the loss of control and will have runners in place with their soldiers to keep them informed of every action. The enemy is of great strength. Even if we attack in full force the fight could rage for hours, or under worse favor, days. By that time, the commanders would be informed of our movements, destroying the advantage granted us by unexpected attack."

"I see." Halta's eyes danced over the rough map as she went through the plan again. "Who will lead our forces?"

"Tepan has given us two hundred Wanoak," Layandria stood. "I will lead them against the lake gods. Once the Chieftains have arrived, we will decide who will lead the main force against the enemy's army. Perhaps they will protest less ardently if I am only to lead a numerically insignificant element."

"What part do we play?" Oslun was tentative. He felt confident in his ability with the sword, but aside from the encounter with the morlt, he had never faced a real enemy. His fear did not revolve around thoughts of his death or injury in battle. Oslun feared deeply that he would be too afraid and would flee the field. He concealed his fear, not wanting Halta to know the shame inside of his heart.

"You will be by my side." Layandria locked her eyes onto the young man. "I do not want any of you, Tepan, Thyso and Rale'en included, to be far from me. I fear that I will need your strength and council before this war has reached its end."

"I will not fail you, My Queen." Oslun spoke the words that he begged himself to fulfill, terrified that he would not keep the oath.

"None of us will fall to fear." Jaxus spoke strongly, his voice giving courage to the Queen and the cup bearer. "Hearts cannot fail when they stand next to those they love."

Oslun felt that Jaxus comment was directed at him, as if the dark warrior understood his feelings for Halta, though he himself did not fully understand them.

Layandria too wondered if Jaxus words were meant for her, but she cast the thoughts aside. Too many lives counted on her strength, and the Wanoak's continued existence relied on her leadership. She could not allow herself to dwell in her feelings for Jaxus.

"I am sure you both want to take rest." Layandria gestured, offering the building she had taken for her bed to Oslun and Halta. "Please find whatever comfort you may. Jaxus and I must go and meet with Tepan and give him the details of our plan."

"Thank you, My Lady." Oslun accepted the offer of bed gratefully, suddenly appearing far more worn than he had moments before. He turned and whispered to Halta, who burst into hushed laughter. Oslun took her hand and they both shuffled off to the building, giggling to each other as they went.

Jaxus and Layandria exchanged knowing glances.

"Let them enjoy the love of youth." Jaxus offered. "They may not have many days left in which to share such pleasures."

"Jaxus, do not speak so!" Layandria stopped him sharply. "Our greatest weapon is hope and we cannot allow even the slightest doubt to enter our speech!"

Jaxus bowed. "Yes, My Queen."

"Jaxus, I love you." Layandria said the words as calmly and as factually as she could. The dark warrior blinked several times at her statement, but his normal impassive countenance did not change. Layandria watched his face carefully. "You have told me several times that you feel the same love for me. Do you wish to recant your declaration?"

"I do not." Jaxus answered.

"Good." Layandria stepped closer to Jaxus as she spoke, laying her hand on the chest plate of his ever-present armor. "I intend to continue loving you long into the future. Have you any protest?"

"I do not." Jaxus repeated the words, though his mind was troubled. For so long had he walked the earth begging for death, to shun the approach of his end now felt a contradiction to his own heart. He could not fully embrace the concept of a future beyond this, or the next battle for that was all he had become. Moving from one fight to the next, hoping that each would be his last.

"Why would you accept less for yourself or others, even if it is just in speech?" Layandria's voice was soft now, her hand still on Jaxus chest, her eyes looking up into his.

Jaxus face did not change, but Layandria had begun to learn that the man's eyes revealed far more than his expression ever did. "You are right, My Queen. I will hold to hope in my actions and speech."

"Hold to me Jaxus." Layandria pleaded softly. "Hold to me as I hold to you."

"I will, My Queen." Though Jaxus did not convey much in tone or cadence, Layandria felt a special twinge in her spine when the man called her his queen. She felt as if he was saying more than a courteous address. He was calling her his own.

28

With attacks of sixty warriors moving out every hour over the past days, Aralias' wolves were exceptionally tired. Early, the losses were minimal, the element of surprise on their side. As the days wore on, the Starrowlanders reacted, taking soldiers off the front lines, pushing back to the rear to protect the supply elements and the losses suffered to Aralias' men increased. Of the fifteen thousand wolves that made the trek to the Argarnoth, more than two thousand had been lost. Entire platoons were destroyed. That great loss of life weighed heavily on Aralias, though the knowledge that his men had killed many more than were lost helped to steady his vision.

Though the enemy began to expect insurgent attacks on their rear elements, they were unable to predict on which position the wolves would fall. Starrowlands soldiers could find no rest with the threat of fast moving, precision strikes always upon them. Lady Kaowith and Lord Brustic had broken their forces down and engaged in similar small element strikes along the enemies opposite front, further fatiguing and degrading the enemies' combat power.

Battlefield intelligence was readily collected as well, the wolves taking many prisoners whose tongues were loosened though certain barbaric means. While these violently gleaned bits of information were of great use, the woman Lord Aralias had recovered from the pleasures of the enemy on the first raid had proven of more use then many spies. Pelnieth, as was her given name, had no direct information regarding names or camps, but her observations of the men and their behavior proved detailed and useful, revealing much of the enemies' structure.

Over a day ago, Aralias had stalked the camp of the battlefield commanders, attempting to confirm the picture painted by Pelnieth's memories. He found that there were four who appeared to direct the front-line units through the dispatch of many runners. Getting to this camp with a large force undetected was unlikely. The commander's encampment was located between the front lines and the rear. Any unit attempting to move to the command camp would have to pass between other elements without raising alarm. Aralias estimated that no more than twenty soldiers could successfully make the trip without being seen.

Twenty soldiers would not be enough to form a meaningful attack against the camp and infiltration with assassination in mind was wildly beyond the limits of time or opportunity. Aralias estimated at least a force of five hundred would be needed to kill or capture all the key enemies. Large scale diversion would be of the utmost import.

The Wolf Lord selected five of his fastest and most skilled men, sending them under cover of the last night's falling to inform Lady Kaowith of her part to play. In nine hours' time, the sun would begin its climb to altitude, signaling the cannons in place on the upper turrets of the Argarnoth. These cannons were loaded with laminated paper projectiles that when ignited, would burn brilliant green as they streaked high into the dawn sky. This was the signal that would begin large scale assaults on both sides of the enemy lines. This mass engagement would take the enemy by surprise and draw the bulk of the soldiers away from the central camps, allowing Aralias to bring his power to bear against the Starrowlands commanders.

The Starrowlanders outnumbered the Arken troops, though the margin was greatly narrowed over the past day's insurgency. Aralias was of the mind that fair fights were an indication of poor planning and in response to this goal, he sought greatly to tip the scales in the favor of

Arken. Were his soldiers able to destroy the enemy commanders, confusion and disarray would follow. The enemy would be starved for direction and would scatter into smaller elements, easily surrounded or splintered off to be prosecuted.

Aralias climbed the long steps to check in with the crews who would be firing the cannons. These ten men and women were all that would remain in the Argarnoth Stronghold, the entirety of the force emptied onto the fields of combat. Most of the units had already moved out, taking up their positions of ambush. Aralias own company were to be the last to depart. The artillerymen were prepared, their instructions clear and their weapons ready.

The Wolf Lord returned to keep, enjoying the cool air on the long walk through the fortress. The woman was still present, bound and seated against the wall of the great room. Aralias approached her softly, kneeling before her. "I and the majority of my forces are departing. After we have left, one of my artillerymen will come to you, your bindings will be removed, and you will be free to go."

"I have nowhere to go." Pelnieth shifted her weight roughly against the ties on her wrists. "My home is far from here."

"I cannot provide you with passage or means to return to your lands." Aralias was as a shadow in the dim light, his voice quiet and soft. "What I can offer you is your freedom. What you do with it is beyond my control."

Pelnieth turned her eyes downward. She had no idea how she would get back to her homeland, or what manner of a home she would return to if she did find a way to get back. Three years had passed since she had been ripped from her family by Axise army. She felt dirtied and shamed by the use she had been put through at their hands. Would her family welcome her back? The young woman was certain that they would not.

"I offer myself to your service, in any way that you choose." Pelnieth believed that securing a place for herself was the only option that would not result in her swift death. Aralias was visibly surprised by her gesture. "You have given me my life, and my freedom. I owe you a great debt that I cannot repay, so I offer you my service."

Aralias pushed his shoulders back and stood taller. "I have only given to you what is yours by right. That right is only forfeit by taking up arms against I and my soldiers, which you have not done, thus I have given you no more and no less than you deserve. I cannot accept your service."

"My Lord, I have nowhere to turn." Pelnieth pleaded with the wolf.

"I am sorry, I have nothing for you." Aralias rose and exited the room with no further word.

He moved through the burned-out halls of the fortress and stepped through the empty doorway, down a spindling staircase, into an expansive courtyard. His soldiers stood in formation, prepared for the order to march. He stood on the stone steps, overlooking the ranks. A strange sort of grim pride took over him. It was a familiar sensation the young commander often carried on the eve of pitched battles. He cleared his mind of doubt and moved down the stair.

Aralias stepped to the front of the formation. All eyes were on the Lord as he took the position of command. "Tonight, we will face an enemy that is strong and experienced. Their blades have slain many Arken Soldiers and they will fell more this night."

The Wolf Lord paused, his thoughts roaming for a moment as he formed the words he would next offer. "We fight this day for those that have been lost. We fight for the citizens of Arken that have seen their families and their homes washed away. We fight to rid our nation of those that would do us harm. But these are not the only things that drive us to battle. This night, we will clash swords not only for our people and our lands, but for the people of all the nations that have been enslaved, persecuted, raped and murdered under the terror of Axise and his barbarians."

"We go now to rid our world of those who disregard the lives of innocent people. We fight for those who cannot hold swords and defend their own. We will not stop until every last one has paid in blood for their crimes." Aralias felt the fervor rising in his soldiers. He pushed forward. "For years I have fought beside you and we have faced death more times than most can imagine. The fight before us is unlike any other we have faced, but I have no care for this danger. There is nothing we cannot do, no foe we cannot triumph over. We are the Wolves of Arken! We are the savages from the north and we will paint the earth red with the blood of vengeance!"

Aralias drew his sword and charged towards a broken gap in the courtyard wall with his final word. The men drew their blades and followed, their rolling cheer climbing into the night. The walk across the desert was long, and the wolves had need for haste. Very soon, the cannons would fire. There was no room for error.

29

Layandria rode across the desert, seated comfortably in the saddle. Her thoughts were heavily burdened under the narrow hope of victory she was leading her army towards. It was a strange thing, to have an army at her command. The Inohamman Chieftains agreed to her plan, allowing her to command the smaller force set to attack the gods at their dwelling on the lake, while Chieftain Barbas' field commander assumed control of the main element. They all reluctantly accepted her as the leader of the Wanoak tribe after testimonials had been offered from several members of the tribe, the most passionate of which were offered by Halta and Tepan.

Wilteph had emerged hours before the army moved, requesting permission to join the Wanoak force. He was a wisp of his former self, weak and sunken in eye. Many of the Wanoak urged Layandria to refuse Wilteph a place among the army, but she could not. She imagined the shame he would feel, being a former Chieftain as he was, were she to deny him the right to fight for his people in their darkest hours, further starved of revenge for his murdered child. She deeply suspected that the disgrace would kill the man.

The moon was high and full, allowing fifteen thousand soldiers to cross the desert without aid of torches or lamps. Layandria was only vaguely certain of the direction she must lead and frequently turned to Jaxus or Halta, who would correct her course. She wondered if her father had ever felt this way as he led the men of Arken into battle. The intense pride that she felt knowing the lives that willingly followed behind her, coupled with the terrible fear that these brave warriors were following her into defeat and death. No one had yet died under her orders and she did not know how she would cope with that inevitability.

The sun stone hung on its chain, resting on her armor. Jaxus had fashioned a small leather pouch to conceal the pendant as its size was uncomfortable if concealed within her chest plate. Nothing appeared to move in the cold desert. She had been told that there were several smaller villages in the land and many hunting parties, but she had seen none of these.

They would make camp under the conifers on the banks of the Bandir River, hoping to arrive just as the sun began to rise in the sky. The Bandir was fed from the mountains, its water clear and wholesome. The next night, the army would move into position in the mountains near to the southern enemy camp and take rest there, waiting the day while Layandria moved her force into position. Both companies would hold again for the enemy ranks to begin their march. The fight felt so close, and yet, riding through the open desert, the time felt to Layandria as if it stretched out far before her.

Thyso and Rale'en had returned in the company of Chieftain Wakkanolh and six thousand five hundred warriors of the Inohamman Xonar just short hours before the entire army departed the Wanoak village. The Chieftain Wakkanolh was suspicious of a foreigner leading the Wanoak, though less insultingly so than Chieftain Barbas. She was constantly under the suspicion of the Chieftains, who had taken to calling her Pulank, which meant whore in the words of old Inohamman.

With whispers hushed just as she approached, word was spread that it was through the power of her womanhood that Layandria had secured her position with the Wanoak. She overheard many of these conversations, taking no care for any, save for those that referenced the hue of her skin. Many believed her to be unworthy of trust, likely to be involved in immoral behavior. The same was said of Oslun, while

Jaxus and Thyso were held in esteem as they bore a much darker complexion than even those of the Inohamman.

Thyso confessed that Rale'en had propositioned him several times in the solitude of the desert. He rebuffed her advances, and she became angered. The young handmaid did not inform his companions of Rale'en's conduct following his rejection. The woman struck him in the throat and took his body against his will. He was overcome by shame and robbed of his confidence, reliving the memory in each night's passing. Rale'en's disposition soured towards the others of Arken, avoiding them and refusing calls to council, though none save Thyso understood the cause. The numbers of those who could be trusted was shrinking at a rapid pace.

"Keep your thoughts well." Halta rode up on Layandria's right side. Her voice was soft, a comforting warmth in the cold of the desert. Halta wore the simple skins that made up her daily vestment, a short cutlass hung at her thigh and a long spear was tied to her horse's flank. Layandria took in her face as the moon light brought out her features, shining off her black hair and revealing her many scars.

"My thoughts are troubled." Layandria let the words out and immediately questioned the action. She never recalled her father admitting his weakness or failing resolve.

"That is natural, Lady." Halta was soothing, riding gently in her saddle as if she was born to horseback. "Stave away doubt and worry. There is a power to thought that many do not see."

"What do you mean?" Layandria inquired, her mind too clouded to focus.

"I have found that when I allow myself to think about the possibility of failure, or to dwell in fear, my actions are swayed by the thought." Halta appeared very wise and experienced to Layandria, though she was only five years her senior. "When I choose to see success and positive outcome, I find that result more attainable. The mind has a way of making its thoughts become truth."

"I see." Layandria doubted that simply choosing to think of success would be possible for her, so heavy was the weight of the lives she now led. Still, there was a logic to what Halta said. "I want to see us through to victory, but if we fail, what will happen to the people in the villages of the Wanoak?"

Halta sighed. "This is not a path that is open to us. Those people and their lives are dependent on our victory. There is no alternative for them should we fail, and so, we must not. We must refuse to think of any outcome that is not our complete triumph."

Layandria tried to internalize the words, but she faltered. "I hope that we can. . ."

Halta cut her off abruptly, her voice strong and defiant. "There is not room in our cause for hope. There is only room for victory. Steel your heart and remove all doubt."

"I am trying, Halta." Layandria was earnest in her words, though she did not feel any more in control than a fish who attempts to controls the sea.

"You cannot try, you must refuse to accept any other thought." Halta raised her arm and gripped Layandria's. "The warriors behind us follow you because they believe you will lead us to victory. Do you know why?"

"In truth, I do not." Layandria turned her eyes down, thinking that she should pass leadership over to one more suited to combat. "Perhaps Jaxus should lead. He has fought many battles."

"Jaxus is not our chosen commander." Halta's words were sharp. "The man is strong and well experienced, but we did not choose him to lead us."

"Perhaps you should have." The Queen was downcast.

"No!" Halta grew angry at Layandria's despondency. "Who was it that rushed to aid the wounded Thyso on the floor of the tunnel? Who was it that moved first to aid the victims of the attack on our village when we arrived? It was not Jaxus, or even Wilteph, who called himself their Chieftain. And who was it that called for patience before riding out to engage our enemies? Who then saw the need for battle and united the tribes to face this enemy?"

"I see the point you are making." Layandria saw her own actions, though she did not see how these choices made her ready to lead an army in war.

"No, My Queen, you do not." Halta softened. "To truly lead, you must have a mind for the people. You must concern yourself with their lives before your own. Wilteph was quick to anger when confronted with the death of our people, but he did not truly feel for the loss of our tribe until confronted with the death of his own child. That is because the anger he felt was not truly for the dead, it was for the damage to his pride. Only when the death was of his blood did he feel its weight. He cannot lead us. Jaxus is powerful, but he feels no loyalty to the Inohamman. No, his heart is yours alone. He will engage in this war, knowing that he may well give his life for it, but were you to stop now and turn away, the man would follow you without question. He cannot lead us. The Chieftains were content to sit back in the knowledge of what happened to our people and do nothing. It was only when they were confronted with knowledge that the Lakemen seek to take lands as their own, a thing that would put the Chieftains own territories at risk, that they acted. They cannot lead us."

"So, there is no one else." Layandria resigned to her role.

"You are starting to see, but it is not for lack of other choice that we elected you. Tepan is wise and strong, he is respected and fit to lead. There are many who would follow me if I asked for their loyalty. You were chosen for reason." Halta let the words sink in before she continued. "You are willing to humble yourself, taking to the dirt to bandage wounds and you easily ask for aid when it is needed. You are strong, and you see to the people before your look to your own aims."

"I do not know if I am strong." Layandria saw the protest rise on Halta's lips but cut her off before she could speak it. "But I will accept the loyalty you give me, and I will give all that I have for you and for those that rely on our victory."

"Good." Halta smiled softly at the Queen. She turned her eyes back forward, gently steering her horse to the left and guiding Layandria in a small correction of their course. "What will you do once we have won and returned to the Wanoak village?"

Layandria took a moment to gather her thoughts on the change in conversation. "I have need to return to Arken, though I do not know what I will find when I arrive."

Halta nodded and spoke quietly, the softness returned to her voice. "Will you take Oslun with you?"

Layandria turned knowingly. She saw love in the woman's eyes. "Oslun is a free man. If he chooses to return with me, he may."

"And if he chooses to stay with the Inohamman?" Halta asked gently.

"I see in him a blooming love for you." Layandria turned her gaze back to the horizon. "If he chooses to stay at your side, he will do so with the blessing of my full heart, though I have heard speech that would indicate he may not be so welcomed."

Halta's shoulders relaxed and an easy smile crossed her face. "In the Wanoak, there is no account paid to love. Warriors are forbidden from it and are banished if found in it. I, being named as a warrior, thought to never find such love, and my tribe will likely put me to the sword if they discover what I share with Oslun, being he of foreign birth and pale complexion."

"I do not understand this." Layandria's voice conveyed her disdain for such injustice. "A person is not the property of the King of Chief they serve. Certainly, there are objective laws, meant to protect the people and encourage the prosperity of the kingdom, but even these laws must be bent at times to serve the people."

"There is no bending in the Inohamman." Halta's voice fell to darkness. "Wilteph was son of the Chieftain, but even that status would not have saved him and did not save his father."

"Such a rigid application of authority serves no one." Layandria's voice was stern. She faced Halta, nearly turning sideways in her saddle. "If your people will not accept your love for Oslun, you are welcome to come to Arken as one of us."

Halta's eyes showed her surprise at Layandria's offer. She thought through the words for a moment. "That is why I choose to follow you, Layandria, Queen of Shadow."

"When we have come through the other side of the days before us, speak to him. I will honor any choice you make together." Layandria did not want to lose Oslun, having great love for the soft boy who was becoming a great man, but she would not deny the wishes of his heart.

The women grew silent, Halta's thoughts on her future with the young cup bearer, Layandria's straying back to the coming fight.

"We were right to choose you." Halta broke the silence, her eyes remaining forward. "In victory, or death, we were right to follow you."

Layandria narrowed her eyes. "Victory is the only option."

30

"No word of Queen Layandria?" Master Hale inquired in a hushed tone. The Whisper Hall was empty, save for Lord Commander Fax and himself. The borum stone walls shone brightly, casting a warm glow throughout the room.

Liam frowned deeply. "No word yet, though we do not know how far the Queen traveled and it may take time."

"Time is not on our side." Master Hale bent low, leaning closely to the Commander's ear as he sat in the throne.

Liam was uncomfortable in the chair, and he was anxious to give it back to the rightful ruler. "There is nothing I can do to hasten the search."

"Of course not, Lord Commander." Master Hale signed and stood. "It is only fear that drives my inquiry. Speed is the one thing that we greatly need, but it is the one thing we cannot control. It has been widely reported that the King is of improving health and that word will certainly reach Lord Nathus. We will soon have to report that Master Pleuin has departed the Arkenhead in route to the Iron Fist. If we delay longer, Lord Nathus will begin to suspect."

"Naturally, Pleuin will not reach the Iron Fist." Lord Commander Fax spoke sternly.

"How will you ensure that Lord Nathus believes his coin master has perished through some other means?" Master Hale was wise in politics and matters of finance, but he had little knowledge in the ways of combat.

Liam folded his hands. A cold countenance took hold of him. "Master Pleuin will depart the citadel in the company of his guards. The guards will be blind to the knowledge that their charge is dead inside his carriage. As you know, the master's body had been laid on ice. It will be placed in the carriage, though it will be accompanied by one of my own trusted men whose voice bears a strong similarity to the coin masters. If any of the master's men inquire on his comfort, they will be strongly rebuffed by their charge. Several of my men will be in place to intercept the caravan, under the guise of savages from the north. They will attack the master's carriage as it passes through the fire fist. My men will leave no survivors, giving much credit to the idea that they were fell upon by savages."

Master Hale broke in. "What will make Lord Nathus believe that raiders from the north have penetrated so deeply into the Wolf Fist?"

"I have already sent a request to Lord Nathus that he dispatch forces to the Wolf Fist to bolster Lord Aralias' lines. Nathus will certainly deny the requisition, as he historically has. This request will be remembered when he is informed of Master Pleuin's death." Liam was certain the plan would work, and he could see no possible circumstance that would cause failure.

"Your actions are sound, Lord Commander." Master Hale weighed in. "Though ordering Arken men to willingly murder Arken men is a crime punished by death. Your choice is necessary, but it does not sit well in my heart."

"Nearly every choice I have made since King Axeleon was wounded has been leading me towards the same fate. Win or lose, I will likely be put to death for what I have done." Commander Fax voice conveyed that he did believe this, but there was no sorrow in his tone.

"And yet you persist?" Master Hale inquired.

"I have no choice but to persist." Liam acknowledged the root of the master's question. "Were I to do nothing, Lord Nathus would march to the Arkenhead to seek out his coin master. He would discover the King's fate and take the throne. I have made it exceedingly easy for him to prove a case of treason. The evidence would lead me to sudden and painful death."

"Though I would be well with this end, the health of the kingdom would be in a terrible state. Layandria would return not to her welcoming people, but to swords. Lord Nathus would attempt to consolidate his power and ensure the loyalty of the Fists. Death and corruption would certainly follow. While I would find my rest in the next life, the ideals I have fought for would die." The Lord Commander stood and walked towards the borum stone wall at the side of the platform. He watched the embers flicker, their light reflecting off his face.

"So, you see," Liam spoke again, though he continued watching the borum stone dance, "while it would appear that I have options before me, I have none."

Master Hale did not respond for a time. He intertwined his fingers with the long, wispy beard that hung from his chin. He watched Liam intently. "You are a good man, Liam Fax."

"Good or otherwise, this bears no weight on my mind." Liam turned and faced the coin master, walking slowly back to the throne. "All that weighs on me is the future of Arken."

31

The sky was dark and heavy with pending rain. Morning had not yet come to light the way. Aralias shivered inside his armor as he hunkered down with his men on the soil. Many tried to find rest, but for warriors about to enter combat, there was seldom luxury. Their minds dwelt on families, past choices, hopes for the future.

Aralias thought about the small chamber he took for his own in the Kanamar Fortress at the center of the Fire Fist, adorned with soft furs and heirlooms of his ancestors. It was not the chamber used by his father and the other Lords over the Fire Fist in the past. He abhorred that room, so large, full of trophies and other adornments. While many said that Aralias personality was quite large, he enjoyed the simpler, smaller comforts of life and found himself uncomfortable in riches.

A low murmur passed through the five hundred wolves on the ground. Aralias lifted his head and saw that several green streaks burned across the atmosphere. As the projectiles traveled, they gave off an eerie glow that would be seen for many miles. The rounds burst, the inner charges touched by the fire that surrounded them, tearing the casings apart and belching green flame into the dawn.

The wolves did not move, the low murmur they emitted dying. They knew that this signal would bring their brothers and sisters into combat. They would wait while the fighting began, allowing time for the camps nearest to them to empty and the bulk of the guards to be drawn off.

Lord Aralias took in a slow breath and calmed his nerves. He began silently counting the time as it dragged by. He focused on small things, the texture of his fingernails, the feel of the dust between his fingers, the smell of the earth. It was a long practiced, personal tradition that allowed him to clear his mind and keep worry at bay. He refused to let his mind focus on anything other than those small things that were real, and before his immediate senses.

Aralias took in all angles that surrounded his men as he rose from the turf. His people stood as well, each stretching as armor allowed, limbering deadened limbs and making ready. Without a word, Aralias began to move, slowly at first, extending his step once he heard the small shuffle of five hundred pairs of booted feet on the dry soil.

They covered the distance well, moving at a rapid pace for just over a half hour. Aralias took in the sight of the enemy position quickly, planning his attack. He turned his formation to the left and wheeled around, keeping a good distance from the camp. The muted armor worn by the wolf soldiers was, though not black, far better at concealment than shadow armor in all but the darkest of nights.

Aralias led into a low defilade, turning the formation again, using the shallow depression to conceal their movement as they drew nearer to the enemy. Aralias stopped and let the ranks reform. There were no words of motivation or fierce cries of battle. There were no heartfelt wishes for good luck passed among the fighters. Aralias eased himself up to the top of the rise, peering into the camp. He could see battle planners and high commanders running about from map table to map table, dispatching runners and barking orders. The commanders were unprepared for the large-scale assault taking place along both combat fronts and there was a certain frantic quality in the movements as men moved about in disarray.

Aralias saw all that he needed. The guards that patrolled the camp perimeter had turned their attention inward, attempting to gain understanding of the panic that was brought on by the runners and messengers. The Wolf Lord eased back down the rise, allowing himself room to stand fully erect. His warriors were prepared, ferocity in their expressions. He took in a deep breath, holding it inside and releasing it with a poisonous rasp. "Kill."

Aralias spun and charged up the dirt bank, sword high. He men surged behind him. No battle calls were given, no war cries went up, but the force of the churning bodies carried the power of an eruption spilling from the bowels of the earth. They met the sentries on the outer perimeter before they could react. Swords penetrated steel, axes cleaved flesh from bone. Screams went up all along the line of attack.

Aralias charged straight towards the center of the camp. He estimated two hundred Starrowland souls remained here and as he moved, he confirmed his count. He did not pause to kill those who stood before him. The enemy he passed would be dealt with by the wolves that came behind. The Wolf Lord knew that they could not risk being stalled on the outer edges, their chief need to prevent any concerted defense from forming, or the enemy leadership element concocting an escape.

A massive warrior, clad head to foot in gleaming armor stood before Aralias, a large axe held in both hands. Aralias was curious as to why the man stood still and did not seek cover. Arrows whistled past the wolf as he moved towards this enemy, his men firing on the silver form. The arrows impacted the chest plate and glanced off, none penetrating. Aralias knew at once that this soldier's armor was too thick for conventional attack. He scanned left and right, slowing his advance and looking for something that would aid him. Several of the wolf soldiers caught up with his slowed pace, blood already adorning some of them.

The distance closed, and Aralias seized on a plan. The man must be taken to the ground. He stepped forward, just inside the ark of the silver enemy's axe. The ax fell, the wolf danced back, letting the weight of the weapon carry it to the ground. He charged forward with his full force, but he did not raise his sword. He drove his full weight into the huge soldier's chest and was rewarded with the impact of another wolf driving into the back of his own armor. Their combined force knocked the man staggering backwards. The heavy armor that was meant to make the man safe from all strike was his undoing before he was able to land a single hit.

The silver warrior impacted the soil with a wheezing explosion of air from lips concealed under helm. Aralias felt the wolf at his back roll off, freeing him to move. Two wolves jumped on the large man's arms, pinning them to the turf. Aralias gripped the underside of the gleaming face shield and ripped it up and away. He drew his knife and barely noted that this impressive warrior in thick, heavy armor was a woman with hair as red as flame. The plunged his knife into the woman's eye socket, wrenching it from side to side before he withdrew the blade and sprang up, raising his sword in one hand, the dripping blade in the other.

The enemy began forming ranks and organizing resistance. Aralias could see through the silhouettes as they moved towards him. Men swarmed the map tables, taking up the documents and destroying any intelligence that the wolves might gain. The Wolf Lord pulled his chain mail hood over his head and dug his boots into the soil, launching into a sprint.

As the man leapt forward, his wolves followed. They ran at full speed towards the loose line of the Starrowlanders. Fear bathed the enemy as the wolves, fueled by the taste of fresh blood, crashed into them. A wolf soldier to Aralias left swung a spiked mace into the chest of an enemy, crushing the enemy's chest plate and taking him down. Aralias smiled wickedly, his teeth barred as the ferocity of the wolves brought rise to the savage within him. His vision expanded as time both rapidly sped up, and simultaneously slowed to a crawl. It was as if Aralias could see every detail of every blade raised against him. He swept swords away, his own slashing and cutting with almost impossible speed as if the blade took on its own hunger for the fight.

An arrow flew in unexpected. The smooth stone head was graced with luck, finding the gap between the chest plate and the armor surrounding Aralias left shoulder. It penetrated deeply, below the joint. The Lord cried out in pain and several wolves pushed in, surrounding him with weapons outward. Aralias dropped his sword and fell to his knees. He raised his right hand and removed the shoulder plate, wrenching against the pain to see where the arrow entered his flesh. The wound was not dire, penetrating low and damaging muscle, but nothing of vital significance. Aralias gripped the shaft and clenched his jaw. He screamed through barred teeth as he tore the arrow from his body. The pain rolled his stomach, but the wolf fought it off.

He stood, finding that his left arm was weak and of no use. He could feel warm blood running down his side, but he paid it no attention. He took up his sword and pressed forward, passing through the shroud formed by his men. The Starrowlanders were collapsing, taking casualties rapidly, bathed in the knowledge that death had arrived for them. Aralias could see a small cluster breaking off and fleeing the battle. He raised his damaged arm, pointing to the cowards, knowing the enemy commanders must be among them. He cried out with all his voice could bring, "do not let them escape!" His voice cracked under the throbbing pain in his shoulder. He ignored it and took pursuit.

The escapees moved quickly, four men in armor that Aralias took to be the leaders, followed by two other men clad in simple clothes who struggled to keep pace, burdened as they were by many large maps rolled tightly. Aralias followed them, two of his fighters just at his heels.

The enemy leaders exited the camp to the east and turned slightly south. Aralias and his companions closed on them as they fled up a low bluff. Wounded though he was, the Wolf Lord brought his sword to bear, ruining through one of the unarmed map bearers as the man screamed in terror. His companions made easy work of the other. The enemy commanders turned back and saw the wolves that pursued them.

A wolf fired an arrow, taking one of the commanders in the groin, expertly finding a weakness in armor. The enemy drew down on the wolves swiftly. Swords clashed and cries went out. Aralias found himself faced by a dull steel-clad commander who wielded twin curved blades. The swords whistled towards him and Aralias dropped his weight, rolling left, coming down hard on his wounded shoulder. He forced himself to ignore the torment brought by the impact as he came to his knees, driving his sword into the man's side. The tip found the armor on the man's hip, scraping upwards until it caught on the downward edge of the man's chest plate.

Aralias lunged forward with one leg, forcing the blade between the plates. It penetrated ferociously, cutting into intestines and lungs. The armored man fell against the sudden intrusion of pain. Aralias could not keep his grip on his sword, lodged as it was in the dead man's armor. He drew his knife and stood, reeling around. Both of his men were down, one bleeding heavily from the under his arm, the pain of coming death concealed under his bestial helm. The other was flat on his back, a Starrowlander stood over him, pulling his sword out of the wolf's chest plate. The other two enemy commanders were also down.

Understanding crept over Aralias. He had one chance to take the man while his sword was still trapped in the dead wolves' chest plate. He shot to his feet and leapt at the enemy's back, his knife high, his damaged arm hanging limply. The enemy caught the burst of movement before Aralias arrived and reacted quickly. The Starrowlander abandoned his stuck sword and swung his arm around like a club, the armored glove striking heavily across the Wolf Lord's face.

Aralias crashed to the ground, intense pain and fog filling his mind. He landed hard on the battered shoulder, destroying his thoughts. Blood filled his mouth and he felt pieces of shattered teeth on his tongue. Aralias rolled to his right and spat. He struggled to stand, gathering his dropped knife from the thick dust. A heavy boot kicked him in the side, sending him sprawling. He landed on his back and blinked hard against the haze that occupied his sight.

The shadow of a man in dull armor filled his vision. He forced his torso up and drove his knife into the man's knee, finding a small gap in armor at the back side of the joint. The man yelped and fell next to Aralias. The Wolf Lord collapsed back into the dust, his strength running away with the blood from his shoulder. The enemy commander dragged himself forward on his elbows, climbing onto Aralias chest as saliva frothed from his lips with rough snarls.

The Wolf Lord wriggled wildly, his left hand useless, his right suddenly empty, having lost the knife. He was weak and without weapon, nothing left in his mind to stop the onslaught as the enemy wrapped rough hands around his neck and began to squeeze. Aralias fought for escape, pushing off the ground with his legs and jerking his hips. The enemy was much heavier than the small framed wolf and he was unable to gain ground.

Aralias did not contemplate his life or think of final words of defiance. He felt his strength leaving him and the knowledge that he would die washed over his mind. His vision began to fail, and he lost sensation from his limbs. White fabric flourished to his left, but the Wolf Lord's diminished vision could not identify the source. He raised his hand in a final attempt to salvage his life and dug his thumb into the man's mouth, peeling his cheek back. The man opened his jaw and bit down on the wolf's thumb. Aralias cried out in frailty, his damaged hand falling to his side. The enemy barred down and Aralias knew it was over.

A small, dark skinned hand gripped the man's hair, just at the top of Aralias vision. The unseen savior pulled back on the man's scalp, lifting his chin. The sudden contact caused the enemy to loosen his grip on Aralias' neck. The wolf lunged his head upward in a final burst of will. He struck the man in the jaw with the crown of his head. The force of the impact dazed him deeply, worsening the chaos of his thoughts, but it did far more damage to the enemy. The Starrowlander bit down hard on his tongue, cleaving off the end of the organ. The man screamed and spat on Aralias, the severed tongue landing with the fluids.

The Wolf Lord was helpless to do anything but watch as the enemy's head was pulled upwards by the hair again. A small, rough knife was drawn across the exposed throat. The weapon was dull and did not cut deeply, bringing pain, but little significant damage. The enemy reeled against the attack, pitching backwards away from the Wolf Lord. Aralias heard a woman scream out as the enemy tumbled on to her. He turned his head to the right, seeing his own knife just out of reach. He rolled and took up the blade, his grip loose and unsure as his hands fought numbness. He tried to stand but his legs failed. The enemy was on all fours, a large rock in his hand, crawling towards the woman in white. Aralias recognized her at once, her dark skin reflecting the light of the new sun and revealing her face. It was Pelnieth, crawling backward desperately as the mad Starrowlander surged towards her.

Aralias dove at the man catching him in the side of his chest and wrapping his arms tightly around the man's armor as both rolled. Aralias swung his hips as the bodies tangled, allowing him to stop the spin to his advantage. The enemy stilled on his chest, face in the dirt. Aralias took his back and did not hesitate. He drove the knife into the base of the man's skull, passing the blade between the vertebrae as a great cry escaped his own lips. The enemy's body jerked wildly as the connection between flesh and brain was severed. Aralias rolled off him and came to his hands and knees.

The Wolf Lord raised his head and found that Pelnieth was coming to her feet. He watched as the woman came to him and extended her small hand, helping him to rise. He did not address her, but moved to recover his sword from the body it took home in. Weapon returned to his hand, Aralias faced his savior.

"Thank you." Aralias managed the words through the pain that washed over him from many injuries.

"You gave me my life," Pelnieth spoke softly, her hand gingerly touching a deep gash on her cheek with the hem of her dress, sopping the blood into its fibers. "Now I have given you yours."

Aralias flexed his fingers, glad to see that after repeated abuse, the digits still responded. He contemplated Pelnieth for a moment. "Do you still wish to serve with me?"

"I have no other place to go." The woman answered meekly.

"You are welcome to come with me and my men," Aralias offered as he continued to work his hand and elbow. "But if this is your choice, do it as a free woman with no debts to be paid."

Pelnieth did not immediately respond. Aralias watched as she approached a dead wolf who had his enemy's sword still impaling his flesh. She wrenched the blade free and turned back to the Wolf Lord. "We should go back to the camp. The sounds of fighting have stilled, and your men will be looking for you."

32.

Layandria rubbed her eyes. She slept in the company of her warriors during the day, but she found no comfort, the hot sun that blazed down on her black armor felt as if it was cooking her alive. The night was more tolerable in temperature, though the long slow walk and the brutal climb into the mountains did not improve her disposition. She was pleased to note that Oslun and Thyso both kept their pace without apparent struggle. She had been worried, especially about Oslun, but the man's heart was stout and with Halta at his side, it was as if he were new, stronger and prouder than he had ever displayed.

Thyso was another pressing worry. Since his return to the Wanoak, the handmaid had barely spoken to any save for Oslun. His eyes were downcast, and he seemed to have no interest in food. Never, in all the years that he stood by her side had the Queen observed this behavior. Thyso had his flaws, as any person did, but bouts of mood were not among them. This troubling behavior occupied the few corners of Layandria's mind that were left available, but she could not find an opportunity to address him.

Jaxus was never far from her side, though he did not show the affection that he had in the desert so many nights past. The dark knight wore the same emotionless expression that he always had, revealing nothing. She had called out to him with her thoughts several times and the man always answered back, but she longed for the comfort of his touch, the feel of his lips on her skin.

They waited now, Layandria and her small band of fighters, prepared to move and strike at the enemy as the final rays of sun light vanished under the tops of the mountains. The Queen felt fatigue and worry wrap around her heart.

The sky was beginning to darken, the deep black of night slowly creeping its ink across the heavens. How would she know when to strike? The day did not die suddenly, but gradually, being beaten back by the blackness one shade at a time. Worse yet, heavy clouds were setting in low. Layandria cursed silently in her head. What point in this scrawling transition was the correct time for attack? She looked around for her knight but did not find him. *Jaxus.* She called out.

Yes, My Queen. Jaxus swift, unspoken response. She called him to join her and the man appeared at once. He sat on the ground, his back against a fallen tree trunk, facing his leader. Layandria took the man's large hand in hers.

She kept her voice low, not wanting any of the Inohamman who so trusted their lives to her leadership to catch wind of her doubt. "I have seen hundreds of sunsets, but it is only now I realize that I do not know the true point where day becomes night."

"You will know." Jaxus gently reassured her. He took in the look of deepening concern on her face. "Though, if you would like, I can tell you when it is time."

Layandria looked markedly relieved. "If you would, Sir Jaxus."

Jaxus smiled. He looked at Layandria and felt himself pulled towards her. He leaned in slightly and brushed his lips against her cheek. He wanted to kiss her with much more of the energy he felt, but he forced himself to resist. Layandria looked unhappy as he moved back. "Rest easy, My Queen. There is still time before we begin."

Layandria did not respond. He leaned in towards Jaxus and rested her head on his shoulder. She could smell his skin beneath his armor, and she wanted more, but she too resisted the desire.

Layandria sat upright at the sound of footballs reached her. Thyso approached softly, concern deep on his face. "Sir Jaxus, I would have a word."

The typical confidence of the young soldier was replaced with some stifling doubt. Jaxus did not want to leave Layandria's side, but Thyso pleaded with his eyes for council. "Of course, Thyso."

Jaxus stood as Thyso lead them off a short distance into the trees, beyond earshot of their fellows. Jaxus waited patiently for the young man to speak. It took Thyso several attempts to make the words come out. "Jaxus, do you think we will see Arken again?"

The dark knight contemplated Thyso's demeanor. It was not fear that gave the young man discomfort. It was something else. "We will, I am certain."

"I want to go home." Thyso said the words, his eyes fixed on the eastern peaks that blocked his home from view. "I want to leave this place and these people far behind."

Jaxus furrowed his brows. "Do you feel so poorly towards the Inohamman, who have welcomed us as their own?"

"Have they Jaxus?" Thyso spoke hotly. "Have the welcomed us? Do you not hear their whispers? They do not accept us as their own. Perhaps Halta and Tepan do, but the others conspire against us."

"I have heard no whisperings of conspiracy." Jaxus responded evenly, not wanting Thyso's emotion to raise his voice to the ears of the Inohamman. "Tell me what you have heard."

The young man continued in a whisper. "The elders of the tribes see you as a threat and several among our force are ordered to kill you if given the chance. One, Warrot is his name, spoke long on the history of your people. He argued for your acceptance, but the others did not care for his voice."

Jaxus smiled softly. "This is not the first time, nor will it be the last that kings and commanders have ordered my death. I do not fear their blades."

Thyso took in a large breath. "Halta and Oslun are not as secretive in their affections as they believe. The Chieftains have already decided that both must be put to death should they survive the battle. The believe that Halta has violated her station by taking a lover and further dishonored herself by taking one who is foreign and of a low complexion. Chieftain Barbas called her soiled and stated that her body must be broken in payment for her crimes."

Jaxus pursed his lips and heavy creases formed on his brow, though he did not speak.

"Of Tepan I have heard nothing. It appears that at least for the present, he has not angered the other tribes. Layandria is, of course, the source of most subterfuge and though I do not know what the Chieftains intend for her. I am not safe either, if they knew what I am, or what transpired in the desert, they would without doubt put me to an unspeakable end." Thyso lowered his eyes in shame and fear.

Jaxus had not seen this look on the proud young Thyso before. It both concerned and confounded him harshly. "What are you that would earn such a grisly demise and what event are you speaking of? I was told of no ill tidings."

"Jaxus, do you not see me for what I am?" Thyso spread his arms as if there were some large mark on his chest that a blind man could easily detect. Jaxus starred at him, his dark features opened in confusion. "Halta and Oslun have found comfort in each other's arms.

Layandria is drawn to you, but I have taken no pleasures in the women of the Wanoak, despite heavy pursuit from one among them."

Jaxus continued his stare. He could not see why failing to bed a woman of the tribe would cause issue, certainly this would save him from reproach if the Chieftains held such a poor view of the foreigners.

"Jaxus, I have no interest in women. I have no desire for the pleasures of the female body. The elders have seen who I look after. Rale'en questioned me on this when I rebuffed her advances and I was honest with her, so welcoming were the Inohamman. This was a snare. She forced me to bed with her. She laughed when I resisted. I can feel her on me still and forever will the sounds of her pleasures haunt my mind."

"Rale'en impressed on me that those of my kind are not welcome to life among the Inohamman. She has kept this knowledge to herself, though I believe she will use it to secure my silence, preventing revelations about her conduct. They will kill me if I am discovered. They will cut my manhood and bleed me until I am dead. It is their way for men like me." Thyso remained in shame and fear.

"For her crime, Rale'en will pay with her life. I and our Queen will ensure this comes to pass. No man or woman has right to take from another's body. Jaxus spoke sternly, though his voice remained low. "This is not a matter for this moment, and I will need your patience. Once the fight is finished, I will bring the vile woman to justice before Queen Layandria."

"Jaxus, you cannot!" Thyso's whisper was raspy, fear ripping the air as it exited the man. "Even in her death, Rale'en will reveal her knowledge of my nature and I will be put to a terrible end!"

"Thyso," Jaxus spoke soft and warm, a hand extended to calm the young man, "tell me plainly what it is that would cause these people to want your death and pain."

Thyso sighed heavily, exasperated. "For all your immense skills of observation, for all your strength, you do not see? I do not find pleasure in women because I find pleasure in men."

Jaxus smiled and relaxed his shoulders. He chuckled slightly, though he immediately saw that his reaction angered the younger man. "Thyso, be still. This is nothing to find shame in. Each man's eyes find pleasure in what they choose. Further still, each man's heart finds its home in the one it chooses. Only a fool fights the true desire of his heart. I have never noted this in your character because it is not relevant to me and changes nothing of the pride I carry for you."

Thyso stamped his foot, barely maintaining control over the volume of his voice. "Jaxus, this is not the law of the Inohamman, and it is not the law of Arken! Your opinion does not carry enough weight to save my life!"

Jaxus remained silent for a moment, letting Thyso breathe and regain his composure. "Layandria is Chieftain of the Wanoak and Queen of Arken. She is of the same heart as I, caring not for whom you love. Certainly, she will put a stop to this ridiculous law. For both you, and for Halta and Oslun."

Thyso looked up, meeting Jaxus eyes. "Jaxus, it is far worse than you imagine. The Chiefs conspire against our Queen. We are fools to accept their loyalty at its value."

Jaxus reeled at the words. He reached out with his thoughts. *My Queen, are you well?*

I am. The response came to him, turning tender in his inner ear. *Come back to me.*

I will, My Lady. In a moment. Jaxus unconsciously reached for the hilts of his twin swords, touching them, but not drawing the blades. *Be on your guard, there are snakes amongst us.*

Jaxus turned his attention back to Thyso. "What have you heard, brave Son of Arken?"

Thyso inhaled deeply, whispering his news at speed. "Wilteph hungers for the title of Chieftain. He has approached the Inohamman Chieftains in secret, and they have bargained on his position. They will allow Layandria to lead the attack against the Lakemen Gods, but Wilteph will kill Layandria and in so doing, be granted his title. The Chieftains fear that if Layandria leads the Wanoak into victory, the people will grow in support of her, giving her sway over their own tribes and strengthening her bid to hold leadership of the Wanoak once the fighting is done. So you see, Layandria has no power and we are all condemned to die if we stay here."

"This is not good." Jaxus mused to himself. "The Wanoak who have come south with us, are they loyal to the Queen?"

"Most are, though a few may have been convinced to betray us." Thyso calmed his speech, delivering the information in a more controlled tone. "The majority who saw the care Layandria gave to the wounded in the Wanoak city are loyal to her. None of their own Chiefs would ever lower themselves such, which has endeared our Queen to them greatly."

"We cannot leave these people to death." Jaxus wrestled with his thoughts. "Were it not for their loyalty, I would gather Oslun,

Layandria and the others to make our escape, but if we leave now, those loyal who have followed the Queen here would certainly die."

"Jaxus, what can we do?" Thyso pleaded quietly.

"I do not yet know," Jaxus brow tightened, "but we have no time to think on it now, the sun is nearly taken to sleep, and we must press our attack. Stay close to Layandria and do not let harm come to her."

"With my life, I will defend her." Thyso answered back resolutely. "Jaxus, do you truly believe I would be allowed to take a lover of my choosing in Arken? I would rather die than be forced to live as I am not."

Jaxus raised his hand to the side of Thyso's neck. "My friend, I will do all in my power to ensure this for you. If you are ordered to death for living as you are, by my word, I will meet that death beside you."

The handmaid took in the oath in silent awe. Confidence and hope sprang up anew. To have a warrior of Jaxus kind sworn to his cause was more than he could have hoped for.

Jaxus slid his swords from their scabbards easily. His eyes grew impossibly dark. "Now, good soldier, we must return to our Queen. It is time to spill blood once more."

33

He had seen her, riding at the head of a large army as it ranged across the desert. Certainty settled on him as he observed. She must be the princess he had been sent to retrieve, shadow armor and flame red hair unmistakable on the desert. He had carved his way across the terrain, keeping to the shadows as he steadily gained ground. She split from the main formation, taking a much smaller number further south. The detachment with the Princess took to rest in the forest and Sahid built a hasty camp, waiting for the cover of darkness. Much caution was required to make safe his approach to the Princess and her men.

She was accompanied by two others in shadow vestments and one man, tall and menacing even from great distance. This man wore a sort of strange armor that made his body nearly invisible. Sahid knew this to be none other than Jaxus. He was well familiar with the camouflage and the shape cut by the dark warrior. They had been friends once, at least as close as Sahid had been to any among the Starrowlands army. He knew Jaxus to be fierce and deadly, utterly without weakness in combat, and strangely devoid of emotion.

Sahid found companionship in the man as he never boasted of deeds behind the sword and took no pleasure in the torment of the dying. Their companionship was bolstered as the dark fighter had once put to death several of his own brothers at arms when he found them abusing the bodies of two young girls who had been taken prisoner. One of the women became with child, and for that, she was killed. Her murderers soon met grisly fates of their own. The other woman was removed from the encampment afterwards, no further pleasure women were brought in, and all understood that Jaxus was not to be tested.

Their friendship was ended prematurely when Jaxus volunteered to infiltrate the royal court of Arken. That was nearly two years before Axise landed on the Elk Fist shores and Sahid knew that much information of vital importance had been passed by Jaxus treachery. In what deception his former friend had engaged to so secure the trust of Axeleon and his court, Sahid could not guess, nor could he anticipate his former companion's reaction when they came face to face.

As evening permeated the sky, he was stirred from his doze by voices close to the brambles surrounding his shelter. He peered through the thicket and saw none other than Jaxus himself alone with one other of the shadow armored men. He began to inch himself out of the brush, moving to seize this opportune moment and make his presence known.

As if triggered by his motion, both men exchanged grim gestures of solidarity and turned off, moving back toward the camp. Sahid moved in behind them, though he was forced to conceal himself as the gathered army began to move. He pursued them, losing sight of Jaxus and the Princess as they moved to lead the battalion. Worry set in. This was an army moving into combat and in this chaos, many whose lives are in need of preservation often perish.

34

On Jaxus return, the Queen roused herself and sent warriors out to ready the others. In short moments, word returned that the small army was prepared. Layandria signaled and the mass of soldiers began to move. They formed loose ranks, staying in line, shoulder to shoulder, Layandria at the lead and center, Jaxus on her left and Thyso, her right. Halta and Oslun were beside Thyso and Tepan was just off Jaxus arm.

The formation moved in relative silence, the terrain moist, easing the sounds of many feet. They made progress quickly, arriving at the outer perimeter of the Lakelands village in less than an hour. The town backed up to a glassy lake. The walls of the city were low, formed of roughhewn logs laying stacked on the ground, bound with heavy rope. The buildings beyond the wall were much the same in construction. Jaxus recognized that the tough structures would provide impenetrable cover for the enemy from arrow fire. The logs, though wood, were safe from fire attack as such heavy timber is not easily ignited. The thatched roofs were somewhat more vulnerable, though the drops of rain that were beginning to fall would likely limit the use of flame.

The army approached the first wall unmolested and without sighting of the enemy. There was no sign of human life as the first rank climbed over the logs and entered the village. Smoke wafted up from stone chimneys, but nothing else moved. Layandria felt great relief, surprise honoring her forces and presenting unaware foes rather than waiting ranks of spears.

A feeling of unease washed over Jaxus as they passed the first row of buildings. They continued through the city, passing building after building and finding no resistance, no life at all. Hushed calls informed the leaders that the hutments were empty. Jaxus suspicions grew within him like a storm of electricity. He could feel the hairs on the back of his neck starting to rise and his senses sharpening. He flexed his hands and renewed the grip on his swords.

Thyso felt it too, fitting an arrow and shooting his eyes to every corner, waiting for the ambush he was certain was coming. Layandria was confused, understanding missing her as she sensed the unease of her fellows. Jaxus had told her that during his scouting, he discovered the center of the city was an open place, ringed by the tenements of the gods of the lake. Her confusion worsened as her eyes laid on this courtyard.

Where she expected to see Lakeland citizens going about their morning activities, she saw rank upon rank of Inohamman warriors filling half of the circle. The four Chieftains stood on a large stone at the center. The Queen stopped short at the sight, her mind unable to conjure any reasonable explanation for their presence. And where were the Lakemen? Her mind reeled in confusion, searching for answers.

Jaxus felt the assassin's approach in the small movements of air and grass. His sense was sharpened by instinct, his suspicion heightened by the information that Thyso provided. Jaxus stepped forward with his left foot and pivoted backwards, bringing Jushash and Ragnashon around. Wilteph had a short knife barred, moving in to strike the Queen low and at tremendous speed.

Jushash passed eagerly into the man's stomach, piercing through his body and exiting his back. As this would be assassin opened his mouth to scream in agony, Jaxus shoved Ragnashon through his chest, diving the blade into his heart and lung. The sound was sickening as Jaxus withdrew his swords from the wailing, dying man. None of the

Inohamman Wanoak warriors near him moved, each starring at the dead man in disbelief. Layandria spun at the sound of Jaxus strike. Her lips formed words, but no sound. The former Chieftain of the Inohamman Wanoak Outcasts, the proud son of Talin, died drowning as his own fluids filled his lungs.

Thyso and Oslun reacted without instruction, turning their backs to the Queen, prepared to repel attacks from any direction. Halta saw the defensive stance and followed suit, stepping in front of Layandria, facing her spear towards the Inohamman Chieftains. Tepan came to her side. The Queen was surrounded on all angles, though Jaxus knew they would not hold off an attack long from the thousands of enemies that had them penned on all sides.

"Chieftain Layandria." Chieftain Barbas called out, his voice so sweet and welcoming that it turned Layandria's stomach like spoiled cream. "Why do you draw weapons against your own people?"

"I have not." Layandria answered, rife with confusion and unable to grasp what was happening. "I have led the Wanoak here to make war on those who slaughtered unarmed people in their own villages."

"We who stand before you have done no such things." Barbas cooed to her across the thirty yards that separated them. "As you plainly see, the Lakemen are gone, there is no enemy here and no need for your weapons."

Jaxus watched the eyes of the Inohamman Wanoak. Confusion and fear covered their faces. He turned his head sideways and shouted towards the Chiefs. "Make your intent clear, waste no time in word play."

"The Chieftains of the Inohamman speak to Queen Layandria of Arken, not her ancient dog." Barbas tone grew into ice as he addressed Jaxus, morphing back into thick, dripping honey as he continued. "Now, good Queen, lower your weapons and treat with us. There is no need for hostility."

"Your words sound well to my ears, but your presence so far south of your target despite our carefully laid plans shows me an ill intent." Layandria pushed past her shock and fought to echo Jaxus confidence. "As my dog has said, make your desires clear."

"Very well." Chieftain Barbas nodded, all pretense of friend dropped from his voice. "You have accomplished something wonderful, something not done in these lands for generations. You have united the tribes of the Inohamman."

Halta spoke up, her voice clear and strong. "For this great accomplishment, you reward with deception?"

"Interrupt me not, outcast." Barbas hissed. "You think that bandaging a few wounds makes you worthy of Chieftain? No. The Inohamman will never follow some crownless Queen from the east."

"I was chosen by the people of the Wanoak!" Layandria bust out, the betrayal before her pushed her surprise and confusion away, fury taking its place.

"You were chosen by the weak survivors of a dishonored tribe. You are no Chieftain and you are no Queen." Barbas stepped forward, coming off the mighty stone. The other Chieftains moved with him, lowering themselves to the ground. "I give you this one chance, Layandria, one chance to save the lives of the Wanoak who follow you."

As Barbas said the words, the front three ranks of the Inohamman warriors behind him drew long bows and notched arrows. Layandria understood at once why the Chieftains had come off the platform. The arrows would be volleyed in on the Wanoak and on the stone, their commanders stood in the way of their firing arks. Layandria felt Jaxus and the others tighten in on her.

Barbas cleared his throat. "You will come forward and kneel before us. You will admit that you are a traitor to your own lands and to the Inohamman Wanoak. You and those who came with you will accept your punishment for the crimes you have committed. The Wanoak will swear loyalty to their true Chieftain. If you do this, the lives of those behind you will be spared."

"What crimes are we supposed to have committed?" Layandria inquired, the anger in her growing to a boil. "All we have done is give aid to those who had none and seek support from their own neighboring tribes!"

"You have brought shame and weakness on them!" Barbas bellowed, "For that, you and all who follow you must die! If you wish to save the lives of the Wanoak, come forward and accept your fate with whatever dignity you can find!"

Layandria was silent, uncertain of what she could say or do. Jaxus flexed his hands on his swords again. Thyso shifted his footing. The ranks of the Wanoak tensed, though none turned against Layandria.

"I see you have no honor." Barbas chided arrogantly. The other Chieftains were absolutely glowing in their triumph, save only for Chieftain Warrot. Layandria caught his eye and saw the slightest, most carefully hidden look of despair on his face.

A gentle calm washed over Layandria's heart. She could see no way out of this fight, knowing that the enemy stood before her in greater number than could be repulsed. The certain coming of death allowed her a sense control over the terms of the thing. She turned her head slightly, not moving her eyes from Barbas. Her voice was as a cool breeze, gentle and emitting only far enough to reach her people's ears. "We are going to die here."

Fear crossed the faces of the warriors surrounding her. Jaxus was impassive. Halta bore only the darkness of a person intent on combat.

"My good Lady," Tepan urged, "Do not accept this fate. Run and we will cover your retreat."

"That will mean certain death for you." Layandria countered. "And the chances of our escape are low."

"No, there will be no running." Jaxus low voice came as a man possessed by dark forces, cold and thick, hungry for the death that was on them. "Today is a good day for our meeting with death."

"Yes, we fight." Layandria agreed solemnly. "There is no escaping this trap, and I would die with honor, not on my knees before corrupted men."

"I am with you, Queen Layandria of Arken and the Inohamman Wanoak." Halta shook her spear, offering her solidarity and power. Her empty hand took hold of Oslun's, the touch carrying all the things that hearts could say if given mouths and words.

"Then let us be on with it!" Tepan shouted, stamping his feet. "I am well prepared for the next journey!"

"Those who are still with me, draw your bows and notch arrows, but keep them low." Layandria cast her eyes on all the Wanoak she could see. The warriors acted out her command slowly, their motions smooth and hidden as best they could. Instruction passed back in sharp words kept low. "When I kneel, loose your arrows."

The Queen turned back to the Chieftains. "I accept your bargain for the lives of the Wanoak."

Jaxus tensed. Chieftain Barbas smiled wickedly. Layandria stepped between Halta and Oslun, moving slowly towards the center of the court. She sheathed Heart's End securely, her steps deliberate.

Jaxus stepped to her side, his swords stowed on his back. "I will join you in this death that I may share with you whatever comes after."

Layandria looked up at him, the minute traces of a wicked smile on her lips. "We will not die this day."

The pair closed within ten paces of Barbas. The man's vile eyes sparkled with the glee of his victory. "You are doing a wise and great thing, for the tribes of the Inohamman are united under one Chieftain. Each has fought their own quarrels in the past, but the shame of the Wanoak has shown us that we can no longer allow the tribes to govern separately. I will lead our people to glory."

Layandria raised her brow in suspicion. "What has become of the Lakemen?"

Barbas chuckled. "Your scout reported the truth, but what he did not know is that my own emissary brokered agreement in our favor. The gods of the lake will return to their holding in their own time, taking a portion of land in tribute."

"So, you seized the misfortune of the Wanoak to consolidate your power over all the tribes?" Layandria asked with admiration oozing from her words. "That is a bold move."

"My brothers know me to be the superior Chieftain. My tribe has more strength and prosperity than any other." Barbas gloated freely, accepting that the empty handed Layandria posed no great threat. "We agreed that no foreign woman would ever be allowed to lead a tribe of our people, and none who assumed this honor would be let to live. It is all according to the laws of our people, though where others lack the will to enforce, I do not."

"You have the strength to rule the Inohamman lands alone?" Layandria fueled the man's boasting.

"There is no other who can." Barbas pride grew. "But we will not content ourselves to sustain on what we have been confined for these many generations. We will reach out. The Lakemen and their so-called gods believe our treaty to be founded in truth, but it is not. The false water gods will return only to find death waiting. The Inohamman will stretch out on this land, taking all that we see as wanted. Perhaps I will lead our armies over the mountains, taking from the iron men what you, who call yourself Queen, could not keep for your own."

Layandria could see the faces of the Inohamman warriors behind Chieftain Barbas. Their expressions reflected confusion, glancing back and forth from one to another as their leader spoke. The Queen chose to push this unsettled energy further. "Have you taken account of the desires of your people? Do they wish for war and conquering?"

"I am their Chieftain!" Barbas blared. "I do not need the consent of those who are beneath me!"

These words brought anger to some of the faces. Layandria could see that if there was ever a time for her to kneel, this was its moment. She let her fury roar out of her chest. "No man who rules without consent will long hold the title. The only way a man can hold the loyalty of his people is to kneel before them!"

Barbas bellowed in anger and stepped towards Layandria with clenched fists. The Queen dropped to her knees with all her weight. Jaxus followed her action, covering her back with his own. The immediate sound of hundreds of bow strings releasing their tension filled the thick air. Barbas was too enraptured in his anger to react. The Inohamman warriors at his back were slow in their understanding. The first volley struck on them with devastating effect. Thunder tore across the dark sky and it opened wide, rain falling in thick sheets. Chieftain Zinan was struck several times, falling in a brilliant show of flailing death. Rank on rank of Inohamman warrior fell against the hail of arrows.

Layandria lurched to her feet, drawing her blade as the arrows flew past her. She dove forward, rushing Chief Barbas with Heart's End at the low ready. Barbas was stunned by the sudden deception, and unable to repel her. The chieftains of the Inohamman did not take to battle with their troops and such as sudden onslaught was beyond their immediate understanding.

Barbas turned his back to flee but he did not complete a step. Layandria slashed her sword across the backs of his thighs in a long cut that gushed freely. The man spun wildly against the sudden loss of control over his legs. He tumbled down, coming to his side and pawing feebly at the wounds.

Chieftain Wakkanolh darted towards Layandria as she turned away from Barbas. A small, black stone knife in his hand. Layandria poised to receive this attack, but Jaxus was faster. The ark he cut with Jushash was swift and vicious, cleaving the Chieftain's arm off at the elbow. Ragnashon followed the cut with a piercing jab that passed greedily into Wakkanolh's chest.

Layandria looked up and saw that the Inohamman were reacting to the change in action. They fired arrows across the courtyard, while they received another volley from the Wanoak. Those in the front most ranks began to spill into the center, moving at speed towards Layandria. The Queen turned to Jaxus, looking for direction. In her movement, she saw that Halta, Thyso, Tepan and Oslun were leading a large group of Wanoak into the center, their weapons ready. She turned back towards the approaching enemy and raised her sword.

Arrows slung at random intervals now, cascading back and forth over her head. The moans and screams of the dying filled the air. Jaxus stepped to Layandria's side. "I am with you."

"Tell me you love me." Layandria said the words without looking at the man. The enemy was closing. Chieftain Warrot stood by, frozen in horror as Inohamman killed Inohamman.

"I will love you for all of my years." Jaxus answered back, just as the first of the Inohamman reached them. Jaxus wheeled, his swords flying in unison, peeling the head of a long spear, jutting upwards and taking the spear bearer across the chest. Layandria dipped her body, avoiding the swing of a stone mace that came in high. She rose, bringing Heart's End into the enemy's belly and wrenching free in a twisting motion that carried her around, blocking the incoming cut of a roughly made sword in the hands of the next attacker.

Halta and the other Wanoak arrived at the front line, clashing viciously in shrieks and crunches of metal on metal. Thyso pushed his sword over Layandria's head, jamming it into the face of a man that was about to strike her back. She reeled and kicked the man, freeing

Thyso's weapon. Jaxus was deeply engaged, spinning and slashing his twin blades in a cascade of blood and steel. Halta's spear found a worthy target in a warrior that charged in with a heavy club held high. The man's own momentum carried him into the spear, his feet slipping on the already drenched turf.

An arrow flew in and caught Tepan in the neck. He roared violently and ripped the projectile from his flesh. He flipped it in his hand, the head now forward, and jammed it into the chest of an Inohamman fighter. The squat wall of a man spun with incredible delicacy and he slammed his fist into the face of another, crushing the man's nose and upper jaw in a sickening crunch. Tepan stepped back to regain his stance, but he found his limbs weakened, blood covering his chest.

Tepan fell. Layandria saw him go down and pulled back, dragging her sword across a man's groin as she moved to Tepan. She knelt at his side and tore a chunk of cloth from his breeches. She wrapped his damaged neck in the fabric and held his hand to it. "Keep pressure on this." She instructed. She turned to two Wanoak, "get him back from the line!"

Layandria rose and readied her sword, but she was not prepared for the stone club that swung in low and fast. The club impacted her chest plate and her feet left the ground. Layandria splashed down hard, her head impacting a stone in the soaked grass. She was dazed and could not regain focus. Jaxus screamed her name and rushed in. Jushash and Ragnashon formed a two-pronged spear that penetrated both low and high on the enemy's chest. Jaxus sheathed Ragnashon and pulled the Queen to her feet. Layandria saw Jaxus eyes go blazingly wide. His grip failed as a sword raked the back of his head and neck. She fell back to the ground.

Jaxus straightened his posture and spun back, slashing his blade in both hands. Jushash crossed the enemy's face, opening the flesh wide, blinding the man. Layandria watched in blurred horror as the man dropped his weapon and fell to his knees, desperately blotting at his wrecked eyes with his hands. A deep wound was clear on the back of Jaxus head, blood mixing with the heavy rain and running in a torrent down his neck, into his armor.

Jaxus engaged another enemy, planting himself before Layandria. The Wanoak gathered, pushing back the enemy and forming a ring around the downed Queen.

Jaxus lunged forward and repelled an incoming sword from striking Thyso's exposed forearm. The man immediately spun around and looked to his Queen. A sword stroke impacted Jaxus back. The Jurin armor that he wore was unscathed by the strike and he ignored the contact as he called to Thyso and Oslun. "Layandria has need for aid!"

So many had fallen. Layandria felt a deep weight drop on her heart as she saw the dead and dying strewn all around. Her companions came to her side. "Help me stand!"

Jaxus sized up the situation and knew there was not enough strength left in the Wanoak to push for the center. Jaxus and Oslun wrenched their royal up from the sopping turf. To her feet, Layandria forced her way between the men as strokes of violence fell all around her. She ripped the leather covering off sun stone. The light that emitted from the pendant was immediately dazzling, shattering the darkness and destroying the vision of all who were exposed to it.

"Do not look at it!" Jaxus shouted to the Wanoak and the others near him.

The Wanoak seized the distraction and struck out, felling many enemies, backlighted as they were by the sunstone. Jaxus surged forward, Thyso, Oslun and Halta at his flanks. Tepan fell back. Layandria stayed just behind Jaxus as they charged towards the flagstone at the center. An arrow glanced off Jaxus armor as he reached the rock and mounted it swiftly.

As Layandria mounted the stone, she held the sun stone in her free hand, stretching it upwards as high as the chain allowed. The sun stone intensified, its radiance forcing the Inohamman to abandon their weapons and cover their faces in great pain.

"Retreat!" Jaxus ordered to the Wanoak. "Retreat now!"

Layandria held her position on the flagstone. The sun stone cast is luminance far, blinding even the rear archers of the Inohamman and rendering their shots useless. She could see Chieftain Warrot laying on the ground, his arms over his head, his face buried in the muck.

The Inohamman fell back, shuffling through the grass and dirt, seeking shelter from the sun stone. For a moment, the Queen considered the life of the cowering Chieftain Warrot. She raised Heart's End, ready to end the man as she dismounted the rock but as she approached him, she stayed her hand, though she could not put words to her hesitation. As her feet touched soggy grass, Layandria dropped the stone to her chest and the group broke into a run, moving for the cover of the wooden buildings.

As the light of the sun stone left them, the Inohamman broke into chaos and disarray. Leaderless, some fired arrows high into the air, hoping to strike the backs of the fleeing Wanoak. They were ineffective. Others abandoned their weapons, lost in the mystery of what they had seen.

Layandria took the lead of the group as they raced off after the Wanoak. A stranger clad in shadow armor stepped out of concealment behind a mighty tree directly in front of the Queen. He held his hands up willing her to stop, but he misjudged her speed and she crashed headlong into him. They rolled to the soil, coming to rest on their backs. Jaxus was on the man in seconds, both swords positioned under his jaw. Recognition flashed through his eyes. Layandria saw her assailant's shadow armor, though she had not seen his face before.

"Jaxus, wait!" Layandria called out and came to her feet, rushing in to stay her man's strike. He did not respond to her.

"Why are you here?" Jaxus hissed the demand as he towered over the prostate from that he recognized at once to be Sahid Hauk Khan.

"I was sent by Lord Commander Liam Fax to find and return Princess Layandria to the Arkenhead!" Sahid shouted the words, begging that his life be not ended on the very moment of his success.

Layandria stepped in over Sahid's head. "The Lord Commander was by my father's side when Axise breached the Whisper Hall. He is surely dead."

"You are a servant of Axise, sent to deceive and bring about the end of my Queen!" Jaxus voice bore all the malice and rage accumulated over his long years. He was as a man become a demon.

"King Axeleon and his men defeated Axise! Lord Aralias of the Wolf Fist broke the siege and I was ordered out to find you!" Sahid begged again as the falling rain pooled on his face. "I bear proof of my word!"

"Show me this proof now or die swiftly." Jaxus ordered, pulling back his weapons enough to allow Sahid to move. He watched closely, ever ready to attack as the downed man removed a black ring from his finger and held it aloft. He did not recognize the ornament in the darkness of the storm ravaged night.

"Lord Commander Fax gave this to me and said you would know with it the truth of my mission." Sahid drank in the falling rain and sat up on his elbows, choking.

Jaxus selected the ring from Sahid's palm and held it before his eyes. He smiled softly as he sheathed Ragnashon and spun Jushash, planting the tip of the weapon into the soil. The ring fit perfectly over the base of the hilt, matching it as if they were one by manufacture.

"The Lord Commander bid that I tell you that it was time for the ring to be reunited with that from which it came." Sahid's voice returned to him and he was gladdened to see that the token was recognized.

"It was dislodged from my sword while competing in the tournament of bones against the Lord Commander. He took it as a prize for his victory." Jaxus reminisced quietly. He looked back up to Layandria. "We may trust his words, My Lady, but we must take in his tale on the move, the enemy is still at our backs."

Layandria nodded and extended her hand to Sahid, helping him to his feet. "It is time to run. Time for stories will come later. Now move!"

The small group took to a swift pace, surging on into the trees. A long line of retreating Wanoak snaked through the woods before them, the head of the column obscured by the trees. The sight gave Layandria hope that a greater number of the Wanoak had been spared from death, but the images of the dead and dying left behind smashed that hope into black shards that filled her thoughts. A deep hatred took hold on her and she could not shake the feeling that she should have been left behind to die with them. That her very survival had cheated them of justice.

35

The carriage bounced along roughly over the hard-packed road while Leighuis rode on inside, ignoring the jarring with ease. The coin master's cart was well appointed, a soft couch lined the wall opposite the door, and a bed, small though comfortable, offered further comfort. The front of the carriage had a table for writing and cabinets that Leighuis found well stocked with fruits, cheeses, dried meats and wine. There was even a fine wooden seat that opened to the ground below for him to relieve himself.

Coin Master Pleuin had always been a difficult man, lording his title and position over any who he deemed beneath his station. This behavior aided Leighuis as none of the guards who followed the carriage as it wound its way back towards the Iron Fist inquired on him. He was able to pass the time easily, enjoying the comforts before him. His only company was the deceased coin master, who though thawing from his time among the ice, was not yet beginning to smell foul.

There were no windows in the cart, though the light of the sun pushed its way under the door, allowing count of the days. The attack was to come on the fourth day of travel, just after midday. Leighuis stood from the couch and stretched. He dined on fruit, strips of dried venison and a small cup of wine. He relieved himself, amused at the thought of those who walked behind the carriage having to step around the stool he dropped onto the road.

Master Pleuin's body rested on the couch, propped against the wall of the carriage. The walls were made of woven strips of thin cut wood, which kept the vehicle light, but did not offer resistance to arrow fire. This type of cart was not meant for use in war, or defense against soldiers dressed as raiders. It was meant for the luxury of masters and councilors who traveled about the realm at peace.

Judging that he had time for another snack, Leighuis sat at the desk and began to nibble at a crust of thick bread. He ran through his escape again. The raiders were to strike at the left of the carriage, opposite the door, pulling the attention of the guards away from that side. He would make his escape quietly, moving to the cover of trees and brush without attracting attention. If all went to plan, no guards would be near to see him exiting the cart. If this was not the case, Leighuis was prepared to kill any who stood in his way.

The deception would only stand if he was not seen, or if none remained alive to bear witness to his presence. The Shadow soldiers were under orders to leave none alive, but the trouble with orders such as this was that unexpected things often took place. Men ran, sought concealment or otherwise escaped death. Such a hard thing to do, leaving no survivors.

36.

They made camp in the same treetop dwellings that the Outcasts had bedded them on their first meeting. Though Jaxus hesitated to linger, Layandria insisted on a rest in the shelter of the high structures and the boughs of the great trees. The many wounded Wanoak had slowed their progress and several died along the roadside. As each one passed, Jaxus had stopped and ordered the bodies buried, then well hidden. Breadcrumbs, he had called them, were not to be easily seen.

It was clear to Thyso that friction was forming between Jaxus and Layandria. The Queen wanting rest for the weary and time to tend the wounded, Jaxus ever pressing forward. The return to the Wanoak city caused even more tension between the two leaders. Layandria wanted to take rest there, but Jaxus refused. The threat was not passed and Jaxus did not want the remaining warriors to be engaged in battle, so weakened were they. Few of the villagers chose to make the trek over the mountains with them, believing that once Layandria and her fellows were gone, the danger to them would be limited. Jaxus argued for leaving the wounded in the city and making haste to the Arkenhead, but Layandria refused. Sahid's tale had set heavily on Jaxus, clouding an already hard read face.

Thyso sat now on the edge of the platform, letting his feet hang off the edge, carefully thinking over the days ahead and their need for haste. Nearly two hundred souls had come with them, many wounded, others far too young or old for speed in travel. The leaders of their party were deep in hushed conversation behind him, deciding the next steps to be taken. The young handmaid felt his voice was overwhelmed and felt unfit to join the conference.

Tepan and Halta advocated for descending into the tunnel and making their way back to the Arkenhead from the relative safety of the underground. Oslun was not eager to reenter the black passages, lobbying for above ground travel. Sahid suggested that he to go back over the mountains, bringing word to Lord Commander Fax, ensuring that the door into the Whisper Hall would be open to the host if they chose a subterranean approach.

Layandria was not interested in the passage, sharing the cupbearer's distaste for the long dark. She feared the morlts would return in greater numbers and that many would fall to them before they could be stopped. Of course, she knew that passing under the stone would keep the party safe from all other foes, and indeed, their movements would hardly be known, but there was power in a return in the sunlight. Layandria agreed that Sahid should be dispatched out in front of their force to carry word back to the Lord Commander, no matter the path that was chosen. He would set out at the first light of the new day. Jaxus had not participated in this discussion, his thoughts unknown to the Queen.

The dark man seemed ill at ease. He had not made eye contact with her since they left the Wanoak village. Of course, she had not been kind following the battle. She was angry, ashamed and barely holding onto herself, but the man whose wisdom and direction she most needed was absent. She needed to be alone with him, to probe him and discover the reason for his separation.

Thyso stood from his position on the edge of the platform and moved silently to Jaxus. Tepan was again expounding on his reasoning for use of the passage while Oslun and Halta listened patiently, but Layandria could not hear his words. Thyso knelt and spoke unintelligibly low to Jaxus, who rose. The pair moved away from the group, mounting a small stair to another platform, disappearing into the shadows of the boughs.

"What is your decision?" Tepan's voice, direct and strong as ever turned the Queen's focus back to the group. Layandria sighed heavily, knowing that she had not the will to decide in her present mind. She was wearier than she had ever known. It felt as if her body had become as the trees, rooting itself in place. Her mind seemed dull and unwilling to respond.

"No choices will be made tonight." Layandria did her best to force leadership and strength into her voice, though it sounded as a child to her own ears. "We must take rest to see clearly."

"My Lady, if you will," Sahid rose his voice to her for the first time since their meeting. "Haste is needed to return to Arken."

"No, my faithful messenger, rest is needed. I am to bed."

The group took the instruction well and readied for sleep. As had become usual, Halta and Oslun lay side by side, entwined in each other's arms. Layandria smiled at their comfort, glad that someone could find something of beauty in all the pain. As she watched them, she realized that they were whispering to each other in secret. Anger boiled hot in the Queen. She was certain they were conspiring, detailing her own failure at the lake, the way she led those who followed her into slaughter.

Certainly, Thyso and Jaxus were now sharing the same words. Jaxus had been in many wars, though he rarely spoke of such things. Layandria was certain he had never seen a greater failure of leadership than hers. Thyso and he must be planning to take their leave of this failure Queen and return to the wild adventures of Jaxus long years.

She wanted to hate them for it, but the rage turned inwards. She had failed those who trusted her. Even the Wanoak, once so gladdened to call her their Chieftain, would undoubtedly turn their backs on her, unwilling to follow one who leads only to death's embrace. Rale'en was taken to shadow in the fray. Her fall was not seen, but no account for her had been found since the battle. Another dear life laid to rest at the feet of the flawed Layandria.

Guilt and sadness set. The Queen was blinded by the suddenness of it and the intensity of the loathing she felt for herself. She knew in her heart that she should have fallen in battle on the flagstone. She silently begged the night for the end of her days. Her mind conjured a cloaked assassin coming on her in the black of a starless night. She would look into his eyes and put up no struggle as he opened her. Uneasy sleep came on her weary body, but her mind carried much pain into her dreams.

"I am concerned for Layandria." Thyso spoke low. "She is not well."

Jaxus considered for a moment, looking intently at the trees, cautious of listeners. "As am I. She is strong and brave, but there is nothing in the known world that prepares a person for such scenes of death. Each will see and carry the destruction in their own way, some taking easier to the burden than others. I have been trying to reach her, but she is closed off to me."

"It is folly for us to take the passage under the mountain." Thyso was adamant. "With so many who have lived their entire lives in the sun, we would never make it whole. Oslun was raised in walls of stone, but the darkness of the passage nearly consumed him."

"I don't believe there to be enough supply for us to survive the journey without the gifts of nature." Jaxus turned his gaze to the moon, slender though it was. "No, the tunnel is not the way. We will send Sahid and a few others forward to carry news of our coming, and we will keep to the sky. Whatever comes to us, good or ill, above ground we can see it approaching."

"What of the Queen? Will she hear us?" Thyso's concern was evident, raising his volume markedly.

"In the morning, the sun will rise. I will speak to her in the light. Now, you must rest."

Thyso nodded and turned away. Jaxus remained rooted, letting his mind find its center. As Thyso dropped from view, Jaxus closed his eyes and focused his thoughts. He could feel the warmth of her skin, smell her essence in his nostrils, but no matter the effort Jaxus put forth, he could not see her face. It was as if Layandria were behind a veil. Close, but beyond his reach.

Oslun rolled over and kissed Halta's cheek. Her eyes were closed, but she smiled at the gesture. She had promised herself to him and he was overjoyed with the sensation of it. Their lives were intertwined, just as their bodies. He knew he needed sleep, but he could not take his eyes away from her.

The sound of soft, mournful singing crossed the platform. A man, deep in loss or pain lifted his voice to the darkness. The words were foreign, but Oslun felt a cold shiver run through his back as the sounds danced among the trees. Halta opened her eyes.

"Jaxus," She whispered to her lover. "He sings for those who fell in battle."

"You can understand him?" Oslun sat up on his elbow.

"Be still my One." Halta placed her hand on Oslun's chest, gently guiding him back to her bosom. "I do not know the tongue he speaks, but I know the hurt in his voice. I know it well."

"It is beautiful." Oslun sank back into her embrace, letting his cheek meet hers. "I hope I never have to sing like that for you."

"Never my love," Halta smoothed his hair and kissed his lips. She too settled in and let her heavy eyes close. "Never."

37

"Lord Nathus! Come quick!" An aid burst into the Lord's dark chamber. "Master Pleuin's guard has returned!"

"What of it?" The Lord demanded from his seat at the end of a heavy wooden table. The juices of his luncheon stained his face.

"My Lord, Master Pleuin is found to be dead inside his carriage!"

Lord Nathus rose suddenly from his chair, sending it clattering behind him. "What do you mean? In what manner did that wretched man meet his end?"

The aid stepped back at the Lord's outburst, "My Lord, he is to be found dead, his neck crushed as in a carpenter's vice."

"Were they attacked? King Axeleon's vassals have reported that savages have pushed ever further south into the infant wolf's territory."

"No, My Lord." The aid stammered, so used to Lord Nathus violence. "The guards report that there was no attack, no incident at all."

"Take me to the body." The Iron Lord commanded sharply.

The aid quickly descended the steps to the ground level, no small feat as Lord Nathus demanded that his chambers and dining hall be moved to the highest level of the north tower. This allowed him to view the entirety of his fortress by simply walking to the balcony or any number of windows.

The fortress itself, called Bradras, was built in a ring, the exterior wall of the ring being made up of two levels of rooms and passages. On each corner of the wall rose a tower, some seven levels high. The space inside the ring was dominated by a large courtyard, training pits for the various soldiers assigned duty here, and an ornate temple where those that held to the gods would take in their worship. Early into his Lordship, Nathus ordered the temple destroyed, but his hand was stayed by his council as they believed such an action would anger the population. The temple endured, but so did Lord Nathus disdain for it and those who took solace within.

By the time the aid reached the main gate and Master Pleuin's carriage, he was panting heavily and sweating profusely. Lord Nathus did not appear to have exerted himself at all on the journey.

The Iron Lord was silent as he first circled the carriage, looking intently over the exterior surfaces. He entered and closed the door behind himself. The aid moved to depart and quench his thirst, but he hesitated. Such is common among the servants of the Iron Lord for his anger was swift and frightening, but one so seldom knew what would cause his wrath.

After a time, which for the aid seemed hours, Lord Nathus emerged, the crown of his balding head exiting the carriage door in time with his massive boot. "Listen to what I have seen and tell me what conclusion you draw."

"Inside this transport, there lies a deceased coin master. His body is cool to the touch, but not stiff as with new death. There are no damages to the exterior of the carriage and of further puzzlement, the man's neck is, as you accurately described, crushed as with a vice. Too what conclusion does this information bring you?"

The aid hesitated again, knowing that even this could bring him pain. He turned the information over in his mind as rapidly as he could. The Lord's impatient eyes fixed on his. The aid forced the words from his lips, "the coin master was killed from within?"

Lord Nathus grunted agreeance. "And based on the temperature and rigidity of his corpse, I would suspect that the master was dead just after his departure from the Arkenhead. Now, what then do you make of this; the master has been long dead, but much food has been consumed, the bed has been used and someone has likely been communicating with the guards throughout the journey, else they would have inquired on the master's condition before their arrival here."

The aid felt his courage rise, as did his excitement in the solving of this puzzle. "Someone with a voice bearing likeness to the master's was concealed inside the carriage with the dead man." The aid paused as he considered the implications of that statement. "But, that would likely mean that the imposter boarded the carriage prior to its departure from the Arkenhead and made his escape under the cover of darkness. Why would anyone go to such lengths to conceal the death? And what must have gone awry with their plan?"

Lord Nathus raised his brow, "What causes you to think that the plan has not gone as intended?"

"My Lord, were I to have cause to fully conceal a man's death in such a way, I would have done as the imposter has done, but I would have also conspired to have the master's convoy attacked by men appearing to be of the northern savages. I would have them fire on the carriage, making sure to pierce its walls, thus aiding the imposter in making his escape, and providing the needed ruse to convince us that the dead man was killed by the bandits."

"Your mind sees clearly." Lord Nathus offered. "Perhaps I have need to take care when you are near, lest you open my throat and make it seem that it was the hand of another. But, you have missed one crucial detail, the reasoning behind all of this. The questions you raise are valid, but easily answered. I ordered the convoy guards to take an alternate course on their return, in case Lord Aralias' reports of savage invasion were not exaggerated. Further, my abstinence from the current warfare in our kingdom has not bought the Iron Fist many friends, so the path was changed without widespread knowledge. That explains the lack of attack and the failure of the ruse. As to the why, Master Pleuin undoubtedly discovered some secret information that he was not meant to carry back to my ears. What could that have been?"

"My Lord, I do not know what news could be worthy of such a deadly affair." The aid dropped his eyes, his confidence gone with his understanding of the situation.

"My vassals report that the king was grievously wounded during the breaking of the siege on the Arkenhead. Yet, they also report that he has made a miraculous recovery, though few have seen him in his chambers. The Princess fled Arken sometime during the battle and has not been seen since. Lord Commander Liam Fax, a worthless man devoted to tradition and ideal, has assumed leadership of the realm, supposedly under the advisement of the recovering King."

"As I consider this, I am forced to determine that Master Pleuin found evidence that the King has not recovered from his wounds, and the princess did not escape, but was rather killed during the fighting. This Lord Commander has assumed control of the throne and seeks to maintain it through deception." Lord Nathus began pacing back and forth in front of the aid. "I have also been told that Lord Aralias has been in the Arkenhead and held audience with the King, whom I believe to be dead. This would indicate that the Wolf Lord is aware of what is taking place and has chosen to support this usurper. There is but one course of action before us. Can you tell me what it is?"

"We must march on the Arkenhead and kill the one who has taken the throne." The aid offered up timidly, hoping that the momentum of his exchange would remain in his favor.

"That is without question. We will marshal the armies and move within the day. Lord Commander Fax sought to seal his place on the throne, but we will seal his tomb."

"My Lord?" The aide questioned timidly, "Is not Lord Commander Fax the eldest of the Lords and the rightful King, if it is true that Axeleon is slain and Layandria lost?"

"Fool." Lord Nathus muttered the word as if rebuking an errant child. "Lord Commander Fax was named to his position by decree of King Axeleon. He holds no noble blood and his family in no higher than yours. He is not fit to be King and more than you, or perhaps the horses. No, title be damned, no low born sword waver will sit the throne of Arken."

The aide sighed relief at not being struck for his query, though he found it odd that Lord Nathus seemed so fixated on bloodlines. His own father was low born but named Iron Lord on his predecessor's death bed. No noble blood adorned Nathus veins, though his aide wasn't nearly foolish enough to admit it.

Lord Nathus took a lasting look on the carriage, becoming certain that his assessment was accurate. "Soon, very soon. The head of Lord Commander Liam Fax will adorn the citadel gate."

38

The Starrowlanders surrendered in less than two days fighting. Lady Kaowith and Lord Brustic remained on the killing fields, mopping up remaining bands of resistance. Surgeons worked tirelessly on Lord Aralias damaged shoulder, but they could not remedy the man. Infection ravaged his tissues, so they took the arm, closing the wound and sealing it with flame. He was also diagnosed to have three broken ribs and a damaged jaw, coupled with shattered molar teeth. This disfigurement would cause him continued pain for the remainder of his life. The Wolf Lord's spirit was not dampened, and his men marveled in his resilience.

The wolves would be prepared to move back to the Arkenhead within the hour, leaving the prisoners, and the dead, to the able hands of the Fire Lady and her Elk companion. Questions remained in plenty. What would be done with the more than ten thousand prisoners? Certainly, they could not be held in Arken forever, and many of them were forced into service at the blade of Axise weapons. The ease with which the Starrowlanders were defeated and the massive numbers who surrendered softened Aralias normally ruthless approach to enemy combatants and he issued instructions that prisoners not be put to death.

For now, these matters would have to be entrusted to Lady Kaowith. There was great need to move north in as much strength as could be mustered. There was yet no word from Lord Commander Fax and any word on Lord Nathus movements would reach the Citadel long before it reached the Wolf Lord. Anxiety grew in Aralias with every passing moment. There were too many liabilities. Were the King discovered to be deceased, and Princess Layandria not returned, Lord Nathus would cease power and likely many heads would adorn the causeway leading into the citadel. Having recently sacrificed his arm, the great wolf did not much desire to give up his head.

The war party would march in two waves. The first being only one hundred men, moving with all swiftness and bearing the Lord's banner. The second being five thousand strong and bearing the banners of both fire and elk. Aralias estimated that with no delays, he would reach the citadel in little more than four days. He would feel more at ease once he had returned to the Lord Commander. With any luck, Layandria would have returned by the time he arrived.

Of course, luck had not shined on Arken as of late. A tingle crossed over Aralias left hand. He flexed his fingers, looking down on the hand, reminded by the empty air that the hand no longer existed. The sensation gave him pause. Was the hope remaining in his heart not but the memory of a limb, and possibly a kingdom lost? Answers could only be found in the Arkenhead.

39.

The sun began its gentle ascent over the eastern peaks. Layandria had not slept well, so disturbed were her dreams. She noted that Jaxus had not returned to the platform, taking his rest alone. She knew it was not unlike the man to desire solitude, but she could not see reason, so overwhelmed was she with grief, guilt and something deeper, more akin to slow burning rage. She was no clearer now than she was in the night about the course of action that should be taken.

The Queen rose and moved to the edge of the platform. The nearly two hundred men, women and children that still followed her were beginning to stir below. Neat little fires crackled as breakfasts were prepared. The smoke rose to the high boughs and Layandria drew in a breath. She had always enjoyed the smell of wood fire. It reminded her of better days in her youth, traveling with her parents as they toured the kingdom. For a moment, Layandria felt lighter, lest consumed by the pain of the past days as the small memories came to her.

His voice interrupted her peace. *"My Lady, I need to speak with you before the others wake."* Jaxus voice in her mind, while welcomed days ago, and desperately needed last night, brought only anger. Why had he waited so long? Why had the man who knew her so intimately abandoned her? Layandria did not respond to his thought but turned to scan the upper platforms for his dark shape. Jaxus was standing on a platform above her own, looking down on her. She could not understand it, but the sight of this man brought a sudden surge of both longing and intense disdain. She stared back at him for a long moment, letting her feelings burn through before she stepped off and mounted the steps to come to him.

"What is it?" Layandria shot at the man as she came up to his level. "What can you possibly have to say that I must hear?"

Jaxus eyes widened in shock at the Queen's outburst, but he quickly regained his composure. "Your Grace, I thought only to speak with you about the best course of action we should take to return to Arken."

"Well, say what you will." The Queen's anger did not subside.

"Yes, Your Grace. I believe it prudent, based on Sahid's words, to separate from the main body of our troop. We should perhaps take Sahid himself, as he is known to Lord Commander Fax. Also Halta, as she has entered the realm over the mountains before and will likely know the best paths. This will give us all available speed and allow the rest to come as they are able without the need for haste. Thyso and Oslun can lead them well, as can Tepan."

Layandria stepped forward harshly. "And what if they are attacked as they climb the peaks? Who will defend them? Not you or I?"

"My Lady, I do not think that likely. The Inohamman tribes are scattered and leaderless. It will be many days before they are able to reorganize and by that time, we will be well into the safety of our own holdings. All of us."

"You did not think it likely that the Inohamman Chieftains would betray us at the lake and that lack of foresight has led to slaughter!" Layandria's inner pain and anguish boiled over, coursing out across her tongue. "You did not think it likely that Wilteph would betray us and his own people. You did not think it likely that Axise would be killed by my father's hand and that your army would fail! I come to think your council is not so wise, and that perhaps you are spying still. Trying to separate me from those still loyal to me so that you may make my end appear to have been by another's hand!"

Jaxus bowed his head at the rebuke. He did not speak.

"Yes, great Jaxus, I know." Layandria let her mind free, no longer in control of her thoughts or words. "Sahid told me of you. Where Oslun was bound to oath and protected you by his silence, Sahid has spoken freely. I know you were heavily engaged and trusted by Axise, taking part in many of his battles. I know you volunteered to come to Arken and spy for my uncle, giving to him much vital information that was likely the cause of our swift downfall. I know you now for what you are."

Jaxus eyes blazed and his voice grew hard as the edge of knife. "You know nothing. Search your memories. I came to the service of your father long before Axise began his conquest. It was your own cupbearer who recounted the day of my knighthood, some short years after your own birth. Rumblings of Axise war reached Arken and your father ordered my infiltration of his camp, gaining his trust that it may serve early warning should Axise seek the throne of his birth. Chance came, and I returned to Arken, passing false details to the enemy. Even as the doors to the Whisper Hall were barred, I sent a false figure, greatly under stating our numbers in the hope that Axise arrogance would cause him to dismiss much of his own strength before making his entry. I am a spy, though not for whom Sahid believes. Do you not see this truth in your heart? In the love you professed for me?"

"I cannot love a man so deeply shrouded in lies." Layandria spoke the words, her body visibly wracked in the pain of her crushed spirit.

Jaxus took the blow of heavy words and deflated, his fire dying and turning to quiet pleading. "My Queen, I have shown only loyalty and devotion to both your father, and to you. I have served and counseled you both to the best of my ability. Your father knew who I truly am. He knew my origins, and the reason I entered your lands, and he trusted me above all others to keep you safe. He alone assigned me to your side, but you still believe me to be a traitor?"

Layandria did not believe it, but anger and hate had taken control of her. "I believe it." She affirmed with a cold, deadly tone in her voice that frightened her.

"Then I must die for my crimes." Jaxus slowly drew Ragnashon over his shoulder, choosing this weapon to be his end, unwilling to sully Jushash, his trusted companion, with his own blood. He held the weapon by the blade, pommel extended to the Queen. "Will you strike me down, or shall I?"

Layandria stepped back in shock. She did not know what to say or what to do. The torment of her mind crashed like a broken dam. Pain, anger and guilt enveloped her thoughts and she could feel nothing else. She said nothing, her face closed and dark.

"My Lady, before my end, I have but one final piece of council and I beg you to hear my truth. No leader should have to witness the slaughter of her people. No doubt you are wondering in your core if there was anything you could have done to save them, and if the faces, the sounds and the weight of the dead will ever leave you. My Queen, the answer to both these questions is no. You had no way of seeing the treachery of the Inohamman Chiefs, while also having no choice but to commit to the battle. Just as you had no choice but to follow your father's command and flee the citadel. You will carry the lives lost at your command for all your days, just as I carry my own dead. Justice was served with the lives of the Inohamman Chieftains running out into the soil, but that will not lessen the weight the lost have gifted to your soul. All you can do is remember why they chose to follow you, why they loved you. That is the gift. The dead remind you of who you are, of what is costs to lead. Remember this sacrifice and you will stay true to virtue."

"I have fought beside many Kings of men. Only those truly worth their title and the loyalty given them so deeply mourn the loss of the lives they command. Feel the loss, remember it and let it make you sharper, but do not let it turn inward or pull you away from those whose faith you keep. You must continue to lead as best you can to earn that trust and love. For my part, I would follow you to the ends of the earth and gladly die by your side." Jaxus hesitated. "Or at your command."

Layandria felt the impact of each word as if it were an arrow, or a stone. Some piercing her through and through, others landing as heavy blows. She could not bear the weight. Jaxus stood, the hilt of his sword within her grasp. Anger crossed his eyes, mixed with the softness and devotion of love. She flashed back to the lake, the images of the broken and dying. The desperation on the faces as they looked for her leadership. There, in the midst of chaos and death were Jaxus, Thyso, Oslun, Halta and Tepan. Steadfast, they swarmed around her, following her command into certain death, but as she recalled their faces, there was no desperation on them. Even Oslun, so recently too meek to handle a blade showed not but steadfast loyalty. There was courage in their eyes, courage and love. For her.

The Queen focused her eyes on Jaxus, willing to die just at her word, knowing he had committed no crime worthy of such an end. She felt so undeserving of it all. Of the love Jaxus gave to her, that a man so traveled and worn would choose her? It felt so wrong. And Oslun, Thyso, even Halta and Tepan. They gave her their lives willingly, though she knew she could never earn the devotion.

Jaxus eyes turned mournful. He relaxed his wrist, letting the hilt of Ragnashon fall to the wood platform. With smooth motions, he notched the tip of the blade under the lower lip of his chest plate. No hesitation existed in the man as he prepared to drop to his knees. He had seen this manner of death performed in the past and was certain he would die swiftly. He did not want the Queen to be forced to bear witness to a long, wailing passing.

"Stop!" She shouted the word as if no other word she had or would ever speak would matter more. Jaxus shuddered slightly at her voice, but he did not rise. Blood ran down the blade of the sword, hitting the man's fingers and spilling over. "Stand up! Put away your weapon!"

Jaxus did as he was commanded, sheathing the sword over his shoulder. He returned his hands to his side and stood still, his face impassive. Blood issued from an unseen gap between his chest plate and armor breeches. Layandria fell to her knees and began to weep.

"You were going to do it!" She nearly screamed the words between her sobs. "Why would you take your own life because of me? Why would any of you put your lives in my hands?"

Jaxus moved to her side and knelt. "We do all that we do because we trust you, Your Grace."

Layandria shook with the furry of the emotion that washed through her. "But why? Why would any of you trust me?"

"My Queen, that is for each one to answer on their own, though such reasons are better left to their keepers. As for my reason, it is much more simplistic than you might guess. I trust you and love you because I must. It is, for me, a fact. Just as the sun will always rise in the east, or that I am bound to the surface of the earth, incapable of soaring into the sky as the birds. Just as I am bound to you." Jaxus gently kissed the back of her head and stood.

Layandria looked at him and felt that she was similarly bound, though she could not understand how or when it happened. She looked again at the blood on Jaxus armor. "You need a surgeon." She offered weekly, ashamed that her anger had pushed her so far.

Jaxus shrugged slightly. "I will live."

"Only just!" Layandria could not hold back from the blatant irony of the statement.

"My Lady, we should return to the others. They will be anxious for your plan and we should not linger here." Jaxus moved back to the steps and descended. The others were awake, several looking at him with various expressions of shock, obviously drawn from the shouting they undoubtedly heard. Jaxus held his finger to his lips, then two fingers to his eyes, shaking his head back and forth. The group understood the signal, and all turned away, busying themselves with packing their beds, donning their armor, feigning ignorance of all they had heard.

Layandria appeared a moment later, coming down the steps and crossing to the center of the platform. She took a seat and dabbed her eyes lightly with her sleeve. She cleared her throat softly. "We should discuss the plan."

All moved to sit in a circle around Layandria. Jaxus took a seat directly across from her, a comforting strength on his face. Layandria managed a small smile, but it faded quickly as Sahid took the seat next to Jaxus right side. There was a tenseness between the men that Layandria could easily see.

"Jaxus." Sahid cleared his throat as he faced the dark warrior. "I have come to learn that while we shared battlefields and tents in service of Axise, you were plotting our failure all along."

Jaxus did not speak but nodded and emitted a rough grunt of confirmation.

"I find it odd that the one man among Axise' army that I did not openly detest is the only one who joins me now in this new life." Sahid extended his hand to Jaxus in friendship. "I desire that we renew the friendship we once shared, though I hope to find it is now less clouded by the dust of an unjust war."

"It will be as you say." Jaxus accepted Sahid's hand and nodded. "Perhaps one day, I will hear the adventure of your turning from the rags of a man forced to fight, to gleaming shadow armor."

"I suspect we have many adventures to share." Sahid smiled deeply, then turned back to the Queen. Silence fell over the platform.

"I know what we must do." Layandria stood. "I will go with Sahid to the Arkenhead. I will bring Jaxus, Oslun and Tepan with me as my guard. Halta has journeyed into our lands and she, along with Thyso will bring our people as quickly as they can manage."

"Your Grace," Sahid's voice grew concerned at the sound of a true plan forming, "I may not be able to make the trek with the haste you require. I have not stopped for more than the barest rest since the day Axise fell on the Whisper Hall. Though it greatly pains me to admit, I fear I lack the strength for the speed.

"Then I will carry you on my back." Tepan growled with pride.

Layandria felt stronger as Tepan's pride shown out. She desperately clung to hope that her people would survive the journey unchallenged. "Begin your preparations to move as quickly as you can. Do not take rest longer than you must. I and my party will depart within the hour."

"Oslun, ready your gear." Jaxus ordered the young cupbearer.

"What need have I to separate from the main body?" Oslun stood from his seat.

Layandria rose gently and smiled. "My dear Oslun, it seems you've found your courage. I dare say, not one month ago you'd never raised objection to the order given by anyone, much less the right hand of the Queen."

Oslun lowered his eyes to the platform. "I meant no offence, My Queen. I only wish to not be separated from. . ."

"You wish not to be separated from the one you love." Layandria softened her voice further. "Though I feel for your heart's longing, I cannot grant it. Tepan must take the front, Jaxus the rear. I am strongest to the right flank, and that would leave our left flank weakened. You have proven yourself of stout heart and I see your strength best suited to our left guard. Though it will separate you from your desired station, I feel it is necessary that you follow Jaxus order."

"Yes, My Princess." Oslun bowed sharply and turned away. Halta came to him. The young cupbearer inhaled deeply and attempted to speak to her, but the warrior raised a single finger gently to his lips. She kissed him deeply. He held her to his chest, unwilling to let go.

Halta spun away from Oslun's arms and walked gracefully to the edge of the platform. Her hand wrapped around a rope, suspended from above, just as she stepped off the edge and she vanished from view. Oslun's eyes stayed fixed on the air left in her wake.

"Take ease, my brother, I will watch over her in your stead." Thyso approached Oslun from behind. He winked at the cupbearer and clapped him on the back. The handmaid strode off to the edge of the platform and gripped the rope Halta had used for decent. He stepped off the edge and began his careful climb down.

Oslun smiled, his shoulders coming back as he swelled with pride. "He called me brother."

40

Liam sat in a simple wooden chair next to the throne. With each passing hour, the weight of his deception and the guilt on his heart grew. He could no longer bear to sit where his King once sat. The death of the King's niece tortured him, coupled with the death of Genif Nitru and the Starrowlands boy. Word had reached the citadel that the Iron Army had formed and marched south. They came with speed and the banner of their Lord flew at the lead.

Few in the citadel knew of the intent behind the Iron Lord's approach. The coin masters were acutely aware, and a smattering of leaders of the citadel guard, but the Lord Commander deemed that none others should be told. A glimmer of hope remained in his heart that the Queen would arrive in time, but with each passing hour, that glimmer dimmed. The Iron Armies were less than a day's march from the main gate.

He knew he must form a plan, some way of forestalling the Iron Lord to give any moment he could to chance of Layandria's return, but his mind was blocked. He felt abandoned and alone. The images of the falling dead boy filled his waking mind in unison with Ilsla's final breaths and the scene of Genif's last grace. He longed for anything that would bring an end to this terrible state he dwelt in.

The great doors creaked with sudden movement. Liam started at the sound and strode rapidly to the edge of the platform. All his senses begged to see the Queen enter as the doors opened. He held his breath tightly, his muscles tense as he leaned towards the slowly groaning door. His eyes saw her, and he called out her name as loud as his strained lungs could bear to support. "Layandria!"

"I'll take that to mean that our young queen has not yet returned." Lord Aralias glided in from the doors, his voice carrying long through the hall. Commander Fax body slumped greatly at the sound of the Wolf Lord's voice. Despair renewed in him. The borum stone walls did brighten significantly at Aralias' presence, but this no longer brought Liam any interest.

"No, she has not returned." Commander Fax made his way back to his simple chair and fell into it. "Nathus is less than a day's march, perhaps closer and our Queen is not found within the borders. I can already feel the life draining from my soul."

Aralias mounted the steps and came to stand directly before the commander. "There is still hope, my friend. Time may yet be bought for our cause and our lives."

Liam scoffed. "Perhaps if we too take the passage under the throne and flee at speed."

Aralias laughed lightly. "I have known you many long years and in that time I had never suspected I would see the great Lord Commander Fax fall victim to despair. Besides which, I find myself unfit for further flight."

Liam lifted his eyes to his friend. The amused countenance of his expression forced a smile to streak across Liam's face. His eyes traced the man's worn and stained appearance. He followed the shape of the wolf pelt and found the sleeve of Aralias' armor had been removed, a metal plate crudely fixed over the space where the arm should have been. "I see that you have left something behind in the Fire Fist."

"I have indeed, though arms are of little use against what we face." Aralias chided. "Of course, the idea that I would ever give up hope until that last second has passed is absurd. There is always one more choice to be made, one more move to be taken. We need only to discover what it is."

"On that discovery, good wolf, I am at a loss." Commander Fax let his eyes pass to the brightly glowing borum stone. As he gazed on the walls, they seemed to grow progressively brighter. So much so that he tilted his head and narrowed his eyes, moving across the blood stone floor to touch the wall. By the time his fingertips grazed the surface, a near inferno was dancing all around the hall. So intense was the fire that the entirety of the room was bathed in the brilliance. "I have never seen such luminance."

"Nor have I, save in living flame itself in the dead of winter's night." Aralias also stretched out to touch the wall. His digits hesitated, expecting to be burned, but the borum stone was flame in appearance alone and cool to the remaining senses.

Footfalls, swift and heavy, filtered through the open great doors. Aralias spun towards the passage and drew his sword, ever strong despite his missing limb. Lord Commander Fax reacted swiftly, drawing Falchon. "Who came to the hall with you? My guards were instructed that none save yourself and Grand Master Hale be allowed to enter."

"I brought none. My men are arrayed at the city gate, prepared to forestall Nathus' rabble." Aralias moved to the center of the platform as he spoke, Liam at his heals.

"Your weapons will not be needed." A strong voice filled the room. "You know who it is that seeks to enter the hall of Kings."

A short, stout man with bronzed skin appeared between the doors. His attire was foreign, simple skins for pants and black fur covering his chest. Lord Commander Fax launched himself forward, nearly flying down the steps and charging across the black floor, Falchon poised to strike the intruder.

Another taller man, nearly invisible save for his head and forearms entered the hall, a third man in ill-fitting shadow armor at his heels. The Wolf Lord snapped to and vaulted the steps behind the Commander, moving to engage the intruders.

Liam drew near the strangers, sizing up arms and strength. "Halt or be cut down!"

"You wouldn't want to attack the Crown Princess." The same voice that announced the entry of this little band of strangers rang out again. A woman stepped into the light of the Whisper Hall, clad in her unique shadow armor, fire red hair cascading over her shoulders. "Such things are rarely taken lightly."

"Layandria!" Lord Commander Fax forgot all pretense of his station. He dropped his weapon to the stone floor and ran to her. As he drew near, he fell on his knees, sliding across the smooth black marble. He came to a stop just before her and he wept.

Aralias stilled his advance and put away his weapon. He approached and took in the Queen. She was well worn for her travels. Dirt, and much of what appeared to be the scrapes of swords adorned her armor. Those she traveled with were equally marked, save for the tall man. His armor appeared to be freshly forged, it's black iridescence untarnished, though a large bandage clung to the back of his head. The short, squat man appeared to be unarmed, though his large hands, covered with the remnants of much heavy use, appeared as weapons in their own. Aralias was awash with the mystery of this man and could find no words.

Lord Commander Fax passed his eyes over each of the Queen' company, taking in their various conditions. Small wounds adorned them all, but the image of the King's cupbearer stuck him the most. He was greatly thinned in body and his face bore the hardness of a man come into his own. Liam remembered well the felling of the innocence that adorned this young man and found himself painfully haunted by the memory of such better times. Liam turned back to Layandria. "My Lady, we have much to discuss."

41.

Hours had passed since Layandria arrived in the Whisper Hall. Word was sent throughout the citadel and riders would be dispatched across Arken at the sun's first light.

Oslun and Tepan were shown into chambers and given rest while a meal of roasted game bird was prepared elsewhere in the fortress. Layandria, Jaxus and Lord Commander Fax had not been seen since just after their arrival, though food and other items were taken into the royal chambers a random interval.

Oslun paced the length of the dining hall. He nibbled at scraps of burnt foul and sipped from a cup of wine as he moved. He could not rest. He expected a great welcome at their return, a proud reunion between Queen and people, with proper crowning to follow. Perhaps accompanied by some sort of honor bestowed on him for the faithful execution of his duties. It was not a lack of award that bothered him, but for these things not to have happened, for no celebration at all, something had to be grossly wrong in the Arkenhead.

Oslun began to take stock of himself as he sipped the drink so often carried, but seldom enjoyed. What had the toils west of the mountains produced in him? He felt no different. Perhaps his body had grown leaner, certainly there was more space in his chest plate and experience in combat had increased his confidence, but he did not feel, in his heart that he had changed. That thought brought him a sort of cold sadness. Thyso had come into his own as a warrior and a strong leader, no doubt headed for much title and honor. Layandria had become a true Queen, strong and kind. Jaxus had not been visibly altered, save for new scars to his skin, though Oslun doubted the man could be moved.

He continued to pace and nibble, turning his experiences over in his mind. He neared the door leading back into the Whisper Hall, not aware of the direction his feet chose. Oslun's ears perked at what he though was the sound of shouting coming from beyond the door. He quickened his pace and drew near, pressing his ear to the wood.

The sound of a frantic voice was unmistakable, though the words could not be discerned. The cupbearer opened the door and stepped out. The soldiers now occupying the Whisper Hall stood in loose ranks. A small woman in shadow armor was running towards the empty throne, nearly screaming.

"Where is the Lord Commander? The Iron Army has arrived at the gates and Lord Nathus demands entry!" The woman continued her charge into the hall, nearly out of breath.

The wooden door leading into the royal chambers opened forcefully. Wolf Lord Aralias, who Oslun had only seen once before this day and had never conversed with, stepped out. The shadow soldier repeated her call. Lord Aralias turned back into the threshold and spoke to unseen persons within the chambers. Lord Commander Fax emerged, having donned his own shadow armor. Behind him was Jaxus, stepping aside of the door frame for Layandria to exit. Her armor was removed, and her skin cleaned, her hair pulled up in a classical style. She was dressed in a shimmering blue gown that flowed softly with her every motion. On her head gently perched the crown of the Queen of Arken.

The Queen approached the throne and took her seat. The two Lords came to stand behind on either side of the great chair. Layandria held her head up in the stately manner she had been instructed since birth, her voice clear and her words precise. "Lord Nathus has arrived?"

"Yes, My Queen." The young woman's words conveyed her fear. Uncertainty filled the city as word of Layandria's return and the King's death passed about.

"Then go at once and tell him that Queen Layandria welcomes him." Layandria's voice conveyed no feeling and she did not move as the woman bowed to her, turned and exited the hall. Once the young soldier had passed through the great doors, the Queen turned her head directly to Oslun as if she had felt his presence. Her voice grew to that of a sharp roar, "to arms."

The cupbearer spun back to the dining hall at once and charged into the room. Tepan was sleeping or attempting it, huddled in a knot against the wall, beneath a large window. As he moved towards the massive man, Oslun raised his voice. "To arms! The Queen calls for weapons!"

Jaxus directed the wolf soldiers into ranks at the base of the white steps. As they took position, some two hundred members of the citadel guard charged through the great doors and took ranks before the wolves. Oslun moved to stand next to Jaxus and Lord Commander Fax at the Queen's right as she stood in front of the throne. Tepan and Lord Aralias stood ready on the Queen's left.

The hall grew silent. Barely a breath shifted the air. The borum stone raged like wildfire. Many treads of heavy booted feet echoed through the passage, drawing near the Whisper Hall.

Iron Lord Nathus rounded the corner through the open great doors and paused. The sight of three hundred warriors standing with weapons drawn was not what he expected. His own guard, halted behind him, numbered only one hundred. He called out, his gruff voice shattering the stillness, "When I was informed that the Queen welcomed me to her hall, I did not expect to be welcomed at the tip of a sword."

"I have no weapon drawn, Lord Nathus." Layandria's voice maintained a regal composure.

"Your hands are empty, but that does not account for the ranked mass before you." Lord Nathus took slow steps towards the throne as he spoke. "What do you call this for a welcome then, Your Grace?"

"Before you stand the Shadow Guard of the Citadel, who are under the command of Lord Commander Liam Fax." With the Queen's words, the citadel guardsmen stepped forward on their right feet and as one motion, their swords cascaded in a twirling flurry into striking pose.

"Behind them stand the warriors of Wolf Lord Aralias Taymrhlyn." The Queen's final word triggered the wolves to take one step forward and to their left, emerging between the ranks of the citadel guard. Their boots impacted the stone as one, rendering a deafening boom that filled the air.

Queen Layandria rose and gently stepped forward to the edge of the steps. The brilliant glow of the ignited walls dazzled in the clear jewels of her crown, casting sharp prisms all through the space as she moved. "Beside me stand my most trusted commanders. We here assembled wish you no harm, Iron Lord Nathus, provided you have reason for marching on your Queen with the Iron Army at your back."

Lord Nathus licked his lips and found that they had gone dry. He knew it could be seen as an act of treason to have brought his army so far south, so long delayed from order. He could feel the pressure of the eyes upon him. He softened his tone as much as possible and took in a breath. "There has been deception in our lands, My Queen. My own coin master was murdered while under the care of the Arkenhead not one week ago. Am I to assume at your presence here that you were aware of this deed?"

"I have been made aware of it yes," Layandria's strong demeanor did not falter. "Though I was not present at the time of Master Pleuin's death."

Lord Nathus face grew hard, casting off his feigned softness. "Further still, Your Grace, word was passed that King Axeleon was grievously wounded in battle and soon to pass into shadow, but this word was superseded nearly the same day by news of a drastic recovery. None I spoke to could confirm having seen the King after his wounds, and those, I have been told, that did make his audience only saw a sallow, pale man who could have, or possibly could not have resembled the King. Am I to assume from your mother's crown sat atop your head that reports of your father's recovery were greatly exaggerated?"

Layandria did not move, her poise perfect. "As for these reports, either the first of the last, I cannot speak, Lord Nathus, for as I have said, I was not present when they were dispatched."

"Pardon my meaning, Queen Layandria, but I do find it deeply concerning that these events have transpired, and you were, where? Certainly, you will not claim to have been south in the Fire Fist rebuffing Axise horde?" Lord Nathus reached the front rank of the Citadel Guard and stopped. There was a cunning hunger clear in his features.

"I was not, Lord Nathus." Layandria felt herself being worked into a trap, but she maintained control over her exterior despite her growing fear. She could feel Jaxus reassuring presence in her mind, but she could not focus enough to hear his thoughts. "I was west, over the mountains, leading the Inohamman Wanoak in a war for their survival."

The Iron Lord stepped closer to the front rank. At once, the inner files pivoted side face, opening a channel in the sea of swords leading to the throne, allowing Lord Nathus to pass. The man quickened his pace and came to the base of the steps. He raised his boot to take the first when Jaxus voice stopped him. "Take caution, Iron Lord. The last to mount these steps against the crown fell to ruin and rot before he could understand his error."

"Who is this who dares address a Lord in this tongue?" Lord Nathus stepped back, but rage welled in his face.

Layandria's face showed none of the emotion she felt, though both anger and fear fought a great battle for her mind. "He is called Jaxus and he is my right hand. He speaks as if it were my own voice."

"Enough of this theatric!" Nathus lost containment on his voice and his anger erupted. "I have come to court with serious allegations of murder and deception, yet you have no answer for this!"

"I am aware of the one who is responsible for these actions." Layandria resumed her regal motif. "But I will not have such talk brokered without due process being paid. The responsible party will be tried in accordance with the laws of my fathers."

"You will broker these words!" Nathus mounted the steps, drawing within arm's reach of the Queen. Those on the platform raised their weapons and moved to strike him down, but Layandria calmly held her hand up, stilling them.

"Put away your weapons. I will not limit the right of our citizens to speak their needs." The Queen commanded those to her left and right. Her voice grew quiet and her poise did not sway. "Speak your mind, Lord Nathus."

"Queen Layandria, you claim to know the identity of the man responsible for the crimes I have outlined, yet you have not set him to justice or revealed his name." Nathus watched the Queen nod her head slowly and took that as confirmation. "You claim to have not been present for, or to have had knowledge of these actions, yet I find you here, in the seat of the King, having crowned yourself ruler of Arken."

Lord Nathus closed the final step to Layandria, his eyes meeting hers at the same level. "I do not believe these words to be true. I believe that you, Layandria Taymrhlyn, conspired with Lord Commander Liam Fax, Lord Aralias Taymrhlyn, and likely the remainder of this rabble who stand beside you to seize this time of war and chaos as your chance to end the life of King Axeleon and seize the rule of Arken as your own! Tell me, Queen Layandria, what am I to make of these things for I see only murder and treason."

"You may see whatever you like, Iron Lord, though I caution you. The treason you speak out so strongly against is very much akin to the treasons committed by your own action." Layandria did not show any reaction at Lord Nathus' words. Oslun did not so ably conceal his emotion.

"It is my right, under the laws of this land, the laws set down by your fathers, to challenge any succession of the crown." Nathus fists clenched tightly. "I deny your crown and charge you with treason, Layandria, daughter of Axeleon and Alandaria. I demand that you remove the crown of the Queen and give yourself over to my custody to await trial! Should you resist, at my one word, I will order my army to flood this city and we will kill all who stand in our way!"

Oslun moved as if he were a release of lightening. He shot towards the Iron Lord and slashed his sword across the man's chest plate. The Iron Lord fell down the steps, coming to rest on his side, his eyes fixed on the Queen's still regal countenance. Oslun lunged down the steps, bearing down on Lord Nathus as a coiled snake takes his prey. "None shall be permitted to make threats on the Queen of Arken! Rise with a civil tongue or my next stroke will bear you to shadow!"

Lord Nathus struggled to right himself on the floor. As he came to his feet, his rough voice found its way out from clenched teeth. "Is this how you will rule, Queen Layandria? Using deception and assault to dispatch any who stand in question of you? I will not, for the sake of Arken and her people, allow this to be our way!"

Lord Commander Fax stepped in front of Queen Layandria and dropped to his knees. "My Queen, I committed the murder of your cousin, Ilsla Taymrhlyn after she became aware that the King had indeed died as result of the wounds he suffered during the battle to retake the citadel. I spread the false rumor that King Axeleon had recovered from his wound. I further took a man by the name of Markols, from his home and poisoned him so that he would remain unable to speak or move, passing him off as the King to aid in the illusion that the Axeleon lived still." "

I murdered Iron Fist Coin Master Pleuin after he confronted me with his knowledge of the true death of the King. I then ordered my men to deceive Iron Lord Nathus into believing Master Pleuin died as result of an attack of Unoathed Men from the north. I have committed treason to the crown and my life is forfeit. Grand Master Hale was witness to my actions and can give full accounting that I acted alone and without aid. He alone was aware of my deeds, but upon confronting me, he found himself sequestered to the dungeons and unable to call for aid."

Layandria stepped back in shock. The Lord Commander had told her of Lord Nathus bid to seize the throne in her absence, but none of his deeds to forestall it. He had spoken on the death of Master Pleuin, but he stated only that the coin master attempted treason and was killed in this action. The death of Ilsla was not discussed.

"All that I did was for Arken, in service of what I believed necessary for the survival of the House Taymrhlyn and the safety of the people of this kingdom." Commander Fax did not pause in his confession. The strain that so dominated his features vanished as his words poured out. "I loved your father. I regret none of my actions and would gladly redouble my efforts to preserve the crown that I have served for my entire life. I only hope now that in the next life, I may find peace."

"You have heard the confession, there can be no doubt to this man's guilt!" Lord Nathus shouted. "If you do not deal the justice owed to this man, you are not fit to rule!"

"Silence, Lord Nathus!" Layandria stepped forward from the throne, resting her gentle hand on Liam's bowed head. "I will decide the justice to be given and you will be still before me!"

Lord Nathus stepped back in shock, unable to believe the strength of the woman before him. He did not expect to find her present, or so groomed and gowned. He predicted dealings with a child, not a woman so well in command.

"My Queen," Liam raised his voice in a gentle, peaceful whisper. "I am guilty, no matter my motives. My soul can no longer carry the weight of the lives I have taken and I can find naught in my sight save the final images of those whose blood stains me. My death can save your rule and our people, I beg of you to be swift and show no hesitation. Send me to Shadow, my beloved Queen."

"Lord Commander," Layandria looked into his eyes, a great sadness washing over her.

Liam cut her off. "I am ready, my Queen. I go to your father's side. Grant me this one request."

Layandria examined Liam's eyes and saw great pain. She turned to Jaxus, who only nodded a small confirmation. She held out her hand to her companion and he presented her with her father's sword. She extended the weapon upward, so all could see. "This is Sword of the Fathers, forged from the blades of Song of the Fathers and Dark Heart. It is the sword of King Axeleon."

"Lord Commander Liam Fax, you have confessed to the crimes of murder, treason and conspiring on the crown. The penalty for these crimes is death." As Layandria spoke, Jaxus moved to Liam's side and gripped his shoulder, a final wordless gesture of affection. "In accordance with the laws of Arken and in honor of her people, I, Layandria, Queen Regent and Lady of Shadow, am prepared to carry out this judgment. Have you any words to say in your defense, that you may stay my hand Lord Commander?"

Liam took in a long, slow breath. He erected his posture and held his head with pride as he turned his back to the Queen. "Long live the Queen of Arken, long live Queen Layandria!"

As the final syllables passed Liam's lips, Jaxus nodded to Layandria.

"Go to rest in the shadow, Son of Arken." Layandria breathed the words as she drove Sword of the Fathers into the base of Liam's neck. The blade wrecked its damage swiftly and the Lord Commander passed his life away before his body fell to the floor.

Layandria lifted her eyes away from Liam's body, focusing on Lord Nathus, no emotion on her face. "The charges you have brought forth have been answered and paid in full. Do you dispute this?"

"The law of Arken has been satisfied." Nathus relented, though his face, framed by his helm, carried lingering hesitation.

"Lord Nathus, your life is forfeit for many crimes." Layandria fought to keep her regal countenance, despite the torment of another life laid at her feet. "Your army was ordered to march in defense of the citadel by my father when Axise arrived on our shores. You refused this order, which was an act of treason. You then brought an army into the Arkenhead with intent to seize the throne for yourself, which you plainly spoke before this assembly. This is treason. Do you dispute these charges?"

Lord Nathus turned his eyes across the Whisper Hall. He could find neither dispute for the charges, nor disagreement in the faces of those around him. He mind reeled to find excuse for his actions, but the strength of this young queen astonished him. The swiftness with which she dealt justice on the Lord Commander, and the integrity needed to deliver the blow herself gave him great pause. He could find no words.

"I will pardon you these crimes, Iron Lord Nathus, but you must swear your allegiance to the crown and withdraw your army immediately. Any future disloyalty, in any from, will be taken as an act of treason. This will bring the armies of Shadow to your doorstep in haste and no mercy will be offered." Layandria sighed softly and closed her eyes. Jaxus took Sword of the Fathers and secured it behind the throne, returning to the Queen's side.

"I do so swear my allegiance, my Queen." Nathus confirmed solemnly, fully knowing that no other path lay before him.

"Then you are to empty the Arkenhead of your forces and return to your holdings. You will put all ill content to rest and make safe the Iron Fist. In one months' time, you will return to the citadel with your masters and councilors. You will bring your patents of succession and your past due taxes to the crown." Layandria resumed a Queenly tone, her poise perfect, though her close companions could sense great stress on her.

"Yes, my Queen." Lord Nathus turned and issued gruff orders to his men, who broke rank and began to empty the Whisper Hall.

"Lord Nathus," Layandria called after the man as he approached the threshold to exit the hall. He turned to face her, his expression unclear to the Queen at the distance. "Any future disobedience to orders or failure to adhere to the laws of Arken on behalf of you or any in your fist will be rewarded with the swiftness of death you have witnessed here today."

Nathus bowed sharply and turned back, exiting the Whisper Hall at a brisk step.

"Empty this hall and return to your posts." Layandria ordered out. She moved to the throne and sat gently as the soldiers of the city guard and those belonging to Lord Aralias exited. Once the last passed through the great doors and they groaned out their closing, she collapsed, her head falling into her hands. Jaxus rushed to her side.

The Queen lifted her head and looked into the man's eyes, her face drenched in pain and despair. "What am I to do now?"

The man grew still, taking Layandria's face in his hand. He could find no words.

"Never in all my life have I known one man of half the character as Lord Commander Liam Fax." Lord Aralias stepped forward and took the Queen's hand in his own. Silence filled the Whisper Hall. "He knew, from the moment that your father was wounded, that his own life was forfeit. No one person can ever earn that level of devotion or sacrifice, and there is nothing that you can ever do to be worthy, so I must insist that you never try. What you must do, my Queen, is strive to give of yourself in the example set by Liam Fax."

"How?" Layandria could think of no other response, so great was her sadness, her eyes fixed on Liam's body.

"To start," Aralias touched the Queen's face, drawing her gaze. "You rest. Then, you rebuild."

42

Thyso knocked gently on the heavy door to Layandria's chamber. Fourteen days had passed since the Queen returned to Arken, eleven since the survivors of the Inohamman Wanoak passed through the citadel gate. Lord Brustic and Lady Kaowith had arrived as well. Much work would be needed to repair the damage in the Fire Fist and Lady Kaowith lobbied for support from the other fists in material and labor. The Shadow Infantry Reserves were drawn out from the fortress at Barang, dispatched to the Fire Fist, that those soldiers native to that land could be granted leave.

In one of her first acts as Queen, Layandria decreed that the reserve forces would never again be settled at Barang, so far away from usefulness in dire circumstances. She ordered new tenements and training grounds constructed in the fields just off the citadel's western gate to house these forces, keeping them close. Barang itself was to be maintained and expanded upon in order to serve as a refuge for the citizens of the realm in events of further war or strife.

Layandria further ordered that land be allocated just off the eastern gate of the citadel, given to the Inohamman so they may construct a district of their own, making it to their liking and fitting with their cultures. The people of the Inohamman embraced this new land immediately, setting to work with ax and hammer to construct their homes.

Many things remained to be dealt with. There were those among the councils who argued for war with the Iron Fist, believing that had they not refused to order to march, first given by King Axeleon, the death and destruction wreaked on the capitol would have been spared.

Layandria largely refused to speak on this matter, saying only that the debts had been paid and oaths taken, the matter settled.

Thyso stood waiting outside of Layandria's chamber, knocking softly again. The Queen would soon be officially crowned, taking the rulers oath and taking the throne in an official capacity. The door opened slowly and Jaxus face appeared.

"Come in, my young friend." Jaxus gestured with an open palm. Thyso saw that Layandria was still in bed, a pained expression on her face.

"Is she still suffering the dreams?" Thyso queried softly. He was aware of the nightmares Layandria carried in rest. Terrible images of her people slaughtered, those she loved casting away their lives needlessly, her failure complete in their deaths.

"Yes, and I doubt they will ever leave her mind." Jaxus voice was grave. He understood all too well, the pain of the dead. "And how is your mind, brave handmaid?"

"My mind is clear, I have no demons in my thoughts." Thyso was deeply concerned for himself. Not for the torment of the images of dead and dying, which seemed to inflict themselves on many others, but for the lack of these images. He worried that something was amiss in his mind that caused him to be unaffected. The only torment he carried home from the war in the west was the terror and shame he found at the hands of a cackling, nude woman. He had not the courage to speak on this pain.

"I do worry for Oslun." Thyso spoke in earnest. "Halta tells me that he wakes up screaming in the night, begging some unknown force to stop whatever devilish cruelty they are acting against him."

"It is not an act against him." Jaxus let his voice fall soft. "Oslun dreams that Lord Nathus is killing his beloved Halta in payment for his assault on the Iron Lord before the Queen."

"Oslun assaulted Lord Nathus?" Thyso was incredulous, having not been told the full detail of the events that took place in the Whisper Hall while he toiled over the mountains with the Inohamman.

"Yes, assault him he did." Layandria rose her head off the pillow and spoke softly, sleep and amusement gracing her voice. "He fairly slapped the man's chest with his blade, sending Nathus tumbling down the white steps."

"Good morning, Your Grace," Thyso bowed to his royal, just as he had on many mornings for the past several years.

"Thyso, enjoy this moment." Layandria sat up on her elbows, her long hair in a tangled mess. "I will require you to aid me in dressing and fixing my appearance, for today, as I am sure you are aware and have thus entered my chamber long before my requested time to wake, I am to be coronated."

"Yes, Your Grace." Thyso bowed again, turning to move toward the Queen's bath, prepared to light the fire under the basin.

"Thyso." Layandria spoke in her sweetest tone, causing the handmaid to turn back to her. "I require your assistance with another matter."

Thyso nodded his obedience.

Layandria let out a wicked smile, poking her foot out from under the blankets of her bed. The damage done to her feet over the long trek through the Inohamman lands was extensive. Many bruises, blisters and cracked nails adorned her. "I will need you to pierce and drain my blisters."

Thyso's stomach rolled at the sight of the Queen's damaged soles. He detested feet and more so, unclean, uncared for feet. The Queen well knew this and had seldom forced her handmaid to attend to them. A small voice in the back of his mind told him that she was toying with him, but he could not get past the terrible foot presented to him.

Jaxus watched the wave of nausea pass over the boy and began chuckling in earnest. Layandria tried her best to suppress her amusement, but she rapidly failed. "Thyso, I am only jesting."

"Thank the Gods." Thyso bowed forward, supporting himself with his hands on his knees.

"Thyso, today I intend to give you a great gift, one beyond your imaginings. For now, take rest in the knowledge that you will never be called a handmaid again." Layandria rose from her bed, wrapping her nude form in a thin sheet wrested from the covers of the bed. "Now, go enjoy the morning. I will prepare myself for the day's events as I find that I am no longer in need of constant supervision."

"Yes, My Queen."

"You are in need of constant supervision." Jaxus voice came in feigned irritation. "But, I am quite glad to take charge of your care."

Layandria giggled and beckoned the man to her side. At this gesture, Thyso quietly took his leave. He returned to his chamber, the same he had held for the last few years, adjacent to the Queen's own. His mind was in turmoil. If he was no longer to be handmaid to Queen Layandria, what station or position was he to take? Why did he feel no sorrow or pain at the memory of the battles he had taken part in, and why did the terrible night in the desert with Rale'en linger so painfully on his heart? He could not understand, and this understanding did not suit him.

Additional trouble was laid on Thyso's mind by the confession he had made to Jaxus in the forest, just before the battle of the Lake. He knew the man to be loyal and true to his word. He also knew Layandria to be of kind heart and fair wisdom, but would she grant him the chance to seek out love in the form he wished? Or, upon hearing of his feelings, would she cast him out? Were the Queen to eradicate the old laws and allow him his hearts desires, would the people of Arken accept him? These things tortured Thyso long as he kept to his solitude.

After a time, a young serving girl came to his door, summoning Thyso to the Whisper Hall in a soft voice through his closed door. He rose from his window seat and stepped in front of a large mirror, checking over his appearance. Satisfied that he looked his best, his armor polished to perfection and his boots heavily glossed, Thyso moved to his door.

As he passed the threshold, he nearly crashed into Sahid. The Fallish man had been given quarter in one of the unused rooms in the royal suites, as had Tepan and Halta, though Thyso did not believe the woman had even once used her chamber as she had not left Oslun's side in all the days since their reunion.

"My apologies, good warrior." Sahid offered sincerely.

"No, it is my error." Thyso offered back, patting the Fallish man on his shoulder. He was dressed in a purple tunic over black trousers, an uncommon combination in a kingdom where purple tones were expensive and difficult to craft. Certainly, this garb was a gift from the Queen's collection, possibly once belonging to her father. "I am glad to see you well recovered from your fatigue."

"Thank you, Master Swordsman." Sahid bowed and smiled. "I am pleased to be an honored guest at Queen Layandria's ceremony. Though, I must confess that I do not know the courtesy of such things. We do not observe them in the same way where I am from."

"Ah, there is nothing to be feared my friend." Thyso laid his arm around Sahid's shoulders as the two moved towards the door to the Whisper Hall. "Anything that is needed from you will be explained and all will be well."

"Again, my thanks." Sahid pushed the door open, gesturing for Thyso to pass before him.

As the handmaid stepped onto the blood stone platform, his stomach dropped. He was late. No doubt the serving girl who had summoned him did so on the Queen's bidding. Layandria stood in front of her throne, Jaxus on her right, along with Oslun and Halta. An empty space was left on Layandria's left side, which Thyso sheepishly moved to, coming next to Tepan. Sahid moved to stand on Tepan's opposite arm.

It seemed that the entirety of the realm's population was gathered in the hall, so full was the room. Lord Aralias, Lady Kaowith and Lord Brustic stood at the base of the white steps, each clad in their Lordly robes, though Lord Aralias still bore his typical preserved wolf head on his shoulder. Thyso noted curiously that the recently pardoned Lord Nathus was not in attendance. That did not bode well. The various masters of the fists were gathered in rank behind the Lords and Lady, while the Captains and Commanders of the armies took the next ranks. Behind them, many of the nations wealthy and powerful mixed with any who had cause to attend. There had to be nearly two thousand citizens gathered in the room.

Seeing her final two guests of honor having taken their places, Layandria nodded to the Lords and Lady. The trio mounted the white steps, Lord Aralias in the lead. As he approached the Queen, the Wolf Lord knelt, Lady Kaowith coming to her knees on his left and Lord Brustic to his right.

Layandria softly cleared her throat and raised her voice to the assembly. "Is it the will of the people of the Elk Fist that I, Layandria, of the House Taymrhlyn, daughter of Axeleon and Alandaria, be so named and sworn as Queen of Arken?"

"It is, Your Grace." Lord Brustic spoke the words and rose. He stepped to Layandria and bowed before turning to face the audience. "I come to you, Layandria of House Taymrhlyn, to give you the oath of the crown. This oath must be freely taken, without coercion from any party. It is binding and can only be removed through death. Do you wish to take the oath of the crown, as your father and your father's father before you?"

"If it is the will of the people," Layandria felt it necessary to include all the citizens of Arken in her coronation, even in absentia, "I will swear it."

"My Lady, raise your hand to your heart and state the Oath." Lord Brustic instructed calmly, unrolling a parchment, ready to provide the written words if needed.

"I, Layandria of House Taymrhlyn, do freely give my vow that I will steadfastly discharge the duties accorded to me as the Queen of Arken. I give my oath that I will be the ever-vigilant protector of this land, all her people and her ways. I give my vow that I will allow no harm to come to this nation and I will seek no personal gain. Finally, I vow that all I am, all that I have and all I shall ever hold will be given unto the people of Arken from this day, until my final day." Layandria silently hoped that she had remembered the words correctly, and that the assembly could not sense her nerves.

Lord Brustic rolled the parchment and affixed it under his arm. "The words of the ancient oath have been taken. I do so name you, Layandria, Queen of Arken, Commander of the Armies of the Fists and Lady of Shadow."

Layandria waited as Lord Brustic moved back to his position next to Lord Aralias and took his knee. "Is it the will of the people of the Fire Fist that I, Layandria, of the House Taymrhlyn, daughter of Axeleon and Alandaria, be so named and sworn as Queen of Arken?"

Lady Kaowith rose and moved to bow to Layandria, before turning to the mass. "The people of the Fire Fist, having born witness to the oath of the crown and holding good faith in Layandria of House Taymrhlyn wish to present the crown of the Queen. To take this crown is to accept that you will hold no other worldly possessions. All wealth, property and successes are owed to the people of Arken. This crown must serve as a reminder that the lives and prosperity of the people rest on you and your leadership. Do you accept the crown, Layandria Taymrhlyn?"

Layandria cleared her throat again, fearing that her nerves would cause her voice to crack. "If it is the will of the people, I will accept the crown as my only worldly possession, I give all that I own and all of my strength to Arken and her people, keeping this crown and all that it represents unto myself."

Lady Kaowith bowed to Layandria, rose and gently laid the crown on her head. The silver setting off the tones of fire in her hair as the pure emerald jewel at the center ignited her eyes. The Fire Lady moved back to her place next to Lord Aralias.

"Is it the will of the people of the Wolf Fist that I, Layandria, of the House Taymrhlyn, daughter of Axeleon and Alandaria, be so named and sworn as Queen of Arken?" Layandria spoke evenly, though her palms were sweating profusely.

Lord Aralias rose and followed the same motions as taken by his predecessors. His face to the crowd, he lifted his high voice. "The people of the Wolf Fist, having born witness to the oath of the crown and holding true faith in Layandria of House Taymrhlyn wish to present the sword of the Queen. It is tradition in Arken that the one who holds the throne will wield a blade forged of the blades of her mother and father."

Aralias somewhat awkwardly raised a fine longsword in his only hand. "This is Hope of the Fathers, forged from the blades of Sword of the Fathers and Heart's End. This weapon and its twin serve as the symbol of your responsibility in all things to protect the safety and prosperity of Arken and her people. This is your foremost duty, and all is owed to this. Do you accept Hope of the Fathers as your weapon and as your promise to do all in your power, to bend all of your will, to the safety and prosperity of Arken?"

Layandria felt herself relaxing, her pulse becoming more manageable as she neared the end of the ceremony. "If it is the will of the people that I be so charged, I accept Hope of the Fathers as my weapon and the ever-present reminder of my first duty to the safety and prosperity of Arken and her people."

The final pieces of ceremony should have been delivered by the Lord of the Iron Fist, but as Lord Nathus had inexplicably abstained from attendance. The Lords and Lady took it upon themselves. Lady Kaowith and Lord Brustic rose, joining Lord Aralias. All three laid hands on Layandria's shoulders and bowed their heads. They spoke the words in unison. "The People of the Fists of Elk, Fire, Wolf and Iron have spoken their will and we do so name you Queen Layandria, Commander of the Armies of the Fists and Lady of Shadow, from this day, until your last day."

On the final word, the entire assembly came to their knees and began their applause. The Lords and Lady each bowed to the Queen and moved back to their positions at the base of the steps. After a short moment, Layandria raised her hand and stilled the applause.

"I come to you now as your Queen, an honor for which I am grateful and one that I will give my all to earn. I come to you on the backs of war and devastation on our people. I give you my solemn word that I will do all in my power to prevent this evil from ever returning to our borders." Layandria paused while again, the assembly applauded.

"Long have sworn Knights protected our realm, though their numbers were few and their charge centered on the leadership of the armies under the direct and sole authority of the King. On this day, I hereby decree that a division of Knights will be formed with the express purpose of providing detection of, and rapid response to incursions into our lands. These Knights will be sworn not to the service of the crown, but to the people. Each Fist will choose five hundred of their finest and most steadfast warriors to be trained and sworn to this charge. From the ranks of Knights, twenty five volunteers will be selected to form the royal guard. No other force will be dedicated to the protection of the crown save for these. The Shadow Fist will be divorced from the Citadel and the Fortress at Barang will be set as the seat for this fist."

Cheers and sounds of great surprise went up all over the hall. Jaxus, standing still next to his Queen, beamed in a great smile.

Layandria waited for the cheers to subside, letting her eyes pass over the faces of those closest to her. She was gladdened to see smiles and hope painted across many of them. She passed a sideways glance to Jaxus and saw that the man beamed. *I owe this great day to you, Sir Jaxus.*

How? Jaxus sole word entered the Queen's mind and she struggled to find the words to express how she felt.

Though the excitement of the audience was beginning to fade, Layandria felt a burning desire to explain herself to the man who had taught her so much and sacrificed much of himself for her. *You showed me your heart. That night, in the desert. I saw through your eyes all the rulers and leaders of the ages of your life. I saw in many good intention, driven askew by false hopes, greed and poor decisions. I saw the destructive power that these rulers held when turned towards the wrong paths. No man or woman can see all ends and no one man or woman should be the sole designer of the fate for so many peoples. I can think of no other way to both protect Arken and who we are, while also preventing my own heart, or any who take up the throne after me from bending towards destructive paths.*

Jaxus took in every word and his heart soared for the first time in his long memory. *Now, without question, I know what kind of royal is Layandria, Queen of Arken.*

With the words of her trusted companion, the hope expressed on so many faces, Layandria felt a great weight being lifted from her. The wounds on her heart did not close, but they felt less raw. She hoped that this new law, this new system of governance would usher in an era of prosperity amongst her people. She willed with all her might that she would never again have to see blood spilled on her behalf.

Layandria took in a calm breath before continuing, letting the tenor of the crowd subside. "Thyso Robith, step forward."

Thyso's eyes went wide at the sudden mentioning of his name. So caught up was he in the passing of this new law and the instant excitement that swept the crowd, he nearly didn't believe it was his name that had just exited his Queen's lips. He regained himself and stepped forward, coming to kneel before Layandria.

"Oslun Panteon, step forward." The Queen's voice was proud and a great smile beamed across her face as she called the cup bearer forward.

Oslun too was shocked to hear his name before this great assembly. He somewhat sheepishly moved to take his place, kneeling beside Thyso.

In short order, Queen Layandria called forth the names of Halta and Tepan, each coming to kneel on either side of Thyso and Oslun. Finally, the Queen lifted her eyes to the back of the Whisper Hall. "Lady Pelnieth, come forward."

There was some confusion in the crowd, as most had never heard this name. In short seconds, there was a slight shuffling at the back of the expansive hall. The crowd parted at the center, allowing an unseen person to move forward. Layandria remained poised in the long wait as Pelnieth found her way to the white steps, pausing at the base. Layandria extended her graceful hand, indicating that Pelnieth should take a position next to Halta on the blood stone. The young woman gently ascended the steps, the hem of her soft green gown, no doubt given to her by Lord Aralias, danced before her footfalls.

"Each of you have committed great deed in the past weeks in service to Arken and her people. It was through your strength and tenacity, as well as your personal courage that the full hand of death's staved off." As Layandria spoke, a myriad of expressions crossed the faces of those kneeling before her. The same was true of the crowd. Many knew who Thyso and Oslun were, though none could imagine that the meek cup bearer would have committed great deed.

"It is my great pleasure as Queen of Arken to honor each of you and bestow what title that you choose within my power." Layandria moved to stand before Tepan. "Tepan of the Inohamman Wanoak, you have shown ferocious loyalty to me, to my cause and to the ideals that demonstrate the heart of Arken warriors. Though you have been outcast from your own, through your loyalty to others who acted in folly, though you have been ripped from your home by war and treachery, I wish to welcome you to your new home, as a citizen and knight of Arken. Do you, Tepan of the Inohamman Wanoak, wish to accept this land and her people as your own, taking the charge of the Knights as your bond?"

Tepan's face broke in shock, he slowly bowed his head, wincing against the still tender wound on his neck. "Your grace, for my part, I am bound to you. Time and again you have shown your great strength and love, not only to your home and the people of Arken, but to all peoples in need. I am proud and honored to call this land my home and to call you my Queen."

Tepan lowered his shoulders further to the floor, turning his face up to the Queen. "As for the honor you bestow on me, offering unto me to be called one of your great Knights, this I cannot accept, in all humbleness and sorrow."

Layandria's eyes softened and she saw that great tears ran down Tepan's cheeks. She moved to him and laid her hand gently on his face. "My friend, there is no need for sorrow. You have well-earned any place that you desire and there is no requirement placed on you."

"Truly, you are the most loving of Chieftains, Queen Layandria." Tepan's voice nearly broke as he offered his words. "I would be honored beyond words to join the ranks of your great Knights, but it is for my old age that I fear I will not be of service to you. Stout of heart, I remain, but the heart cannot forever keep strength in the body. I am proud to serve you, for the rest of my days, in any way that seems worthy to you, my Queen, but I ask only that an old man be allowed to put away his weapons and serve not in blood."

Layandria lowered herself to the floor, coming to Tepan's level. Several murmurs shot through the assembly. Never in any life present had a royal of Arken lowered themselves before another. "My friend and brother, I offer to you a position on my council. You will be given chambering in this very citadel, the freedom to move as you please, and a seat at my table that your wisdom may ever grace this land as it has through many trials at my side. Does this suit your heart better?"

"My Queen, I am yours and I am honored beyond all that words could express." Tepan's tears were replaced with freely running happiness.

Layandria stood, letting her hand pass over the great man's head. She smiled and came to stand before Thyso. "Thyso Robith, long have you stood by my side, accepting the title of handmaid and performing your duties without fail. For that alone, you are deserving of great honor, but I know what desires you whispered in the shadow of the night. I offer to you the posting as the Commander of my personal guard. In this role, you will, in cooperation with me, select and train the Knights of my guard. You will stand by my side in battle, should war return to our lands and you will be granted a seat at my council. Do you wish to accept this posting?"

Thyso was nearly overcome by his emotion at the Queen's speech. He had so long desired to be sworn as a Knight of Arken, long before he was named to Layandria's service. His body shook and he could barely bring his voice up. "With all my heart, Your Grace, I accept."

Layandria beamed in pride at her faithful friend. "What is the name you have chosen for your blade, good Thyso?"

"I have not named my blade, Your Grace, as it has chosen for itself." Thyso felt silly saying these words before this large mass, but he could say nothing else aside from the truth his heart believed. "In the long dark of the passage to the land of the Inohamman, I discovered that the greatest strength of a warrior does not come in his skills at single combat, but in the energy and passion that he pours into his companions. This thought has resonated in me and I cannot separate form it. In the battle at the Lake, we faced a numerically superior enemy and held no tactical advantage, having been taken by surprise."

A rumbling interest passed through the room, most in attendance being unaware of the events that had transpired west of the mountains. Thyso paid it no mind. "Though we were, by all measuring, doomed to pass into the shadow, we were saved from this defeat not through strength of arms, but through love for each other and an unwillingness to see those we called our own to be slain. Thus, I have found that my blade is to be called Keeper, for within it exists the power to keep safe those dear to me."

Layandria took to tears, so transformed was the once arrogant and prideful Thyso. "Your words grace us all and ring true for every man and woman of Arken. I am proud to call you, Commander Thyso Robith of the Queen's Guard. May your name, and Keeper, the name of your blade, be written into the books of Arken histories and added to the lists of the Knights of Arken."

Thyso shook with emotion as the Queen moved to stand before Oslun. "Oslun Panteon, you once served my Father, King Axeleon, as his cup bearer. In this position, you were seldom noticed and often overlooked. I have found in you a great power and surely the heart of a warrior in keeping with the highest traditions of Arken. You are a man of many great skills and many paths are open to you. I will give you whatever you ask, as it is within my power."

"Your Grace, I ask only for one thing, after which I will serve in any manner deemed worthy by the crown." Oslun turned his face up to his Queen. Halta had discussed this day with Layandria several times over the past days and she in turn had shared her knowledge with her beloved, allowing him much time to prepare his thoughts. "I ask that I be allowed to marry Halta of the Inohamman Wanoak and that all in Arken be given right to marry any they choose, having no law to prohibit."

Layandria stepped back a pace in shock, this was not at all what she expected from Oslun as he well knew she supported his love for Halta. "By what law are these loves prohibited, my good and faithful friend?"

Oslun cleared his throat and summoned his courage again, desperately hoping he would not anger the Queen, or his brother Thyso. "My Queen, there exists in Arken a law that forbids man to marry man or woman to find love in woman. Additionally, there exists a law prohibiting a citizen of Arken from engaging in marriage with citizens of those nations not named as allies. I believe the former law to be unjust and having no bearing on the security or prosperity of Arken, while damaging the individual happiness of many citizens. While the later law is necessary, currently the Inohamman are not recognized as allies."

Layandria started. She was not aware of the first law and had never considered such relationships to be any different that any she had seen. Without hesitation, the words spurted from her lips. "I will have the historians strike this law from the records immediately."

A great commotion went through the assembly, some voices raised in anger. Thyso was frozen in complete shock, while anger too welled in him. He turned his eyes to Oslun and bored into him. Layandria stepped forward again, taking her place and raising her arms to still the crowd.

"There are many laws in this land that were written long ago. While I will not dispute the reasoning for my forbearers to set these laws down, as I do not know their minds, I do know that the Arken we will build is not one of restriction and oppression. I will form a council and we will examine the laws, abolishing any and all that restrict the right of the people of Arken to live as they see fit. We will build a nation where no man has hold over anther and all peoples are free so long as they do not seek to oppress or limit their fellows."

"On this day, I can see no reason that a citizen of Arken should be limited in the love they hold for another, given that their chosen mate has age and ability to choose as well. As such, I, Queen Layandria of Arken abolish this law and it will be stricken from the records." Layandria tremored with nerves, unprepared as she had been for this type of request. Next to her, Jaxus pleasure deepened, his trust in her proven again. Thyso found that he could not stop trembling with joy. "And yes, the nation of the Inohamman Wanoak is to be hereby recognized as an ally to Arken."

"As for your posting, Oslun Panteon, I offer to you a seat on the council of the law as I have described it. You will aide me, along with the Lords and Lady of the Fists in reviewing these laws and determining which are unjust. Once completed in this task, you will take post as a Knight and member of the Queen's guard. Do you accept this posting as I have offered you?" Layandria silently begged the cupbearer to accept without rebuff, not wishing for further surprises before this large mass.

"I do accept, and I will serve with all strength that I possess, Your Grace." Oslun felt Thyso's great emotion next to him. He did not understand why his brother would be so overjoyed by the Queen's proclamation, though, as he examined his memories of his companion, Oslun found that he had no knowledge of Thyso's interest in romantic entrapments. Perhaps there was something there that he did not see.

Layandria sighed her relief and regained her composure. "Do you wish to continue carrying the Sword of Amyus Colth, known as Devil's Song, given to you by my father, King Axeleon?"

Oslun wasted no time in his response. "I do, My Queen."

"It is my great honor to name you, Oslun Panteon, Knight of the Queen's guard. May your name, and Devil's Song, the name of your blade, be written into the books of Arken histories and added to the lists of the Knights of Arken." Layandria moved to stand before Halta quickly, preventing Oslun from raising any additional words of controversy. She did not fear this, but only wished to speak on these matters with her advisors before being forced to answer before much of her public.

Halta beamed with a great smile, clearly having known that which Oslun intended. Her countenance gave Layandria comfort, knowing by the expression that the young man had at least discussed his intent with Halta before levying it on the Queen.

Layandria allowed herself a smile as she looked down on Halta. "Halta of the Inohamman Wanoak, you have rapidly proven yourself a trusted advisor, confident and a steadfast friend. Over many days we have shared much of our hearts and grown to know each other's mind. I find that there is but once posting befitting one in whom I find such faith and trust."

Halta's face never broke from her smile and her eyes shown brilliantly as Queen Layandria spoke. "To you I offer a post that has not been used in Arken for many generations. In days of old, the Hand of the Crown was the most trusted advisor and often served as the word of the King. In this post you will never be far from my side and will not be denied access to any part of our realm. As you speak, it will be as the words of the crown. Do you accept and wish to serve in this post, Halta of the Inohamman Wanoak?"

"To be known now as Halta of Arken is an honor I joyously accept and while I ask for none other, I gladly accept that which is offered." Halta's voice was strong, full of the vigor and power of a warrior of her kind. Her face shone with a radiance to match the borum stone and Oslun's eyes were frozen on her in love as she addressed the Queen.

Layandria's voice rose in power as if feeding off Halta's energy. "I am honored to name you, Halta of Arken, the Hand of the Crown. Let your name be written in the histories and added to the lists of those who have born the title. This is a list of few names, but it carries the memory of many who served this realm in greatness."

Halta lowered her head in honor to the crown as Layandria stepped to stand before Pelnieth. The young woman was still filled with uncertainty, having heard the gifts bestowed on the others. She was certain no such titles would be given her as she had never spoken to this beautiful Queen and had performed none of the deeds described.

"Lady Pelnieth of Gilfring," Layandria spoke in a regal tone, her eyes not on Pelnieth, but fixed on Lord Aralias. "Much have I heard of the suffering you endured at the hands of Axise soldiers. Much have I heard of the devastation they wrecked on your homeland and on your own body. Though it may unknown to you, there stand before you two men who bore witness to these great crimes."

Pelnieth raised her eyes from the blood stone and followed the Queen's gesture to see both Jaxus and Sahid standing before her, having moved silently to flank the Queen as she spoke. She recognized both at once and in her memory, saw the vengeance Jaxus wroth on Axise men who abused her and her sister. She also recalled Sahid's kindness, giving her shelter in his own tent and on many days, caring for her wounds after she had been abused. Tears ran freely and overcome by the sight of these two men who showed her kindness when others offered her naught but pain.

Jaxus knelt before the breaking woman. "No person in this world should be made to endure that which has been given to you. Most would be utterly broken by such atrocity, but in you is a greater light. Rest easy in the knowledge that your tormenters have been put to the soil and never again will you suffer."

Sahid knelt as Jaxus moved away. His own face drenched in pain for the young woman. Sahid's voice failed him and it quaked as he spoke. "For the death and torment that you have endured, I cannot offer you peace. I can offer you only my solemn vow that should you choose to be taken as a Daughter of Arken, long will you live while those who made you suffer rot away."

Pelnieth dropped her head to the blood stone, her body racked with waves of emotion. A gentle hand came to rest on her back and she turned her eyes to find Lord Aralias having come to her, his remaining hand giving her comfort. The man spoke no words, but his eyes conveyed much compassion.

Layandria knelt for a second time, though much less shock came to the assembly. She laid her hand on the back of Pelnieth's head. "Much has been spoken on the pain and suffering you have endured, but today is not a day of sorrow for deeds already written. Much has also been said of your conduct in the battle for the Fire Fist and the courage you showed in the saving of Lord Aralias from certain death, at great risk to your own life."

"Pelnieth, I offer to you, in honor of your great sacrifice and courage, to be taken as a Daughter of Arken, given full right as a citizen of this realm. Further, Aralias, Lord of the Wolf Fist has asked that you be named as his personal guard. In this post, you would be the left hand of the Lord, never far from his side and aiding him in all things."

The young woman's breath caught in her chest and she could not stop sobbing. She turned her face to the Queen, seeing not but love in her expression. She took in Lord Aralias and saw much affection in his eyes, accompanying the many tears that bathed his youthful face. She swallowed hard, quelling her emotion. "Long I have wished for death, believing this the only respite I could have, but here, in this land of warriors who give mercy and royals who show love, I find that I am truly home."

Pelnieth cleared her throat and took several slow breaths, composing her thoughts. "This man has given me life. He has renewed my hope and showed me that there remains kindness in this life. I would ask for no other thing than to be allowed to remain at his side, in the shelter of his protection and giving him what aid I can offer."

"Let all sorrows pass away and let all hope be restored in the light of the new sun." Layandria raised her voice to the assembly, nearly every gathered heart taken in by Pelnieth and her emotion. "I name you Pelnieth of Arken, hand of the Wolf Lord. Though you will often be away from this place, as your Lord travels, know that you have forever a place in this hall and that if ever you are in need, you may come to me without delay."

"Thank you, Your Grace." Pelnieth broke into sobs again, the feeling of release so overpowering her. Lord Aralias remained at Pelnieth's side, wrapping his arm around her shoulders and the woman quaked.

Jaxus and Sahid both remained standing, flanking the Queen. Layandria turned her eyes between both as she addressed the assembly.

"These two men have both already been named as Knights of Arken and both have performed great deed on behalf of our people. Though their actions are not known to most, the continued survival of Arken would have failed in entirety save for the efforts and sacrifice of these two warriors."

The Queen let the words hang in the air, Pelnieth's quiet sobs still giving gentle backdrop to the cold room. "There is nothing I can offer that would properly honor all that they have given, so I ask of you, Sahid Hauk Kahn, what can I give to you? I will give to you anything you desire if it is in my power."

Sahid faced the Queen and knelt, but Layandria touched his chin gently, raising him back to his feet. Her voice came to him softly, and full of a grateful heart. "Neither of you shall ever bow before me, or any other for the rest of your days."

"My Lady," Sahid spoke in bewilderment, as with nearly every action he had seen from the royals of Arken, she proved herself of the highest quality. "My homeland was destroyed by Axise conquest, most, if not all of my tribe killed. I do not know what will await me upon my return, but I find that my heart will not grant me rest until I have seen the fields of the Fallish Realm and found what remains of my people. I ask only to be allowed to return to that land."

Layandria smiled, hiding her personal disappointment. She had found Sahid to be wise and full of youthful energy. She had hoped he would stay in Arken, perhaps taking a position under Commander Thyso in the Queen's Guard, but she would not deny him. She knew far too well the pain of longing when separated from her own home. "I will have our finest ships carry you home."

"Thank you, Queen Layandria." Sahid's heart felt much relief and he let his shoulders relax.

"Though," Layandria took the man's hand, "should you return to the Fallish Lands and find that it is no longer the home of your years, you will forever be welcomed as a Knight of Arken and your name will grace the lists for all the ages of this kingdom."

Sahid could not help but bow low to this young, but great Queen. He watched her in amazement as she returned his gesture, and releasing her grip on his hand, turned to Jaxus.

"Jaxus, to you I wish to give anything your heart desires, but I find in this moment that my heart cannot bear the chance that you would choose to separate from my side." Layandria felt her composure break and her fears took into her heart.

Jaxus took her hand, much as she had done with Sahid. His eyes met hers and she felt the warmth and love in his gaze wash over her. "My Queen, I am yours, for all of the days that remain before us and for all that we may endure."

Layandria could find no words to say and she felt a sudden desire to be free of the eyes that focused on her. She breathed deeply several times, stilling her emotion, before turning to face the audience. "All that has been said here today, in this mighty hall, is the beginning. We will build in Arken a nation of free people and a great strength. We will shine as a beacon for all the world to see, that all peoples may find an end to the toils of oppression."

Somewhere in the middle of the hall, a single voice went up. "Long live Arken! Long live the Queen!"

This unseen speaker continued, repeating the verse. Several voices joined in and a fervor built in the hall as nearly every voice joined in.

Long live Arken! Long live the Queen!

Epilogue

"Yes, My Lord," Chammelman Kerrick, a Knight of the Iron Fist spoke to Lord Nathus in the Iron Lord's personal chamber. The shades were drawn over the windows and the only light emitted from a small fire off to the side of the cold stone room. "She has sworn to abolish many laws of Arken, though which laws she will strike from the records is not yet known. She did, on that day, abolish the laws banning marriage between man and man, or woman and woman."

Lord Nathus said nothing, his eyes dark and his fist clenched around the handle of his fork. He did not eat, but repeatedly tore at a chunk of lamb that bled on his plate.

Chammelman drew in a drink of strong wine and continued. "Further, My Lord, the Queen has named several not of Arken blood to positions of high rank and title. The worst of which being that she has restored the ancient post of Hand of the Crown and named some unknown woman from west of the mountains to the title."

Lord Nathus drove his fork into the lamb with such force that he bent the tines against his plate. He did not speak, his jaw clenched with such force that his teeth ground together.

"Finally, My Lord," Chammelman nearly held back his final piece of news, seeing the intense fire of Nathus anger, but he thought it better to endure the Lord's wrath now than to come under his heal later were it discovered that he had not revealed all. "As I was taking my leave of the citadel, I gathered word that Queen Layandria intends to marry a man who is known by the name of Jaxus. I am told that none know of his true origins, only that he came to the service of King Axeleon within the last ten years."

"She wishes to make this Jaxus our King?" Lord Nathus growled as he pushed his plate away.

"Yes, My Lord, though this was only rumor and no announcement has been made from the royal court. I can tell you only that the Queen honored this Jaxus before the assembly at her coronation and the exchange between them carried much uncommon tenderness. I also have been told that Jaxus resides within the Queen's own chamber." Chammelman was relieved to see that his Lord had, at least in part, maintained control over his temper.

"And how did the assembly receive these pronouncements from our beloved Queen?" Lord Nathus stood slowly from his chair and began pacing across the length of the table.

"My Lord, I dare say that her orders were well received. Before the Queen retired to her chamber, nearly the whole of the court began chanting for her. By all appearances and all talk I gathered, I believe that the people find the Queen's actions to be well." Chammelman allowed himself to take a bite of the meal before him while Lord Nathus' back was turned in his pacing.

"So, Layandria wishes to destroy all that was built by her forefathers and usher us into a new era." Lord Nathus continued his pacing. "And the simpering sheep of the fists will embrace their Queen and call her well in their sight. This cannot be allowed."

Chammelman went cold. He knew his Lord would be angered by the decrees of the new crown, but he did not expect sedition to follow. "Are we to raise war banners, My Lord?"

Suddenly Lord Nathus gripped the table in both hands and threw it crashing into the fireplace hearth. Wine ran down the stone and blood from the lamb adorned the rug. The mess smothered out the fire plunging the room into darkness. All Chammelman Kerrick could see was his Lord's silhouette and a sinister gleam of his eyes.

"War against the crown is war we cannot win." Lord Nathus barely moved, and his voice came as that of a deadly cobra. "The four fists would come to her aide and we would not survive. No, this whore queen must be dealt with in ways that will not only lead to her death but ensure that the only memory of her is one of disdain. Before we kill her, and we will kill her, we must break her."

Dedication

To my Bride, I thank you for the countless nights where you went to bed alone, knowing that you would sleep to the endless ticks of keys and hushed whispers as passages were read aloud in the other room. Your excitement for this journey and the input you have offered have been crucial. I find no words that will aptly convey my appreciation for all that you are and the countless ways you amaze me.

To my parents, I am profoundly grateful for the unfailing support and guidance that you have given as you watched me pass from one adventure to the next folly, back to another grand idea. There are many elements of this narrative, and certainly of my entire life that I owe to both of you. I wish that someday, parent and child will cherish this book in the way we cherished so many.

To Lunchbox, I must thank you for the nights in your flat that were filled with too much cigarette smoke, five dollar pizzas and wild ideas about stories we could tell. For the years spent shoulder to shoulder though challenges, triumphs and all our glorious mistakes. I'll look forward to your debut novel, or whatever magnificent thing you do next. Your victory is here and now warrior. It asks only for you to grab it and never let go. Oddly, whiskey asks for the same.

For all the others who have stood by me, who have inspired, shared laughs and adventures, please know that were I to allocate all the pages of this work for my sincere words of thanks, I would find it insufficient. Every voice matters and every moment shared contains profound significance. Never lose sight of the power you hold inside.

About Jack

Music that inspired and aided in the sanity of the writer during the production of this work includes but is not limited to: The Animal In Me, Asking Alexandria, As I Lay Dying, Bad Wolves, Bloodywood, DMX, Eyes Set To Kill, Halestorm, Lady Gaga, Lupe Fiasco, Oh Sleeper, Snoop Dogg, Taylor Swift, T.I., and Wyclef Jean.

Jack is an avid supporter of Veterans of all eras, branches of service and occupational specialties. He is a fan of General Raymond Odierno, General James Mattis, Command Sergeant Major Raymond Chandler and Command Sergeant Major Daniel Daily, from whom he draws constant inspiration and wisdom. He is profoundly grateful for the sacrifice given on the altar of freedom by all the proud men and women of the United States Armed Forces.

Athletics are a very important part of Jack's life and he ardently follows the Colorado Rockies, Colorado Avalanche, San Francisco 49ers, Portland Trailblazers, Helio Castroneves, Graham Rahal and Tanner Foust.

Jack Keesling

For more information on this novel or any other works by Jack Keesling, please visit facebook.com/jackkeeslingbooks.

Made in the USA
San Bernardino, CA
20 July 2020